THE SWORD

BY ZOE SAADIA

At Road's End
The Young Jaguar
The Jaguar Warrior
The Warrior's Way

The Highlander
Crossing Worlds
The Emperor's Second Wife
Currents of War
The Fall of the Empire
The Sword
The Triple Alliance

Two Rivers
Across the Great Sparkling Water
The Great Law of Peace
The Peacekeeper

Beyond the Great River
The Foreigner
Troubled Waters
The Warpath
Echoes of the Past

THE SWORD

The Rise of the Aztecs, Book 6

ZOE SAADIA

For more information about this book, the author and her work, please visit www.zoesaadia.com

ISBN: 1537360434
ISBN-13: 978-1537360430

AUTHOR'S NOTE

"The Sword" is historical fiction and some of the characters and adventures in this book are imaginary, while some are historical and well documented in many accounts concerning this time period and place.

The history of that region is presented as accurately and as reliably as possible, to the best of the author's ability, and although no work of this scope can be free of error, an earnest effort was made to reflect the history and the traditional way of life of the peoples residing in those areas.

I would also like to apologize before the descendants of the mentioned nations for giving various traits and behaviors to the well known historical characters (such as Nezahualcoyotl, Tlacaelel and many other), sometimes putting them into fictional situations for the sake of the story. The main events of this book and the followings sequels are very well documented and could be verified by simple research.

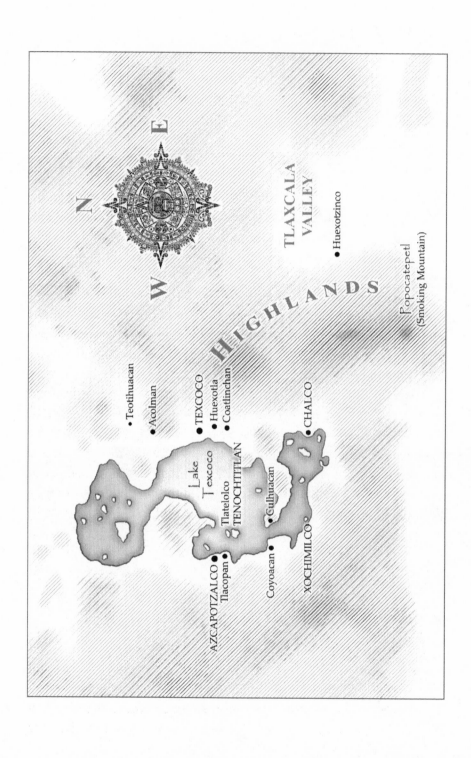

PROLOGUE

City of Texcoco,
1431

The silhouettes slipped through the small opening in the wall, as silent as ghosts, disturbing no object. For a heartbeat they froze, surveying the darkness, listening. The silence was deep, encompassing.

Apparently satisfied, they moved along the plastered wall, following the curt gesture of their leader. Silvery moonlight reflected on the bright smoothness of their knives, out and ready, glittering strangely. These were no obsidian daggers, but blades brought from the far south, made of bright metal, not as sharp as obsidian but more durable, easier to use; and very, very rare. The rest of the light was swallowed by the darkness of their clothes.

Following another gesture, two of the men crossed the spacious room, avoiding its sparse furniture – a cluster of low tables, mats, and cupboards. Their destination lay behind those, on a high reed-woven podium, the only place the dim moonlight managed to reach.

Hesitating, they eyed the uneven surface, suddenly unsure of themselves. The object it hosted poised there, wrapped in a cotton cloth, hidden, yet its shape was obvious, unmistakable. A long, massive sword, ominous even when not exposed, the magical carvings concealed, yet still there, still full of power.

The men glanced at their leader once again, sensing his hesitation. He shook his head and gestured resolutely, sending them toward the doorways leading into other parts of this relatively small dwelling. The Acolhua Chief Warlord was about to finish rebuilding the mansion he intended to occupy, but for now, he lived here, in the respectable neighborhood between the Great Plaza and the marketplace. Not a bad location for a fairly rich and influential person, but far beneath the status of the War Leader of Texcoco and its provinces, the man closest to the Emperor himself. Easy to break into too, especially since the dangerous man was out tonight, attending the celebrative feast in the Palace along with other nobles and guests.

Long summers of the Tepanec oppression had harmed Texcoco badly, turning the once-beautiful, important *altepetl* into a provincial town full of crumbling, neglected roads and public buildings, the last bout of warfare on the city's streets adding to the destruction. Full of great spirits, Nezahualcoyotl, the returning Emperor, seemed to be determined to correct all that, bursting into an extensive rebuilding program. Still, there was much work to be done, much effort to return the city to its previous glory, a task that progressed not as fast as the ascending ruler wished, so even the Chief Warlord had to make-do with a relatively humble sort of dwelling. The great ceremony to celebrate Nezahualcoyotl's taking the throne was to be held in less luxury than of yore.

The leader of the intruders shook his head, clearing his mind of irrelevant thoughts. It was now or never.

Crossing the room in one powerful leap, he reached for the revered object, his hands touching it, feeling the firmness of the carved wood and the smoothness of the obsidian, the razor-sharp spikes whispering danger, warning his flesh through the soft material.

Holding his breath, he picked the sword up, careful not to let its covers slip. There must have been a good reason for it to lay there concealed, wrapped in cotton. Maybe if one glimpsed the ominous carvings one would die, or weaken, or summon the owner of the dangerous weapon, somehow.

He muttered a prayer. Tezcatlipoca, the powerful deity of war and jaguars and the night sky, among his many other celestial responsibilities, must take care of this aspect until they reached their destination, safely out of Texcoco and down by the shores of the Great Lake. The mighty god should keep them safe while carrying the dangerous relic, taken away on that rare night when the Warlord was out, busy in Texcoco Palace. Too busy to come home, or to keep his magical sword with him. Such rare luck! But they paid the spy in this household for a reason. It took nearly two market intervals, half of twenty long days filled with fraying patience, for their generosity to pay off.

Soundlessly, he slipped back into the deeper shadows, the weight of the ominous weapon slowing his step, weighing him down. Was it his fear or was the sacred object actually hindering his progress? He pushed the troublesome thoughts away and muttered another prayer.

Back by the gaping opening at last, he tucked his precious cargo into a large padded bag, then gestured to his companions, welcoming the draft of the cool breeze upon his sweaty face. It was dangerously near dawn. They were expected to break in earlier, in the dead of the night, but the members of this household had gone quiet truly late, preparing for the upcoming ceremony, probably; the children running around at the time they should not be awake at all.

A last glance at the dimming moon and he reached for the windowsill, but as his companions turned to follow, there was a sound of sandals dragging upon the stone floor and they froze, held their breath, now nothing but dark shadows.

The light of a torch flickered, came closer. A figure appeared in one of the doorways, wearing no cloak. A slave. A woman. She hesitated for a heartbeat, as though sensing that something was wrong. Slowing her step, she peered into the room, then thrust her torch toward the faintly lit podium.

Her gasp barely disturbed the darkness, cut short by the knife buried expertly in the cavity of her chest, between her upper ribs. She was dead before she knew it, but the man next to her, holding her with one arm, preventing her fall, made sure to cover her mouth, just in case. The other rushed to catch the torch. Putting this house to flames was not a part of their orders.

Stifling a curse, the leader watched them, painfully aware of his growing uneasiness. It all went perfectly, according to the plan, until he touched the gods-accursed sword. He clutched the bag tighter, then gestured for them to put out the light and dump the damn corpse. It would have to stay as one more piece of evidence. It wouldn't spoil their mission, as they had been paid to make the sword disappear mysteriously, leaving almost no trace. *Almost*. That's why their services had been sought. Otherwise, any criminal, thief, or robber could have tried to do that, accepting a pitiful payment as opposed to what they had been paid. Five full-length cotton cloths of the best quality material and a bag stuffed with cocoa beans, close to a hundred in amount. Real riches for some, but a regular payment for them. Not many knew of their existence, and less could afford their services.

When the darkness prevailed once again, he breathed with relief. The damn maid might have proved a problem. If she had managed to scream, it would have spoiled the entire mission. The house of the Warlord might have been relatively abandoned, but the clamor their hasty retreat would have created was sure to make the fuss their employer made clear he wished to avoid. They had better get out before anything else happened.

Clutching his dangerous cargo, he hopped over the windowsill, light and sure-footed, hearing his companions doing the same.

"We go back the way we came," he breathed, when they were beside them, washed with the blessed freshness of the retreating night.

They hesitated, not accustomed to changing their plans on the spur-of-the-moment. This was not how they worked, having planned for every step before setting out on their rare, special, and very exclusive missions of theft or killing.

He nodded curtly, and they hurried, afraid to argue. He was not a person to permit a dispute of his decisions. The tale of his ruthlessness went ahead of him.

While scaling the wall, he remembered one more thing. His knife made no sound, slipping along the damp stones, slicing into the soft ground. He pushed his regrets away and went on, remembering what a staggering amount of cocoa beans he had been given to do this.

Clutching the cumbersome bag, he jumped onto the cracked stones of the road, seeing his companions there, waiting impatiently. A new gust of wind brought the slightly damp odor from the Great Lake's shores, not very far away, where the hired man was waiting for them in a large, sturdy canoe, to carry them and their magical cargo. But the darkness was dispersing rapidly, too rapidly. Was it not too early for that? Since touching the accursed sword, it had all started to go downhill, the unexpected maid, the elements, and now the forced change of plan.

And there was something else. He peered into the darkness, his skin prickling. No sound disturbed the night, no silhouette appeared, but something was out there; he could sense it peering at them. Not something dangerous, his instincts told him, but something alive, watchful, maybe terrified. Just a passerby? Oh, mighty Tezcatlipoca! Was he to fail this time? But for the damn sword and the nearing dawn, he would have lashed out, making sure to leave no living witnesses. As it was, they would just have to detour once again.

Never mind, he decided, turning away and motioning to his companions to follow. He would deliver this cargo, and having been paid so highly, he would disappear into a new life of a rich man, to enjoy the fruits of the last few summers of work, the murder of the previous Mexica Emperor included. The people who paid him now were not the same people who had paid him back then, but he didn't care for the politics and the squabbles of the ruling classes. All he wanted was the means to live in style and freedom, to do whatever he wanted, and he was going to reach it all now.

CHAPTER 1

The royal feast in Texcoco Palace progressed loudly, shaking the night air with the trill of flutes, clatter of plates, bursts of laughter. Such a merry affair. Tlalli suppressed her smile. They would be feasting into the next dawn, she knew, amused and relieved to leave the clamor behind.

The royal celebration provided the perfect opportunity to sneak out, an opportunity she was not about to miss. No need for explanations, reasoning, or making excuses; no facing the scandalized frowns of the servants, the disapproval of the guarding warriors, the smirking pleasure of her fellow concubines, other women of her status.

Nothing of the sort, she thought, satisfied, walking down the paved avenue in the thick darkness that always preceded the gray of the dawn, her hair flowing free, her spirit soaring. They were too busy with the festivities and the preparations for the Great Ceremony, which would be held through the first part of the nearing day. A very solemn ceremony, but for now, the multitude of noble guests, the visitors from all over the Great Lake, were busy eating and drinking, with enough food and *octli* to set their spirits free. Texcoco was regaining its past glory, but she wanted to get the taste of this *altepetl* uninterrupted, to abide her private curiosity and to watch the sun coming up from behind the Great Pyramid.

Oh, yes, the Acolhua capital was beautiful, she had decided earlier, through the previous day, watching the Great Pyramid from the other side of the Plaza, in the shade where the litter-bearers stopped upon her request. However, traveling with the litter, being taken from one memorable location to another at the whim of her bearers and bodyguards, was not the same as the ability to tour the city free and unhindered.

She had heard so much about this *altepetl*. Father had loved Texcoco, describing its refined beauty, the decisive lines of its buildings, its delicate mosaics and paintings, the elegant curves of the roads, the eloquence of its inhabitants' poetry and music. Being a second-class Tepanec trader, he had traveled far, bringing goods from the rich eastern side of the Great Lake. Even after Revered Tezozomoc, the greatest emperor of them all, conquered the Acolhua, turning Texcoco and all its towns and lands into yet another Tepanec province, even then, Father insisted that the Acolhua people remained the aristocrats of the Great Lake, subjected now, yes, but still noble people who knew how to run an *altepetl*.

She remembered how she would hold her breath, listening to the tales of the Great Plaza and the huge, buzzing marketplace, and the high ridges and mountains of the savage highlands to the east, towering, watching with their eyes narrowed, wary and dangerous. He told her that even Texcoco itself, once upon a time, many summers and moons ago, belonged to the Chichimecs of the Highlands. She had relished such stories, fascinated, wishing to see them all, the highlander savages and the aristocratic Acolhua, biting her lips, hoping that Father would take her along when she was old enough to travel such distances, as he promised her more than once.

How was she to know that Father would not live to see the last Tepanec Emperor coming into power, dying by the hand of this despicable man's cronies; and that, not much later, Azcapotzalco, the invincible Tepanec Capital, would burn, conquered by the same Acolhua, along with the Highlanders and the savage Mexica Aztecs?

She shook her head, pushing the troubled memories away. It was all in the past now, all the good and all the bad. While the path she had taken did bring her here, to Texcoco, and in the state she would not have dreamed to travel back when her family and the Tepanec Empire had still been alive and prospering. And if she was disappointed, it was only a little, not a deep disappointment. Texcoco *was* beautiful, even if not as refined as she expected, not as rich or colorful, but not an ugly city at all, with a definite touch of nobility about it, much better than the businesslike, ever-growing, earthly Tenochtitlan.

Now the Mexica-Aztec *altepetl* had been a true disappointment! She stifled a giggle, bringing Tenochtitlan's Great Plaza before her mind's eyes. Oh, even the attempt to compare these two seemed like blasphemy.

Pressing her cloak tighter around her body, to keep the pre-dawn chill out, she swept along the main road, guided by the dark silhouette of the Great Pyramid somewhere to the east. Even if humbled quite thoroughly by her own countryfolk, Texcoco was rebuilding, but in a grand manner, while Tenochtitlan was just busy building, period. Everything to make it stronger, larger, more impressive, neglecting the subtle elegance, the beautiful fineness along the way. The city of pushy newcomers, but what were those Mexica Aztecs, if not exactly that?

On the crossroad, she hesitated, trying to recognize the way to the Plaza. Was this the same road she had seen earlier in the day while carried in a litter, on their way to the marketplace, the favorite place of the visiting ladies? The silly fat fowls! As though she wanted to spend her time buying stupid trinkets. There were slaves to do that, to bring her pretty clothes and good food, and sometimes unnecessary jewelry that she never bothered to wear. Tlacaelel paid no attention to sparkling gems, so she discarded those too.

Tlacaelel!

She smiled to herself, paying attention to the way she walked. He wouldn't be pleased with her independent excursion through the Acolhua Capital, but he was too busy now, drinking and feasting with the other nobles. It would be a long time before he might be requesting her company. Surely not before the Great Ceremony, and by then she would be back, with no one the wiser. And even if someone found out and told on her, he would understand. He always understood, because he was the wisest man in the whole World of the Fifth Sun. The wisest, the strongest, and the kindest too, with that beautiful smile of his, and this sometimes mischievous spark lightening his eyes; a rare spark reserved only for her, she was sure of that.

Oh, if only they knew how heartily the arrogant, greatly feared Head Adviser could laugh, how boyish he could turn when teased with just the right amount of insolence and challenge, how wonderful his love could be. But they didn't. Not even his wives, not even his older concubines! They all thought him to be cold and aloof, passionate about his work, caring for nothing but Tenochtitlan and its future, shaping the new Mexica Empire day and night.

Well, he was all that, of course he was. But not always, and never in the privacy of her quarters.

Choosing to follow the wide, well-paved avenue that, to her estimation, should have brought her to the Plaza, she suppressed another smile, remembering how the litter-bearers had frowned this morning, when she had insisted on strolling it and some of the marketplace's alleys on foot. Ladies of her status didn't do that, but she paid their feeble protests no attention, hard put not to laugh. Gone were the days of Azcapotzalco's marketplace and the dirty rag displaying her pretty carvings, gone the times of running barefoot along the dusty, cozily warm alleys of Coyoacan. The favorite concubine of the second most powerful man of Tenochtitlan was not expected to stroll around, marring her elegant feet and her pretty, bejeweled sandals. Not even when visiting the great *altepetl* of Texcoco to witness Nezahualcoyotl ascending the throne, assuming the burden of the reign officially, at long last.

Oh, benevolent Coatlicue, the Mother of the Gods, she thought, pausing to rest, leaning against the wall of a rich two-story-high dwelling. *Thank you for your continued kindness; thank you for being wonderful to me. And thank you for making him take me along this time.*

He had traveled so much, on campaigns and all sorts of political missions, but without him, Tenochtitlan was unbearable, the luxury of the Palace or not. The ever-busy, ever-growing island-city lacked the refinement, the finesse, the subtlety, no matter how important or noble or worthy the pushy newcomers thought themselves to be, how gleefully they smirked while conquering on and on, determined to subdue all cities and towns previously ruled by the Tepanecs. Never thinking it would be possible, she had found herself missing Azcapotzalco from the most basic of aspects, while breathing the perpetually damp air or while drinking the slightly different-tasting water. Not to mention the hatred.

She shrugged, trying to shake off the irritating memories. It had been close to two summers since Azcapotzalco and Coyoacan fell, bringing the entire Tepanec Empire down, crashing like a cluster of rocks shaken by the wrath of the gods; close to two summers since she had betrayed her people by helping him, the leader of the conquerors, showing him how to reach Coyoacan by surprise, to take it more easily, with lesser losses for his men; two summers since she had avenged herself and the death of her family against filthy Maxtla. Convinced by him, the Chief Warlord of the Aztecs, she had helped the conquerors, while he had helped her. They had both gotten what they wanted.

Yet, somewhere along the way, their initial desires changed, their lives entwined, and their hearts had spoken. Or so she felt. When Maxtla died, Tlacaelel should have sent her away, rewarded and taken care of, as promised. But he did not. Instead, he took her to be his woman. Not the way warriors take women to have their pleasure and go away—she would never have yielded to that!—but the way lovers take their loved ones, in the fashion of the best storytellers to whose tales she had never bothered to listen while a child. Love stories were for silly girls, to make them giggle and sniffle with their noses and wipe away tears of excitement, a waste of time. However, the real thing proved to be wonderful, better than anything she had ever heard of. It made her head reel.

So she dived into their newfound love without looking back, traveling with him to Xochimilco, when he had finished reorganizing Coyoacan and went on to subdue that other strategically important *altepetl*. The spoils and the prisoners, and the other loot of the crumbled Tepanec Empire were sent to Tenochtitlan long since, but she went with him, nearly against the custom, as the women the conquerors chose to keep as concubines were sent back home along with the spoils. However, neither of them were ready to separate, not yet, and so she had traveled far, to the far south, to the lands even her father may not have reached.

Oh, what wonderful moons those were! He had been very busy, the Chief Warlord and the leader of this campaign, with his Acolhua and the Highlander allies leaving for their homelands – the Acolhua to liberate their towns and provinces, the Highlanders to enjoy the fruits of the war, carrying away an impressive amount of spoils and considerable political promises.

It left the Mexicas to face the remnants of the resisting Tepanec Empire alone, but no one was worried. Tlacaelel led his people to nothing but victories. Everyone had known this. Her high opinion of him, apparently, was shared by the entire Mexica army, to her immense pleasure and pride.

Oh, he was wonderful, this glorious man of hers. And as busy as he was, he did find time to be with her, enough to make plenty of love, and to teach her to read scrolls, like he had once promised her he would do.

So, with the passing of time, it had been easier to wait for him when he was busy reorganizing her people's former empire, shaping it into his vision of the encompassing Mexica domination. What he had in mind seemed impossible, not with his pitiful island-city and its people, the Tepanecs' most despised subjects of yesterday. And yet, if anyone could do it, it was him. Somehow.

So when Xochimilco refused to give an open battle, but chose to block every possible access to the city, making Tlacaelel irritable and greatly occupied devising his new best-fitting strategy, Tlalli surrounded herself with scrolls of *amate paper* and attacked her lack of ability to decipher the glyphs. It was a real war, as without his guidance and his helpful, even if often annoyingly amused, explanations, she had to work twice as hard, poring through so many scrolls, comparing so many glyphs that her head would buzz and reel toward each evening, and her hands were hard to restrain from tearing her hair out.

However, by the time the Mexica warriors stormed

Xochimilco's walls with such vengeance, the defenders surrendered before the first of the attackers had a chance of threading the city's stones, she had finished her first scroll, hard put not to whoop with joy. It was an account of some tribute due, or maybe already paid, to Azcapotzalco, but there was a report of a trading expedition that went with the tribute collectors. A lot of symbols for numbers, but enough glyphs to describe the places where the goods were taken from, and the happenings when some of it was not handed over in time, along with the traders reporting of their part of the expedition. A large enough story, and she had read it all!

Pleased to the point of barely stopping herself from running right into the middle of the battle to let him know, she didn't notice that it was all over, with one more adversary losing to the unstoppable Aztecs, surrendering unconditionally. Later, she had learned that this time, the once-again-victorious Mexica spared the city, not even bothering to enter it. They were either tired of looting or in a hurry, with Tlacaelel eager to return home, to start his reforms, the reorganization of his own beloved *altepetl*, to make it fit its newly gained status of importance among the nations of the Great Lake.

Thus, Xochimilco was fined with providing an extensive force of workers to speed up Tlacaelel's numerous construction projects of rebuilding Tenochtitlan, in addition to the full recognition of the Mexica supremacy, and the unconditional agreement of a high annual tribute to be paid.

Not wasting his time, or giving the conquered the opportunity to come to their senses and possibly consider something silly, he had commenced the building of the new causeway between Coyoacan and Tenochtitlan, to connect his city to the mainland in yet another location, he had informed her, scratched and battered, gray with fatigue, but still desirable, dashingly impressive, washed and clad in loincloth only, busy deciphering a dispatch by torchlight.

However, she had her own news to share, so she came up to him and took his scroll away, determined, as full of triumph as he was. His gaze flickered, amused, expectant, challenging, misinterpreting her gesture as a prelude to intimacy, dalliance, lovemaking, the demand of a woman to have her due. He did neglect her for a full market interval while divulging the way to make Xochimilco crumble.

Yet, avoiding his seeking hands, she knelt beside him, thrusting the parchment closer to her face, leaning into the circle of light the fire created, peering at the glyphs covering the smooth brownish surface, desperate to understand. To her relief, it was covered with symbols that clearly meant numbers and people and some goods, a tribute figures probably, or maybe a list of spoils, people and materials designated for his projected causeway. An easy work. Victorious, she read his scroll to him aloud, glyph after glyphs, putting their possible meaning together, encouraged by his stunned silence.

Oh, he was surprised, and oh-so-very-proud of her. His eyes glittered with not a trace of his usual slightly superior amusement, and his smile was everything she had hoped for. That night, lying in his arms, she knew she had gained more of his respect, more of his admiration; that she was not just another woman for him to enjoy and discard after a while. He might have been a mighty conqueror, the second most important man of the growing Mexica empire, but he was her man, to love and to talk and to laugh with, and to tease sometimes, to read scrolls by the campfire with, and to listen to his fascinating stories about history and politics and gods and great men of the past. Oh, but he did love talking to her, airing his thoughts aloud, enjoying himself, yet not as much as she did while listening to him.

Hiding her smile, she went on, relishing these memories, smelling the scent of rain in the air. Nighttime Texcoco was even more beautiful, more alluring than in the daylight. Slowing her steps, she lingered by a small one-story pyramid, enjoying the sight of the colorful stones washed by the last of the moonlight. It was cold, but smooth, freshly painted, very pleasant to touch.

Quickly, she mounted the low stairs, reaching the temple, touching the inscription upon its base, eager to read it as she always did. The ability to decipher glyphs still filled her with pride, to attack and conquer every time anew. It might have belonged to Coatlicue, her favorite goddess, whose temple she hadn't managed to find in Tenochtitlan.

Tenochtitlan!

The thought of this *altepetl* made her frown. Oh, how she had anticipated her first visit there, how expectant she had been. The famous island-city was about to reveal itself, to welcome her into her new home, to offer a new beginning. What a thrill.

Well, reveal itself it did, disappointing her greatly. No special sights, no riches, no refinement, no wonders of architecture like in Azcapotzalco, not even the calm good-natured coziness of Coyoacan. Just a plenitude of wharves and buildings, dusted roads with wide, smelly canals twisting alongside many of them, with canoes hurrying and people hurrying, all busy and purposeful, with the perpetual dampness of the air irritating, permeating one's lungs. The famous *altepetl* of the fierce Mexica Aztecs, the conquerors of the Tepanec Empire, turned out to be no more than a large sprawling town. No beauty, no elegance, no dignified bearing, but buzzing like an anthill. So many people! Azcapotzalco was larger by far, and yet it never seemed to be as crowded as Tenochtitlan, as cramped, as overwhelming, as gushing and hostile.

And hostile it had been, indeed. She had learned all about it upon reaching the Palace and the quarters allocated to her. A pretty suite of two rooms and a balcony. What riches! Was she to live like an emperor's Chief Wife?

Well, the Emperor's wives lived elsewhere, she was to discover, as the Chief Warlord's and the Head Adviser's quarters were located in the other wing of the Palace. A richly furnished, extensive space, with its own courtyard, fountains, and alleys lined with exotic trees. Tlacaelel's women lacked no luxury, neither his highborn wives, nor the neat collection of his concubines. The wives had their own quarters, some children, and an army of slaves to order about, while the concubines shared suites and servants and plenty of time spent in idleness and boredom. The second most powerful Mexica man had been too busy to entertain his women. He was mostly away, working day and night, his concubines discarded long since, not thrown out of the Palace due to a simple generosity. A life of loveless luxury was apparently preferable to the tough reality outside the Palace's walls, especially for those who bore him children, quite a few women.

Stupid fat fowls, each and every one of them, was Tlalli's conclusion, as she would pace her very own prettily furnished suite of rooms. What lack of pride! Of course, she would leave the moment he tired of her. What kind of life was that, to just sit and wait for him to maybe appear, to notice one of them again for a quick, indifferent bout of lovemaking, gossiping through the long days, nibbling sweetmeats and getting fatter? Did they think he was interested in any of this?

She would have run away from the very beginning but for his frequent visits, but for these wonderful nights when he would stay with her until just before dawn, until it was time for him to break his fast with some food and a cup of fresh water and go about his work. Oh, how she wished she could have gone with him! To help him all she could, to do something useful. Like back at Coyoacan and Xochimilco, with no spiteful women all around, watching her every step, gossiping, hating her with all their hearts.

And did they hate her! His wives, his concubines, all of them, even the servants, they all felt that she was the effrontery to this wing of the Palace, if not to the whole of Tenochtitlan; a foreigner, a commoner, a hated Tepanec with no sense and no fineness, not strikingly beautiful even, with her being too small and too slender, with no pretty curves, and her face marred by a twisted scar, the reminder of her revenge on despised Maxtla. She was nothing but a pushy foreigner who didn't want to learn her rightful place, a woman he favored too openly, while neglecting the rest of his refined, exquisite, aristocratic collection. What insult!

She tried to pay them no attention, holding her head high and sleeping through the days, as the nights were too precious to spend on mere sleep. His company was more than enough to keep her happy. She needed no friends, anyway. In Azcapotzalco she'd none either, apart from Etl, but now she had books and no need to struggle for meals and survival. No need to carve figurines, unless for her pleasure. She didn't do it very often these days. The books were better, and he made sure to send her whole chests of those, accounts of old battles and calendars, and even some poetry he used to help her decipher between their spells of desire and longing for each other's touch.

So when he would leave the city – too often for her liking – spending many days away on political visits, pacifying yet another conquered region, reorganizing their affairs, campaigning sometimes, like that time when the Acolhua reminded the Mexica of their promise of help in recapturing Texcoco, she was not at all miserable, because by then, she was very busy, fully occupied, determined to learn the mystery of writing. And not by just drawing a glyph or two, like her noble-born rivals did from time to time, but to draw quickly and accurately, like the scribes did, recording important happenings. Because she intended to write a book, her own account of the fall of Azcapotzalco, to present him with upon his return.

Her stomach would convulse, and she would stifle a gasp of delight every time she imagined how surprised he would be, how appreciative. Maybe he would even remember that night on the outskirts of Coyoacan, when he had told her about the different ways to tell the same event, written down at the whim of the author and according to his or her point of view. Oh yes, he would be happy to know that she remembered, remembered all of it, every single word of what he had said, because his words were as precious as his deeds. Maybe he would even ask her to write his account of the same event, and this would force him to spend more time in her company.

Battling her excitement, she would plod on, crouching on her balcony or in her rooms, working by the light of the torch at night, the way she had seen him do many times, the ambitious project filling her days and nights fully, destroying many pieces of expensive *amate*-paper the slaves were required to bring in with the same frequency they had been supplying sweetmeats and beautiful cotton cloths to the other dwellers of this wing of the Palace.

By the time Texcoco was re-conquered, she had completed her project, and oh gods, had he been surprised! Not so much by the long scroll and its contents—this lack of appreciation disappointed her greatly—but by her unexpected ability to do so.

Eyes narrow, he had made her squat by the low table, sweeping refreshments aside and ordering a fresh piece of paper to be brought, along with the pile of sharpened charcoal.

"Write it down," he had told her, beginning to describe the opening stages of the Texcoco campaign, how he had led five hundred elite Mexica warriors out of Coatlinchan, past Huexotla, all the way toward the southern parts of Texcoco.

She was on the verge of tears, finding it impossible to keep up. She didn't even know the symbols of the mentioned towns, barely remembering the glyph describing the *altepetl* of Texcoco. This one appeared in her Azcapotzalco account, but only briefly, when she had mentioned the entering Acolhua. Oh, he must have thought she could do miracles, and he would be so disappointed.

However, all he did was laugh heartily, with no condescension, and not even his usual baiting amusement. She did not badly at all, he had told her, one hand pulling her chin up, making her face him, the other encircling her sagging shoulders, warm and supportive. For a person who had just taught herself to write, she wrote surprisingly well, accurately, even if not quickly enough. She had much to learn yet, but he would see to it, he assured her, that she would get her daily lessons until she was able to write like the best of scribes. A treasure like her, he had said, a person with so many talents and ambition could not be left to her own devices. He should have begun teaching her in the first place.

Safe in his embrace, snug in his warmth and this familiar, wonderful scent of his, she remembered her excitement welling, threatening to explode and kill her with too much happiness. He did appreciate her surprise, even if not in the way she intended him to.

"But what about my book? What about the fall of Azcapotzalco?" she had asked later, lying beside him, spent and elated, not wishing to drift into sleep and have these precious moments with him end, not yet.

"What about it?" His voice trailed off, either sleepy or deep in thought.

"Did you like it? Was it written well?"

He shifted, losing some of his relaxed abandonment. "Yes, it was not done badly. I've yet to read it in detail, when I find time to do this, that is." Propping his head on his arm, he peered at her, suddenly serious, free of their post-lovemaking euphoria. "But you should not spend your time recording the past. History is being made now, in these very moments, and it's worthy of recording, every little detail of it." His eyes clouded, turned unreadable. "The past isn't of any interest. It does not exist anymore. It will go away, and no one will ever remember."

There was something about the way he had said it, about the way his face closed, lost its usual sincerity. He looked this way, sometimes, maybe often, but never with her.

"But all those scrolls you sent for me to read. They were about the past events, old wars, old calendars. They were written down for people to remember. We want to remember our past. We can't pretend yesterday did not exist."

His face cleared of shadows. "Yes, of course. I'm not telling you to forget anything. Your past is yours, to cherish or to hate, the way you prefer. But," he shrugged again, "our present and our future are those that are important enough to spend the expensive paper and beautiful colors on. Don't waste your time writing about Azcapotzalco and the times when the Tepanecs ruled. The new world is upon us, and you'll spend your amate-paper and charcoal better recording the history you witness, the life you live, the life I live." He smiled broadly. "Learn as diligently as you did until now, and if you write fast and accurately enough, I will use you as my scribe, sometimes. Not around the city, it would be too much of an affront to every custom and tradition, but I will be taking you along on some of my journeys, to record history as it unfolds before your eyes." The mischievous spark was back, flickering in the depth of his eyes. "You wouldn't want to come to Texcoco when they get around to celebrating Nezahualcoyotl's ascending the throne, would you? It might be boring for you to be there, to witness it all and maybe write it down."

She found it difficult to breathe. "You would...you will...Would you, truly? Oh, gods!" The words refused to formulate, as she grabbed his arm with her trembling hands. "Would you take me there with you?"

He raised his eyebrows, clearly pleased with her response. "I may, if you write fast and accurately enough by then. How about that challenge, eh? You have at least three, maybe four moons, depending on Coyotl's ability to put his people to work." His chuckle shook the air as he dropped onto his back, to stretch luxuriously and to lie still for a moment. "He is going to be the Emperor, at long last. He waited for too long. But the aristocratic brat wants it all perfect, wants to see his Texcoco as beautiful as it used to be before the Tepanecs, for him to reclaim his birthright. So I predict he will drive his people insane for the next few moons to come, building and rebuilding, spending the last of the spoils and everything he might put together as a means of payment to all these craftsmen and regular workers." Another chuckle. "He should have stayed for the Xochimilco campaign. Then he would have enough free labor to hasten his projects. As it is, Tenochtitlan's new causeway will be finished long before Texcoco will be done polishing its pyramids' cracked edges. Good for them." A soft nudge of an elbow into her ribs. "And good for you. You will have enough time to turn into the fastest, most accurate recorder I've ever had."

And now, huddled under the dark mass of a stone wall that was sheltering someone's dwelling, watching the towering silhouette of Texcoco's Great Pyramid, she smiled, knowing that she had done a good job of learning the scribes' trade. She was not yet as fast as she, and he, wished her to be, but she was clean and accurate, and her records were already praised and copied. Well, some of them. He did not make her work as often as she wanted.

About to resume her walk, she shivered, then pressed against the cold stones, her heart missing a beat, then beginning to pound in fear. Holding her breath, she watched a figure appearing above another wall, not far away from her shelter. As black as the night, it froze for a moment, watching intently, barely visible against the last of the moon. *A ghost? A dark spirit of the night, coming from the*

Underworld of Mictlan, or maybe heading back there now.

She could not get enough air. Stifling a cry, she shut her eyes tight, knowing that one was never to watch such spirits. However, this way it was even more frightening, with only the moaning of the wind surrounding her, overcoming the wild pounding of her heart.

Sick with fear, she opened her eyelids a fraction, seeing again only the dark mass of the stones and the graying sky above it. The creature was gone, but how far?

Not far, apparently. She could sense it somewhere there, beneath the wall, while another black apparition took its place, then another. That last one moved less gracefully, struggling with a large bundle it seemed to carry.

Her heart fluttering in her stomach, she pressed deeper into the cold stones, wishing to disappear inside them. Oh gods, what had she been thinking, running around all alone in the nighttime city? A veteran of living on the streets, she had taken the regular dangers of the large city into account, bringing along her knife and knowing which areas were better avoided. Yet, who would think the Acolhua *altepetl* was full of ghosts and dark nightly spirits!

The silhouette on the wall lingered longer than the first, clumsier, having less of the ethereal way of gliding like the ghost it was. If not for it being so strangely black, she would have thought it was a mere thief scaling someone's wall. There were plenty of those around Azcapotzalco's marketplace.

Encouraged a little, she watched the figure gesturing with its free arm, then jumping down, to be swallowed by the darkness. The sky was brightening rapidly, but she didn't dare to breathe, clutching her sweaty palms together, trembling.

No sound reached her ears, no shuffling of footsteps, nothing. The creatures disappeared, swallowed by the night, to dive back into the depths of the Underworld. Oh, mighty gods!

CHAPTER 2

Tlacaelel's head pounded, heavy with drink and lack of sleep. Replete with food, he fought his exhaustion off, knowing that the luxury of lying down was not a thing he was likely to enjoy, not until the second part of the next day, maybe. Until after the Great Ceremony.

Pleased to have a moment of solitude, he sought Nezahualcoyotl's tall figure with his gaze, finding him squatting by the nearby cluster of low tables, conversing with a group of richly dressed people, his Acolhua subjects most probably, either from Texcoco itself or the delegation from one of the provinces.

There were plenty of those all around, crowding the great *altepetl* to the brim, excited by the impending ceremony. At long last, the line of the Acolhua rulers was to be restored, and with none other than their beloved champion, the surviving heir of the previous emperor, Ixtlilxochitl, now-dead, killed by the Tepanecs more than ten summers earlier, dying together with the Acolhua independence.

Grinning, Tlacaelel reached for his cup, remembering those turbulent moons. He had been a mere youth back then, the son of the Second Mexica Emperor, Huitzilihuitl, a legitimate heir, but with no hope of achieving *his* birthright. His mother was not the First Wife but the minor one, second, or third, or whatever was the count, a mere background to the Emperor's power-hungry Chief Wife, a Tepanec, the daughter of Tezozomoc, a favorite daughter at that. She had been the one responsible for the reduced tribute Tenochtitlan was paying to its overlords back then, allegedly having pled with her powerful father, because up to these times, Tenochtitlan was a mere subject city, stuck on an island, with nowhere to grow and nowhere to expand, groaning under the heavy tribute, despised by everyone, the aristocratic Texcoco included, with not even fresh water to drink. Its first Emperor, the much-admired and revered Acamapichtli, did his best to put his *altepetl* on the regional map, to keep it safe from the Tepanec appraisals and to make it grow slowly but steadily, yet the heavy tribute kept his efforts curbed.

Well, all of it had changed when his heir, Huitzilihuitl, acquired his Tepanec royal wife. The tribute was reduced to one-fourth of what it had been before, and the water construction was permitted to be built, bringing good drinking water to Tenochtitlan all the way from the mainland by the elaborate construction of clay pipes and earthen bridges.

Tenochtitlan was free to grow, but there was a price to pay. The Tepanecs demanded unwavering obedience. The Mexica Aztecs were to do as they were told, to take an active part in all Tepanec wars, to do as they were bidden. The Emperor's Chief Wife had seen to it that her father's wishes were deferred to and that no insurrections were forthcoming. She had also bore the Mexica Emperor a son, Chimalpopoca, who was to inherit, of course.

Even though being a mere youth of less than twenty summers, Tlacaelel had been wise enough to cherish no illusions, careful to attract no attention from the power-hungry woman who seemed not above disposing of the people who might have threatened her son's inheritance. He had still been less than twenty, out of *calmecac*-school, busy acquiring his first battle experience by doing his shield-bearer duties, dreaming of great warriors' deeds, when the Tepanec-Acolhua war broke. In the beginning, Huitzilihuitl had managed to avoid an active participation, not willing to betray his old friends and allies of Texcoco, but not coming to their aid, either. Some summers passed with the Mexicas fence-sitting, maneuvering and struggling to stay neutral, but also enjoying the benefits of the increasing trade that their neutrality in the raging war had brought them. Tenochtitlan kept growing, and so did Tlacaelel's ambition. He wanted to be a great warrior, a great leader; he wanted to be remembered. His *altepetl*'s neutrality hurt his pride.

Apparently, it seemed that his father, the Emperor, shared the same sentiment. Wavering and vacillating for moons, secretly sympathizing with his Acolhua neighbors, who warred on and on, with varying success, at one point even invading the Tepanec lands, he had held his breath along with the rest of Tenochtitlan citizens, most of them no lovers of the Tepanecs and their oppressive rule. It might have came to Tenochtitlan joining the war, backing the Acolhua, maybe, but then, the still relatively young Mexica Emperor died, with no reason and no explanation, having never been sick or unwell.

Wild rumors flooded the grief-stricken city, while his successor, a boy of barely twelve summers, took on the burden of the reign, backed and assisted by his mother, the all-powerful Tezozomoc's daughter. The Mexica people frowned, but could do nothing, while Tenochtitlan's policies changed, dramatically at that. Now the island-city sided with the Tepanecs openly, devotedly, sending its warriors in time to help them squash the rebellious Acolhua and to conquer Texcoco and all its provinces.

The war was over, and peace once again came to the lands of the Great Lake, with the Tepanecs turning yet more powerful, unquestionable masters of the entire valley and all its surroundings. Humble and afraid, the Mexica kept very quiet, not daring to anger their overlords, but yet again enjoying the fruits of their forced betrayal, with a new source of income coming from Texcoco that was granted to them as a prize for their good behavior.

"I wonder what grand plans are to come from this deep thinking." A loud voice tore Tlacaelel from his reverie, bringing him back to the elegance of Texcoco Palace, the re-conquered Acolhua *altepetl*. Blinking, he looked up into the beaming face of the Acolhua Chief Warlord, the notorious Highlander, a friend of many summers. "Or had the glorious leader fallen asleep with his eyes open?"

Gesturing to the maid that was passing by with a tray full of plates and cups, the Highlander squatted on a vacant mat, his beam one of the widest. As always, the enormous amounts of *octli*

consumed by this man did little more than put an additional
spark to the widely-spaced eyes, although, for once, his speech
did seem to slur lightly. He must have been drinking the entire
night.

"To tell the truth, I was musing about the past this time, not the
future." Refusing another cup of drink, Tlacaelel picked small
tamale, grinning at his friend, challenging. "It was nice to have
your Texcoco paying us tribute. We put that income to good use."

"Oh, yes, you greedy Mexicas got the best out of this whole
mess. Every turmoil had you, cunning bastards that you were,
coming out on top of it, did it not?" His chuckle light, non-
committal, the Highlander's face clouded nevertheless. "Those
were some times to remember. Tenochtitlan was not a boring
place, to say the least. I was lucky to survive that ugly *altepetl* of
yours."

"Speaking of coming out on top of every overturn, you could
teach a class in *calmecac* about it. No matter what happened to
you, you always came up, heading for better positions."

The man laughed heartily. "Yes, you can put it this way, too."
His gaze swept over the spacious hall. "I regret nothing.
Tenochtitlan gave us enough adventures to recall when we are old
and useless, sitting by the fire, telling old stories, boring our sons
and their sons to death."

"And we still have a lot of work ahead of us." Stretching,
Tlacaelel eyed the hubbub in his turn. So many people, and still
the marble-lined hall didn't look cramped or overcrowded.
"Coyotl finally got what is rightfully his, against all the odds, eh?
This man enjoys benevolence of the gods, but he had to work hard
to achieve his ends. His struggle changed him in many ways."

"Coyotl will make a great emperor. Texcoco and the Acolhua
provinces will prosper like never before." The Highlander's face
held none of his usual light-hearted mischief. "He has so many
projects, so many ideas. It would make your head reel." The
mischievous spark was back. "Oh well, maybe not your ever-busy
head, but that of any other ordinary person." Another assessment
of the glittering eyes. "You have even more plans buzzing around
that stubborn skull of yours. I'm prepared to bet my newly

acquired wealth on it. Even the great house by the Plaza that is yet to be rebuilt for me to show it off and make my wives happy."

Receiving a friendly nudge into his ribs, Tlacaelel grinned. "I'm glad to have your faith in my abilities, old friend."

"So what are you up too, old fox? A causeway to connect Coyoacan with Tenochtitlan, I understand. A sound, good idea, especially if built at the expense of Xochimilco. I do see why you had to make this *altepetl* submit. But why are you eager to head farther to the south?"

Against his will, Tlacaelel frowned. "Your spies are good. I hadn't talked about it to anyone of importance yet."

"You mean Itzcoatl doesn't know?"

"He knows, of course he knows. There is little that escapes our revered emperor's squinted eyes." He measured the Highlander with his gaze, taking in the decided handsomeness of the broad face, the newly acquired scar running down the high cheek, the tough spark to the widely spaced eyes. "Won't you join us in that campaign?"

"Well, yes, maybe. I haven't talked to Coyotl about that yet." The man narrowed his eyes. "I can see what's for you there in the south. You need to make your point, establish yourself as the firm heirs to the Tepanec Empire, before anyone foolish enough to assume otherwise does something silly." A shrug. "But us? I don't know. What will we do with Cuauhnahuac or the surrounding towns?"

"I will find out who your spies in my palace are," said Tlacaelel, not amused by the fact that his friend knew even the exact location of his projected campaign. "What's for you in the fertile valley of Cuauhnahuac? Think about it, oh Honorable Warlord. Fields upon fields of cotton, sown and harvested every year. What, indeed, would you do with all that?"

"Cotton, eh?" The Highlander studied his cup thoughtfully. "I see your point. Yes, I suppose we might benefit by joining you there in the south."

"And make the re-conquest of Acolman wait?"

A pair of indignant eyes flew at him. "Your spies are not that bad either, Mexica Head Adviser."

Tlacaelel just grinned. "Why was he in a hurry to proceed with the ceremony now, rather than wait for Texcoco to take a better shape?"

The Highlander shrugged again, but his eyes turned cagey. "I suppose he wants to get the formalities over with."

"You suppose, eh?" Laughing heartily, Tlacaelel accepted the offered cup, this time brought to them by a prettier maid. "Want to know what else my spies have been telling me?" he asked, when the slave was again out of hearing range. The obvious discomfort of the glorious warriors' leader was too tempting not to explore. "They say that not all is well in the Acolhua ruling circles. They say some of the older Texcoco nobility are not happy about the policies of their young ruler. Legitimate heir or not, they seem to think he should confer with them more." Biting into his tamale, he discovered it was filled with mashed turkey, his favorite meat, softer and easier to chew than the dogs that ruled Tenochtitlan's menus. "They say that even the great ruler's favorite sister is giving him trouble, threatening to leave the capital."

The gritting of the man's teeth could be heard on the other side of the hall, of that Tlacaelel was quite sure.

"She won't be leaving any time soon!" The Acolhua Warlord's voice had a stony ring to it, the cup clutched tightly between his rigid palms, the drink in it forgotten.

"What's troubling her?"

The man rolled his eyes, then emptied his cup in one gulp.

"If you want to know, it's your own revered emperor. Itzcoatl. Her hatred for him knows no bounds." The man shrugged. "I'm not overly fond of him myself. I would rather have *you* ruling Tenochtitlan. But I accept things as they are, the way you do, the way Coyotl does. While her? Oh, she hates this man passionately. She wants him humbled, or better yet, dead. She can't say his name without spitting in rage. Her hatred is blinding her."

His own drink forgotten, Tlacaelel studied his cup, remembering her vividly, the beautiful woman in her mid-twenties, as exquisite as a stone statue, with her skin as creamy as the foam of a chocolate drink, and her eyes as dark as polished

obsidian, glittering as magnificently. Passionate and forceful,
bubbling with life and coveted by many, first the minor wife of
Tenochtitlan's Second Emperor, then the Chief Wife of his
successor, young Chimalpopoca, the Third Mexica Emperor,
murdered in his prime, by the Tepanecs, allegedly. But not really.
Tlacaelel knew better. And so did she. And so did her current
husband, the Chief Warlord of Texcoco, the notorious Highlander,
with whom she was reported to have been having a love affair
since times immemorial, while belonging to Tenochtitlan's
emperors.

"She is not the ruler of Texcoco," he said mildly, immersed in
the study of his polished golden cup and the way it glittered,
reflecting the flickering lights of many torches. "She is neither the
empress nor a member of the emperor's family now." He
shrugged, hiding a grin. "You should control your wives better,
Honorable Warlord."

Another grunt told him that his friend was not nearly as
amused as he was. "I can't keep her away from politics, not when
Coyotl lets her have her way, time after time."

"He does that, doesn't he?" Glancing up, Tlacaelel sought the
tall figure of the Acolhua Emperor once again, now conversing
with the ruler of Tlacopan, squatting together with this third
member of the Triple Alliance, the conquerors of the Tepanec
Empire, set on ruling the valley of the Great Lake instead of its
previous masters. In this powerful gathering only Itzcoatl was
missing, too busy to attend, sending his Head Adviser in his
stead.

The valley of the Great Lake? He hid his grin. The Tepanec
Empire would be nothing but an unpleasant memory of a small
local power when all was settled and done, when he had finished
with his projects and plans. His Mexica people would rule the
known world, from the distant Mayans to the no-less-distant
lands of the Purepecha or Huastecas. His Mexica Empire, Triple
Alliance or not, would be strong, efficient, not like the realm of
their predecessors. History was being made in these very
moments, he reflected, watching the two rulers conferring, talking
calmly, reservedly, wary of each other. It was unfolding before his

eyes, with him playing a major part, not satisfied with being just a small tidbit of it.

Tlalli should write it all down, he thought, a familiar wave of warmth spreading at the memory of her, washing through his limbs. Her attempt to record the fall of Azcapotzalco was naïve, an artless work full of errors and cumbersome, improperly drawn glyphs. But it was her first work, and she had done a brilliant job of teaching herself the secrets of the written word in such a short span of time and with no help.

Oh, this woman was a treasure! As pretty and vital, as untamed and not fitting as on the day he had found her hanging under his balcony in the conquered Palace of Azcapotzalco, she made his senses thrill, with her slender but delectable body as much as with the unpredictability of her mind. When, in the burning ruins of Coyoacan, he'd made the decision to take her as his woman, believing that she was his talisman, his sign of the new path he and his countryfolk were about to take, he hadn't thought of any practical aspects. She was a woman to enjoy and to please, a personal gift from the dying Tepanec Empire. But oh, benevolent gods, she was so much more than this. From an illiterate commoner, she had turned into almost a partner; now, two summers later, well-versed in history and laws, even in the ways of planning campaigns, devouring scrolls by the hundreds, deciphering the meanings of the elaborate clusters of glyphs almost as accurately as he did—he, who had been renowned for his ability to read faster and more accurately than anyone!— already writing these down as fast as some scribes.

Oh, she had so much potential, a treasure to cherish and enjoy, to maneuver wisely, since unsupervised, she could do silly things. Like writing a book on the fall of Azcapotzalco, and from the Tepanec point of view, of all things! What a strange, unacceptable idea, when the Tepanec history was to be forgotten, erased from the records, if possible.

"I support Coyotl in his policies and in whatever he intends to do." Once again, the Highlander's voice tore Tlacaelel from his thoughts. "He is wise and farsighted, and he listens to good advice. He will make a great emperor. He has always been thoughtful and studious, but the last half twenty of summers turned him into an incredibly wise man. I think he is the best ruler Texcoco can ask for, my personal loyalty to him as a friend notwithstanding." The man's eyes were also on the conversing rulers, assessing them calmly. "He is wise and worth listening to. I think you, the Mexicas, are doing right by listening to his opinions."

"But not all of his subjects think that." Shifting to ease his aching back, Tlacaelel studied his friend closely. "What is the main complaint of those who disagree with his policies?"

The Highlander's gaze met his, firm, unwavering. "His close association with your people, with the Mexica who betrayed the Acolhua in the first Tepanec War, and who made a tremendous profit out of it. That is their main complaint."

"I see." He stood the piercing gaze. "You do agree with them, to some extent."

"To some extent, everyone agrees with them." The wide shoulders lifted in a shrug. "But it is of no importance. The past is no concern of mine. If I let it rule my mind, I would not be here in Texcoco at all. The Highlanders, my true people, were at war with the Texcocans for decades and more. But they put their differences aside, letting the past rest for the sake of the future. And this is what we all need to do." The smile blossomed, a mirthless, somewhat cold grin. "You Mexicas are the natural ally to the Lowlanders, whether they like it or not. To start a war on you would be unwise. Both of our nations need to fortify their current achievements first." Nodding, the man shrugged, gesturing to the passing maid, demanding more *octli*. "Many Mexica and Acolhua understand that with perfect clarity, even if some are not entirely happy about it. My Chief Wife, for one. But she won't be listened to. Not in this matter. Coyotl is wise, too wise to let anyone rule in his stead, even his favorite sister, the force of nature that she is." Another shrug came accompanied by a mirthless grin. "She won't leave Texcoco, and she won't join those who will. I can promise you that."

Impressed, Tlacaelel nodded in his turn. "Good. I'm glad Coyotl values your opinion. You are a wise man, Chief Warlord of

Texcoco, even though you usually don't bother to show any of it."

A wide grin was his answer. "You must be desperate to compliment me in this way, oh Honorable Adviser, second most powerful man of Tenochtitlan. You, Mexicas, are yet to develop more subtlety. But yes, you can count on me sounding my good opinions of that foul-smelling island of yours." Ducking out of Tlacaelel's elbow's reach, the man avoided a rough push into his ribs, but barely, too drunk to enjoy his usual catlike agility. "No subtlety, as I said."

"Oh shut up, you wild Highlander. Speaking of savages, where are your countryfolk? Went back home?"

"Yes, they did. They seek no glory with the dubious allies like your Lowlanders. They fancy having no part of your history and the questionable way you are going to write it down."

"Oh, yes, with the spoils they carried out of Azcapotzalco, no wonder they are keeping low. They cleaned the Tepanec Capital more thoroughly than the street rats clean a corpse on the summers of famine."

But the Highlander's grin widened, refusing to take offense. "Without them, you would never have taken the annoying Tepanec Capital at all, so stop complaining. They did their part, helped to rid you of the Tepanecs, and now they are home, enjoying themselves. And fortifying their towns too, probably, just in case. Who knows if you, sneaky Lowlanders, are not nurturing wild ideas concerning our mountains and the valley beyond it. Eh?" Now it was Tlacaelel's turn to receive a friendly nudge into his ribs. "I'll bring my Acolhua warriors to help you expand into the south mainly to make sure you are not sneaking glances toward my hills."

"I'll sneak my glances wherever I want." Suppressing his laughter, Tlacaelel motioned to the slave with a tray full of foamy chocolate drinks. "But yes, talk to Coyotl and make your famous sword ready."

Refusing the simmering cup of spicy chocolate, the Highlander snatched a rolled-up tortilla.

"My sword is always ready." His smile spread wider, turned dreamy, as though remembering his first lovemaking. "Just to think that I never fought without it. I got it in my very first battle, when not even a warrior, just a wild youth of mere fifteen summers. It happened more than half of twenty summers ago, old friend. Think about it! So many spans of seasons, so many battles, and this wonder held on. Oh, mighty Tezcatlipoca!" The man's admiration was strangely open, unconcealed. "A regular sword would have cracked and split long ago, wouldn't it? You replace the obsidian all the time, but the shaft would be rotting after so many battles. It has to! But not this one."

"And the carvings?" asked Tlacaelel, fascinated. The sword had been the talk of Tenochtitlan for many summers, covered with strange-looking carvings from its handle to its tip, decisive lines running between the obsidian spikes, blood-freezing figures and symbols, eerily alive, threatening, filled with darker shades where the blood had soaked in, not always wiped away quickly enough.

The Highlander's eyes clouded. "I don't remember how it all started, but at some point, yes, I was carving them. Not because I wanted to, but because I *had* to."

I bet you did, thought Tlacaelel, disturbed. *Those images could not be just fancy carvings, and this sword did keep you safe through quite a few deadly adventures, lucky son of a rat that you are!*

"I'm glad this sword, its magic, and its owner are with us," he said, studying the familiar face, pleased with what he saw.

Oh but this man was a true asset, the best warrior of the entire valley, his instincts perfect, his reactions swift, his thinking clear, his battle experience unmatched. A talented leader too, but not someone he, Tlacaelel, would promote to the highest level. Too much impulsiveness, too much independent thinking, too much improvising. Itzcoatl was right about this man. Tenochtitlan needed well-disciplined leaders, now that he was about to reorganize its warriors' forces into tightly controlled units, closely observed and meticulously guided. The brilliant Highlander was best used as an Acolhua ally. There, he could do as he pleased with the forces he brought along, just like in Azcapotzalco's campaign. As an ally. Not the leader of the entire enterprise.

He watched his friend, recalling his last escapades in

Tenochtitlan, still remembered well in the city, the alleged murder of the Third Emperor notwithstanding, although Tlacaelel knew it was not his friend's doing. The tale of the eerie killers clothed in black, swift, lethal, invisible in the darkness, carrying strange knives, still made his hair rise. The Highlander had, indeed, been there. Maneuvered into trying to murder the Emperor by Itzcoatl himself, he had witnessed the actual assassination, telling Tlacaelel all about it later through the same night. And he still carried that strangely bright, glittering knife he had managed to take from one of the killers.

Oh, what days those had been, running around Tenochtitlan, making it ready for the Tepanec invasion, turning a blind eye to its internal upheavals, knowing better than to try and stop the projected death of his own half brother, the Emperor, but trying, at least, to save his friend and his family. One good deed, among many heartlessly calculated ones. He shook his head, hating those rare waves of remorse. He had done many bad things, but the safety of this man's family was one of his good deeds.

"How are those wild twins of yours?"

"Oh, don't even ask!" The Highlander's face lit brighter than the Palace's hall illuminated with too many torches. "Wild, unruly things. Tenochtitlan is lucky to be rid of this pair."

"Put them in *calmecac*. They are of an age." As fond of the wild pair as he had been, Tlacaelel still felt irritated by his friend's obvious neglect of the necessity to discipline his promising sons.

"I did. Of course, I did. They have been in *calmecac* since we reorganized this establishment, doing surprisingly well, come to think of it. Coatl, that is. He is bright and eager, very strong, very adaptive. A good boy. He'll make a great warrior." The broad face darkened. "His brother is a different matter. He went completely out of hand." Shrugging, the man looked away. "That knee he had broken before we fled Tenochtitlan did not heal right. He limps, and it's driving him insane like nothing else would." He shrugged again, then got to his feet. "He will be all right. In the meanwhile, it's already near dawn, and Coyotl's great day is upon us, so I'll better be off, making sure his ceremony is well underway, as perfect as he deserves it to be."

CHAPTER 3

Tlalli watched the man fishing bundles of maize husks out of the steaming pot, his fingers glowing red, unheeded of the heat. A little girl crouched on the mat next to the cooking facilities, guarding a pile of wooden plates and some older stock of food, mainly cold tortillas. Absently, Tlalli winked at her.

This alley was quieter, not as busy and bubbling with life as the main avenue of Texcocan marketplace, she had discovered, wandering about since sunrise. She had been tired and hungry, still unsettled by the vision of the Underworld creatures she had witnessed just before dawn, emerging out of the darkness and disappearing into it, leaving the dwelling of mortal beings they visited with undoubtedly some sort of trouble. Had someone died or been carried out of that house? She had been curious, yet too tired and afraid to go back and see for herself. What if the dark forces were still there, lingering, refusing to leave?

Also, with the ceremony soon to begin, she resolved to make the best out of her independent, even if unauthorized, excursion into the heart of the Acolhua *altepetl* by staying to watch. The visiting dignitaries were all invited, offered the best places to see and participate. But whether their staff, the servants, the scribes, or the concubines were allowed to go or not, she didn't know, didn't want to find out. She would attend as just one of many, with the multitude of commoners crowding the Great Plaza. Even if her absence was noticed, Tlacaelel would understand. He was too busy to bother with her way of spending time, anyway.

The aroma of cooking tamales made her stomach growl. She hadn't eaten since the evening before. Worse still, she hadn't thought to bring along any valuables, nor some cocoa beans. Two summers of Palace's life had spoiled her into forgetting that outside one had to pay for everything one needed. And so now she could not even afford to buy herself a meal.

Shrugging, she turned to go. Another half a day of hunger would not kill her, although the rumbling stomach and the general air of the busy marketplace brought back the memories of Azcapotzalco in force. The good and the bad. She had been so young back then, so lonely, frightened, and unhappy, devastated by the death of her family but full of life too, busy planning her revenge. And there had been Etl, her only friend, the man who loved her. She hadn't known it back then, being just a silly girl, but she knew it now, and although she did not love him back in the same way, she knew she would have done anything to save him, to help him carve his place in the new world of the Aztec domination. If only he had not been so warlike, so stubborn, so convinced of the Tepanec superiority.

She sighed, blinking away a single tear. He had died together with Coyoacan, of that she was sure. If he had lived, he would have let her know. He had died, while she had gone on a new path, happy, loved by the most powerful man in the new rising empire, full of purpose, anything but an insignificant woman. She had done the right thing, but as happy and fulfilled as she might feel, her duty to the memory of Etl and her dead family was clear. She was to remember and to make other people remember the glory of the Tepanecs. She would write the history of Azcapotzalco, but unlike her first writing attempt, she would make her scrolls readable and easy to decipher, so even the less literate people would be able to read and understand.

The aroma of cooking tamales dissolving behind her back, she made her way up the alley, in the direction of the Great Pyramid, its silhouette clearly visible against the glow of the high morning sun. Atop it, the priests must have been busy for some time, but the ceremony was not about to begin, not yet. Still, being just a part of the crowd, she had to make sure to find a good place to watch, and to be prepared to fight for it too, vacating it to none of the pushy dwellers of this great *altepetl* and its guests.

"Come back, you rotten bastards!"

A scream made Tlalli jump, startling her from her reverie. A thickset middle-aged man, obviously an owner of the nearby mat with various objects displayed upon it, was on his feet, waving his hands at the scattering boys, maybe three or four of them, running away as fast as a bunch of scared forest mice; or rather marketplace rats.

"Stop them! They stole my goods," yelled the vendor, hopping about, obviously finding it difficult to decide which one of the culprits to chase. Taking in his age and complexion, Tlalli decided that his chances were slim no matter which direction he decided to take. Yet, now more onlookers were displaying an interest, with one of the boys avoiding being grabbed by mere luck, slipping out of the passing man's grip.

"Get the dirty rats!"

Two other boys charged up her alley, their eyes glittering with fright, faces round and young, covered with sweat. Her heart went out to them. A veteran of Azcapotzalco's markets and streets, she knew what their punishment would be if caught. Theft was a grave crime, no matter one's age, with marketplace courts quick and efficient, not lingering and not inclined to be merciful, taking no mitigating circumstances into consideration. Back in her time, she had happened to steal some food, but after witnessing the stoning of a woman who had been caught doing the same, she had preferred to starve or to eat half-rotten things thrown in piles after the vendors would go home. It was a terrible thing to watch, the trial and the punishment equally humiliating, but not equally painful.

"This way!"

One of the boys headed toward her, his hands clutching something, probably the stolen goods, his face more determined than frightened. He was tall and broad-shouldered, surprisingly clean, obviously well-fed, maybe ten summers old or older, with his eyes narrowed and an air of grim resolve surrounding him. It was easy to imagine him getting away, yet something was wrong with the way he ran. There was a slight limp to his gait, barely noticeable but there, slowing his progress. Maybe against the fat vendor he could have made it, but with one of the marketplace frequenters hot on his heels, the boy's chances seemed to diminish rapidly.

Her compassion welling, she watched the little rascal sweeping past her, changing direction, charging toward the wall separating this alley from another, scattering a pile of fruits on his way, adding to his growing list of crimes. Women's indignant screams joined the hubbub. Yet, aside from the additional mess it created, the fleeing criminal's last action seemed erratic, made out of panic, unless he intended to climb the wall, which didn't seem like a possibility, not with the way he limped while running.

Her instincts decided for her the moment the pursuing man swept past, concentrated on his prey, making an additional effort, sensing his victory. At the precisely right moment, her foot stuck out, making the sweaty man bump into it, waving his hands wildly before toppling over into the dust beneath her feet. A sweet victory. From the corner of her eye, she saw the boy leaping up the wall, scaling it with the natural grace of a monkey, damaged leg or not. Apparently, he was quite a climber.

The man was up, cursing loudly.

"What is wrong with you, you dirty *cihua*?" he yelled, pressing so close she had to take an involuntary step back to avoid being pushed off her feet.

She glared back at him, beginning to be afraid. "Nothing!"

"You made me fall!" His face thrust so near, she could smell the odor of hot beans on his breath.

"You ran into me," she said, the effort not to move back taking some of her precious strength away. "You were running like a person possessed. You stumbled over me, and you almost made *me* fall!"

He gasped, lost for words, but her senses screamed danger, the people surrounding them now, blocking her route of escape. What if they tried to drag her to the court? What did she know about the laws of this *altepetl*?

"What happened?"

They seemed to be talking all at once, newcomers pressing forward, trying to see better.

"Dirty boys stole my goods," cried out the fat owner, indignant and fuming but also seemingly pleased to be in the center of the attention. "The rotten good-for-nothing tried several times before. Oh, what I will do when I catch them!" A savage grin stretched the man's lips. "They won't get to the court in one piece."

"Yes, I remember them," said another vendor. "They stole tortillas from my stall some dawns ago. They were three or maybe four, from the local *telpochcalli* school, obviously."

"Yes, yes," contributed more voices. "They are running around here too often to be from a noble school like *calmecac*, although that little brat that is leading them looks well-fed and way too well-dressed."

"He can't be from *calmecac*! No children of nobles would go around stealing things. They are from the local school."

"Maybe we should go and ask—"

"Go to the court and lodge a complaint anyway," suggested a woman with the scattered vegetables. "You have enough witnesses."

"That boy who is leading them, I think I've seen him before," contributed another woman, her eyes gleaming with excitement. "But he wasn't limping, and he *was* in *calmecac*."

"How would you know?"

She confronted the doubting crowd, her hands on her hips. "I deliver my goods everywhere, including the noble establishments."

"Oh, yes, that you do," laughed someone. "Nobles don't need your rotten tomatoes."

The woman cursed and advanced toward the loudest of the doubters, ready to fight for her good name.

"And anyway, what is a tomato or a tortilla compared to an arrowhead?" cried out the momentarily forgotten owner of the stolen goods. "The rotten bastards got away with two of those and a knife into the bargain. They're worth a fortune, unlike the silly tomatoes of yours."

Amidst the growing commotion, Tlalli began to ease away. Having no intention of being a witness in the court that was sure to be located somewhere near, in full session by now, she knew she would be better off putting as much distance as she could between herself and the agitated marketplace frequenters of this unfamiliar *altepetl*. In Azcapotzalco, foreigners did better by being careful, by infringing on no customs, and she wasn't sure she did not break a law by making the man chasing that boy fall. She shouldn't have interfered.

A fresh gust of wind welcomed her, cooling her sweaty face. Hastening her step, she bypassed the scattered tomatoes and the overthrown basket of glaringly red chili peppers. The end of the alley beckoned. Before they would know she was gone, she'd be back in the Palace, safe and sound.

"Wait, you, where are you going?" The shout echoed behind her back, the voice belonging to the man who accused her of making him fall trembling with rage.

Frightened, she didn't turn to look, beginning to walk faster, instead.

"Don't let her get away! She is a witness."

Hearing the hurried footsteps, she hesitated no more, breaking into a run, thinking no more. She just *had* to get away from this place. The excursion into the heart of Texcoco was proving too wild. It was stupid of her to overestimate her abilities to get along in a foreign place. Maybe she had survived Azcapotzalco when a commoner of no significance, but two summers of luxury in Tenochtitlan had apparently made her lose something vital, turning her into a spoiled noble *cihua*, oh yes.

Her heart pumping, their yells making her double her step, she darted into yet another alley, relieved to see it spreading ahead, wide and full of people, not a dead end. Thank all the benevolent gods! She could not climb half as well as the limping boy, the real thief, damn his eyes into the lowest level of the Underworld. Why did she try to help him in the first place?

Mats and stalls and people swept by, but their yells still reached her ears, as she turned into another alley, a wide road lined by low, wooden constructions. Oh gods, was she heading toward the warehouses or the lakeshores? At the busy areas of the wharves she would be lost, at the mercy of her pursuers.

She tried to suppress the welling panic, concentrating on the earth sweeping beneath her feet, her heart thundering in her ears. Why was she running, anyway? She had done nothing wrong back in the marketplace, only helping that boy, but in a quiet, unobtrusive manner. Still, it was stupid of her to get involved, and even more stupid to run away as though she were the one guilty of theft.

Exhausted, she didn't dare to slow her step, now fleeing along a narrower road, desperate to have the silhouette of the Great Pyramid back in sight. Anything that would bring her near the Palace. Or, at least, the Plaza and the ceremony that might have already begun by now. Tlacaelel would be there, even if her falling upon him in this way was sure to make him angry.

Dizzy with exhaustion, she looked around once again, suddenly recognizing the place. Yes, she was heading in the right direction, as she had passed those richly colored walls while wandering near-dawn Texcoco. *The black spirits crawling along one of these dwellings.* Oh gods! She brought her trembling hands up to wipe the sweat away, then saw a litter springing into her view, too close to halt her pace or to avoid the collision.

"What in the name of the mighty gods—" The sturdy man cursed, wavering and pushing her away with his elbow as she crashed into him full-length. "Stupid *cihua!*"

Gasping for breath, Tlalli tried to catch her balance, grabbing the cold stones of the wall for support. The same wall from the night! Or was it? Her heart pounded along with the cursing of the litter-bearers, desperate to steady their cargo.

The curtains of the litter were opened, allowing the view of a pleasantly looking woman who clutched onto the low border, trying not to slip off, her other hand pressing a frightened child, a cute round-faced little girl.

"You dirty, slimy piece of..."

Having been successful at steadying himself and his burden, the man Tlalli bumped into paused, evidently taking in her clothing and jewelry. She wore very little of the precious stones Tlacaelel had bestowed on her from time to time, but still, her neck was encircled by a necklace of topaz, matching the deep blue of her cotton blouse.

The woman in the litter was staring at her now too, wide-eyed.

"Are you all right?" she asked finally, her voice husky, surprisingly deep for the slender form wrapped in the prettily embroidered cotton.

"Yes, yes, I think I am." She wished her heart would stop thumping so wildly. It made her feel nauseous, and the world was blurry, swaying in an annoying manner.

The woman turned toward one of the servants. "Go back inside, and bring a cup of water." She glanced back at Tlalli. "You don't look well. Maybe you better go in with my maid; you could rest a little and eat something. I wish I could attend to you myself, but I am in a hurry." A fleeting smile lit her face, smoothing the grim expression. "The Great Ceremony will begin soon."

"Oh yes, the ceremony." Pressing her lips, Tlalli made an effort to control her breathing. "I was going there too. I...I'm sorry, sorry for making all this trouble."

The woman's smile widened, but her eyes were still shadowed, troubled as well. "You made no trouble. Well, not to me or my household, anyway. Unless..." She shook her head, then brought her hands up, brushing her palms against her face. Taking in the dark rings surrounding the large, prettily tilted eyes, Tlalli remembered the previous night and the Underworld spirits slipping over this very wall.

She straightened up, pleased to feel the trembling lessening. "I thank you for your kindness, but I better be on my way." For the life of her, she was not prepared to enter this particular house. Who knew what still might have been lurking there in the shadows? "I'm sorry for making you late for the ceremony."

"Do as you please." Absently, the woman leaned back against her cushions, just as the young maid came out, carrying a flask of water and a cup. "Pour the lady her drink, Yolotl, and attend to her needs if she asks for something. Then catch up with us on the Plaza."

The Plaza! Tlalli caught her breath. What better way could there be to get back than escorted and protected?

"May I follow your litter, lady?" she asked, accepting her drink with a forced smile. "I need to be on the Plaza too, but I'm afraid I lost my way."

The woman straightened up. "You were going to see the ceremony?"

"Well, yes, I..." Frowning, Tlalli stood the openly puzzled gaze. Who was this woman to question her deeds? She owed explanations to no one, save Tlacaelel, maybe. "Yes, I was going to watch the Great Ceremony."

"Well," the woman hesitated, one eyebrow arched, eyes sliding down, appraising Tlalli's clothing again, "then why don't you ride with me? There is enough space in my litter, and although you seem to have no trouble traveling on foot, I can't have a lady of your status following me like a servant."

"Oh, no, please, I can't intrude in this way..." Wistfully, Tlalli eyed the cushions spread upon the wooden platform, her tiredness welling. It would be a wonderful way to solve all her problems.

The smile was back, reaching the woman's eyes this time, glittering in their depths, as though reading her unexpected companion's thoughts.

"Come. The Plaza is not far away, but we need to hurry."

Frowning, the litter-bearers lowered their cargo, keeping it steady, not swaying in the least. When Tlalli neared, the little girl pressed further into the woman's skirts, as though trying to disappear there, leaving plenty of space for the intruder to take. Sliding in, Tlalli stifled a sigh of relief. But for a quick snack, she would have declared herself happy, indeed. The wild adventure was over.

"You are so very generous, lady," she said, squatting carefully, glad to busy herself with rearranging her skirts, embarrassed at the dirty, wrinkled state of the expensive material. "I'm grateful."

"There is no need for gratitude." The woman eyed her guest calmly, her smile reserved, hands caressing the girl's shoulders, as though trying to relay calmness and a sense of security to her child. "In my time, I've been through similar situations. Alone in foreign places, lost. Having met nothing but kindness, I do feel obliged to repay—err, how do I put it?—my debt to the benevolent deities; those who sent only good people to cross my path."

Fascinated, Tlalli eyed the delicate face with no touch of the yellow cream or other sort of tricks that the noblewomen applied to their skins in order to make themselves prettier. The thick, braided hair might have been washed with indigo this morning, for it shone magnificently in the rays of the high morning sun, but the rest of this woman was real, genuine, honest, curiously calm, even though deep inside, she seemed to be upset with something. Was she a foreigner to this *altepetl*, too? She certainly had some sort of an accent, not speaking like the Acolhua people in the least.

"There are many foreign delegations in the city these days," the woman was saying. "You must have arrived with one of them."

"Yes. Yes, I did." Shaking her head, Tlalli tried to get rid of the strange sensation. "I should never have wandered around the way I did. It was silly of me."

"Why did you?"

"Well..." Against her will, she winked, meeting the pair of widely opened eyes at the level of the woman's skirt. The child gasped and dived back into the colorful rectangles of the soft cotton. "I...I was just curious. I wanted to see Texcoco as it is. I've never been here, but I've heard so much about this *altepetl*."

"Of course." The woman nodded, politeness itself. "They say it used to be the most beautiful city around the Great Lake, full of elegance and grace. The Tepanecs and the Mexicas ruined it. Maybe on purpose. They didn't dare to destroy it, as they wanted the Acolhua Lowlanders tamed, because of the tribute, but they tried to make it as unimportant as they could." The woman shrugged, strangely indifferent, as though approving of the deed. "I daresay they succeeded in that. Like you, I expected much from Texcoco when coming here for the first time, but, well, maybe unlike you, I was disappointed. It's nothing but a large town; there's nothing special neither about this *altepetl* nor about its dwellers." A shrug, a fleeting, somewhat guilty, smile. "But our Emperor, of course, will revive its past glory. I predict he will make it shine as never before. If anyone can do it, he is the man."

The Acolhua Emperor? Tlalli tried to remember. She hadn't chanced to meet the famous ruler in person this time, but Tlacaelel had often talked about Nezahualcoyotl through the last two summers, usually with a good measure of respect and appreciation. Also back in Azcapotzalco's Palace, after the night of the conquest, she was forced to serve the food, while still belonging to the man with the carved sword. The maids thought that her captor fancied her, so they made her bring the refreshments, and thus allowed her glimpse the conquerors for the first time, three tired young men full of jokes, bubbling with the sense of well-being, so very pleased with themselves. Oh, how she hated them back then!

"No, I was not disappointed," she said, mainly out of politeness. All she wanted was to close her eyes and rest, the monotonous movements of the litter making her sleepy. "Tenochtitlan was a real disappointment. But Texcoco is not too bad."

The woman's eyes widened in surprise. "Where are you from? I thought you came from one of the provinces."

The little girl was staring at her again, but this time, Tlalli didn't dare to wink, afraid to scare the cute little thing again.

"I came from Tenochtitlan. I live there now." She shrugged. "Since Azcapotzalco fell."

"Oh!" The woman dropped her gaze, as though feeling guilty for prying into someone else's affairs.

For a while, they rode in silence, with Tlalli looking around, enjoying the view of the widening road and the pretty houses adorning this rich neighborhood, adjacent to the Plaza. The sounds of the people crowding it reached them, growling like a distant thunder. The Great Pyramid loomed ahead, casting almost no shadow.

"We should have come earlier," muttered the woman, as their litter jerked time after time, coming to a halt, then moving on, the bearers having difficulty clearing the way in the flow of agitated people. Many were pushing and cursing. "It was silly of me to refuse the escort, but I thought to be here before the crowds."

"Are you looking for a good spot to see the ceremony?" asked Tlalli, enjoying the advantage of an unexpected protection and the additional height. She would have no chance of pushing her way any nearer, she knew, no matter how determined she might have been.

"We will have to clear our way through the worst of the crowd." The woman shook her head, frowning and pulling her girl closer, since, in the commotion, the little thing actually seemed to lose some of her shyness, looking around happily, leaning outside so far that Tlalli was afraid she would fall off. "We need to reach the base of that other pyramid."

"So close? You have no chance."

"I have no choice but to do that, either." The woman's laughter trilled, sudden in its appearance, clearing the lines of worry off the delicate face. "I will not miss my husband's big day. He has worked hard to take Texcoco back from the Tepanecs. Without him, this day would not have happened at all."

Tlalli felt the air escaping her lungs. "You are one of the Emperor's wives?" she whispered, aghast, thinking about the things she might have said without care.

A hearty laughter was her answer. "What? No, of course not! Do I look like an emperor's wife to you?"

The giggle from the little girl made Tlalli feel worse.

"I don't know," she muttered. "The emperor may take whomever he wants to be his women. He is an emperor."

"Mother is not an empress," said the girl. "And she wasn't the empress before, either. Not even in Tenochtitlan."

"Mixtli!" said the woman, still laughing.

"The Second Mother was the empress," insisted the girl. "She was, she was!"

The woman shook her head, her mirth spilling. "Yes, the Second Mother was. But I wasn't." She turned back to Tlalli. "Mixtli has too many happenings in her life, too many changes, too many strangely high relatives and connections. But the daughter of the emperor she is not." The large eyes sparkled proudly. "And yet, her father is very important, and without him Texcoco would be still a Tepanec province, ruled by Azcapotzalco and not even Tenochtitlan."

"My father is the leader of all Acolhua warriors," contributed Mixtli, her eyes gleaming as brilliantly as her long, uncut hair, clearly having been washed with indigo too, so dark it shone with the streaks of blue in the sun. "He conquered the Tepanec Empire with his magical sword."

The air again felt too thick to breathe. Tlalli struggled not to gasp, fighting the urge to jump out and run away. She remembered that sword well, long and massive, glowing viciously against the flames of Azcapotzalco's temples, ferocious, bloodthirsty, as unstoppable as the beasts of the Underworld.

Clutching the edge of the litter with all her might, she clenched her teeth, trying to make the vivid images go away. This man had saved her, and he was kind to her in his own indifferent manner. He had made sure she was tended to, and he never forced anything on her. He gave her to Tlacaelel, yet not as a chattel. Content with his friend's extraordinary idea of making a guide out of her, he went along the routes she had shown them, scouting the countryside, making it ready for their warriors' forces to follow. He was a good person, and yet the memories were always there. Whenever this man was mentioned, all she could remember was terror, pain, and humiliation; that bottomless desperation of the terrible night in the burning Azcapotzalco.

"I think...I believe I should go," she mumbled, making an effort to concentrate, to meet the woman's eyes. "I don't, don't feel well.... The ride, it made me nauseated. I should go now that we've reached the Plaza."

But her hostess was not looking at her at all, her face turned away, drained of color, white teeth making a mess out of the full lower lip. "Oh, I'm sorry, what did you say?" she mumbled, concentrating with a visible effort.

Forgetting her own agitation, Tlalli watched her, wide-eyed. "Are you all right?"

"Yes, yes, of course!" The woman took a deep breath. "You were saying?"

"Oh, well, I said I had better go now that we have reached the Plaza..."

"Not here, surely." Her companion raised her eyebrows, as the litter kept jerking, clearing its way through the thickening crowds. "Where were you heading?"

"Umm, I don't know." Glancing at the hordes gushing around their feet, Tlalli hesitated. "I thought I would just find a good spot."

The woman smiled again, polite and well-meaning, although, like back in the alley, her eyes took no part in the smile. She was troubled, oh yes, reflected Tlalli. Trying to be brave for the sake of the little girl, maybe.

"You would find no such spot now, and even if you did come early, you would be pushed away. The Lowlanders of Texcoco are fierce and brutal, and they do take whatever they want, if allowed." The smile widened, turned warmer. "Why don't you stay with us? This way you will see the entire ceremony from a good vantage point, next to the base of the Great Pyramid but far enough not to let it hide what is happening upon its top. We don't mind your company, Mixtli and I. Eh, Mixtli?"

The girl nodded eagerly, clearly recovered from her initial spell of shyness.

Tlalli forced a smile, liking the woman a great deal. "You are too kind to me, lady."

The smile faded. "I'm not. Truth to be told, I'm in need of good company. This crowded Plaza is the last place I want to be as of now. The very last place in the whole World of the Fifth Sun." Face twisting, the woman turned away, biting her lips again. "Something terrible happened," she murmured, almost to herself. "I sent the word to my husband, but I wish I knew how to deal with it by myself."

Tlalli's stomach convulsed violently. *The evil spirits of the Underworld!* It was one thing to think of an unknown family visited by those, but quite another to face a person who had undoubtedly found the traces of their presence; and paid the price.

"Someone died this night?" she asked quietly. "Someone of your family?"

The woman looked up abruptly, frightened. "No, not of my family!" she said sharply, her arm tightening around the girl's shoulders.

"Then what did they do?"

"Who?"

"The spirits of the Underworld."

A pair of momentarily terrified eyes stared at her. "What are you talking about?"

"They visited your house just before dawn. I saw them."

"You what?" It came out as a muffled shriek.

Taken with compassion, Tlalli leaned forward, taking her companion's hand between her palms. "I did. They were shadows, moving soundlessly, leaping in the air, coming from behind your wall. I've never seen anything like that before. But then, I'm not usually strolling around at night. I heard so many stories about the Underworld Spirits that wander the darkness, but I never saw them for real. Until last night." She pressed the lifeless palm, feeling it cold and painfully small. This woman was truly too slender, thinner than Tlalli even, who seemed to never be able to put on weight like Tlacaelel's other, neglected, wives and concubines did.

"Who are you?" whispered the woman, too terrified to try to take her hand away, although it was trembling now.

"It's not of any importance. I'm not important, and I'm not a healer or a person who converses with the dead. It happened by... by a coincidence. I went out at night. I shouldn't have done this, but I wanted to see Texcoco, and there was no way I could get away during the day. No one would allow me to do that."

This time her companion straightened up, tearing her hand from Tlalli's grip, which caused the child to press back into her mother's skirts.

"But what were you doing outside *my* house?" she demanded, challenging.

Cursing her silly impulse to talk, Tlalli stared back, afraid now. Would she be accused of sorcery now, in addition to her non-existent marketplace theft?

"I was there by chance, I just told you. I went toward the Great Pyramid, and your house happened to be there, on my way, between the Palace and Plaza."

"So now you do know where the Plaza is!" It came out as an outright accusation. "Earlier, skulking around my house, you were all lost and helpless."

"I was not! And I was not skulking around your house. I was on the marketplace, and there was trouble there. I didn't want to be involved, so I ran away." She glared back, enraged by the unreasonableness of all this. She was just trying to help, for all the gods' sake! The stupid *cihua* had no reason to turn all accusing. "And yes, I know it was silly of me to run away the way I did, but well, I just didn't want to be involved. Those boys stole things, and I didn't want to be a witness in the court. And—"

"What boys?" The woman gasped again, returning to her previous colorless state of terrified staring.

"What?"

"What boys? What did they look like?" Suddenly, it was the woman leaning forward, grabbing Tlalli's hand. The girl's eyes were clinging to her too, more expectant than frightened. Unlike her mother, who seemed to be ready for the worst.

"I don't know. They were boys, *telpochcalli* boys, very young. Troublemakers. They stole a knife and some arrowheads, and ran away like real marketplace rats." Understanding some theft, on the other hand, like any former vendor, she hated thieves, although back in Azcapotzalco, her unpainted carvings attracted no mischief, being neither food nor anything of great value.

"Oh, *telpochcalli* boys." The woman seemed to be relieved, focusing on the most irrelevant part of the story.

"Well, yes, and they stole goods and ran away, and one almost got caught, and I should not have helped the dirty thief, but for some reason, I did. And so the disgusting troublemaker climbed a wall and got away, but I almost got in trouble because of him."

The woman tensed again. "He climbed the wall?"

"Yes, he did." It was irritating, the way the annoying *cihua* kept clinging to the most immaterial parts of the story. "He could not run well. He was limping or something."

Now the woman stared at her as though Tlalli were the shadow of the Underworld, springing before her out of nowhere, determined to carry the silly woman away.

"He was supposed to be in *calmecac*," she muttered in the end, making no sense whatsoever. Yet, Tlalli had gotten used to it by now, and anyway, they reached the base of the opposite pyramid, the litter-bearers breathing with relief, diving into the shadow and the vacant space reserved for the highest nobility, guarded by warriors.

The crowds gushed around, not daring to push against the guards, who were armed with spears only, clad in their colorful attire. Spearmen looked more impressive than other warriors, Tlacaelel had explained to her once, and their long-reaching weapons were more comfortable to keep away an unarmed crowd, however agitated it might grow.

Uncomfortable, Tlalli stood the curious gazes, as their litter had been carried past the others, already placed in the shadow, in relative coziness, the ladies leaning on their cushions, nibbling on refreshments, or sipping from exquisite cups, their feathered fans swaying lightly, expertly managed by slaves.

The Warlord's wife acknowledged the greeting with the same reserved politeness she bestowed on Tlalli back near her house, in control once again, although her shoulders were stiff and her smile obviously forced.

"This boy," she asked quietly, when their litter was placed in the shadow. "What did he look like? Tall? Broad-shouldered?"

"I think so, yes." Tlalli tried to remember the leader of the rascals, the way he ran, concentrated, determined, not as afraid as the others. "He was the one who stole the things."

The woman seemed to groan. "Why would he do this?" she asked, helpless.

"I don't know."

The anguished gaze was back up, suddenly concentrated. "You helped him? How?"

Tlalli winced. "Well, you see, the boys scattered. He was running past me, and the man who was after him was going to catch him. And, well," she hesitated, embarrassed, "I put my foot forward. It made him trip, and the boy got those few heartbeats he needed to scale the wall." Grinning at the memory, she chuckled. "He climbed very well, like a monkey. But he is a bad runner."

"His knee is damaged. It was broken, once upon a time." The woman straightened her gaze, in control once again. "Thank you," she said quietly, sincere.

Tlalli felt like laughing. This *altepetl* and its denizens were strange.

"Why would the Chief Warlord's son run around the marketplace, stealing things?" she asked, unable to hold her tongue.

"Because he is a wild ocelot," declared Mixtli, quite forgotten in her corner between the cushions until now.

They both turned to stare, with Tlalli unable to stifle her laughter. It erupted loudly, attracting the attention of other noble ladies, so she pressed her palm against her mouth, her eyes locked with those of the giggling girl. This whole day and night were just too much, but at least she was safe and on her way to Tlacaelel, his spacious, richly furnished quarters and his protection.

"No one can tell Ocelotl what to do," went on Mixtli, proud to be in the center of the stranger's attention. "He doesn't listen to anyone, not even his *calmecac* teachers. He listens to Mother sometimes, but not always."

"Mixtli!" The woman glared at the girl, not amused. "Yes, our family is anything but ordinary," she said, turning to Tlalli, composed once again, back to her reserved, distant self. "It's been through much, thrown around along with the upheavals of our Great Lake's various empires. And, well, it's difficult for the children, sometimes. Difficult to teach them proper discipline and behavior." A shrug. "The Warlord's household has more than one difficult child."

"Citlalli," cried out Mixtli, triumphant. "Citlalli is difficult, too!"

The woman just shook her head, her smile only partly amused.

"How many wives does the Warlord have?" asked Tlalli, curiously comfortable to venture prying questions. "How many concubines?"

The woman's face twisted. "Two wives. That's all."

"Where is the other one? Didn't she come to watch the ceremony?"

The smile widened, but didn't fill with more mirth. "She is watching, of course she is. But being the favorite sister of our

Emperor, she has a better spot than ours. I won't be surprised to see her up there, on the Great Pyramid, standing alongside the men, participating in the ceremony."

"No woman can do this!" cried out Tlalli, aghast.

"Well, yes, maybe not this, but you have yet to meet Iztac-Ayotl. There is little in this World of the Fifth Sun that would stop her from doing whatever she feels should be done. She is a law unto herself."

Oh, yes, why not? thought Tlalli, turning to watch the Plaza and the Great Pyramid, as the monotonous beating of drums began rolling down the massive stones, interrupted by trills of various flutes. The priests were about to begin, clearly visible even from such a distance, their cloaks black, their hair matted and long, flowing freely. An unsettling vision.

Narrowing her eyes, she tried to find Tlacaelel among the richly dressed dignitaries, their majestic figures atop the magnificent construction outlined against the brightness of the sky, as imposing as stone statues, with no human weaknesses to them. A spectacular vision!

Taken by the grandeur of this view, she shivered. Could it be that they turned into gods for the duration of the ceremony, or maybe until all the matters are settled and the lands around the Great Lake calmed under the new rules, new masters, new empires? She knew all about Tlacaelel's vision, no one better. He loved to talk about it as much as she loved to listen. He wanted his Mexica people to inherit the Tepanec Empire, but that was only a part of his plans.

The Tepanecs were sloppy, he would say again and again. They conquered, intimidating their neighbors into obedience, but they didn't bother to manage those whom they subjugated. Their tribute system was sporadic, robbing some out of existence, taking next to nothing from others, distributing conquered cities among their allies with no pattern and no sense.

This was no way to run an empire, he would say, staring at the distance, or sometimes smiling at her, challenging to ask questions. A tribute system should be well-organized, leaving the conquered to prosper, enough to produce this tribute and to be content, but not enough to think silly thoughts of rebellion. Take the *altepetl*, change its ruler, put a tamed person who would be accountable to you, the conqueror, and then leave it be. Don't force the regular people, the minor nobility and the commoners, to give up on their way of life. Leave them content, well-fed and well-clothed, to go on with their lives, enriching themselves and you, the conqueror, producing the tribute, contributing to the might of your empire. Oh, how wise he was!

She strained her eyes, trying to see against the fierce glow, but they were no more than the distant silhouettes, maybe immortal beings, but only for the short afternoon. They had their human weaknesses, plenty of those. The women all around the base of that other pyramid could testify to that matter.

She glanced at the Warlord's wife, the woman's gaze focused on the ceremony too, but not seeking, not staring, wandering the realm of her inner thoughts and feelings, instead. Worrying about that troublesome son of hers, was Tlalli's conclusion. And the dark spirits that visited her house just before dawn. What did they do to make this woman so downcast, so worried? If no one died, then what happened?

The girl crawled closer, her body warm, pressing against Tlalli, a pleasant presence.

"They are appeasing the gods," she said importantly. "They sacrifice Tepanecs."

"Warriors, yes," agreed Tlalli, not liking the way it was said. "For a warrior, it's a glorious death, Tepanec or Acolhua, it doesn't matter. Not all Tepanecs are bad."

The girl stared at her, aghast. "But they are!"

"No, they are not. I am a Tepanec. Am I bad?"

The roundness of the girl's eyes matched that of her face now. "You are a Tepanec?" she squeaked.

"Yes, I am. And I'm a guest in your *altepetl*. Also," suppressing her smile, Tlalli tried to look grave, "I saved your brother this morning. What does that make me? A good person or a bad one?"

The round face squeezed with an attempt to decide, making Tlalli's effort not to burst out laughing more difficult.

"Does your brother always make trouble?" she asked, trying to change the subject, to ease it for the little thing, who seemed to be more confused with every passing heartbeat.

"Ocelotl? Oh, yes, he does." The girl beamed, her qualms about the Tepanecs forgotten. "He is frustrated, Mother says. I don't know what frustrated means, but he is angry many times. Coatl is not like that. He makes his *calmecac* teachers proud."

"Who is Coatl?"

"My other brother."

"Oh."

"He is the best boy ever!"

"Is he the oldest?" Glancing at the gentle profile of the Warlord's wife, Tlalli found it difficult to think about all this multitude of children. She seemed young enough to have Mixtli alone. Another child, maybe, yes. But more?

As though sensing the inquiring gaze, the woman smiled. "The boys are of the same age. They were born together," she said, revealing that, deep in thought or not, she had been listening. "Our household is mixed, strange and out of the ordinary," she added, laughing lightly, again more amused than troubled. She was changing fast. "You will have to forgive Mixtli. She has met many peoples, Highlanders, Acolhua, Mexica, but the Tepanecs are new to her. She needs to get used to them." A shrug. "Although she does have Tepanec blood in her, whether she likes it or not."

"How?"

"Her father is half Tepanec."

"Oh!"

But of course. She remembered how calming it was to hear the Warlord's Tepanec-accented Nahuatl, alone among the conquerors. Reassured she was not, not then and not later, but still, the way he had spoken pleased the ear. She remembered that most clearly.

"His other half is Acolhua," she said, making it a statement.

"No," said the woman lightly. "None of us are Acolhua. Aside from his other wife, who is half Tepanec herself."

Tlalli found herself staring like the little girl had before. "Then who are you?"

The smile widened, again not reaching the woman's dark eyes. "I came from the Highlands. As did the Warlord."

The wild highlanders? She tried not to stare. "But how?"

"Oh, it's a long story. Too long and too complicated to tell it all now." Turning back to watch the body of the first sacrificial offering tumbling down the Great Pyramid's stairs, the woman shielded her face. "I wish it would be over soon," she muttered, talking to herself again as it seemed. "I truly need him to come home."

CHAPTER 4

Tlacaelel shifted his weight from one foot to another, sighing inwardly. A pleasant night of feasting, being entertained in the most exquisite manner that only the Acolhua Capital knew how to provide, followed by a long morning of organizations and preparations, made him so tired he could barely see. Itzcoatl's ceremony of enthronement three summers earlier had been easier to get through.

He grinned, trying not to squint, watching the crowds splashing far below his feet. The Great Texcocan Plaza was packed to the brim, the lake of people wavering, spilling into the nearby alleys and pathways, flowing around the base of the Great Pyramid and the lower constructions as well. So many people! Tenochtitlan's ceremony was attended by a quarter of this amount or worse, while now, the Acolhua Capital was overflowing with exuberant dwellers and visitors. Still, the next emperor of Tenochtitlan would come into his reign under even a greater ceremony than this one, he decided. Whoever it would happen to be.

Not me, he thought, shifting his weight once again. *They can argue and press and beg, but I love my current position. As a ruler, I would be restricted. It is not my style of doing things. Or so Tlalli would say.*

His grin disappeared, replaced by a nagging worry. The unruly woman had, once again, resorted to doing whatever she liked, not waiting for him to arrange an appropriate way for her to watch the ceremony. Did she think he would neglect to make sure she could attend?

Damn her independent streak into the first level of the
Underworld, he thought, worried. She could have talked to him.
Asked about it. Pled even. But, of course, that was not *her* style of
doing things. Her way was to sneak into the city unattended, to
run around like the commoner she was. Elevated to an exalted
position, she had no right to behave like the marketplace *cihua* she
probably used to be. And what if something happened to her?

He pressed his lips together, scanning the crowds once again,
too distant to see particular faces or even heads, yet hoping
against hope. She had better be back by the time the ceremony
was over. Unharmed and unruffled. Because if something
happened to her, the rebellious Acolhua elements of Texcoco,
those who did not want to see their Emperor cooperating with the
Mexicas of Tenochtitlan, would get what they wanted. A damn
outright war! Because he would tear that snotty *altepetl* apart if
they dared to harm her. And yet, all the same, it was her fault, and
if she made it back unharmed, he would find a way to scold her in
a manner that she would not forget in a hurry.

With an effort, he forced his thoughts off the trouble, watching
Nezahualcoyotl as the tall man strolled toward the very edge of
the platform, undeterred by the height, standing there proudly,
his arms stretched out, legs wide apart, addressing the crowds.
With the gods already appeased, satiated by the life forces of
twenty high-ranking prisoners, it was the turn of Texcoco citizens
to be appealed to.

"Why won't he get it over with already?"

The murmur of the Highlander standing next to him was
barely heard, but it startled Tlacaelel all the same.

"What?"

Puzzled, he watched the stony face, the clouded, stormy eyes,
the clenched fists of the Acolhua Chief Warlord, the entire being
of the man radiating an air of dark fury. What troubled that one?

He hadn't seen his friend since they parted their ways at the
near-dawn mist of the reception hall, with the Highlander
hurrying off into the city, to make sure the Great Plaza was
secured properly, by plenty of warriors responsible for making
the crowds behave. A leader of his status could have let his

subordinates do such mundane duties, but that was the best thing about this man. Like Tlacaelel, he preferred to do the bulk of the work himself, trusting no one to carry out his enterprises.

However, whatever happened in the city between the night and the high noon must have been truly bad, as it had been summers since he had seen his friend in that kind of deadly rage. Three summers ago, in Tenochtitlan, was the last time it had happened, when the previous Emperor died, having sentenced the pushy foreigner, this same notorious Highlander, to death by stoning, accusing him of small, non-existent charges, not saying the real reason aloud – the Highlander's affair with the Emperor's Chief Wife preying on the minds of those who knew. Worried for the woman he loved more than for his own troubled situation, the Highlander had lost all sanity, and in the end, the Emperor died, and this man and his family had to flee Tenochtitlan, just as the war with the Tepanecs was breaking. At the best of timings, as it turned out. Back in his native highlands, with Coyotl finding refuge there once again, both had been able to work most efficiently, bringing the hordes of the fierce Highland warriors along with the encouraged Acolhua to reinforce the Mexica forces against the might of Azcapotzalco. So this particular misadventure ended up surprisingly well. However, now something was seriously wrong again. What?

He glanced at his friend, meeting the rigid face and the unreadable, clouded gaze. Later, he decided. It was neither the time nor the place, but he would make an effort to discover what happened at the more appropriate time. Troubles in the Acolhua Capital bode him no good. They could influence his undertakings as well.

Mictia, the leader of the black-clothed killers, forced himself into stillness, watching the slivers of light coming from behind the shut screen, slipping through the densely placed planks of the wall. The darkness did nothing to upset him, offering protection, as always, but the air in the vast building stood stale, suffocating, accumulating heat.

He had been pacing this warehouse since they had reached this place in the early morning, having been forced to detour, unwilling to take their chances by going straight for the boats as it had been planned at first. The dawn had broken too soon, forcing them to seek cover. They could not run around in their black outfits, carrying magical swords, having just broken into the dwelling of this *altepetl*'s Chief Warlord. They needed a place to hide and to regroup, to rethink their plans, so this warehouse, one of the smaller ones, situated on the outskirts of the busy marketplace area, had to do.

"Curse their eyes into the deepest level of the Underworld," he muttered, hating the heat and the way his loincloth clung to his body, making him feel filthy. They should have been out in the cool breeze of the lake now, rowing, putting as much distance between themselves and Texcoco *altepetl* as possible. Not baking in the airless warehouse, surrounded by filth and the noise and the smells of the nearby alleys adjacent to the marketplace.

Nacatl, his associate, stirred, looking up briefly, perturbed. The possible failure would affect them all, not only the leader responsible for the mission. And a failure it did, indeed, began looking like now, curse this filthy *altepetl* to rot until this World of the Fifth Sun would end.

"Why does it take the motherless rat so long to come back?" he growled, wishing to explode like a thunderbolt in the best of the summer storms. The third man had been sent to the wharves long ago, to apprise the boat's owner of the change in plans; that is if the cowardly rat hadn't already sailed away, having arrived at the wrong conclusion.

"It must have taken him a long time to talk the filthy fisherman into staying," muttered Nacatl. "Also, the roads would be packed now. Because of the ceremony."

"I'm aware of the ceremony and the difficulty it adds to our mission." Desperate to control his temper, Mictia stopped, eyeing their improvised shelter, trying to think of a way out of this mess. "If not for the gods-accursed ceremony we would have gone to the wharves now." He frowned at the aroma of cooked food brought with an obvious breeze just outside the wall. It made his stomach growl. "The rotten son of a whore is useless. I should have gone out myself."

"Yes," muttered Nacatl miserably, changing into a better position in the filthiness of his corner.

Mictia shifted to make himself more comfortable too, his hand seeking the smoothness of his special knife's handle, finding none. Another aggravation. He would have to make sure to get a high enough price for this particular sacrifice. Fancy asking him to leave that sort of evidence. He snorted. The people who paid him must have been desperate. And then there was the witness. Someone had been there in the alley, hiding in the darkness, watching them. He had felt it in his bones. But for the rapidly approaching dawn, he would have dashed into the shadows, killing the filthy onlooker. It was not wise to leave witnesses, the scary looking outfits and the appearance of the Underworld Spirits or not. He should have lingered for a few more heartbeats, taking care of this matter. But on top of the interrupting maid, it would complicate their mission further, take more precious time, make them linger where they were not supposed to be.

But then again, were they in a better position now?

No, they were not, the deed still unaccomplished, the magical sword still here in Texcoco, possibly about to spring into action, to punish the thieves all by itself.

He saw his companion's gaze fixing upon the bundle, watching it as one might watch a dangerous beast, not knowing when it would pounce. Against his will, his eyes followed, appraising the patterns of the wittily interlaced rectangles embroidered upon the smooth cotton. Such an expensive cloth! The best quality, the material and the colors applied to it. But not like the object it hid. They didn't dare to uncover their cargo. It would be pushing their luck too far.

"Ocelotl, wait!"

A cry from the outside made them both jump, reaching them along with the shuffle of running feet and the gasps of panted breathing. Freezing, they held their breath, their knives out and ready, instincts honed.

"What?"

This voice clearly belonged to a boy who not only stopped next to their wall, but actually leaned against it, with only the wooden planks separating their backs from that of the intruder.

"Where are we going?" Two more pair of feet made a screeching sound, halting next to the one called Ocelotl.

"I want to sniff around the food alley. Ilhuilt might be somewhere there now. I saw him running this way."

"The fat trader will get us!" cried out one of the other boys, his voice trembling with fear. "We can't go back there."

"I didn't say we will go back to the stupid fat trader." The first boy was still gasping for breath, but there was no fear in his voice; and no uncertainty. "I say we sniff around, at a safe distance. Just to see what is up with them, to find Ilhuilt."

"Maybe he got caught. Maybe they dragged him to the court. Maybe they are looking for us all over the marketplace now!" The third boy seemed to be on the verge of panic.

There was the sound of a sandal crashing against the wooden planks. "No one is looking for us, you stupid piece of dirt. And no one got caught." Ocelotl's voice peaked, vibrating with rage.

"You almost got caught."

"I did not!"

"That other man was sure to get you before he fell."

By the sounds and the changing light seeping through the wooden planks, Ocelotl must have grabbed his accuser, pushing him hard against the wall.

The little rascals will soon be punching each other, thought Mictia, getting to his feet, as soundless as a true ocelot. And it would draw unwanted attention to their quiet corner of the alley. Not good!

Gesturing to his companion to stay where he was, he slipped toward the doorway.

"No, no, he would never get you." It was the first boy, his words gushing in a breathless rush. "Ocelotl, stop it. Let him go. They'll find us if we make trouble."

Good thinking, reflected Mictia, pausing near the shut screen.

The dirty little thieves were stupid to fight their differences here, in the place they clearly needed to escape.

"You will never come with us again, you stinking rat," hissed Ocelotl after a long pause. "You are a coward and a traitor, and you are not a part of our group anymore. Is that clear to you? Stay away from us from now on!"

The sobbing of the assaulted cub made Mictia let out a breath of relief. The violent leader was obviously holding his followers in thrall, demanding, and getting, a proper respect. He shrugged. Killing those boys would complicate things even further, when all they needed to do was leave the gods-accursed city, the sooner the better.

"Are you coming to look for Ilhuilt?" The words shot out angrily, piercing the air like sharpened arrowheads.

"Yes, yes." The first boy was so obviously afraid, Mictia could imagine him taking a step back, pressing against the wall, maybe.

"We'll come from behind the baths and down the walled alley." Ocelotl sounded somewhat mollified, busy thinking. "If we don't run into him anywhere there, we'll go by the courts."

"What if the fat trader went to the judges already?" The trembling voice of the assaulted thief contributed to the conversation.

"Shut up and go away." The tough leader's verdict brought the sobs back. "You are not with us anymore, traitor!"

"No, please."

"Go away before I make it impossible for you to go anywhere at all. The fat trader's knife needs to be tested, so why not on you, eh, you dirty coward?"

The sobs melted away as though by magic. Mictia suppressed his grin, then turned to go back to his previous corner, his thoughts on the boats again. Why was it taking the man he sent to the wharves so long to return?

"The damn arrowheads cut my hand all over." The aggressive thing outside the warehouse was cursing again. "We need to hide them before we go. But I'll keep the knife. It's a nice-looking thing, eh?"

"No, we should hide it all in there." The suggestion of the

remaining member of the gang made Mictia freeze again. If the boys entered the warehouse, they'd have to die, and he would be stuck with two rotting bodies until the darkness fell.

"Only the arrowheads." The voice of the leading boy drew toward the doorway.

Rotting bodies, oh yes. Mictia turned back with a sigh of acceptance. But surely they would be able to leave no later than nightfall.

"No one will see us entering anyway." The wooden partition screeched. "They are all on the Plaza now." Suddenly, Ocelotl's voice lost its self-assurance. "I should be there too," he muttered in the pitiful way of the child he probably was.

"Your father will be so angry. He will blow like the Smoking Mountain." The other boy seemed to gain confidence as fast as his tough friend seemed to be losing it. "He will kill you."

"He won't." Not sounding too convincing, Ocelotl poked his head in, scanning the place through narrowed eyes. After the brilliance of the outside, he obviously could see nothing but darkness. Mictia held his breath, the knife, a regular short obsidian dagger, relaxed in his palm.

"The Warlord will kill you, if your *calmecac* teachers don't do it before him." The other boy stepped inside the warehouse, sounding pleased with himself.

"I piss on the stupid teachers!" cried out Ocelotl, slipping in more carefully than his friend did. "And Father never beats me or my brother."

They stood there, hesitating, two silhouettes outlined clearly against the brightness of the entrance.

"There is always a first time, you know." The second boy squinted, then took another step.

"No, wait. Something is not right here." This time it came as a whisper. That Ocelotl boy was good.

Mictia hesitated, digesting the information. Could the little piece of dirt be a son of this or that war leader? It didn't seem possible. *Calmecac* boys did not run around markets, stealing things.

"What?" The other boy stopped abruptly.

"I don't know," whispered Ocelotl, his firmness returning. "But something is wrong. Let's get out of here." The sense of danger brought the leader of the marketplace rascals back, his confidence, shattered by the reminder of the influential but now angered father, seemed to be returning.

"What?" Another step brought the boy so close, Mictia could feel the warmth the young body radiated. Couldn't the little piece of excrement feel it, too?

"Wait!" Ocelotl's warning came a fragment of a heartbeat too late, with Mictia's knife darting out, sinking in the second boy's chest, forcing its way upward, straight toward the heart. His other hand caught the body, not letting it fall and possibly slip out of the lethal contact.

Satisfied, he felt Nacatl pouncing from the darkness, covering the distance to the entrance with one powerful leap, catching the leading boy by his shoulder. Holding his own victim tight, feeling the thin body slowing its squirming, Mictia heard his companion cursing as his prey slipped out of his grip, bolting toward the safety of the outside, as nimble as the marketplace rat he was.

"Don't let him get away," he hissed, pushing the now-limp body away.

Nacatl grabbed the boy again, by the edge of his short cloak this time, pulling sharply, making the wild thing lose his balance. Still, the little beast fought, squirming and kicking, managing to free himself once again, leaping toward the brightness of the outside for the second time. But for Mictia blocking the entrance, tearing the screen shut with a loud screech, the tough rascal might have even made it. What a beast! Even now, cornered and with no chance of getting away, the tall boy turned to face them, holding his pitiful knife out, full of enough fighting spirit.

"You filthy son of a whore." Nacatl was upon the would-be warrior, crushing the thin body against the wall, his hands wrapped around the boy's neck, lifting him up, paying no attention to the feeble attempts to use the knife.

"Wait."

Still not sure of his reasons, Mictia came closer, studying the struggling cub.

"Put him down."

"Why?" called out Nacatl, perplexed.

"Just do it!"

The boy slipped onto the floor, coughing and retching, gasping for breath. Grabbing the collar of his cloak, Mictia pulled him up, feeling the quality cotton under his palms. Could it be that the boy truly belonged to a wealthy family, a son of some important leader?

"Who is your father?" he barked into the wide, pleasantly round face, now contorted with fear.

The boy blinked, then pressed his lips tight.

"Answer me!"

As the demand was accompanied by a rough push into the planks of the wall, it was answered by an involuntary groan. He bettered his grip on the cotton collar, then dragged the boy toward the sprawling body of his friend, shoving him into the bloody heap of limbs and the stench of fresh blood and discharges it radiated.

"Want to keep him company on his Underworld journey?"

The boy gagged, pushing with his hands, trying to roll away. A vicious kick brought him back.

"Is your father the warlord?"

"Yes." The word came out muffled, seeping through the clenched teeth.

"Which one?"

Another kick made the answer come faster. "The Chief Warlord."

"The stinking brat is lying," muttered Nacatl, contributing a kick of his own.

"Maybe not." He pushed his companion away. "Stop beating him. Let me think."

Quickly, he tried to put the pieces of the mosaic together. The Warlord, indeed, was reported to have sons, a pair of strong, healthy twins, another miracle, as though one of the sword was not enough. Their informant was forthcoming with information. They paid the filthy slave generously, while intimidating him along the way. A good combination that brought results. After two market intervals, they had known this household's routines, all the comings and goings.

Not that they were interested in anything beyond the movements of the powerful leader himself, but some information kept coming without them having to ask, so by now, they knew not a little about both Warlord's wives, the haughty sister of the Emperor and the commoner from the wild highlands, the one who ran his household, in charge of everything. Two chief wives, of all things. This man was a law unto himself.

"He has twins in *calmecac*." Scratching a mosquito bite, Mictia frowned, then leaned forward, trying to see the boy better in the darkness. "How old are you?"

The little brat was staring at the body of his friend, speechless. Or maybe asking for another kick. Mictia obliged, then contributed a resounding slap.

"You better answer me in a hurry, boy," he said conversationally, dragging the wild thing onto his feet. "I have time to extract all the answers I want. In the end, you will beg of me to do to you what I did to your friend, to put you out of your misery."

There was still enough defiance in the pair of huge, terrified eyes, so he reinforced his words by bringing his knife up, to glisten dully against the little light that managed to get through. It had the desired effect. The boy's eyes glazed over and grew impossibly wide, watching the glittering blade.

"Now, will you tell me what I want to know, or will I have to cut your eye out first?"

"I'll tell you."

Against his will, he admired the cub's courage, whose voice and limbs shook, but bearably so. Even the toughest rat of that age would be howling by now, smearing snot and crying for his mother.

"You are the Chief Warlord's son? One of the twins?"

The boy nodded, lips trembling, pressed too tight to part for an answer.

"Where is your brother?"

A shrug.

He slapped the unshaved head viciously, and again admired the boy's attempt not to fall, or cry out. "You'll have to talk more than that. How old are you?"

"Half twenty of summers." A convulsive breath was drawn noisily through the bloodied nose. "Almost half twenty."

"Was your brother with you, making trouble on the marketplace?"

The bruised face closed. "No."

"Where is he?"

"I don't know."

Another slap. "Yes, you do."

But the pair of glittering eyes fixed upon him, gleaming with what seemed a measure of new determination, accompanied by a fair amount of hatred. "I was busy. I don't keep an eye on my brother. He doesn't do these things."

The wild brat may have a point there, thought Mictia.

"You were busy, oh yes, busy stealing things and running a bunch of other little thugs like yourself." For good measure, he added another slap, not as vicious as the previous ones.

"Tie him up, and don't hurt him more than necessary," he said to his companion, who stared at them, puzzled.

"What for?"

"Just do as I say." He frowned, contemplating his associate before letting his mind wander back toward a new plan. "The powerful Texcoco War Leader may wish to pay generously to see his son back."

CHAPTER 5

"Tell me exactly what happened!"

The powerful shout rolled down the corridor, making Tlalli jump. Although safe in the coziness of the inner rooms, surrounded by low tables, mats and cushions aplenty, she tensed, her eyes darting toward the opening in the wall, checking for a possible route of escape.

It had only been a short while since they had arrived back at the haunted house, in the rich neighborhood not far away from the Plaza. She should have been heading for the Palace, she knew, but toward the end of the ceremony, she had been dizzy with hunger and thirst, and probably the lack of sleep, truly unwell, so the Chief Warlord's generous wife brushed her protests aside, taking her back to her own home, to eat and rest before letting her go.

It was nothing that good food and maybe a boiled root of tomato would not fix, maintained the kind woman. Claiming knowledge of healing, she said she would know, so Tlalli didn't argue, too exhausted to think of talking her way back into the Palace, or facing the obviously enraged Tlacaelel, disappointed by her behavior. She would do it later, during the afternoon, when she felt stronger and back to her forceful self.

Yet, when they arrived here, in the troubled house, she regretted agreeing to come. The place was clean and pretty, richly furnished, cozy, inviting, but the memory of the Underworld Spirits flying over these very walls made her fears return, reinforced by the frightened looks of the servants.

Escorted in, made comfortable in the spacious rooms clearly

belonging to this woman—by now she had discovered that her benefactress's name was Dehe, outlandish but pleasant, like the woman herself—they had been served food and drinks. The Mistress of the House hardly touched any, but Tlalli and Mixtli had dug in, devouring freshly baked tortillas, dunking them in the spicy sauces or bowls filled with honey, attacking the plates with sliced avocado and other vegetables, drinking plenty of water to wash the rich assortment down.

"I want my chocolate drink," demanded the girl, her face smeared with honey. "Can I? Please?"

But her mother shook her head, deep in thought. "Not this time of the day, Mixtli," she muttered absently. "You had your chocolate in the morning."

"No, I didn't!" protested the girl. "Don't you remember? Nakaztli was dead, and everyone was busy running and yelling and looking for Father's sword."

The woman's face lost the remnants of the color it had gained while spending the hot noon hours in the sun.

"Oh, gods," she muttered, shooting an anguished glance at her surroundings.

As though about to vomit, she pressed her hands to her mouth, got to her feet and fled, leaving Tlalli rigid with a new wave of cascading fear.

"I want my chocolate drink," mumbled Mixtli, her lips beginning to quiver. "I didn't get it in the morning. I didn't!"

"You will get your chocolate. I'm sure you will." Helplessly, Tlalli reached out, caressing the plump little hand, desperate to prevent a crying fit. This girl's mother didn't need any of that at the moment. "We'll make sure of it. Later on, when it all calms down."

"When?" whimpered the girl.

"I don't know when, but later. Today." Holding the tearful gaze, Tlalli smiled. "Today. We'll make sure it happens today." She pushed the bowl of honey across the table. "Here, have more of this for now. It might make you feel better."

The little thing pressed her lips, hesitating.

"Who is Nakaztli?" asked Tlalli after her offer was accepted and more honey smeared all over the round cheeks.

"Nakaztli? Oh, Nakaztli is good. She is Mother's most favorite maid. She smiles, and she has sweets, always. Mother loves her." The large eyes fixed on Tlalli, full of importance. "She is dead now."

"How did she die?"

"She was lying in the big room this morning. Sleeping on the floor." The girl frowned. "Then they all were running, and screaming. And Mother was crying, and they were looking for Father's sword. And..." The round lips began to quiver once again, as the girl's eyes filled with tears. "I want my mother! *Nantli!*"

Sniffing loudly, the little thing sprang to her feet and bolted out of the room, as hastily as her mother before her. Tlalli felt like cursing. How silly of her. She should have kept her mouth shut. But then, it was nice to be alone for a little while, to relax and to think.

Leaning against the cushions, she sighed, replete and exhausted. So the black spirits did steal a life in the pre-dawn mist, when she watched them leaving. The life of a favorite servant. No wonder the mistress of this house was upset. But then, they could have taken the lives of her family members, any of the children, or the woman herself. Or maybe the Warlord. What if the Chief Warlord died on the day of the Great Ceremony? It could have been a terrible omen for the Acolhua Capital, of that she was sure. So, come to think of it, it was good that only a servant had died.

She picked up her cup, then jumped, spilling its contents, as the roaring voice erupted, coming from the central rooms, rolling through the entire dwelling. She remembered it too well, this Tepanec-accented Nahuatl, sometimes cold, sometimes laughing, sometimes vibrating with anger, but never, not even in the worst moments in Azcapotzalco or Coyoacan, holding so much bubbling, melting rage.

"Tell me exactly what you found!" the man bellowed again, as loudly as before.

She could hear others, talking in a rush, the voice of the

Mistress of the House overcoming them, her speech flowing rapidly, but calmly, not afraid.

"I can't believe it!" Something went flying across the room, crashing with a thud. Some furniture probably. She could hear Mixtli beginning to howl. The man was outside, barking orders at his warriors. She could hear their voices too, quiet and subdued.

Slowly, she got to her feet, pondering her possibilities. To sneak through the opening in the wall would save her another encounter with this household's family, but it might make her face the Warlord, and in the worst of ways, getting out of his house like a thief after one of his most precious possessions was stolen. It was enough that she didn't dare to show her face on the Texcoco marketplace anymore. Straightening her shoulders, she strolled toward the central rooms. Maybe she would be able to go unnoticed in all the commotion.

"Who of the servants went to sleep last?"

The man was back inside, as impressive as she remembered him from Azcapotzalco days, but more dignified, his shoulders broad, laden with jewelry, his warrior' s lock immaculate, his cloak crisply fresh, a pattern of vivid colors, a massive necklace glittering dully against the wideness of his chest. A war deity, a creature of the battlefield, his current expression in a perfect accord. So much fury!

"Stop shouting," said the Mistress of the House firmly. "You are scaring everyone." She stepped forward and stood before him, small and delicate against his width and height. "I made all the inquiries already. I know all they know, so ask me, instead. And stop yelling. You are scaring the children."

Clutching onto her mother's skirt, Mixtli was howling lustily, now a vision of puffy eyes, running nose, and worse.

"Tell me," he said curtly, taking a deep breath, obviously trying to control his temper.

"We went to sleep later than usual last night," said the woman, now perfectly composed, her previous state of distress gone, or well-hidden. "Because of the impending ceremony. After you left for the Palace, the children were excited. And the servants, too. All of us, we were getting ready for today. So it was not until after midnight that the patio and the central rooms cleared of people. Maybe even later." She paused, collecting her thoughts. "Citlalli was difficult, with her mother being out there in the Palace, so I allowed her to sleep in my rooms, with Mixtli, and the children went quiet unusually late. But of course, the servants were wandering much later than that. And then, with dawn, we were all up, having found Nakaztli." The woman swallowed hard, frowning, making an obvious effort to communicate her report eloquently and clearly. Tlalli's heart twisted. "So it must have happened somewhere in the later part of the night, in a short period of time, and," she paused, swallowing again, "and I suppose we were watched for our activities. Maybe not only this night, the only night you spent outside this house without the sword."

The Warlord seemed to turn into stone, listening with his lips pursed, jaw tight, formidable fists clenching and unclenching – an image of a mountain about to erupt with the terrible smoke and flames, like Popocatepetl, the Smoking Mountain, clearly visible from Texcoco shores.

"Nothing else disappeared and no one else got hurt?" he asked finally, barely moving his lips.

"No, nothing. We found no traces, no marks. It was as though the spirits—" Suddenly, the woman gasped, turning to Tlalli, her eyes wide and frightened, for the first time since they met. "You saw…you said you saw…" Her stare was unnerving in its intensity, her eyes huge, glittering, full of genuine fear. "Tell him what you saw!"

The Warlord's blazing gaze leapt to her too, frightening with the fiery heat it radiated. Tlalli felt like taking a step back. Or maybe a few steps. Like back in the marketplace, the temptation to turn around and run welled.

She licked her lips. "I, well, I'm not sure what I saw, but…" They all were staring at her, even Mixtli. "I was outside, and it was near dawn, and I didn't mean to be here or anything—"

The Warlord's face came back to life with a puzzled frown. "You are Tlacaelel's woman!" he cried out, not trying to hide his surprise. "What are you doing here?"

She felt terribly silly. "Well, it's another long story. You see, I went out, and yes, I know I'm not supposed to be here…"

The Mistress of the House blinked. "You know her?"

"Yes, yes, of course." The foreboding expression was back, freezing the Warlord's features once again. "Tell me what you saw!" It was an order.

Tlalli took a deep breath. "Well, I was outside. I went past this house. I didn't know who lived here. I just wanted to see this *altepetl*, you see?" She hated the way she sounded, like a frightened girl. "I saw dark shadows slipping across the outside wall. They were no people, but spirits. They were black, and they made no sound. Underworld Spirits. I could see this much."

"When?" he asked curtly, eyes narrow.

"Just before dawn." She hesitated, trying to remember. "It was turning gray. The sky, I mean."

"How many?"

"I don't know. Maybe three, maybe more. I didn't look all the time. You see, the Underworld Spirits are not be watched directly, unless—"

"What did they look like?" He seemed to pay no attention to her words, listening to his inner voices, instead.

She fought the wave of frustration. Why, why did she have to open her stupid mouth in the first place?

"I don't know. They were black, just dark forms. The spirits, they have no human form, as you must know."

He didn't seem to listen, his eyes narrowed into slits, concentrated, obviously thinking hard.

"Father!"

Now it was Tlalli's turn to stare, as the boy from the marketplace burst into the room, his face flushed, as pleasant-looking as she remembered, but clean and calm, despite the excitement, which was no wonder, of course, as no one was chasing him now. Although tall and broad-shouldered, he looked more like his mother than his Tepanec-looking father, his eyes large and slanted, turning upwards at their edges, his features gentle. She remembered him running from the enraged merchant, doing his best not to falter, but now he walked easily, with no visible effort and no limp, followed by a slender girl of about the same age.

Not deterred by the stares of everyone present, he rushed toward the Warlord, his palm up. "You have to see this, Father."

"I found it, not him!" called out the girl, enraged, trying to grab the object the boy was offering.

"Who cares?" His arm shot sideways, avoiding the girl's attempt to recapture the artifact. "Father, it looks like your knife, but it isn't. Look!"

"What is it?" growled the Warlord, not amused. He looked at the boy sternly, but with an obvious affection, then his eyes widened, taking in the object as it glimmered dully on the spread palm.

Fascinated, Tlalli watched the strange-looking knife, its blade glowing, so smooth it reflected the light like a polished mirror, like no chopped obsidian would do. Its handle was marvelous, looking like a face crowned with a high headdress.

"I found it," cried out the girl again, not daring to resume her snatching attempts, not under the incredulous stare of the Master of the House.

"Where?" It was quite a bark, which made them all jump.

The girl gasped, taken aback, her eyes filling with tears. "I just saw it...it was under the wall...on the ground." She frowned, clearly gathering the remnants of her courage. "It is not your knife. Coatl said it, too."

"Yes, Father," said the boy hurriedly. "Yours has a different handle."

Coatl? Then she remembered. Oh yes, the woman told her that Mixtli's brothers were born together, on the same day. So it must be the other boy, not the troublemaker from the marketplace.

The Warlord paid both children's words no attention. "Show me exactly where you found it," he ordered, taking the girl by the shoulder, not aggressively but firmly. She seemed as though about to argue, so he silenced her with a fierce glare. "Now, Citlalli!"

She complied with no further argument, subdued and resentful at the same time, with Coatl in tow, following without being invited.

"She did nothing wrong, Father," they heard him saying, hurrying after the silent pair. "It is not your knife."

Although still crowded, the room seemed to empty. Tlalli looked at the Warlord's wife.

"Is that about the sword?" she asked quietly. "Is it gone?"

"Yes." The woman stood frowning, biting her lips, her palms clenched, the delicate jaw tight, the smaller version of the Warlord's stance before that, one hand stroking Mixtli's hair.

"The sword with the carvings?"

"Yes." The troubled gaze flew at Tlalli, concentrating. "Who are you? How do you know my husband? Why did he say you were Tlacaelel's woman?"

Regretting speaking up for the thousandth time through this wild, insane day, Tlalli stifled a sigh.

"Because I *am* Tlacaelel's woman. He brought me along, after Coyoacan fell." She shrugged. "Your husband saved me. I owe him my life, and…and my honor. He saved me from the warriors on the night when Azcapotzalco fell. They wanted to…to do me harm before killing me."

The woman was staring, wide-eyed again. "He did this? He didn't let the men…? Oh!" The large eyes filled with tears. "Oh, he is the most wonderful man in the entire world!"

Amused against her will, Tlalli found herself staring again. He was a good man, the Warlord. But wonderful? Oh, this woman must truly love him to be so easily excited about his deeds, and after he scared the life out of her own household and made her children cry.

"Was his sword so important?" she asked, mainly to change the subject. Azcapotzalco and the night of its conquest was not a subject she was ready to discuss, neither with friends nor with strangers. "He is the Chief Warlord. He can get plenty of new, and better, swords."

But now even Mixtli stared at her, scandalized, and the servants were gaping as though she had just laid an egg. Irritated, she returned their gazes.

"It is a very special sword." The woman was the only one to

react with a measure of reasonable thinking. "It's revered by many. It's believed to have magical qualities. It served my husband for more than half twenty of summers. This sword is very important and had never been touched by anyone but him."

The way it was said, in a calm, matter-of-fact voice but with such deep conviction, made Tlalli shudder, bringing back the memory of Azcapotzalco against her will, the way the Warlord had stood upon the stairs of the burning pyramid, after besting its defenders, killing them all and not even getting scratched; the way he had brushed his hand along the wide shaft and the vicious spikes, not afraid to cut his own flesh, murmuring something that looked like a prayer, or maybe an address, talking to the evil weapon as if to a special person. Oh, how this sight had terrified her back then!

"This whole *altepetl* believes in the magic hidden in this sword," the woman was saying quietly, as though talking to herself. "It is so very important. It can't be gone. People would be unsettled when they hear. They might lose their confidence, warriors and some of Texcoco citizens, too." The small teeth sank into the full lower lip. "How could it have happened? To think of someone breaking into the Chief Warlord's house in order to steal the most revered relic in Texcoco and the provinces. It's impossible!"

"No one dared to touch that sword?"

"No one. Of course, no one."

Tlalli's stomach tightened. "Unless not human."

The haunted gaze shot at her made her regret her words.

"And they killed Nakaztli." The tears were back, filling the beautiful eyes, threatening to spill out.

"Please." Unable to keep from doing so, Tlalli took the woman's hand in her own, pressing it lightly. "It will be all right. The Warlord, he will solve it somehow. Tlacaelel thinks of your husband so highly. He holds him as the bravest, most resourceful man in the entire valley of our Great Lake. He will find the way to solve it."

"But it hurts him so!" Not attempting to retrieve her hand, the woman looked away, her lips quivering. "He doesn't deserve this pain. This sword was always with him, always. He believes in it wholeheartedly. What if he gets hurt without it?"

"Where is the body of your maid?" The Warlord was back, sweeping through the doorway, as forceful as a storm cloud, and as unstoppable, followed by the children, both breathless and wide-eyed.

"In the back rooms." The Mistress of the House's attempt to compose herself was admirable, reflected Tlalli, liking the woman more with every passing heartbeat. She tried to be strong for the sake of her man.

He was gone again, waving the children away as he ran.

"Where is your brother, Coatl?" asked the woman, smoothing her hair tiredly.

"I don't know," said the boy quickly. Too quickly. Amused, Tlalli noticed his eyes clouding, turning blank.

The girl by his side smirked, not trying to conceal her grin. "He went back to *calmecac*," she said.

"Why would he? The school is closed for the days of the ceremony." The woman's eyes turned piercing. "He was with you and the *calmecac* boys on the Plaza, wasn't he?"

"Yes, of course."

The boy's eyes were anywhere but on his mother, and the girl was having a difficult time stifling a giggle. She was slender and tall, pleasant to look at, but somehow strange, appealing and unsettling at the same time, with her face narrow and her eyes of the most unusual color, bright and yellowish, catlike in a disquieting way. An outlandish creature. Fascinated, Tlalli studied her covertly, having every opportunity to stare as both children's attention was on their interrogator.

The woman's face darkened with foreboding that promised no good for the lying boy, but before other questions or accusations came, the Warlord was back, more furious than before, if that were possible.

"Tell me about those dark shadows you saw," he demanded, stopping before Tlalli, making her jump with the surprise of his advance.

Against her will, she took a step back. "I told you all about it already."

"They were black? All of them?"

"Yes, yes! They were black, just a part of the night. They were no people."

He ignored her last remark. "Do you remember where exactly they were? Can you show me the place?"

She just nodded, lost for words.

"Come!"

A curt inclination of his head demanded her to follow as he turned around, charging back toward the outside.

Would he dare to grab her by her shoulder had she argued like the yellow-eyed girl had before? she wondered numbly, not pleased with being ordered about, not in this way. Still she followed, wishing to be of help in spite of herself. This family was in trouble, and they were nice people, even the Warlord himself. If someone, people or spirits, had stolen something that precious to her, she might have been as aggressive, as put out and demanding as he was. After all, she owed him her life as well as her honor, and Tlacaelel appreciated and liked this man greatly.

CHAPTER 6

The wooden chests were everywhere, some low, some high, too high to see their insides without using something to stand upon. It made one work to get to the riches, but of course, those who spent their time in this wondrous place were not to be deterred.

Tlacaelel smiled, inhaling the peculiar smell of *amate*-paper as he pored through the stack of scrolls and folded pages. Nezahualcoyotl's private library was the talk of Texcoco, and he had heard about it in Tenochtitlan, too. Expecting much, he was still surprised to find it so large, so well-organized, so rich in content. Twenty times twenty books and more were stored here, placed in an inviting manner, to pick and choose your desired read, to sit comfortably on the clusters of mats and cushions, to read to your heart's content.

Sophisticated bastard, thought Tlacaelel, pulling one thick bundle out carefully, afraid to damage the fragile material covered with glyphs. His fingers slid along the wooden planks that held the folded paper, preventing it from closing up for the comfort of the reader. How had Coyotl managed to organize all this in the short time since he got his Texcoco back?

The book presented an account of Nezahualcoyotl's father, the last Acolhua Emperor, and his part in the first war against the Tepanecs, when the Acolhua won such a decisive victory, throwing the invaders off the local shores and then crossing the Great Lake themselves. In the long run, it did Acolhua no good, because Tezozomoc, the Tepanec Emperor, regrouped and then invaded again, in a more calculated manner, to squash the Acolhua presumption once and for all.

Still, here they were, reflected Tlacaelel, studying the glyphs, deciphering them rapidly, at the speed only he could read, absorbing the knowledge. Oh, yes, here they were, half twenty summers later, with the Tepanecs finished for good, and the Acolhua capital back in the rightful heir's hands, to return to its previous glory and made to evolve into something even larger and more influential, probably. A glorious *altepetl*, yes, but not as glorious, not as powerful as Tenochtitlan would be, he thought. His city would be the one to evolve into unheard-of grandeur, with Texcoco possibly following, but at a respectable distance.

He eyed the multitude of chests. Oh yes, some history would have to be rewritten. The Tepanecs were not important anymore, so their history would have to go.

"Honorable Master." One of his servants coughed delicately, uncomfortable at disturbing the great man's thinking process.

"Yes, Maitl?"

"The Acolhua main engineer you summoned is on his way, Honorable Master. And the priests are waiting in your quarters." The man shifted uneasily. "Our delegation will be ready to depart with the first light, if you wish to order our departure."

Tlacaelel looked up. "Did the lady come back?"

The servant's frightened expression gave him the answer before his lips did. "No, Honorable Master, not yet."

"Send a group of slaves accompanied by some warriors and a local guide. Search for her through the city." He held the man's gaze, not attempting to conceal his fury. "Find her." Trying to curb his worry, he glanced back at the scroll, his concentration gone. "Greet the engineer when he arrives, and make the priests comfortable. I will see them in a short while."

"Yes, Revered Master." The servant fled, relieved.

He tried to read on, not willing to let his worry distract him or consume his precious time. There was so much to do, as always. The famous Acolhua head engineer must be convinced to go back to Tenochtitlan with them, tempted by a challenge or a rich reward, or both. Provided Nezahualcoyotl was willing to lend the man and his services for, at least, a short span of time. Another thing to mention while meeting with the newly anointed Texcoco

Emperor tonight.

Then there were the priests – self-assured, powerful, not easily intimidated individuals – who had to be convinced, pacified, persuaded. These men held a certain power of the Mexica throne, and there was nothing he could do about it, not yet. Still, his reforms regarding the gods and their worship could not wait, so the priests' cooperation would have to be secured by any means possible. Huitzilopochtli, the special Mexica god, needed to be elevated above the other deities. It would unite Tenochtitlan and its people, would strengthen his beloved *altepetl*, would place it somewhat apart from the surrounding nations and communities. One more step toward the leading position the Mexica were to take in the Great Lake Valley's affairs.

The colorful glyphs stared at him from the old, slightly yellowish paper, telling the story of the battle upon Texcoco shores. So many warriors, so many boats, the symbols of the Acolhua forces victorious, full of valor. Quite a biased account. The Tepanecs looked insignificant and small, just a few glyphs, drawn tepidly, dull against the Acolhua colorfulness. He remembered Tlalli's attempt at writing a book. Oh, the Tepanecs did look heroic and brave in her glyphs. Another account lacking in detachment. *Where was she?*

With an effort, he pushed her out of his mind, aware of his churning stomach. Hungry he was not. Damn it. If something happened to her...

He folded the book carefully, defeated. If he could not read, at least he would explore the wonders of this library further. Maybe another book, something rare and fascinating to occupy his mind to the full extent.

Fully immersed in poring through one of the lower chests, he didn't hear the footsteps until the woman swept into the room, her head high, steps rapid but royal, her high-soled sandals making a pleasant sound against the stone floor.

"Wait outside!" she ordered her maid impatiently. "And prepare my litter. I'll be going home after I'm done here."

She turned around, then saw him and stopped dead in her tracks, a beautiful vision of shiny pulled-up hair, a pair of large eyes so black they glittered like obsidian, golden, creamy skin and a face that looked as though chiseled out of polished stone; a work of art. Clad in a richly decorated turquoise blouse and skirt with matching bracelets and anklets, the haughty noblewoman looked as stunning as he remembered her, although more than three summers had passed since he had laid his eyes on her. The daughter of the late Acolhua Emperor and his highly exalted Tepanec wife, the granddaughter of Tezozomoc, the Second Wife of Tenochtitlan's Second Emperor, the Chief Wife of his successor, the favorite sister of the current ruler of Texcoco, now the wife of the Acolhua Chief Warlord, the lady was highly aristocratic, wonderfully connected, annoyingly involved.

"Tlacaelel, the Mexica Head Adviser, it's a pleasure to see you," she said, composing herself with an admirable swiftness. It was anything but a pleasure for her, he knew. She had not forgotten what happened to her previous husband, whose murder he could have tried to prevent but hadn't.

"The honor is all mine, Revered Lady," he answered, getting to his feet, not liking her any more than she liked him. This woman was a force of nature, too beautiful, too smart, too forceful, and, of course, too spoiled, accustomed to getting her way, to being listened to, speaking her mind in the most unladylike fashion. Even the Highlander had not enough strength, or willingness, to tame this wild beast.

"I'm glad you found the time to enjoy my brother's private library. This place is a wonder to behold, isn't it?"

"Yes, it is. Nezahualcoyotl is a remarkable man who finds time to indulge in literature and arts, while rebuilding his *altepetl*, leading it to its future glory."

"A time for refined arts should always be found. Is it not what makes us into civilized people? One should not think of conquest and battles alone. A yearning for the beauty of art, music, and poetry is what marks a civilized *altepetl* and its people."

He watched the pretended innocence of her gaze, indifferent to her barbs.

"There is time for everything, Lady. Time to war, to shake off an oppression or to strengthen one's people's stance, time to make laws aimed at the general welfare of people, all people and not only the privileged ones, those who can read or appreciate the refined arts. Plenty of work for rulers like my emperor. Or like yours. Our sovereigns may have different visions, accomplishing their goals in a different manner, but we are yet to see which path proved more efficient, worthier to take."

He stood her glare, knowing that his coldness and indifference should anger her if nothing else did. He didn't care if she was angered or not, but her haughtiness was annoying at times. He knew what she thought of his Mexica people, the pushy newcomers with no subtlety or finesse. Many peoples around the Great Lake shared this sentiment of hers, but it was all about to change. Oh, it was changing now, with her aristocratic Texcoco being a perfect example. It needed Tenochtitlan more than Tenochtitlan needed it, refined arts or not, and this balance of powers would only deepen with the passing of time.

She didn't grow visibly annoyed or offended. "You haven't changed, Tlacaelel," she said softly, almost sad. "Talking to you brings back memories I wish to forget."

"I'm sorry about that," he said, contemplating the best route of retreat. The engineer might have reached his quarters by now, and the priests were sure to grow impatient being kept waiting for so long.

"You have no cause to feel sorry. You were not the one to do the deed. Or to order it." Her eyes clouded, and he recognized the fire behind them, remembering similar occasions. "The ones responsible will pay in the end."

That arrested his progress.

"Can I be honest with you, Iztac-Ayotl? For the sake of old times."

Her face closed. "Of course."

"Your brother is one of the wisest men I know. Against all odds, he achieved the impossible, returning your people to their previous glory. By courage, wisdom, and cunning, by patience worthy of a great man, he made Texcoco into a great Acolhua capital once again, an independent, powerful *altepetl*, the way it used to be during the time of your father. Nezahualcoyotl is a great ruler, a perfect leader to bring your people to an even greater future. Do not make life difficult for him. Help him achieve his goals, instead." He raised his hand as her eyes sparkled and her lips pressed in a thin line. "Your husband is another exceptionally wise man. Of a different background, he is a law unto himself, but under the façade of a reckless warrior, he is a politician. His loyalty to your brother is unquestionable, nothing will shake that. It makes him loyal to your people as well. And he is another man who knows what should be done in order to bring Texcoco to the greater glory." Seeing nothing but stubborn resentment, so familiar since the days of the Third Emperor of Tenochtitlan, he held her gaze, hoping against hope to make her listen. She was a wise woman, even though she allowed her emotions to rule her mind. "Do not make life difficult for both these great men," he added, knowing he was not being listened to. Like the good old times. "I heard you wield some influence. Why not use it to help them?"

She looked like a mountain about to be hit by a storm, like those beautiful snow-covered peaks one could see from the shores of Tenochtitlan when watching the mainland, covered by swirling dark clouds.

"You talk well, Tlacaelel. You always have. But under the beautiful words remains the fact that you do not care for my people or their *altepetl*. Tenochtitlan and its glory are the heart of your passion, and you will stop at nothing to achieve its supremacy. We are not standing in your way now, but if one day we do, you will turn against us with no second thought." Her breasts rose and fell as she took a deep breath, her head proud and high, gaze challenging. "My brother and my husband are fond of you. They think highly of you and your talents and abilities, and I do not disagree with them. But I do have my doubts as to the decency of your intentions. It suits you to be on our side now, but it may not always be the case. And worse so, I detest your emperor and everything he stands for. I will do everything in my power to sway my brother's opinion of the Mexicas as his partners."

For some reason, her words hurt. "As long as I lead

Tenochtitlan, my people will not betray Nezahualcoyotl or his people. You do not need to doubt my decency."

Her eyes softened. "I do not doubt your decency, Head Adviser, but I do doubt the decency of your elected emperor."

Some election, he thought. The council of the elders, representatives of Tenochtitlan's districts, had little say in that particular matter back three summers ago. On the brink of war with the still-invincible Tepanecs, the city had been in turmoil and afraid, needing a strong, weathered leader and not this woman's late husband, a youth of a mere twenty summers. Itzcoatl had made it all ready, striking at precisely right moment, just like he planned and schemed for a long time.

He stood her gaze, suppressing a shrug. "And yet, a further cooperation, a true alliance and friendship, will benefit both our people. You should let the past rest."

"My people will do better alone, with no cooperation of the people led by a man they cannot trust," she said stubbornly, her eyes blazing. "Many important people are sharing this opinion of mine, and there will be more of these soon. My brother will be made to listen."

"Neither your brother nor your husband will do anything to change their policies."

"You may be surprised."

Something in the way she said it made his skin prickle. She was up to something. He knew it now. Something more tangible than a pure hatred and a desperate wish to sway Coyotl to her side. The ruler of Texcoco was a pleasant man of great manners, but he was not a person to have his policies dictated to him. If Tlacaelel might have had any doubts before the battle of Azcapotzalco and Coyoacan, he had learned what the well-mannered Acolhua was made of. A pure marble, very hard, even if beautifully polished, pleasant to deal with, but impossible to break. Nezahualcoyotl would not be told what to do, neither by the influential Texcocans nor by his favorite sister.

As to his Chief Warlord, this woman could move the Smoking Mountain of the Highlands sooner than she would make her husband betray his most trusted friend. He was not a man anxious to please his women to that extent, letting them tell him what to do. He would sooner send her packing. Unless…

He watched the beautiful face, trying to find a clue. *What devilment do you have planned, or maybe have already done?* he thought. Oh but he had better set his spies in this palace to work at once.

"I wish we could reach an agreement," he said, non-committal, anxious to escape, to think it all over. She would not yield any more information, he knew. She had told him too much already. It was there in her eyes, suddenly worried, guarded, apprehensive.

"I hope so, too." A reserved nod of the royal head and she headed toward the closest cluster of mats, her maids trailing behind, ready to serve her refreshments or find a scroll the mistress may wish to read.

Waving his own escorts away, Tlacaelel hurried down the corridors, deep in thought. Something was not right here. Something had already been done. What made this woman so sure of herself? He would have to talk to the Highlander. And then to Coyotl. One after another, but in this order. The Highlander was more of a friend and not only a peer, and he needed to be warned, but carefully, without offending the man by having an open suspicion cast on his own Chief Wife, the woman he had evidently loved, passionately enough to fight for her back in Tenochtitlan, to endanger his life and his warrior's status among the Mexica forces. Oh, no! The Highlander might turn indignant and defensive, like any man in this situation, so someone else would have to be blamed for a possible conspiracy that he didn't even know existed for sure.

"Find out if the Acolhua Chief Warlord is in the Palace," he said to one of his warriors. "If not, send a word to him. Let him know that I need to talk to him. And hurry. It's a matter of importance. I want to see him as soon as possible."

However, he didn't expect his wish to be granted so soon, as the moment he settled to speak with the engineer, the Highlander burst through the doorway, leading a trail of appalled, protesting warriors, Tlacaelel's personal guards.

"I will kill Itzcoatl!" he bellowed, his face twisted, flushed, glittering with sweat, his cloak askew and dust covered, the wide chest rising and falling as though the man had just run through half of Texcoco, his fists clenched so tight their knuckles went white. "I will strangle him with my bare hands! I swear, I will do it. I promise you, I will find a way to get to him personally. I will not hire filthy killers and thieves to do it, not the way he does. No, I will do my own dirty work. I will take the satisfaction of killing him myself. I'll cut off his limbs one by one, and I will pull out his treacherous heart, to feed it to the marketplace rats. And then I will be back, cutting his flesh into tiny little pieces, to feed the rats some more. The dirty rotten son of the meanest whore, how dare he? How dare he do it?"

Dumbfounded, something that did not happen to him often, Tlacaelel just stared, listening to colorful descriptions of entrails spilled out and limbs cut off, all promised to be done to the object of that savage, unrestrained rage. The appalled engineer and the flabbergasted warriors left, following his gesture, and still the litany continued, with short but frequent pauses for breath. The man had been gasping when he arrived, and the screaming did not help to restore his ability to breathe.

"What happened?" asked Tlacaelel eventually, deeming a somewhat longer pause a good time to interfere. His friend truly needed to breathe. The glaring color of his face promised no good. He might drop dead right here at Tlacaelel's feet, complicating the already complicated political situation.

"What happened? Your filthy emperor, that's what happened! That rotten son of the dirtiest whore, that sickness-stricken rat of Tenochtitlan's canals, that two-faced stinking piece of excrement!"

The bellows of the Acolhua Warlord could be heard on the other side of the Great Lake, of that Tlacaelel was sure. He frowned, knowing that soon the Palace's dwellers would be here, Coyotl in their lead, and probably many of his advisers, family members, and influential guests – on the afternoon following the Great Ceremony, the Palace was still bursting with foreign visitors. He needed to find out what had happened before more people arrived to witness the scene currently on display.

"Calm down!"

Grabbing his friend by the shoulders, he shook him violently, ready to stop a blow that might have come. About the same height, although more slender, he trusted his power, clutching with all his strength, not letting the surprised man shake his hands off, or push him away, for that matter. Heart racing, he peered into the darkness of the widely spaced eyes, trying to get through the insane rage. "Calm down, for Huitzilopochtli's sake!"

"Get your hands off me!"

In one powerful movement, the Highlander broke free, and for a heartbeat it seemed as though he was going to strike his offender, thus putting an end to the friendship of many summers. He, Tlacaelel, would kill the dirty bastard if so. No one dared to lay a finger on the second most powerful man of Tenochtitlan, the conqueror of Azcapotzalco, Coyoacan, and Xochimilco, the former Chief Warlord and the current Head Adviser.

A few more heartbeats passed as they just stood, staring at each other, gauging one another's possible reactions. Then the Highlander's eyes cleared and the sanity flowed in, bringing back the man Tlacaelel knew and liked.

"I will calm down, but not for the sake of that strange Mexica god of yours," he said, wiping the sweat out of his face, smearing it with dust and the fresh earth his hands seemed to be marred with. The generous lips twisted in a mirthless grin. "Sorry for bursting in upon you in this way."

"What happened?"

The question wiped away the grin, and for a moment, Tlacaelel was afraid it would bring a wild flow of colorful curses back.

"Itzcoatl, that dirty son of a whore," hissed the Highlander, wiping his face once again. "He stole my sword!"

"What?"

Now it was Tlacaelel's turn to gape. But for the spectacular entrance, he would have burst out laughing, appreciating his friend's silly joke.

The glaring eyes and the anguished face in front of him told him that it was no joke, impossible as the allegation might sound.

"Wait. Tell me exactly what happened." Trying to find a foothold in this lake of unreasonableness, he went toward the low tables, not wishing to summon a slave to pour their drinks. "Here."

But the Highlander shook his head forcefully, not making an attempt to take the offered goblet, standing there with his fists clenched and his eyes haunted, disclosing the depth of his desperation. "I'm not touching the drink until I decide what to do."

"How do you know it was Itzcoatl?"

"Oh, I know; believe me, I know!" The air hissed loudly, bursting through the widening nostrils. "He might have thought he had covered his tracks, but he did not. His favorite bunch of killers was not as careful as they used to be in the days when they murdered Chimalpopoca." A mirthless grin flashed. "They grew sloppy, come to think of it. Or maybe they just didn't care enough."

"These men?"

In spite of himself, Tlacaelel shivered, remembering the tale of the Third Emperor's murder, carried out by the men who climbed like jaguars, as though having powers out of the humans' sphere of abilities, clad in black clothes, impossible to see unless very close, and in this case, most chances were for the witness to die, not living long enough to tell his story. Only one man had faced them, had fought the two of them and survived. This same Highlander. And now, three summers later, these men had broken into his house, stealing his most priceless possession, the magical sword that no one but them dared to touch.

"Was anyone killed?" he asked, thinking about the Highlander's first wife and the twins, having a soft spot for this particular family, given his contact with them on these same eventful days prior to his half brother's murder.

"Luckily, only my wife's favorite slave." A shrug. "I suppose she wouldn't have died either, but for happening on them at the wrong moment. They came to steal, not to kill."

"How do you know? I would expect such highly trained killers to leave no trace of their presence."

A slightly mischievous, if still mirthless, smile lightened the haggard face. "Your woman saw them."

He found himself staring again, as dumfounded as before. "What woman?"

The smile widened, obviously pleased with the effect. "How many did you bring here with you?" Another lift of the wide shoulders. "Your Tepanec woman."

He put his *octli* down, having hardly touched it. "What was she doing there?"

"Well, you should ask her that. Unruly females take time to get used to, you know. I've learned all about it." The smile was gone, replaced by the fierce glower. "Itzcoatl did it. I know it. He used these black killers before, and he used them again now. And they are good, damn good. They must have been watching my house for some time to have been able to pick the only night I wasn't there but my sword was." A clenched fist hit the side of the table, making the flask and the cups on it ring. "They sneaked in, took the sword that no one would dare as much as to look at, let alone touch, killed the poor slave that must have happened there by mistake, as it was just before dawn, and went away. So disgustingly easy." Another punch at the helpless furniture. "I should have thought about something like this. I should have guarded the damn thing. Should have put warriors around it, or at least some armed slaves. It's my fault it happened!"

Watching the familiar features, now distorted with unconcealed anguish, Tlacaelel felt his heart squeezing with compassion, but his stomach was churning, turning as though he had eaten something rotten.

"What was Tlalli doing in your house at night?"

A shrug was his answer. "Ask her. All I know is that she was outside, near dawn, she said. There were black shadows climbing over my wall. She insisted they were Underworld Spirits."

"Maybe they were. How do you know they were Itzcoatl's killers?"

"The stupid rats lost this." A large palm shot forward, offering a long, strangely glittering knife. "Recognize?"

Making no attempt to touch it, Tlacaelel studied the dagger, having seen it from time to time, in his friend's arsenal of weapons. Brightly reddish, peculiarly smooth, it reflected the light in a way that hurt his eyes, its handle made of the same material, but fashioned in the form of a head crowned with a magnificent headdress, wonderfully detailed.

"It's not your knife."

"No, it's not! That's what I'm telling you. The dirty sons of a whore lost it while climbing my wall, and who would use those knives if not the black killers? I'd never seen such a weapon, not until I got one for myself from another bunch of these dirty murderers, and not again in all these summers – until now."

It all made sense, the small details comprising a worrisome picture. Yes, Itzcoatl had used the highly trained killers before, while disposing of the previous emperor. And he might have used them again, of course. Who else could handle such a mission – the theft of the most famous sword around the Great Lake? And yet, why? Why would Itzcoatl do this?

"Did you talk to Coyotl?"

The Highlander grunted. "Not yet. I'm trying to decide what to do."

"Do nothing for now." Standing next to the man, he looked into the clouding eyes, which were again sparkling dangerously, ready to lose control. "Give me time to make my own inquiries. Until the next dawn." Catching the dark gaze, he held it, trying to relay confidence he didn't feel. "Promise to give me one day!"

"I can promise you nothing." The Highlander's voice was growling again, then the man closed his eyes, making a visible effort to control his temper. "But I will not do anything rash without telling you first, I promise you that. Anything that might affect the relationship of our people, I'll talk to you first before I act." A mirthless grin was back, stretching the bitten lips. "How handy for some of the Acolhua discontents. This incident came right in time. Itzcoatl could not have done them a better turn."

"Itzcoatl has no reason to do this—"

He gasped, stopping in mid-sentence, the beautiful face of the Emperor's sister leaping before his mind's eye, hovering there, refusing to leave. *My brother will be made to listen,* she said, and she was not worried about her husband, either.

No, he thought, clenching his teeth. It can't be. She wouldn't do this. She was not devious enough to come up with such a plan. And even if someone would advise her, one of these important discontents she mingled with, why, she would not do something like that, not to her husband, the man she was reported to love for many summers, long before coming to his household.

"I will go out and make my inquiries." Adjusting his cloak, he snatched up his own very regular sword, tying it to his girdle hastily. "Give me one day to do this. I ask for no more. I will not leave at dawn as planned, but if neither of us have found out anything of importance, we will leave for Tenochtitlan together, later that day." He grabbed the resisting hand, seeing the Highlander's eyes sparkling again, with an obvious protest. "You make your inquiries, I'll make mine, and we will meet here tonight. Or better yet, in your house. Or anywhere else where we can talk freely." He held the bleak gaze again. "We'll solve this problem, and we'll find your sword. We need it for our upcoming campaign, after all, don't we? So find it we will."

A reluctant smile was forming in the corner of the thinly pressed mouth. "Until tomorrow at dawn."

"Until tomorrow at midday."

"Why do you need so much time?"

Now it was Tlacaelel's turn to shrug. "I don't know. I'm planning ahead. Like always. In case something comes up."

"You and your grand plans!" But this time the Highlander's smile held some of his usual warmth. "Midday it is, then." He smoothed his creased, muddied cloak. "I better talk to Coyotl, then go back, if for no other reason than to take this filth off." He shook his head as though finding it difficult to believe any of it. "My wife promised your pretty Tepanec love to deliver her back here in a litter. So don't worry about her anymore. If you ever noticed she was missing." The spark in the widely spaced eyes was brief but unmistakable, that old cheeky, challenging glitter. "You should control your women better, oh Honorable Adviser. A lady of her status, running around Texcoco at night? Unacceptable, I would say. Not in our civilized *altepetl*."

"Oh, shut up! Speaking about controlling women and wives, you are doing no better, oh, Honorable Chief Warlord of the

Acolhua. The troubles my women make are nothing compared to some of yours."

Especially if your beloved Chief Wife has any part in your current trouble, he thought, hoping for the sake of his old friend that she was not involved. Or at least not heavily.

CHAPTER 7

Mictia watched the crowded Plaza, his senses alert, but not overly so. Clad in a loincloth only, without his pitch-black clothes, he blended with the excited commoners, drawing no attention whatsoever.

Having discovered the fascinating activities in the center of the city while heading back from the wharves, unable to solve their sailing problem, and therefore in the worst of moods, he had slowed his pace, then dived in, determined to hear the possible gossip. Had the rumor about the disappearance of the sword made it to the Plaza or the markets already? The crowded center offered possibilities, packed to bursting, but with no dignitaries upon the Great Pyramid, no sacrificial victims, no priests. Only the excited, sunburned people remained, to stroll around, talk, gesture, watch the performers or listen to music, replete with the free food offered at a multitude of stalls.

That was an interesting ploy to make the Texcocans and their visitors happy, thought Mictia, unable to resist the temptation, his hunger getting better of him. Whether the newly anointed ruler wanted to win the crowds, or was he determined to just make his big day remembered, Nezahualcoyotl had managed on both scores. A fascinating undertaking.

Lingering, he waited patiently by the more populated of the food stalls, not joining the vigorous elbowing of those who didn't want to wait. Groups of warriors could be spotted in the hubbub, although now those were also busy eating and drinking, more concerned with their own welfare than their responsibilities of keeping the crowds well-behaved. The ceremony was over for good, with the exalted Texcocans and their noble guests back in the Palace, so it was less important to keep the commoners from brawling. And not that any spicy beverages were offered to make the spirits soar. Drinking in public was against the law, punishable most harshly, whether purchased for favors or cocoa beans or offered for free by the authorities. Still, Mictia had recognized the slightly drunken spark in some of the milling commoners' eyes. Forbidden or not, the cheap *pulque* was always in high demand.

Careful to draw no attention, he had stayed for enough time to eat heartily, stealing a carelessly thrown bag and stuffing it with some food for his associates, but in a discreet manner. The commoners were there to enjoy themselves, not to carry the food away, of that he was sure. There was no need to create trouble. He had enough on his hands as it was.

He tried not to succumb to a small wave of panic. The good large boat that was supposed to take them away was gone, having probably left at dawn, when they failed to appear as planned. The cowardly lowlifes! Oh, how angry he had been upon his associate's return, his fury helping him to conceal his fear. They were stranded in this barely familiar, hostile *altepetl*, and with the most dangerous cargo that was to be delivered at those very moments. The people who had paid the staggering amount of cocoa beans and full-length cotton mantles had surely expected to receive their goods with no delay.

Not the Mexica people of Tenochtitlan, of course. But this even his associates didn't know. Only he knew what their true destination was, guessing the identity of the real recipients, local people of some importance, people who wanted the magic sword to pass into their possession. Or maybe just to leave the possession of its rightful owner.

For what reason? He didn't know; didn't care to ask. It was none of his business. He was to take the payment, compensate his associates to some extent and then go away, truly away, traveling far, rich and unconcerned, because to stay in the vicinity of the Great Lake, in either of the two powerful *altepetls*, was not a wise thing to do. The storm that would hit these shores upon the discovery of his deed would make the Tepanec War look small.

However, first he needed to leave, losing neither his loot nor his men, if he could help it. And maybe the hostage, too.

He thought about the boy, the way the little beast had huddled in the far corner since being captured, gazing at them with his eyes blazing, dark and haunted, a cornered jaguar cub. There must have been a reason he was called Ocelotl. A courageous little thing, the boy had made no sound, didn't cry or try to beg for his life. He just squatted there as comfortably as his ties would allow, radiating more hatred than fear, a ball of dark energy.

There was only one point when the wild thing lost all his composure, turning horrified and looking as though about to faint. A son of the magical sword's owner, he had clearly no trouble recognizing the cloth covering the dangerous weapon, its shape obvious, on a relatively open display with no bag to hide it. The boy grew so terrified, Mictia felt his own scant body hair rising, watching the sword, expecting it to spring from under its covers and cut them all into twenty little pieces, maybe. Cursing, he kicked the prisoner into a far corner, ordering him to stay there unless he wished to join his friend in his Underworld journey. Which the little rascal did, keeping very quiet.

Biting into a deliciously crisp tortilla, Mictia shrugged, actually liking the boy. A truly wild brat, a force of nature, just like his powerful father, maybe, as there were plenty of stories about the infamous leader, foreigner in himself, a dangerous man. But why would a son of the Chief Warlord run a bunch of street thugs on the marketplace? At this age, he should be in *calmecac*, learning to be a great warrior. Was the boy of value to his powerful father at all?

He contemplated this matter while heading back, watching his surroundings, more careful now. Not killing the unexpected intruder on a spur-of-the-moment inspiration, seeing the possibility of a good ransom, he knew he has to rethink the matter now. Again, he had acted hastily, grabbing too many opportunities at the same time – a weakness he knew himself to be guilty of. A kidnapping could bring in a good payment, yes, but they were here in Texcoco for another reason. A reluctant hostage would turn into more of a liability than an asset when it was time to sneak out in the darkness, crossing the major parts of the city, heading for the western roads, leaving the capital on foot, having no other choices. The accursed sword would hinder them, maybe, the way it had since he had laid his hands on the precious item. It was enough in itself, without the fierce offspring of the magical sword's owner making trouble of his own.

No, it would be wise to kill the boy and get it over with. The cub was too wild, and the Warlord may not even pay them in the end, having another son and wives to sire more male children

"Tell me exactly what happened!"

The curt order made Tlalli shrink back. He didn't look angry, indignant, or even disappointed. Had he scolded her, yelled at her, or maybe even threatened her, she would have known what to do, but the distant, cold indifference left her lost for words, even afraid. Had he cared at all?

Gathering the remnants of her courage, she met the coldness of his gaze. "I went along the main road, the one leading from Texcoco Plaza to the marketplace and the temples behind it. That brought me to the Warlord's neighborhood." She took a deep breath. "You see, I wanted to walk Texcoco. To walk it for real and not just to ride it in the litter, taken to buy silly things like other women. I wanted—"

"I didn't ask why you went out." His voice rang stonily, the voice of a leader interrogating an insubordinate warrior of the lowest rank, cutting, lacking in emotion, ominously calm. "I want you to tell me exactly what you saw outside the Acolhua Warlord's house."

She clasped her sweaty palms together. "There were black shadows, maybe two or three of them. I thought them to be the Spirits of the Underworld." It was unbearable to see the freezing chill of his eyes. If only he would smile at her, just a fleeting smile, at least that. "They appeared on the Warlord's wall, and then they went down, to disappear into the darkness." She made an effort, collecting her thoughts. He would appreciate a crisp, detailed account. "It was turning gray already. It was almost dawn."

"And then?" His gaze didn't thaw.

"And then I went away." She frowned, beginning to feel the buds of rising anger. He had no right to be so cold and commanding. "I was on my way to see the city. I had no reason to spy on the Warlord's house. I happened to be there by accident."

He turned away, eyeing the papers spread all around him.

"But you did come back later on." It sounded like an open accusation.

She felt her hands beginning to sweat. "Yes, it happened much later, and it was the most silly accident. It should not have happened."

"A lot of accidents, Tlalli. Too many, if you ask me."

"Yes, I know. But please, you have to let me explain."

Encouraged by the slight decrease of hostility in his tone, and by the way he did use her name after all, as though recognizing her presence, not holding her to be just an insubordinate underling, she leaned forward, not daring to come closer without some sort of an invitation, but hoping that he would turn around and take her into his arms, like he always did.

"I don't want your explanations." His back was still facing her, wide and uncompromising, his voice returning to its cutting edge. "You did what you did for your reasons, and I don't want to hear any of it." At last, he turned, his face a mask cut out of stone. "Tell me about your later visit in this household."

She took a deep breath, gathering the remnants of her courage. If he wanted an impartial account, he would get one.

"The Warlord's household was troubled, of course. His magical sword was gone and no one knew how it happened." Pleased to hear her own voice ringing firmly, with no visible trembling, she went on, returning his frosty gaze as best as she could. "The servants were scared, the children unsettled. But the Mistress of the House is a very pleasant, kind woman with much strength. She made sure everyone told her their accounts, and so when the Warlord came, scaring everyone with his shouting and his kicking at the furniture, she was able to calm the spirits and tell him exactly what happened." She hesitated, remembering the woman, so small and fragile, but so determined, not about to allow anyone, even the powerful Master of the House, to upset her family. "She was able to calm him, so he went on making his inquiries in a more peaceful way."

"What kind of inquiries?" He seemed to thaw again, clearly impressed with her account of the events. Was she like the Warlord's woman, standing up to the powerful leader? The thought gave her strength to go on.

"He wanted to know everything, so she told him. And she asked me to tell him about the Underworld Spirits I saw, so he made me to go out and show the exact place. Which turned out to be the place where the children found the knife."

"The strange knife with the beautiful handle?"

"Yes." She gazed at him, surprised. "Have you seen it? I had never seen anything like that before."

"Yes, I have." His face closed once again. "Tell me about the other wife, the Chief Wife. What did she do all this time?"

"The Chief Wife?" Puzzled, Tlalli peered at him. "The Mistress of his House is the Chief Wife. The woman who talked to the Warlord. She manages his household, and she is listened to by all."

He frowned with impatience. "He has another wife, the Emperor's sister. Wasn't she there?"

"Oh, the highborn lady, the former wife of some other emperor? Oh, yes." She remembered Mixtli's chattering. "No, she wasn't there with us."

"Too bad!" He glanced back at his scrolls. "Anything else?"

Her stomach twisted. "Not anything that I can think of. If I remember something, I'll tell you."

He didn't look up, his face again a stone mask painted with dark colors. "Do that."

The interview was clearly over. She hesitated for another heartbeat, her feet heavy, as though made out of marble. "You don't need me anymore?"

There was a sudden tension in his shoulders, as though an

invisible spasm rushed through his limbs. "No, I don't. Go back to your quarters and stay there. We will be heading back to Tenochtitlan in a day or so. Until then, stay in your quarters. You are not allowed to go out anymore."

She gasped, prepared for anything but that. How dare he? She was a free woman, not a slave and not even one of his noble wives to be restricted in this way.

"You can't treat me like that!" she called out, welcoming the confrontation. It was better than his stony indifference. "I'm not your slave to be ordered about."

His eyes were upon her, blazing with the suddenness of lightning, burning her skin. "You very well could have been, woman! So don't try my patience any longer. I will deal with you later, when I have time. When the matters of real importance are solved and the trouble with our allies prevented. Until then, stay in your quarters and try to behave like a respectable woman." There was frustration in his eyes, she could see that most clearly, but his rage was much stronger, making her skin crawl with fear. He was never angry with her, never, let alone that greatly enraged. "Now go." His hand shot out, palm up, preventing what she might have tried to say in protest. "You are not allowed to speak to me, either. Go away!"

She clutched her hands to stop them from trembling, holding the tears back, determined not to let them show. Not in front of him! Because they were tears of rage, not of fear or desperation. The desperation would come later maybe, when she would miss him and his touch, and his amused half-serious, half-teasing remarks. She was missing it already, wishing nothing more than to relax in his embrace, to tell him all about her stupid adventures in this strange, busily rebuilding *altepetl*. Oh, how she craved to run back to him.

But oh no, she thought, clenching her teeth. He was too unreasonable, too stubborn, too blind, determined to see nothing but his side of the story, suspicious of her activities and unwilling to trust her as he always did. Why, he had trusted her more readily in Azcapotzalco, with the hidden route to Coyoacan, when they had been nothing but enemies, the wary conqueror and the unyielding conquered. But now, after all they had been through, after the wonderful love of two summers, he was ready to throw it all away because of a simple mistake, a silly deed committed out of impulse, an unauthorized excursion that brought no harm to anyone. Was it that wrong to go into the city all by herself? She had done it many times, in Tenochtitlan too, before finding her purpose with scrolls and papers. Admittedly, he had been out of town on all those occasions, so maybe he didn't know, but she was not his slave. She was a free woman, and she would go wherever, and whenever, she pleased. And if he didn't like it, well, he could just dismiss her and she would be gone, never to return.

Head held high, she crossed the spacious room and went out of the doorway, ignoring the gaping servants who gathered outside, agog with curiosity. They could all rot together with him. Them and this gods-accursed Acolhua *altepetl*. It was not as pretty or as charming as her father had led her to believe it was. It was dangerous and unjust, unreasonable, unfair, full of angry people and bad spirits. Even the good people she met, the Chief Warlord's wife with her sweet little girl, were not locals. The pleasant, kind woman admitted to coming from the Highlands, as foreign to Texcoco as Tlalli herself.

Hesitating in the corridor, she sent a direful glance at the slave who seemed as though determined to steer her toward her quarters. What to do?

To go to her rooms tamely and wait for him to come there and "deal" with her when he had found time between his important dealings, or to do something, anything, a useful activity that might keep her busy, too busy to think about his unfairness? She cursed softly. One thing was sure. She should never have come here in the first place. This *altepetl* was nothing like she thought it would be.

CHAPTER 8

The shadows were deepening, closing on the emptying alleys of the marketplace, which were now filled with armies of cleaners, anxious to sweep the mess away and be gone. Tlacaelel watched them, his mood as bleak as that of his friend, who squatted opposite from him, not comfortable at all, ready to spring to his feet and rush off, his face as dark as the deepening dusk, and as stormy, his hand not straying from the hilt of a sword, a regular, ten-spike-long affair that adorned his girdle.

"I know you deem it a waste of time, but I wanted to meet here because I want to talk to you without being overheard."

The Highlander sighed, his attempt to relax his limbs almost visible, impossible to miss. "Yes, of course. I appreciate your concern, Old Friend," he said, his smile flashing for a heartbeat with the old familiar charm, gone almost as quickly. "So what did you find out?"

"Well, I would rather hear your findings first."

He watched the owner of the food stall, a nimble middle-aged man who rushed to refill their cups, his other hand balancing a plate of fresh tamales he had made a young woman, probably his daughter, prepare in a hurry, although it was obvious that they had been closing their business for the day. No vendor would dream to spurn such important customers. It was not every day that the food stalls of the marketplace were honored by the highest of the nobility.

"I found nothing. Nothing!" The Highlander's voice rose, shaking with rage. "What did you think I would find? The sword itself? The filthy thieves who stole it?"

"Stop yelling." Glancing at the stall owner and his pretty helper, both looking alert and listening, Tlacaelel pursed his lips. "I would think you would find some trace. Something they might have left. Anything. Anywhere. They were no dark spirits, unless Tlalli is right, so they would have to pass through some parts of the city, even if they lost only one knife at your place."

The sound of her name made his stomach heave, his thoughts straying in an inappropriate manner. He had more important things to take care of, didn't he? And yet his doubts were nagging. He had treated her harshly. Yes, women of her status were not to sneak out, touring foreign cities at night, unsupervised and unescorted. Besides chancing running into trouble, how was one to know such a woman was not intriguing with men? She was not a marketplace girl anymore, and after two summers of being a favorite concubine of a powerful man, she should have known better. And yet...

He ground his teeth. And yet, had she been that regular, reasonable woman like many of them, he would have lost interest in her, would have discarded her long since. Her fierce, untamed spirit was what kept his attraction to her strong. Combined with a keen mind and a strong, delectable body, it kept drawing him back to her rooms, even now making him think about her and not about more important matters. He forced his mind back to his friend.

"Traces? Do those people leave traces? Did they leave any while killing your previous emperor?" the Highlander was saying, his fist crashing against the helpless table. "They left no traces back then, and they left none this time. Aside from the gods-accursed knife, and I wonder what made them so sloppy as to drop that priceless thing." The plate of tamales remained untouched, the man's cup of *octli* forgotten beside it, a highly unusual sight. "I sent my warriors everywhere. They checked the wharves and the more distant shores where the fishermen sail. I even sent a group to investigate the roads, in case the filthy pieces of excrement tried to sail from any of the villages." The large fist rose again, banging against the hard wood of the table, making the cups clatter. "They found nothing. Nothing! The filthy lowlifes disappeared without a trace. As though they were truly just spirits, like your Tepanec woman thought they were."

Shrugging, Tlacaelel picked the crispiest looking tamale. "What were the chances of someone seeing them, moving at night, wearing nothing but black?" Against his will, his eyes drew to his friend's girdle, taking in the regular sword and the easy familiarity with which the Highlander's palm rested upon its hilt.

"They didn't leave at night. Your woman saw them climbing my wall near dawn. Even if running all the way, they would be reaching the wharves after the first light, when the people are already out and about."

"Maybe they didn't leave. Maybe they are still here in Texcoco." The replacement sword forgotten, Tlacaelel frowned, thinking it through. "Maybe something went wrong, as stealing anything, let alone the famous weapon of the most prominent leader of this *altepetl*, should have been done in the dead of the night, not just before it ended."

The haggard face twisted again. "Of course something went wrong. My wife says they all settled to sleep very late that night, and then her favorite maid surprised them. Together, these things might account for the lateness of their visit."

"Send your warriors to guard the wharves and the roads out of the city."

The Highlander pursed his lips. "Of course. The warriors who scanned the city and the roads stayed where they are, watching. Although I don't believe the filthy thieves are still here." For the third time, the fist landed on the helpless table, but as painful as it might be, the man didn't even wince. "We are wasting our time, Tlacaelel! I believe my sword is already in Tenochtitlan. Or at the bottom of the lake. Your damn emperor might have wished to just get rid of it, if not to try to use it himself. Oh, gods!" The man buried his face in his hands, his massive shoulders sagging. "You have no idea what I will do to this man. He will wish he had never been born!"

"It's not him." It took him all his willpower to stand the wild gaze that leaped at him, full of so much rage and pain his heart twisted with compassion. "Listen to what I have to say." The fierce glare was his answer, but he held the burning eyes, determined to get to the man in spite of it all. "Itzcoatl has nothing to gain from any of it. He doesn't have a reason to do that. He simply doesn't. Yes, he would have done it if it suited his purpose, but it does not. In fact, it does exactly the opposite, and if he heard of this incident he would be rushing to put his own spies to work, to find out who did it and why. Not because he is fond of you or Coyotl, or his Acolhua allies, but because he needs this *altepetl*'s cooperation. He cannot have you angered and hostile, not now. Maybe in the future it won't matter that much – although I believe we will always work closely, your people and mine – but it does matter now." He raised his hand, seeing the protest forming, flashing out of the veiled, haggard eyes. "Please, listen to me now. What I want to tell you is important."

Taking a gulp from his drink, he put the cup down, unwilling to let the spicy beverage blur his thinking.

"You brought up the murder of Chimalpopoca, Tenochtitlan's previous Emperor. Think about it. It was made to look as though the Tepanecs did it, wasn't it? All the clues pointed in that direction, with dirty Maxtla going around, murdering other rulers as well. It was easy to believe it, wasn't it? But we both know that it was not Maxtla who paid the murderers. We both know it for a fact, but even had we not known the details, pure common sense would tell us that Maxtla had no motive. As simple as that. Just like you and me, Maxtla knew who the next emperor would be, the strong man who was able to oppose him, to challenge him on the battlefield, while poor Chimal would never have even tried something like that. So Maxtla has nothing to gain and everything to lose from Chimalpopoca's death. Still, was he not blamed for this murder? Oh yes, he was, because the smart person who did it made sure it looked like Maxtla's doing."

Detecting the frown and the spark in the dark depths, he breathed with relief, encouraged. Oh yes, the man was listening.

"And that is what has happened now. I'm sure of that. Someone with a motive to break the Acolhua-Mexica relationship has stolen your famous sword, and made it look like Itzcoatl's doing, counting on you arriving at the conclusion you did, indeed, very promptly, arrive at." He shook his head, pleased with his friend's narrowing gaze. "What better way could there be than to make the Acolhua Chief Warlord furious beyond reason, with the Acolhua Emperor just as indignant, backing his most trusted leader and friend up, causing a breach between the two allies, too deep to bridge. Is it not a good plan?"

"The dirty manure-eaters who make life difficult for Coyotl," growled the Highlander, words seeping with difficulty through his clenched teeth. "This co-called 'old aristocracy' of Texcoco."

"Yes, I would bet many cocoa beans it was their group who paid the black-clothed pieces of rotten meat to do the deed."

The dark eyes flickered, now mere slits in the broadness of the man's face. "What is your solution?"

"We will look elsewhere. Not in Tenochtitlan, but in the Acolhua towns. Coatlinchan would be my first destination."

"Because this is where their resistance is the strongest," said the Highlander instantly, his forehead clearing of creases.

"Yes. According to my spies, they are congregating there, stirring trouble."

"I know that!" called the Acolhua Warlord tersely, almost his old self again. The shadows were still there, the dark rings under his eyes deep, the pallor of the strong face startling. Still, the worst of the desperation seemed to lift, or at least to retreat a little. "Coyotl is well aware of what is going on, but he knows his supporters are larger and stronger, with the warriors on his side. So he lets those manure-eaters talk freely for now." The handsome face darkened again. "But not for much longer. You have my word on that."

"Yes. Such open resistance should be squashed. Coyotl was careless to let it blossom. Too careless or too sure of himself." Shaking his head, Tlacaelel picked up his cup, then put it back without touching it, gesturing to the stall owner, instead. So much talking made him thirsty, but *octli* was not a drink to quench that. "I know he has his way, and our methods are different, but to allow the bunch of influential traitors to go around freely was somewhat extravagant of him." He waited for the man to bring cups full of clear water, then glanced at his friend. "So what will you do now?"

The Highlander snatched his cup eagerly, emptying it in one gulp. "First, I'll go home and think about all this while sending more warriors to guard possible routes out of the city, the wharves and the land roads. Then I'll talk to Coyotl. Then, if convinced, I'll go wherever we decide first thing in the morning." The familiar warmth was back, pouring out of the widely spaced eyes. "You will be heading for Tenochtitlan tomorrow, won't you? If so, will you make the inquiries there, just in case?"

Tlacaelel grinned. "Maybe I won't be returning so quickly. A short delay will not hinder our southern campaign preparations, and it would do me nothing but good to visit your other Acolhua towns, to assess their mood, while keeping an eye on their hotheaded Chief Warlord. I hear he is a bloodthirsty bastard, that one."

"Oh, shut up!" The flicker was unmistakable this time, bringing his friend back in force. "You will not be able to stop me from killing the manure-eater responsible for all this, your emperor or not. But I could use that clear thinking of yours, Old Friend. So come along, by all means."

For a few heartbeats, they kept silent, sipping their drink, with the Highlander still attached to his water, not stealing a glance toward the neglected cup of *octli*.

"No *octli* until you get your sword back, eh?"

The man nodded, deep in his thoughts.

"Don't talk about our plans or suspicions." Tlacaelel took a deep breath, knowing that he might be treading on a dangerous ground now. "Aside from Coyotl, no one needs to know. And maybe not even him."

The face of his friend darkened again. "I trust Coyotl wholeheartedly!"

"I know, and I don't doubt him, either. But you never know whom he can share this information with, or who may overhear you two talking about it." He held the defiant gaze. "No one is to know that you may suspect anyone else but Itzcoatl. No one! Not your most trusted warriors. Not your wives even, especially the more noble-born among them."

"Iztac-Ayotl has nothing to do with it!" It came out stonily, in a cutting voice.

"I didn't say she does. But she is connected to the people we suspect, so it's better she knows nothing." Anxious to contain his friend's growing anger, he raised his eyebrows. "She is impulsive, fierce, loyal. She may do silly things trying to help. Now your first wife is a pure treasure, so if you must, confide in her. She cannot help us, but she can try and keep your other woman, the force of nature, busy while we are solving this problem. I heard they are getting along surprisingly well."

The Highlander shrugged, back in his gloomy thoughts. "They are all right, both of them. Why not?"

"You never appreciate what you have." Tlacaelel grinned without envy, remembering thinking that again and again, since he had met this man more than half twenty summers ago. The lucky beast had always enjoyed more than his share of good fortune, taking everything he got for granted. "Wives do not get along, not usually, especially when they share the title of a chief one, like only your household could do. A hierarchy helps things work out easier, with the natural ascendancy of one wife over another. But oh no, you let both your women rule however they see fit, and surprisingly, it works, even though one of them is a headstrong creature that could not be tamed even by Tenochtitlan's royal family before that. Still, all is shiny in your household, and you, lucky frog-eater that you are, have no idea what a miracle it is."

The grunt was his answer, but the Highlander's eyes filled with warmth once again.

"That's Dehe. She is like the most talented leader; she knows how to make it all work, from slaves to the highborn peers above her status, she can make everyone do whatever she thinks has to be done, and her plans are always good, always working." A smile dawned. "Come to think of it, she is a small version of you, oh highly aristocratic second most powerful man in the rising Mexica Empire. Content to run her tiny realm from the shadows, she holds all the power, and she never brags about it."

Against his will, Tlacaelel roared with laughter. "Well, thank you. I'm flattered. This particular lady always held my highest admiration." He sobered again. "But she can't help us in this, so I would prefer you don't talk about any of it in the vicinity of your household."

There is no telling what servants may be running to tell your high-strung and high-born royal cihua of a wife if they hear anything worth telling, he thought, knowing that some suspicions one should keep strictly to himself. If the Emperor's sister and this man's beloved wife was implicated, as he, Tlacaelel, believed she would be, his friend would do better having found this out all by himself. The sparks would be flying high, burning every bystander in the vicinity, especially those who would dare let the disillusioned husband know.

CHAPTER 9

Nightfall had barely arrived when Mictia gestured his associates out of the warehouse's safety, following them promptly, probing the darkness with his senses. The clamor of the marketplace and its flickering lights reached them here, but faintly, not disturbing the murky gloom of the back alleys.

"Now lead," he whispered, pushing the boy forward, but making sure his grip on the thin shoulder was as tight as before. He leaned closer. "Remember, one attempt to alert anyone and your guts are out there, spilling down your legs. Like your friend and the other man, but more slowly, with a lot of pain." To make sure his message was appreciated, he moved his knife lightly, letting it slide against his prisoner's ribs, mildly painful yet drawing no blood.

The boy shuddered, stifling a gasp, his face just a black mask of pressed lips and glittering eyes, barely visible in the darkness. Not that Mictia expected anything else. The fierce cub was a fascinating thing to watch, his reactions predictable by now. Nothing but a carefully calculated hatred and desperate attempts to survive. A remarkable creature.

Earlier, coming from his excursion into the city, he had distributed the food between his companions, giving Nacatl a larger portion, which was his way of letting the other man know of his dissatisfaction. The good-for-nothing piece of dirt could have been more efficient in his morning trip to the wharves. To come back empty-handed, with no boats and not even worthwhile news to share was unforgivable. His own, Mictia's, later trip produced much more – food, some needed supplies, and a plan.

They would leave on foot, the moment the darkness fell, wearing regular clothes, blending with the festive crowds that were still sure to fill the city. It wasn't as safe as their original plan of sailing on the night of the theft, but given the circumstances, this was the best he could come up with.

So, as the scowling man was eating his smaller share, not daring to sound an argument, Mictia rethought his plan, shrugging. At least they were not stranded in an island-city like Tenochtitlan, having land avenues of escape as much as the water ones, with their destination lying on the same side of the Great Lake, anyway, not truly far and not a dangerous journey unless pursued.

Would they be pursued? He tried to imagine what the formidable Warlord would do, or maybe already had done by now. Did he spread his warriors in order to block the roads? No, not likely. The man would assume the obvious, that they were long since gone, sailing for Tenochtitlan.

Tenochtitlan! He suppressed his grin. Was the fierce leader sailing there now, bent on confronting the ruler who was supposed to pay for that theft? Had he brought along warriors? How many?

It was a war, oh yes, but he didn't care. His job was done, or almost done. He would be far away before this entire region sank into another bloodbath, with the conquerors of the mighty Tepanecs going for each other's throats. A stupid idea, but those who paid him had wished it so, and he was not a person to argue with his customers.

"Give me that tortilla." Not waiting for the second man to comply with the sudden request, he snatched the warm pastry, then strolled toward the far corner where their prisoner curled up, a dark heap of limbs, making no sound.

"Get up, boy," he said, appreciating the hate-filled stare that followed his advance. "Do what you are told," he added, when not obeyed instantly, administering a kick to drive his point home.

The boy got to his feet, reeling but catching his balance, clearly not willing to be helped, either good-naturedly or with more beatings. Grabbing the cub by his upper arm, Mictia turned him around, seeing the large eyes widening, filling with terror, following the progress of the knife. Satisfied that the wild cub still took him seriously, he cut the ties, then pushed his prisoner back to the ground, tossing the tortilla into his lap.

"Eat and make no sound," he said. "Stay in that corner, and don't even try to think of moving a limb."

The narrowing eyes met his gaze, over their initial fright again.

"I need to pee. Do I do it right here?" The boy's voice was husky, but not trembling, not having the sound of tears in it.

Amused, Mictia found it hard to suppress his laughter. "Didn't you already?" he said, turning to go. "If not, keep it in. You'll have your chances to piss on yourself soon enough."

Too bad, he thought, heading back to his associates, thoughts again on his plan. The boy has huge potential. It would be a certain waste to kill the wild thing, but what choice did he have? They could not slip around the night streets of the alerted city, dragging a prisoner of such a fierce disposition. They were sure to get caught, and the magical sword was of greater importance than the wild son of the sword's owner. No man in his right mind would pay much for such unruly offspring, having another, as good as this one, and wives to produce more heirs. No, the boy would have to go.

"We begin moving in a short while," he said to Nacatl, making a point to give a dark look to the other man. "The moment the darkness spreads. Clean the bag, in the meanwhile, as best as you can. I don't want it to be oily and full of crumbs and smells."

The tall man nodded, offering no argument, bright enough to understand without the need to explain. The bag he had stolen to carry the food would have to contain their black clothes and the rest of their gear. In order to blend with the crowds, they would need to look as normal as they could.

"You," he turned to his other one, "did you find a better way out of the city?"

"It depends if we are heading north or south," mumbled the man, keeping his eyes low, his fear obvious, marring the suffocating semidarkness of their shelter.

"What do you think?" growled Mictia, his anger raising, threatening to get out of control.

"South, yes, of course, south," cried out the man, stammering. "But we can't go on foot. We just can't. We'll get caught and —"

In one leap Mictia was beside his frightened associate, grabbing him by the cloak, slamming the trembling body against the wall.

"What are you so afraid of, eh?" he hissed, controlling his temper no longer. "Did you betray us already? Did you?"

The man moaned, a long, desperate howl that he was quick to silence with his fist. His victim's quivering jaw made a cracking sound, as the pain shot through Mictia's wrist, resounding in his arm, rolling all the way up his shoulder. He stifled a curse, feeling the assaulted body sagging against his. His knife made a quick work, knowing exactly where to sink to silence the groans that may escape the torn lips.

Taking a step back, he let the body fall, bending to clean his knife against his victim's cloak. It gave him time to compose himself, to stop the cursing. The filthy coward's uselessness and fear were unforgivable, but his own loss of control was not an admirable trait, either. The man was turning into a liability, yes, his fear making him prone to a fit of panic at the worst of moments, when they would have to cross the more populated parts of the city. Yet, the disposing should have been done quickly and efficiently, involving no beatings and no damaged wrists.

He moved his palm, causing some of the pain to return. Damn it.

"You are not familiar with Texcoco, are you?" he asked Nacatl, pleased to see the tall man still busy with the bag, unperturbed.

"I am. A little. I can try to find means to avoid the Plaza on our way to the southern parts."

"Good." Kicking the body away, he made it roll toward the second boy's corpse, already stiff and beginning to smell in the accumulating heat. "You can finish his food after you're done cleaning the bag." He glanced at their prisoner, still huddled in the far corner, now a dark form turned to stone, not even breathing, as it seemed. "Give the whelp the rest of the food if you don't want all of it."

Nacatl hesitated. "Do you still want to bring him along?"

"He might have brought us a nice reward." Leaning against the wall, Mictia massaged his damaged palm, twisting it lightly despite the pain, trying to find the dislocated bone. "But no, we can't bring him. I'll dispose of him before we go."

The silence prevailed, interrupted by Nacatl's ministering to the bag as he turned it inside out, shaking it vigorously, beating against the stiff material with his palm, making the reluctant crumbs fall away. It wasn't going to be large enough to carry all their weapons, thought Mictia, exasperated. He should have stolen a larger bag.

"I know where you can steal a boat." The boy's voice tore the silence, making them almost jump with surprise. He saw Nacatl freezing, holding his breath.

"What?"

"I know where you can... can get a boat," repeated the boy quietly, his voice trembling.

"You do?" Getting to his feet, Mictia felt like cursing again, his wrist on fire now, worse than before. "What are you trying to tell me, boy?"

The cub watched him nearing, his eyes huge and terrified, his arms clutched around his knees, hugging them in a protective manner.

"Speak up." He contemplated kicking the wild thing again, mainly to remind him of his place, then decided against it. That one had clearly seen all the evidence he needed to behave in a reasonable manner. "Well?"

The boy drew a deep, somewhat convulsive breath. "If you don't kill me, I'll show you the way to the place where you can steal a boat." It came out breathlessly, in a frantic rush.

Mictia studied his prisoner carefully. "I've been to the wharves. No one leaves their boats there unattended."

"It's not the wharves," said the boy hurriedly. "It's where the fishermen do their fishing."

"Where?"

"Far from the wharves. Where the shore is all sand."

"How far?"

"Not very far." The boy pressed his arms tighter, his eyes not leaving Mictia's face, boring into it, very anxious.

"And you know how to get there without running all over the city?"

"Yes, yes! It's all the way behind the colorful wall of the marketplace, where the loose women are. Then you just go with the trail, up until you reach the lake." A hesitation, a nervous lick of the cracked lips. "I can take you there."

"You can take us there, eh?" He peered at the boy sternly, thinking the offer over. Sailing was always the most preferable solution, sure to get them away from the warriors with which the Warlord might have stuffed the city by now, blocking the more obvious roads of escape. And if possible to reach without passing through the most crowded parts of the city...

"You don't want to get killed, do you?" He let his gaze harden, seeing the boy swallowing hard. "Well, lead us to your boats. But one squeak in order to alert someone's attention, one attempt to get away..."

With his good arm, he dragged the boy to his feet, pushing him toward the sprawling bodies, making him stumble into the revolting mess, the odors of rotting flesh mixing with the stench of the fresh blood and discharges.

"See this? See their bodies? Yours will be the same the moment I suspect you are trying to do something silly. Understand?"

The boy scrambled back to his feet, gagging, his entire body shaking, his sobs muffled, out of control. Mictia caught his shoulder once again, stabilizing him as he did.

"Now relax and stop mewling. Or we'll be finding your trails behind the alley of the loose women all by ourselves." He pushed the prisoner toward their corner this time. "Go get some food. You might be of use now, so make sure you are strong enough to guide us quickly, with no fainting fits halfway there." He suppressed a grin. "Loose women, eh? What does a cub like yourself have to do with them? I bet you were sneaking there to watch, you and your pitiful bunch of other marketplace rats."

And now, heading down the narrow alleys that the boy seemed to recognize with no special effort, sensing their way more than seeing it, clearly familiar with the twisted paths, he contemplated again what a wild thing this son of the Texcoco Chief Warlord was. How could a noble offspring turn into something like that? Didn't the powerful leader try to discipline his own son? Why allow the cub to run around in such a loose manner?

The boy had claimed to be a *calmecac* pupil, but if in *calmecac*, how did he come to know the marketplace slums so well, running a gang of other little thugs, instead? Did he prove too unruly even for the stern teachers of the best school in the city? And there was another thing. Only now, walking the streets, Mictia noticed that the boy limped. Not enough to hinder their pace, it was a slight totter that made his gait cumbersome, lacking the cat-like grace his other movements suggested.

He remembered the morning encounter. Was the boy's leg damaged while receiving a rough treatment at his own and his associate's hands? It didn't seem so. The boy's step was easy, self-assured, as though accustomed to walking this way. Curious.

He shook his head, his senses reaching out, probing their surroundings regardless of his thought process. No, he decided. The powerful Texcoco War Leader would not pay for this not only unruly, but also a damaged little thing. Not while having another, clearly better, son. They would have to dispose of the boy before sailing away, no matter how promising the wild cub was.

Or maybe not, he mused, hastening his step. With the useless manure-eater of his third associate gone, maybe they might have enough space in the boat to take the little beast along. So much presence of mind, so much courage, so much negative energy, and in such a young thing could be of use, come to think of it. The boy could not be tamed, but he could be taught to channel his anger in useful ways, turning into a priceless tool if used correctly.

CHAPTER 10

Tlalli took her eyes off the beautiful woman and watched the servants bringing in steaming plates, her stomach churning again. Since high noon and the tamales that the kind Warlord's wife made her eat while coming back from the ceremony, she had touched no food, busy fuming in her room, pacing it from wall to wall, furious.

He had been so unjust, so unfair in not letting her even try to explain. He had never dismissed her this way before, never snapped at her, never threatened, but now he did all of it, letting her know that the love was the thing of the past. One silly slip and she was dismissed like his other women, sentenced to an empty life of no importance and no thrill.

The tears that flowed while back in the privacy of her quarters shamed her, made her despise herself. No better than the rest of his women, really.

She had bitten her lips into a bleeding mess, until the new pain pushed the deeper one away. No, she would not have any of it. If he didn't want her anymore, she would go away, never to return. She could take care of herself, the way she had done back in Azcapotzalco. And she would do much better now, having more wisdom and more skills. She could do many things, working for her living the way the commoner women did. She had never been the noble lady he was trying to turn her into, anyway.

With this resolution, the tears stopped completely, and she took care of her appearance, while thinking about her plans. To leave now or to wait for them to return to Tenochtitlan?

She shrugged. She had formed no attachment to the island-city, so Texcoco might be as good a place to go away as any. He would find it difficult to track her here. More so than in Tenochtitlan, should he bother to look for her at all.

The thought of him worried, maybe even sad, made her feel better. He would be sorry in the long run, missing her even, maybe, when not working day and night as he always did.

So, washed and dressed in new garb, careful to tuck a favorite necklace into her bag, a sheet of clean paper and a small stash of charcoal, along with another change of clothes and a pair of additional sandals, she had waited for the slaves to clear the outer rooms, then sneaked away, rushing down the corridors, unwilling to be detected. He had told her that she was not allowed to leave her rooms, but he evidently didn't bother to put a guard to make sure his orders were obeyed. He truly didn't care!

At the spacious courtyard she slowed her step, unwilling to be stopped or asked for her purpose with so many people walking around, warriors of a higher rank in their designated cloaks and the high-soled shoes, nobles clad in embroidered cotton, sparkling jewelry, pretty women aplenty, their clothes brilliant waves of colors, with slaves of all sorts rushing about, ready to serve.

Carefully, she went on. Just to reach the gardens and the gates of the outer wall. Then she would be gone forever, never to see any of them again. Well, not him, for sure. If she stayed in this *altepetl*, she would see its nobility from time to time, but not that of Tenochtitlan.

Her stomach twisted. He would be gone tomorrow, for many summers to come, too busy to pay a visit to his Acolhua allies and friends. She pressed her lips tight, then went on, determined. Maybe he would be sorry to find her gone. Maybe he'd even send his warriors to look her up.

Deep in thought, she didn't notice the Acolhua Emperor until she almost bumped into him as he stood there, listening to a strikingly beautiful women, surrounded by a few of his nobles, some warriors, some scribes, many of them watching his company with as much curiosity as they watched the mighty ruler himself.

Fascinated as well, Tlalli slowed her step, peering at the impressive pair, safe in doing so, just a part of the admiring crowd. Not that the Acolhua Emperor would have recognized her had she stood there alone, waving her hands and shouting her greetings. She had met him only once, in the Azcapotzalco Palace, on the day the magnificent Tepanec capital had fallen. He had been there with his friends, as tired and spent as they were, but unlike Tlacaelel and the Acolhua Warlord, he was half asleep, never noticing her there serving their food. But Tlacaelel noticed. Oh, she remembered his curious gaze resting on her, encouraging even back then, when she thought him to be nothing but a cruel conqueror.

Biting her lower lip, she pushed the memories away, putting her attention back on the newly anointed Acolhua ruler. Broader, more imposing than she remembered, the man stood there proudly, radiating authority, a wide turquoise decoration piercing his eagle-like nose, adding to the prominence of his features, the royal diadem encircling his head, making him look imposingly tall. An emperor for sure!

The woman was talking rapidly, in a breathless rush, her face an exquisite mask of polished gold, but a perturbed mask, not a calm one. Suddenly, Tlalli wished she could hear their words. It was about the magical sword, she realized, having forgotten all about this affair while brooding over his unfairness. She pushed her way closer.

The emperor shook his head, stopping the woman's current of words with a light wave of his hand. His face hardened, and not hearing them yet, Tlalli knew he was refusing the woman, and in a most decisive manner at that.

The nobles around her watched covertly too, she had noticed, and they seemed to hold their breath, trying to overhear.

"You must hear me out, Coyotl!" the woman was saying angrily, less beautiful with her lips pressing into a thin line, her voice strong enough to be heard even at such distance. "You cannot dismiss me as an unimportant petitioner."

The emperor answered her quietly, his face cold, but his hand reaching out, touching the woman's arm in what looked like a reassuring manner. As he turned to go, Tlalli held her breath.

"Go home, Iztac," he was saying, still patting the woman's

arm, which she made no effort to take away. "Your husband needs you now. Not as an adviser but as a woman. After I deal with this crisis, come back to the palace and advise me on the matters I will ask your opinion on. But for now, be a good wife and go home."

"You haven't listened to a word of what I said, Coyotl, have you?" The woman followed, oblivious of everything. "You are dismissing me as a man dismisses an insignificant woman!" Her eyes were very black, blazing with anger.

The closed-up face of the newly appointed ruler did not change its expression. "I heard you, sister," he said quietly. "I listened to every word you uttered. Having always been respectful of your opinions, I will never dismiss what you say lightly." His eyes narrowed, turning colder. "Yet, it is neither the time nor the place to argue about the matters of the state. You should not forget your place, sister."

The woman drew a sharp breath, but her voice dropped, and her next words did not reach either Tlalli's or the surrounding noble's ears. She could feel the curiosity around her welling, turning tangible, filling the air.

"She will make him listen," whispered a man beside her, addressing someone above her head.

The other man shrugged. He was tall, very richly dressed, with his jewelry sparkling, hurting the eye in the rays of the afternoon sun.

"The emperor's sister has much influence," insisted the first man. "And this time she has more than her mere words to use. The emperor will listen."

"I'll offer on the altar of mighty Tlaloc for that to happen." The richly dressed man exhaled loudly. "The traitorous Mexica will not enjoy Texcoco friendship for much longer."

"Will the Chief Warlord cooperate now?" asked another man, his tones hushed. "He has to, doesn't he?"

The gaze the richly dressed man gave the speaker made Tlalli shudder as well, so angry, even threatening it was. The other man quailed.

"The emperor's sister is speaking her mind, that is all," said the first man, trying to calm the spirits. "Nothing out of the ordinary. With the despicable theft of our War Leader's most revered weapon, she is allowed to share her concerns. And so are we."

"Later, later," muttered the tall man, refusing to calm. "If we are not invited to share the emperor's evening meal, meet me beside the temple, behind the colorful wall. Both of you."

The royal pair was drawing off, the emperor's hand again patting his sister's shoulder, as though urging her to leave, but in a polite, well-meaning manner. The woman, Tlalli noticed, made tremendous efforts to keep the anger off her face, but it was still there, manifested in the creases lining the wide forehead, in the tightly pressed lips, in the darkness of the troubled eyes. It was not purely the fury, realized Tlalli. The woman was genuinely troubled, but then, why shouldn't she be?

She thought about the other wife of the Warlord, so worried and desperate, even if still kind and pleasant, trying to run her household and her children as though nothing happened, grieving over the murdered maid. Did Mixtli receive her chocolate drink after all?

The thought of the talkative girl made her smile. The cute little thing hadn't wanted to let Tlalli go, not until the promise to come back soon was made. So maybe she should pay this household another visit, to see if they had found out something new in the meanwhile. This whole *altepetl* seemed to be concerned with the sword's disappearance, from the emperor to his influential sister, to his nobles and guests, Tlacaelel included; they all were anxious to know what would happen now. Why? How was a sword, even a magical one, important enough to influence this people's alliances and wars?

The talk of the nobles around her indicated that it had to do with the policies concerning Tenochtitlan, and indeed, Tlacaelel seemed to be greatly concerned, wishing to know everything she had heard or seen, putting the troubles she caused aside for the sake of this problem.

Her previous anger cooling rapidly, she thought about it now, watching the emperor's back disappearing up the path leading back toward the Palace, surrounded by many subjects now, his sister nowhere to be seen. Maybe Tlacaelel wasn't as unfair, as indifferent as she assumed him to be. Maybe he was just concerned with the problem the disappearance of the sword might create between the Mexica and the Acolhua capitals. And if so, he might welcome the recollection of the conversation she just overheard.

She hesitated, frowning. It was such a small piece of information that he probably had known already. He was too busy for that, and she was not allowed to go out, or to speak to him without permission.

The anger rose, then subdued again. She was already out, breaking his dictate. Therefore, there was no reason not to do something useful, like visiting Mixtli and her nice mother again and maybe finding something of interest to tell him afterward. Maybe he would understand and forgive her later on, when she came back with more news.

However, what she did not count on was that the other wife, the emperor's powerful sister, would be there too. Obviously riding a litter, the highborn lady reached her home long before Tlalli, who had taken her time strolling around the afternoon city, enjoying the long, unhurried walk, reaching the Warlord's house when the dusk was already nearing.

And not that the woman was rude or impolite. She had actually smiled and greeted their guest nicely, when introduced by the Mistress of the House. But she was troubled, preoccupied, probably still seething over her interview with the emperor, which precluded any light conversation or questions Tlalli was actually glad to avoid. She wanted to spend her time with the other woman, anyway. But the Mistress of the House was also busy, supervising the preparations of the evening meal, occupied with the quarreling children, so Tlalli found herself ensconced in the inner rooms again, with Mixtli for company.

Not the worst of feats. The girl was very excited, chattering with no pause for breath, retelling the happenings of the morning and the afternoon again, talking rapidly, her eyes shining.

Father was very angry, the girl had said, hopping all over the place, dragging her toy-canoe, a wonderfully carved likeness of the long war boat, upon the floor tiles. He needed to find his sword, and fast. No one was allowed to touch it, ever! But some bad people did, taking the magical weapon with them.

"Oh, Father will punish them so hard when he finds them!" The girl's eyes glittered excitedly, like a pair of round coals. "He will teach them that no one touches his sword."

"What will he do to them?" asked Tlalli, amused. The child provided the kind of company she needed the most for now, the comfort of a warm, unconcerned human being, with no complications and no necessity to keep her guard up. She needed time to think.

"He will kill them," declared Mixtli, holding her head proudly. "He can do it. He is the greatest warrior in Texcoco! Don't think he will not find them. He will, he will!"

"I don't doubt that." Hard put not to laugh, Tlalli made sure her expression was suitably grave. "I'm sure he will find his sword. Do you think he knows who took it?"

The girl nodded, bursting with importance, her toy boat forgotten. "He was so very angry today."

"Yes, but what did he say? Who took his sword?"

"Oh. . ." The round face twisted, frowning in the funniest of manners. "He said...he said it was a serpent that took it. Yes, a serpent." A victorious spark. "I remember it now! A serpent."

A serpent?

"It must have sneaked into the house in the middle of the night." Suddenly, the girl shivered, her excitement dying away, replaced by quivering lips. "What if it comes back? I don't want to go to sleep tonight."

Tlalli fought the urge to press the sweet little thing to her chest, knowing that the child's mother may not like strangers hugging her treasure.

"I don't think a serpent took it," she said instead, smiling as reassuringly as she could. "It doesn't sound possible. And anyway, your father will find it and kill it, you said it yourself."

"Yes, but what if it comes back before he finds it?" The tearful eyes clung to her, afraid and expectant at the same time. "He said it was obsidian serpent, so it's hard and sharp. What if Father can't kill it?"

An obsidian serpent! Itzcoatl, the Mexica Emperor, whose name meant just that— Obsidian Serpent. It dawned on her all at once, and she held her breath, remembering the nobles of the Texcoco Palace whispering about the end of the Acolhua cooperation with the Mexicas.

So that was that! The Warlord, and apparently other influential Acolhua, believed it was Itzcoatl, the Aztec Emperor, Tlacaelel's sovereign, who was responsible for the thieves, the dark shadows wearing all black, stealing the important relic. Was that what the Warlord's other wife was telling the Emperor?

"Do you think it will come back?" The girl stood before her, her eyes almost round, glittering with tears.

"No, it won't. It's not that kind of a serpent."

"What kind is it?" The ready-to-flee pose did not relax.

"Not a real one." She took the plump little palm in her hand, pressing it lightly, trying to reassure. "He is called that, but he is not really a serpent, you see. It's a man, and your father will be able to take care of that, because his friend will help him."

The thought of Tlacaelel made her stomach flutter. He wouldn't let her leave him, and he wouldn't behave unreasonably anymore. He was just concerned with the possible trouble between the two great *altepetls*, anxious to prevent the war between the allies. It was more important than the grief she might have caused him by going out all by herself. He would not stop loving her because of that.

"When?" Mixtli was peering at her, calmer now but very expectant, her hand comfortable in Tlalli's grip.

"Soon. Very soon. What else did your father say?"

"Oh, he was yelling a lot, but Mother told him not to. He said the Serpent will wish he had never been born. He said it was a despicable traitor and a real snake."

Oh, gods! Was the war between the Acolhua and the Mexica people about to break?

"And then he ran out to look for his sword." Full of her former self-importance again, Mixtli frowned, looking funny, a small version of a grownup woman. "And now Mother is worried. And

Citlalli's mother is worried, too. And Citlalli was yelling at Coatl like she never did before, and he told her to shut up. They had such a fight just before you came."

"What about?" asked Tlalli absently, aware that something was strange in this story, something was missing. Something to do with the noblemen's talk back in the Palace. She should have been more enterprising, should have tried to overhear what the Emperor and his sister were talking about.

"Citlalli said that Coatl should have hit someone when they went to look for Ocelotl. She said Ocelotl would have done that; he would beat someone and get all the answers. That's what she said."

"Oh."

She tried to listen to the voices outside, both wives of the Warlord talking somewhere in the kitchen areas, arguing. About the evening meal or about more important matters?

"And when Coatl told her to shut up and mind her own business, she started to yell at him. She tried to hit him too, but Coatl is so much stronger. He is the best boy ever, the funniest and the strongest."

With an effort, Tlalli made her thoughts focus, concentrating on her animated company. "Citlalli yelled at your brother?"

"Yes, oh, yes! She was so angry with him."

"Why?"

"Because they went looking for Ocelotl, and they didn't find him."

She tried to make sense of this flood of information. "Who is Ocelotl?"

"My brother." The girl's brow was furrowed with creases again. "Coatl and Ocelotl are my brothers."

"Oh, the twins!"

"Yes, they were born together, and they look the same, but I can always tell them apart. Always!" A victorious spark made Mixtli look like a mighty conqueror, clutching her toy canoe above her head, as though it were a powerful weapon. "Even when they were small and liked to fool people with their looks." A frown was back. "I like Coatl better. Ocelotl used to be funny, but he never plays with me anymore. But I want him to come home, anyway. Citlalli and Coatl think something happened to him."

She remembered the boy from the marketplace, leading a bunch of other rascals, self-assured and determined, running badly but scaling the wall like a real ocelot would.

"He usually comes home?"

"No, of course not!" Mixtli's eyebrows created a solid line above her puzzled eyes. "He is in *calmecac*, with Coatl."

"Then maybe he is there now."

"No, he is not. There is no school for the days of the ceremony."

Tlalli wanted to laugh. "How do you know all that?"

The round face turned ridiculously smug. "I know everything."

"Oh, good for you." She thought about the yellow-eyed girl. "So Citlalli and your favorite brother went out to look for him?"

"Yes, they did. Right after Father left. Citlalli found a magical knife under our wall, and she was angry with Coatl for taking it and showing it to Father." The girl giggled. "She wanted to keep it to herself."

"Citlalli is your half-sister, isn't she?"

The girl looked puzzled again. "Citlalli is good. She plays with me sometimes. And when Mother will allow, she promised to take me to the marketplace." The smile that stretched the small lips was full of mischief. "She doesn't listen to her mother, and to Father himself, even. She says he is not her father, so he should not tell her what to do. She says he is not noble enough to order her about, but she doesn't dare to tell him that in his face." The girl giggled again. "Citlalli is not afraid of anyone, and she likes to make trouble. But my mother knows how to make her listen and behave." Another giggle. "She and Ocelotl are fighting all the time, but they are best friends, always together, making trouble."

"Oh."

Tlalli let her thoughts drift, as the girl chattered on, hopping excitedly, relaying family gossip. Nothing out of the ordinary, as the noblemen's families were always complicated, having two, or often three wives, with a mixed issue to raise. The Warlord might have had more children, or maybe more wives. What he had was not that impressive. Tlacaelel had more wives, more children, more concubines. And they did get along somehow, mainly by avoiding each other. He had a Chief Wife, of course, the most noble of them all, and the most mean, as the gossip had it. Tlalli had never met her, which was a relief, for the concubines, even the favorite ones, did not mix in the noble circles, unless of minor nobility themselves.

Tlacaelel. Her stomach shrank once again. Was she still his favorite woman? What did he think when he found her gone? Was he angry or maybe sad, just a little? Was it a good decision to go out without permission again?

No, she thought, pushing the troublesome thoughts away. He was too busy with the magical sword, and maybe the tottering alliance of his own and the Acolhua people to notice her absence. He must have known by now that Itzcoatl was blamed for that theft. His emperor, his sovereign. But why would Itzcoatl do something as scandalous, as sensational, as shameful? And why behind *cihuacoatl*, his most trusted adviser's, back?

A question that sounded aloud the moment the evening meal was finally served.

"Why would the Mexica Emperor do that?" asked the Mistress of the House, squatting gracefully on one of the mats, after making sure all was in order, with the children being fed and sent away, and the three of them ensconced in the cozy privacy of a spacious alcove with plenty of mats and two low tables, served a rich variety of foods, their every need taken care of. Still, it was not a merry meal. Both hostesses seemed to be troubled too deeply to fake a genuine interest in polite conversation with their uninvited guest. Not that Tlalli minded any of that. She wanted to listen rather than to be heard.

"Oh, please, Dehe," exclaimed the Emperor's sister, a plate in her lap lying lifelessly, its contents untouched. "You don't know that ruler the way I do. He is capable of worse deeds, believe me on that."

Dehe's pleasant face clouded, turned unpleasantly stubborn. "I know that he is capable of many things. I had my dealings with him too, just to let you know. A very long time ago." She pushed her plate away, as though irritated with it sitting in front of her, reminding her of yet another obligation to perform. "But what I'm saying is that this particular deed doesn't make any sense. He is capable of worse, of course he is. But why would he do that? Why antagonize the Acolhua, eh?"

The Emperor's sister waved her hands in desperation. "Maybe he doesn't want to cooperate with the Acolhua anymore. Maybe he wants war. Maybe he thinks he can conquer our *altepetl*, or at least try to do that. This man can't be trusted. I keep saying it, but no one listens."

"It's not true, Iztac-Ayotl. They are listening to you. From our husband to your brother to many of his nobles and advisers, they are all listening." The fragile shoulders lifted in a shrug. "I listen to you too, if you value any of that. But your brother cannot let you rule in his stead. He is a very wise man. His subjects, nobles or commoners, trust him. Our husband trusts him. The whole of Texcoco trusts his judgment. And so should you."

The royal woman stared at her plate, her long manicured fingers playing with a small tomato, rolling it around the edges of the painted pottery.

"Don't be naive, Dehe. My brother is loved and trusted, but not by everyone. Some people are not happy with his continued cooperation with the traitorous Mexica. Many are disappointed, dissatisfied, disillusioned." She frowned, then pushed her plate away. "His reign is not very well-established, not yet. He cannot rule as though no one else's opinions matter."

But now it was the turn of the Mistress of the House to wave her hands in the air. "That is not true. Ask our husband! The people you refer to are a small group who cannot see beyond the immediate. They are sounding their opinions loudly, but they are nothing but a few discontents and some misguided nobles with personal motives." Suddenly, she reached out, touching the other woman's palm, pressing it warmly. "You have your private reasons for hating Itzcoatl, sister, and I respect that. For myself, I am with you on that. I will never forget what both of us went through back in Tenochtitlan. But your brother and our husband are right. Our *altepetls*' further cooperation is essential. It's for our mutual good, theirs and ours. We cannot tear those bonds, not now. It would be disastrous if we tried. The past is in the past. You should not let your hatred rule your mind."

"I do not let my hatred for the despicable Aztec Emperor rule my mind," exclaimed the royal woman hotly. "I know a thing or two about running an *altepetl*. I did this for some summers, as you may recall." She took a deep breath, as her face closed all of a sudden, turned wary, lost some of its passionate vitality. "Yet, now Itzcoatl has done the unspeakable. He has stolen the most precious possession our *altepetl* has. He has stolen our husband's sword, Dehe! So when his Chief Warlord, his closest friend and most loyal supporter, comes to my brother, demanding justice, he will have no choice but to listen and help."

"Help to do what?"

"Help to do anything he demands!"

Now both women's eyes were locked, flickering darkly, a pair of sharp, polished obsidian as opposed to the brighter hue of a firm stone. "Like what?"

"Do I have to tell you to what lengths he will go to get his sword back?" There was a trace of superiority in the beautiful woman's tone now, a smug, unbearable arrogance that made Tlalli angry, wishing to contribute to the argument.

"I know him as well as you do." The Mistress of the House's voice had a cutting edge to it, which pleased Tlalli immensely. "And I'm telling you, you don't do him justice now. He is not the simple warrior he pretends to be from time to time. If he fooled you with this aspect of his appearances, then you do not know him at all. He will go to great lengths, yes, but he will not harm the policies of your brother."

More of the thundering silence, then the Mistress of the House remembered her guest, turning to Tlalli, striving to appear calm.

"I'm sorry. We've been so impolite." She smiled, but it was a forced smile, and the shadows in her eyes were deep, full of misery. "Please, have more food. Xochitl," she called, looking at the doorway, "bring us another plate of tamales and vegetables. And a chocolate drink."

"Yes, I can do with a cup of chocolate," agreed the Emperor's sister, reclining more comfortably, her smile dawning. "So how do you like Texcoco?" she asked, turning to Tlalli. "Have you been taken around? I hope they provided good guides for you."

Tlalli suppressed her laughter. "Well, yes, I've toured the city, with guides and without them." A conspiratorial glance toward the Mistress of the House produced a hint of a smile in the worried eyes, and it pleased her. The poor woman was worried so, and now she realized why. The other twin must have been still missing. "Texcoco is beautiful," she went on, smiling at the Emperor's sister politely, liking her too, almost against her will. With the anxiousness and the arrogance gone, this one was too pleasant a sight to look at. Such a beauty!

"Oh, Texcoco is nothing compared to what it used to be," exclaimed the royal woman, turning animated, some color creeping back into the chiseled cheeks, her eyes sparkling. "It was the most magnificent *altepetl* around the shores of our Great Lake, before Tezozomoc ruined it. It was so elegant, so refined, so rich in beauty and brilliance. You are too young to know that, of course," she added with a charming smile. "How old are you?"

"I've seen close to twenty summers," said Tlalli, adding to her age. They had no way to prove otherwise, and she didn't want to be treated like an insignificant girl. It was enough that Tlacaelel had ordered her to her rooms as though she were a disobedient child. "But I lived in Azcapotzalco for some summers. Now that was a magnificent *altepetl*."

The woman's gaze lost some of its friendliness. "Azcapotzalco was a very large city, yes. I visited this *altepetl* once, attending Tezozomoc's funeral." A shadow crossed the beautiful face. "This city was impressive, there is no argument about that. Yet, it lacked the refinement, the elegance of the old Texcoco." She shrugged. "My brother will return this capital to its previous glory."

"Yes," agreed the Mistress of the House. "If anyone can do it, Nezahualcoyotl is the man." She cast a meaningful glance at her fellow wife. "But to do that, he needs a few summers of peace at his disposal. Warring on his allies will keep him busy elsewhere, with his funds diminishing, not spent on refining or rebuilding."

"Oh, please!" The Emperor's sister waved her arms in the air.

"You asked me to leave the politics for our men to solve, but you keep bringing it up, Dehe. Don't try to convince me you won't be talking to our husband about any of it."

"He will ask for neither mine nor your opinion on that matter," said Dehe calmly, but her eyes narrowed, as her attention was caught by the raising voices of the arguing children, coming for the depths of the house. Her shoulders sagged. "I need his help on a different matter," she muttered, the shadows returning to her eyes.

"Oh, Ocelotl!" exclaimed the Emperor's sister instantly, her gaze softening. "I'll send another group of slaves to search the marketplace and the surroundings of his *calmecac*."

"It's of no use. I sent a party of servants already. They came back not long ago." The dark eyes looked up, full of misery. "We need to inform our husband. He will know what to do."

"He must be in the Palace now." The royal woman sprang to her feet, smoothing her skirts with a brisk efficiency. "I will take my litter and go there now. If he is not there, I'll talk to Coyotl. He'll help us find the boy. There is no need to worry."

"If he was all right he would have come home by now," muttered Dehe, but her eyes lit, clinging to the other woman's face, filling with hope.

"If he is not, then there is more urgency to get my brother involved," said the Emperor's sister briskly, offering one elegant foot to a servant armed with a pair of richly embroidered sandals.

The troubled eyes of her hostess brushed past Tlalli. "Would you like to ride along with Iztac-Ayotl?"

The question hung in the air.

"Where to?" asked the Emperor's sister, puzzled.

"Back to the Palace," mumbled Tlalli, unsettled. What was the better way to return?

The arched eyebrows climbed up in a silent question. "Why?"

"She resides in the Palace, in the guest quarters of the Mexica visitors."

The pair of obsidian eyes narrowed, turning to Tlalli. "Whose woman are you?"

"Tlacaelel's." It came out weakly. She cleared her throat,

enraged with herself. "I belong to the Mexica Head Adviser."

"And now you decide to let me know?" The accusation was shot in the direction of their hostess, ringing loudly.

"There was no time for a proper introduction," said Dehe, unperturbed, getting to her feet too, clearly about to go to the arguing children, as the shouting voices were now joined by Mixtli's loud howling.

"But there was time to let me run away with my tongue, wasn't there?" The Emperor's sister shook her head, her elaborately braided hair jumping. "Well, Tlacaelel's woman, come along. And I will appreciate if you don't run to him right away, telling him everything I said. He knows my views, no one better, but I would still appreciate a measure of discretion on your part."

"Yes, of course, Noble Lady," muttered Tlalli, greatly perturbed, suddenly sure that she didn't want to share a litter with this woman. She saw the questioning gaze of her hostess, poised on one foot, ready to go. "May I stay for a little while? I'll return to the Palace later, by other means."

There was no hesitation on the woman's part. "Yes, of course. We are honored to have you here." A small smile flashed, reserved but still somehow warm, inviting. "Would you like to come along? Mixtli will calm sooner with you around."

The Emperor's sister shook her head. "I will never understand you, Dehe," she said, with a light amusement and not a hint of animosity. "But what is new about that?"

A soft rustling of the embroidered skirt and she was gone, the beautiful goddess, full of power and purpose.

"Like I said earlier, she is a law unto herself," muttered Dehe, as good-natured as her fellow Chief Wife, turning around and inviting Tlalli to follow with a light nod of her head.

Two chief wives, thought Tlalli, amused in her turn. Fighting and getting along in the fashion she remembered herself and her brothers doing, with an equal measure of fierce rivalry and a mutual liking, if such a thing were possible between anyone but siblings. She shook her head. This household *was* strange.

CHAPTER 11

The darkness was still at its thickest, not much past midnight, as Mictia hastened his step, not worried. Reaching Coatlinchan so swiftly and without a hitch was a good sign, he decided, sliding along the narrow alleys, a black shadow again.

Coatlinchan was no Texcoco, although it seemed to be almost as large these days, bubbling with life, benefiting greatly from its elevated status in the decade of the Tepanec rule. Tezozomoc, the conqueror, while giving Texcoco to the Aztecs as a symbolic gift, had taken Coatlinchan and Huexotla, making them into the principal towns of his newly conquered Acolhua province, finding Coatlinchan's large portal facilities of a great use, and Huexotla's roads satisfactorily wide and well-maintained to boost the trading activities that he had been eager to pursue. It was a good base to mount the invasion to the Highlands too, but this one project never came to bear fruit, with the fierce Highlanders fortifying their mountain passes and the mighty Tepanec ruler getting old and not as forceful as of yore.

Well now, after the re-conquest, Coatlinchan remained an important town, sprawling far and wide, full of life and activity, but lacking the might and the majesty of the Acolhua Capital, especially now that the new emperor was busy uniting his former provinces under his undisputed leadership, sometimes too forcefully for the influential Coatlinchan citizens' taste. Not everyone of importance was happy about it. Some voiced their opinions loudly, regretting the loss of their previous independence. Nezahualcoyotl, legitimate heir and universally loved or not, was a relatively young man. He should be watching his step more carefully, should be listening to his advisers' opinions more often, was the local aristocracy's verdict.

So the troubles, if they arose, would occur here, in this businesslike Coatlinchan, speculated Mictia, indifferent to the politics but liking to know which way the winds were blowing. Nezahualcoyotl should handle the problem with his Warlord's magical sword carefully, by either going against his Mexica allies and with his own most discontented aristocracy, or by disciplining his subjects with the ruthlessness he was reported to be capable of. There was no midway through this.

Oh yes, even an extremely expensive killer-for-hire understood that, thought Mictia, amused, calculating his way toward the large two-story house not far away from the central plaza, in the best neighborhood once again. But was renowned Nezahualcoyotl capable of dealing with this internal crisis?

The outcome of the problem he was paid to cause might have been interesting to see, but first, he needed to deliver his cargo. So, pressing his bag tighter, he hastened his step, hurrying on, anxious to get rid of the dangerous spoil, glad that while having no majesty of the Capital, Coatlinchan presented none of its dangers either, with hardly a warrior outside and no night patrolling at all.

The cumbersome bag hindered his step, burning his skin with every brush. Oh, it would be wonderful to part his way with the gods-accursed thing, he thought, nearing his destination, studying the wall in the faint moonlight, pleased to be alone, safe in the surrounding darkness. It was easier to move this way, with no need to coordinate one's actions, not even with as good a subordinate as Nacatl, who had stayed behind to guard the boat; and the hostage. The boy could not be trusted to sound no alarm given half a chance, so Mictia had left them near the shore, with the strictest orders not to move anywhere for any reason; to wait even if it took him days to come back.

Scaling the outer wall was an easy feat, he had done it while still deep in thought, landing soundlessly, disturbing no leaf. A quick search for the opened shutters and he was inside, freezing for a few heartbeats, listening to the silence.

The master's sleeping quarters must have been on the same floor, he decided, sliding along the wall, his senses probing. Quick scanning of the smaller rooms showed a few slaves sprawling on the mats, deep in sleep.

He slipped on, careful to make no sound. Killing wandering servants was not a part of his plan. It was crucial to disturb nothing, to harm no one. He hadn't been paid yet. Scaring the people who owed him so many goods should help, while harming them would do the opposite. These were rich, influential people.

To his immense relief, the leading opposition of Coatlinchan slept alone, not sharing his cushioned mats with young beauties to ward off the chill of the night.

Mictia halted, studying the sprawling man in the scant moonlight. The fat, middle-aged body lay half hidden by the covers, one fleshy arm out, its palm well-groomed, shielding the wrinkled face, exposing the rolls of fat on its upper parts, leaving the plumpness of the neck temptingly open. It would be so easy to kill this man, waking no one, leaving no trace.

Shrugging, Mictia covered the rest of the distance, placing his dagger under the pudgy chin, squatting comfortably, his other hand ready to silence the scream that was sure to erupt.

It didn't happen. The man swallowed and didn't move, staring at the intruder wide-eyed, too terrified to scream.

"Don't move a muscle," whispered Mictia firmly, trying to sound reassuring. An impossible feat under the circumstances.

The man let out a held breath, but had enough presence of mind to keep still, his mouth beginning to twitch, sweat rolling down the fat cheeks.

"I'm not here to kill you. I want to talk." He peered at the man closely, gauging his reactions. "Tell me you understand. Say it quietly!"

The man tried to say something and failed, his lips quivering, limbs jerking, out of control.

"Just nod!" ordered Mictia, wondering if he had taken it too far.

However, having failed to appear at the agreed-upon meeting place on the previous day, he had no other option but to go straight to the source. No matter how careful these men were, contacting him through various intermediaries, he had made sure to find out who had paid for this mission before accepting, wasting no time on the irrelevant messengers.

The head twitched in what looked like a nod. He studied the gaping eyes, taking in a sudden blink, the resemblance of sanity flooding in, making the enlarged pupils return to their normal size. That should do, he decided.

"Now listen to me, and listen carefully." He shifted, but left the knife where it was, just in case. "I brought what you paid me to bring. The magical sword. It's here."

The man shivered, but his eyes turned more concentrated, filling with apprehension.

"Now that we've established where we both stand," went on Mictia, outwardly unperturbed, but inwardly pleased, knowing that he'd gotten the man's attention, "you will sit up and we will talk." He shrugged. "The possession of the stolen artifact puts us on the same footing, doesn't it?"

The man's eyes told him that he saw the implication of the position the presence of the sacred weapon that had just been stolen and was most assuredly already sought after, put him in. Oh yes, he understood it well.

Satisfied, Mictia moved a fraction, taking his knife away, but ready to use it should the need arise. In such circumstances, some men might succumb to panic, acting unreasonably against better judgment. Narrowing his eyes, he watched the man sitting up, still trembling, clutching onto his covers.

"Do you want to talk here?" It came out as no more than a whisper.

"Yes, this place is as good as any. Unless you have indiscreet slaves. Then you may be in trouble, as I won't be talking in riddles."

The man shot a quick glance at his surroundings, as though expecting to see a multitude of eavesdropping slaves advancing on them.

"I would prefer to talk elsewhere," he breathed.

"I see." Mictia nodded, hiding his grin. Of course he would.

"But I will say my piece, because when we meet tomorrow at noon, I will expect you to come in person and accompanied by no one, carrying nothing but the compensation I am about to receive."

"A compensation?" The man's frown was almost painful.

"Yes, a compensation," repeated Mictia patiently. "A payment. My payment. I received a part before I began, but it was only a small part." He shrugged. "What I have been promised was not nearly enough given the dangerous nature of the mission. To cover the risk and the casualties I suffered, I would have to receive more." He let his gaze harden, wishing to make himself absolutely clear. "I worked very hard, endangering my life, losing one of my associates, and I cannot stay in the area with the full knowledge of what happened. I will have to go away, taking your secret with me. It will be an expensive enterprise."

The man's eyes hardened, the terrified look fading a little, giving way to suspicion. "How much?"

"Ten full-length cotton cloaks, two bags of cocoa beans, about four hundred in amount, and a few bags of golden dust thrown in."

"It's too much!" breathed the man, aghast, forgetting his fear.

"Too much to ensure my eternal silence? I don't think so." He played with his knife, spinning it around his palm and between his fingers, letting it slide elegantly, showing his expertise. "I'm not a trader from your marketplace, and I'm not a politician with whom you can haggle. I don't have to deal with you. I can take the magical sword along and leave, finding another influential Acolhua ready to betray his lawful emperor. It won't be difficult to find here in Coatlinchan, will it?" He let his real grin show, a mirthless, dangerous twist of lips. "Quite a group of disaffected Acolhua have gathered here, eh? Plotting against the emperor, thinking they could do better than that remarkably able man."

The round face was losing its color so fast he began fearing the man would drop dead or faint on him, solving nothing. And yet it was a pleasant sight to see. They really thought him just a simple killer for a hire. Stupid nobles.

"I suggest you gather that payment quickly, before the sun has reached its zenith tomorrow. It would work better for you and your group, a wiser course of action. Send me away safely, well-satisfied, not interested in the affairs of this side of the Great Lake anymore, while keeping the sword and letting your ruler think that the Mexica Aztecs have stolen it, eh?"

A terrified gasp was his answer. He hid his grin. Those highborn and high-flying snakes thought themselves so very smart, expecting him to do the deed without figuring out the whole scheme, as though he were nothing but a simple thief? Haughty bastards.

"What do you say, Honorable Acomitzin? Will I meet you or your trusted servant in one of your warehouses, the one closest to the shores of the Great Lake, that place with a painted wall, when the sun reaches its highest?"

"I can't…can't promise," groaned the man. "I need time…time to gather all this together. So many cocoa beans! How can I obtain it in less than half a day?"

"Make an effort." Grinning, Mictia got to his feet, causing the man to back away in horror, his eyes again widening as though about to pop out of their orbits. "I will not wait. By midday, if the goods are not at the warehouse, ready and packed as I asked, I will be sailing back to Texcoco, without the sword to hinder my progress this time. The Warlord can come and fetch his most prized possession all by himself."

By the opened shutters, he turned around, casting a last glance at the curled-up man. "And don't try to do anything foolish. My spies are everywhere. Before you send one single summon to any of your minions, I will know all about it." A casual wave of his hand. "I'm not your lawful ruler. I'm much more dangerous than that, as my eyes and ears are everywhere. Just bring what you owe me, and I will not stand in your way." He pulled the shutters open, casting a last glance at the bag, now thrown carelessly upon the floor, discarded. "And careful with the sword. It has a spirit of its own, and its magic is powerful."

CHAPTER 12

"Take however many warriors you need, and go to Coatlinchan."

Nezahualcoyotl did not turn around, but kept peering out of the wide opening in the wall, studying the dark gardens as though fascinated with the scenery.

"Why Coatlinchan?" asked Tlacaelel, when the Highlander didn't bother to respond, deep in his gloomy thoughts.

The three of them were ensconced in the spacious room that somehow managed to look cozy despite it being crammed with chests of books, stacks of paper, and piles of boxes containing colors and other writing materials, with very little furniture or anything irrelevant like statues or plants. A working room, but not as austere as Tlacaelel's in Tenochtitlan. This one had a typical touch of the Acolhua elegance and taste.

"He knows why," said Nezahualcoyotl, turning abruptly and moving away from the window. "Don't you, Warlord?"

The Highlander stiffened. "Yes, I know, but I'm not as certain as you are."

"Don't tell me you believe it was Itzcoatl's doing?" The Acolhua Emperor's eyes narrowed, sparkling coldly, reminding Tlacaelel that with all his preference to solve the problems in a diplomatic way, with all his refinement, his literacy, his politeness and wit, Nezahualcoyotl was a dangerous man, a tough warrior and a shrewd ruler, with his private toll of bodies lining his way to the power as high as those of Itzcoatl, maybe. The half twenty of summers that marked this man's way back to the throne had not been an easy road.

The Highlander let out a held breath. "I know you both don't believe it. But for myself, I'm not convinced. All evidence points in that direction."

"Carefully planted evidence, I must say." It was high time he contributed to the conversation, decided Tlacaelel, turning to face his friend. "I know you know my reasoning, but I would love to hear Coyotl out."

The Acolhua Emperor shrugged. "Like you, I'm convinced that your emperor does nothing without a good reason and thorough preparation. I don't see why he would jeopardize our relationship, nor why it would be done in such a sloppy manner, leaving so much evidence a child could have found all of it and more."

The Highlander's jaw jutted. "There is not that much evidence, and it was not lying out there for everyone to see. The lost knife was sloppy, I admit that. But without another clue, a clue that Tlacaelel's favorite woman provided, we would not have arrived at our conclusion so easily. Whoever planned this could not have taken into account the strange woman's wish to explore the nighttime Texcoco. Just as they could not have known that, based on that particular knife and the killers' peculiar outfits, I would have no difficulty identifying these men. How many people know about my encounter with those killers some summers ago, at a place I should not have been present at all?" The man waved his hands in the air. "The people who know this part of my history I can count on the fingers of one hand, two of them are present in this room." A fleeting grin flashed, a mirthless affair that was still laced with a measure of mischief, so typical to this man. "Unless you, Tlacaelel, were the one to plan it in order to incriminate your emperor. Want the throne to become yours, eh?"

"If I had planned something like that, no one would be asking any questions," said Tlacaelel, grinning back. "You both are lucky to have me on your side."

"Or so you've kept telling us over the past half twenty summers." Nezahualcoyotl shook his head, his grin light, but his eyes full of shadows. "But you overlook one more aspect, Old Friend," he said, turning back to the Highlander, who seemed to lose his brief amusement again, refusing to be lifted out of his rage and despondency.

"What do I miss?"

"You miss the motive." The Acolhua man picked up a piece of paper, eyeing it absently, his eyes clouded, wandering unknown distances. "Itzcoatl has none. Think about the people who do."

"People who hate you."

"Yes, people who hate me. People who don't want to see me ruling Texcoco and its provinces. Those are no Mexica Aztecs, Old Friend. They are much closer. But luckily for us, they feel safe enough to voice their opinions loudly, to concentrate in one location."

"That bastard Acomitzin and his Coatlinchan's so-called town council!"

"Yes, although there are quite a few of them here, in Texcoco, sniffing around my capital and my palace, thinking themselves safe." There was a savage glint to the Acolhua Emperor's eyes now, his face anything but the pleasant mask it usually wore. "They think they can criticize me openly, fearing no reprisals. They think they can rule Texcoco better than I can, me, the First Son, the lawful heir!" A fierce grin stretched the thin lips. "They will regret this!"

"Filthy rats!" growled the Highlander, his fists clenched. "To try to get to you through me, using my sword, my family, to achieve their petty political goals."

"There is nothing personal in it, Old Friend," said Tlacaelel, pleased with the atmosphere of old comradeship despite the trouble. Like good old times. "They used you because you and your sword were there." He shrugged. "They thought it would be simple. Steal the sword, make the warlord and the emperor angry, drive the wedge between our *altepetls*, the two victors whose relationship is not yet very well-established, thus making life difficult for Coyotl. It would come to war, eventually, and while engaged in the long campaign he can't win, the opportunities to get rid of him would be endless."

The Highlander strolled toward the window in his turn, peering into the gardens, his broad shoulders so stiff they seemed to be made out of stone. "I'm trying to work out how such a devious plan was created. Those people cannot know some very private things about me."

Unless they are very close to you, living with you, having spent many summers as a part of your life this or that way, thought Tlacaelel, watching Nezahualcoyotl instead, wishing to catch a glimpse of this man's real thoughts. Would the highly perceptive Acolhua ruler see the obvious?

"There are ways to find out, to gather as much information as you need," said Coyotl, addressing his friend while answering Tlacaelel's unspoken question. "Your Tenochtitlan history can be easily flushed out. Yes, even your involvement in Chimalpopoca's death. People with enough patience, willingness, and resources can discover anything they want to know, even your childhood habits and deeds. Am I not right, Mexica leader?"

"Yes, you are." Tlacaelel sighed inwardly. No, the Emperor was not prepared to see the obvious, anymore than his Warlord was. And they would not be willing to listen to the accusation of the only possible culprit, no matter how well-based and logically presented. They were too closely involved, emotionally and otherwise.

"So you think it was taken to Coatlinchan," said the Highlander finally, turning back and crossing the room in his long, impatient stride.

"Yes, I think that." Putting the scroll back, Coyotl straightened his shoulders, his face unreadable.

"And while combing the filthy town, looking for my sword, I am to clean it of all sorts of unwanted elements, am I not?" The Highlander's face turned as impassive, a cold marble mask, a deadly one. "Openly or covertly?"

Curious, Tlacaelel held his breath. Had they forgotten that they were not alone now, these two old friends? To talk so openly was not wise, no matter how much unconventional history all three of them shared. They were the rulers of the new world now, and needed to behave as such.

Nezahualcoyotl's quick glance told Tlacaelel that the Acolhua ruler was thinking the same.

"Do as you see fit, Chief Warlord," he said mildly, eyes blank. "I trust your judgment. As always."

Sensing the currents, the Highlander's eyes narrowed, then lit with a brief yet familiar spark. "Of course, Revered Emperor," he said, his grin light. "I'm honored by your trust."

"Of course you are, my most obedient subject." It was Nezahualcoyotl's turn to stifle a smile. Then his face cleared of mirth. "What is your advice, Tlacaelel?"

"I see your course of action as a wise one." He let his gaze linger, holding the Acolhua man's eyes, letting him know that he knew and approved. "I plan to return to Tenochtitlan tomorrow, but if you need me, I will delay my departure."

"Thank you, Old Friend. I always cherished your advice." Coyotl picked a stick out of a pile of charcoal, studying it absently, his thoughts far away. "I may seek your advice before you go."

"Do so."

There was no familiar easiness, no delightful banter, no lightness around this room, when only the night before they all joked and laughed, throwing good-natured insults, enjoying the easy comradeship, familiar from their days in Tenochtitlan and Azcapotzalco.

He watched both his friends, now haggard and pale, closed up in their worries, their frowns deep, looking older than they were, no boyish lightness around either now, their despondency obvious, each over his own trouble, and together over the mutual one.

Would Nezahualcoyotl keep his throne? Suddenly, he was not so sure. His most loyal friend and supporter, an unstoppable force of nature, was now too busy with his troubles to think lucidly, to behave in a reasonable manner. Maybe he should have been sending another man to Coatlinchan? The Highlander would be there, looking for his sword and for the men who dared to steal his most prized of possessions. He would not be thinking as the leader and strategist, not this time.

"It looks as though you and some of your warriors will be flexing muscles before joining us in our southern campaign," he said lightly, on the spur-of-the-moment. "Maybe some of my men and I, myself, could use the exercise. Let me know if you would like me to detour by Coatlinchan on my way back."

"You are always welcome to join me!"

There was no mistake about the glint in the Highlander's eyes and the wariness of Coyotl's glance. Both reactions expected. The Warlord welcomed the company of the old comrade, Mexica or not, while the Acolhua Emperor wished no foreigners prying into his internal affairs.

"You are wonderfully generous, Old Friend," the Emperor said. "But there is no need to bore you or your men with such a mundane mission. There will not be enough warfare to provide exercise for even a small group of warriors. If the most prized possession belonging to my friend was not involved, I would not be thinking even of wasting my Chief Warlord's time in this way."

The Highlander raised his eyebrows but said nothing, staring ahead, back in his troubled thoughts.

"I'll be leaving with the first light," he said quietly, as though talking to himself.

"Come to see me before you sail." Coyotl narrowed his eyes. "Will you manage to organize it all in what remained of the night?"

The Highlander nodded, but his face closed as the lines of worry upon it deepened. "It'll be a busy night, yes."

And suddenly, the Acolhua Emperor's face softened, sparked with worry. "Your boy, did they find him yet?"

"No, not yet." The man's jaw tightened. "It's probably nothing. He must be up to his usual mischief. But his mother is worried sick. Between the sword's affair and those bastards breaking into my house, killing her favorite maid, I wish the young rascal chose another night to enjoy his wild escapades."

"What happened?" asked Tlacaelel, puzzled.

The Highlander shook his head, as though trying to clear it, his face straining to assume some of its former lightness, not making a great job out of it.

"Ocelotl, one of the twins, chose the worst night to go missing. He is not in *calmecac*—well, naturally, the school is closed for the celebrations—nor at home, and no one knows where he is. My bet he is somewhere in the dirtiest corner of the marketplace, enjoying himself, up to no good. But his timing is bad. He should have picked a different night." Another forced grin. "When he is back, I don't envy him. His mother will go hard on him."

"Ocelotl is the wild twin, isn't he? The one who is not doing well?"

The Highlander's eyes flashed. "He is doing well! He is smart and strong, and very, very fierce." A shrug. "He is doing well according to his view, and he will live up to all your standards and expectations, when he decides to do so. Not a heartbeat before. I know that type."

"Oh yes, you do," said Coyotl, his smile wide, reaching his eyes for the first time through the entire evening. "I daresay you know all about *that* type."

"And so do all of us." Getting to his feet, Tlacaelel grinned, glad to finish the gloomy meeting on a lighter note. "All those who came in contact with a certain wild thing who, once upon a time, came down his mountains, bent on changing our history."

"Oh, please!" The Highlander leaped to his feet without his usual forcefulness, the shadows not clearing from his face. "To see the real wilderness one needs to go no further than your devious Lowlanders' politics. To survive that takes skill." Brushing his palm against his face, he hesitated for a heartbeat, as though deliberating his next move. "I'll be off now. If I don't leave with the first light, I'll come to see you both. If not, have a safe journey, Mexica Head Adviser." A fleeting smile that did not reach the clouded eyes, and he was gone, disappearing into the semidarkness of the corridor, soundless as a forest beast.

"He is worried about the boy," said Tlacaelel, eyes on the doorway.

"Yes, he is." Coyotl was still toying with his charcoal stick, eyeing it thoughtfully, as though trying to devise the best way of using it. "The sword, and now the boy... It was not a good day for him. The day of my Great Ceremony..." Suddenly, the whole pile of writing material went flying, hurled to the floor, to roll over the cold stones, breaking into helpless little pieces. "The day I waited for, for so long! Fifteen summers, Tlacaelel! Fifteen summers of wandering and begging, living in shame, smarming to influential people, gathering allies, pleading alliances that were not of my choosing, me, the lawful heir to the Texcoco throne, swallowing my pride, doing everything that was necessary. And fighting, always fighting, and scheming, careful not to offend, doing things no future emperor should have been asked to do." Both fists clenched so tight their knuckles went white, the man peered at the pile of paper as though he had never seen it before. "And now that my day is here, that I'm finally the emperor, ruling Texcoco and most of its provinces, sitting on the throne that was always rightfully mine, now my great day is ruined, spoiled into insignificance, with my capital looking no better than any provincial town, my main province rebellious, my nobility daring to criticize me openly, presuming to tell me how to rule, and my best friend's possessions and family are not safe in my city any more than it was when he first came visiting it while still just a boy from the Highlands." The dark eyes came to life, flashing with fury, dangerously fierce. "Well, I won't have it! I'm the emperor now, and I will have my edicts obeyed, my policies implemented. No one will rule Texcoco in my stead, and no one will harm my most loyal friends and followers. Nor will they make me war on my allies. The despicable worms will rue the day they decided I'm not strong enough to stand up to that much-praised old Texcocan nobility. They will pay for it with their very lives, and no one will dare to voice a squeak of protest, or they will face my wrath. *I have had enough!*"

Eyes blazing, his hair no longer shaved in a warrior's fashion but combed backwards, to fit the emperor's diadem, he stood before Tlacaelel, impressively tall, his eyes glowing fiercely, radiating power only perceptive people, wise enough to pay close attention, could sense in this generally pleasant, easygoing man.

No longer a youth, and no longer a refugee, but a man of power, he reminded Tlacaelel of the day when Coyoacan fell, when this Acolhua, covered in sweat and blood, had grabbed the captured Maxtla, the last dirty Tepanec Emperor, by the hair, dragging him up the burning pyramid, determined to tear out the filthy heart of their most important captive with his own hands, with no ceremony and no customary procedures.

Backed by his fiercest follower and friend, as always, he had

had his way back then, with him, Tlacaelel, giving up on that argument, shrugging but glad to learn the real depth of his ally, the man he intended to keep as such, to conquer the Great Lake's surroundings and to rule them side by side for many summers to come. He had known it in those very moments, suspecting it all along, but getting his final confirmation only then, on the burning plaza of Coyoacan. The pleasant Acolhua was no man to take lightly. He had the ruthlessness, the brutality, the conviction. He was a born ruler, an ally to cultivate, a partner to use.

Holding the blazing gaze, he pressed his lips together, liking what he saw.

"I've known it all along, Nezahualcoyotl. Even back in Tenochtitlan, when we both were no more than hotheaded youths, I knew. You received what is rightfully yours, and you will overcome these difficulties as you did until now, with patience and cunning and ruthlessness when necessary." He allowed his own impartial grin to show. "You do the right thing, Acolhua Emperor. Strike the opposition down, and do it quickly and efficiently. You are the emperor; you owe no reasons, no explanations. Some of your subjects have behaved traitorously. That is enough to warrant their punishment. And thus, the others will see what I see, and they will heed the lesson."

Coyotl's face was smoothing, returning to its previous state slowly, hesitantly, as though ashamed of the outburst.

"Thank you, Old Friend," he said finally, his smile reserved, but his eyes friendly, gleaming with genuine warmth. "Your patience and your continuous support are greatly appreciated. You are an exceptional man. There could be no greater friend, nor fiercer enemy, than you."

"So what about his sword?" asked Tlacaelel, uncomfortable with too much frankness. It was safer to change the subject.

"We'll find it."

"And if not?" He raised his eyebrows, watching the man's reaction. "I mean, yes, I know what a relic this sword is, how highly it's praised, how cherished, how feared. But should it disappear for good, will it make a difference? Will it cause your warlord to leave the battlefield?"

The Acolhua man frowned, chewing his lower lip. "No, it will not. Nothing will stop this man from fighting. He is a born warrior, a born leader. He has been a full-fledged warrior since he was a mere youth, long before the customary age. But when was there anything ordinary about this man?" A warm grin dawned. "No, he will curse and rage, and he will do anything he can to find and get his sword back, but if it's gone, he'll get over it and find another weapon." The man leaned forward, dropping his voice. "I should not be telling you this, but you will find it out anyway, sooner or later. He has been using a different sword already, as his revered weapon is not strong enough anymore. He is hiding it, reluctant to let it be known, but after so many summers, the wood got cracked in too many places. He cannot trust it not to fall apart on him and in the worst possible moment, in the middle of this or that hand-to-hand. So he carries it along into battles, but more as a talisman these days, not as an actual weapon to use." Another know-it-all grin. "So yes, he'll get over this loss. Never fear. I won't lose my most trusted leader of the warriors, and you won't lose a valuable ally and a friend."

"Good." Turning to go, Tlacaelel frowned in his turn. "And yet, he is upset now, in no condition to make sound decisions." He glanced at Coyotl, his eyebrows arched. "In Coatlinchan, he will have to act wisely, with a measure of subtlety I would credit him with but for his current mood. The theft of the sword aside, if one of his boys is involved, hurt or possibly dead, he may not be able to summon enough detachment to act as your representative should, without letting his temper get the better of him."

Coyotl's nostrils widened as he drew a deep breath. "I cannot trust anyone else with this sort of mission." He stood there, an air of stubbornness surrounding him, eyes narrow, legs wide apart. "Also, I can't offend him by showing my doubts. He wants to go after his sword, while going after my enemies at the same time. To take it away from him would be a terrible offense."

"I did not suggest you should be giving this mission to anyone else. He is the perfect man for this and many other actions. And yes, he is your closest friend and you owe him much more than he owes you." Seeing the indignant glint, he rushed on, not willing to get into a side argument. "What I suggest is simpler, easier to implement. Just a backup plan, really." He raised his hand, preventing Coyotl's possible protests. "Now, I know you don't want outsiders prying into your Texcocan affairs. Yet, I got involved, because you two did not wait to talk in private, rushing to discuss your problems in front of me. So now I know more than I should. Therefore, I'm offering my help." He watched the narrowing eyes, pleased with how his words were received. "I don't mind detouring by Coatlinchan on my way back to Tenochtitlan. I'm not in a hurry, and my help can be significant, given the circumstances." He paused, letting his gaze harden. "You see, your Acolhua status as our friends and allies is important to me, to my policies, to my plans. Therefore, now I offer my help as Tlacaelel, a private person, an old friend of you two, not as the Mexica Head Adviser." The deepening gaze of the Acolhua man let him know that his message was received well. No indiscreet, maybe embarrassing, information from the Acolhua provinces would reach Itzcoatl, the Mexica Emperor, no friend or admirer of either of the two men. "Your Warlord would not mind me coming along. He would welcome my presence gladly, as a matter of fact. "

"I'm aware of that." Coyotl nodded, his face again a pleasant, yet unreadable mask. "He had invited you earlier, in this typical reckless fashion of his. I wish he were more refined, less straightforward. His behavior is not always fitting that of the Chief Warlord, the Emperor's closest adviser, the second most important man in Texcoco." His grin widened, along with Tlacaelel's. "But then, he would not be himself if he behaved with any decorum, any consideration to other people's idea of a proper behavior. I won't be the one trying to make an impeccable nobleman out of him, even if it were possible, which, of course, is not. So the things will go as they are, and our refined old aristocracy can frown all they like."

"And I bet they are frowning." Amused, Tlacaelel thought about how he would have handled this man if he were an emperor. In about the same fashion, he decided, but not as such a close friend. More like a person for special missions. Like those black-clothed killers, come to think of it, such an exclusive group.

"Well, you are very generous with your offer of help, Old Friend," Coyotl was saying, "and yes, I receive it with gratitude. I hope to repay it all when the time comes. Our *altepetl*s will remain friends and allies. We will see to that."

CHAPTER 13

Holding her breath, Tlalli froze, listening to the booming voices of the passing men. It was dark and windy in this part of the marketplace. Yet, shivering with cold, she welcomed the freshness of the breeze, preferring that to the stench of the other side of the colorful wall, in the revoltingly filthy alleys full of drunk men and scantily clad women, with the strong odor of *pulque* and spicy foods, and so much noise she wanted to cover her ears and flee. She had never been to such places, not even on Azcapotzalco marketplace through her worst days.

She pressed deeper into the shadows, waiting for a group of drunken men to pass, praying silently, asking Coatlicue, the Mother of the Gods, to conceal her presence well. She could feel the boy freezing too, holding his breath, invisible in the darkness. He had been the one to bring them here, following familiar paths, sure-footed, knowing exactly which alleys to turn down and into which corners to peek, an unfitting knowledge for a boy of his age and status.

"How do you know these alleys so well?" she had asked him earlier, relieved to get away from the boisterously loud gatherings with swaying men and toothily grinning women in loose gowns. They had sneaked past them, dangerously close, and her heart raced in alarm. What if any of those people saw them? After the night of Azcapotzalco's fall she knew what some men were capable of. Terrible things!

The boy shrugged, as uneasy as she was, peering into the darkness.

"Neither you nor your brother should be running around these places, you know that?"

He glanced at her fleetingly, his eyes large, flickering with defiance. "We are not running around these places," he said after a pause. "But my brother meets his friends here, sometimes, so I thought we should check it."

"Yes, of course. And that's why you know every alley as though it were the corridors of your father's great house."

The way she said that made the boy giggle, his features smoothing all of a sudden, turning irresistibly charming. The tough expression did not suit this young cub, she realized. No more than it suited his mother, whom he resembled greatly, having inherited her gentle features along with his father's impressive width and height.

Earlier this evening, after the meal was over and the aristocratic Warlord's wife departed for the Palace, Tlalli had watched the quarreling children and the way the twins' mother dealt with them, firmly and efficiently, even with the defiant Citlalli, the yellow-eyed girl who, according to Mixtli, was not even the Master of the House's daughter.

And if not his, whose daughter was she? wondered Tlalli, impressed with the way the slender woman made the girl listen, calm and polite but unwavering, not about to take a "no" for an answer. The yellow-eyed thing scowled and muttered angrily, but did as she was asked by retiring to her mother's suite of rooms, clearly respecting the Mistress of the House, shooting furious glances at the twin, who was not impressed in the least, answering with his own murderous glares.

But later, when the woman took Mixtli to her rooms and stayed there, comforting the little girl who was afraid to fall asleep, talking about the obsidian serpent again, the children spilled into the quietness of the patio, needing each other's company, quarreling or not.

The early night air was pleasant, the breeze bringing aroma of cooking food, unusual for this time of the day. Contemplating her next step—to return to the Palace or not?—Tlalli went out too, leaning against the doorway, listening to the children who were careful to argue in hushed tones, not wishing to attract attention.

They glanced at her with suspicion, but soon were back in the depths of their heated discussion.

"You can't go. Even Ocelotl wouldn't go there at night," hissed the girl, waving her hands in the air, agitated.

"He might be there now," maintained the boy stubbornly. "Or at least some of his friends. If I get one of them, I'll know where he is."

"Oh, yes, like you got anything out of that stupid coward earlier," she said, her scorn obvious. "He mewed and squealed, and you just let him go!"

"He didn't know where my brother is!" cried out the boy, his fists clenched. "There was no point in beating him up any further."

"Maybe he just didn't want to tell you, eh? He looked guilty. I saw it! He was afraid, all sweaty and shaking. He knew something, and you didn't squeeze it out of him. Ocelotl would have, you know? If you were missing, Ocelotl would have found you already."

"Oh, shut up, Citlalli! Just shut up!" The boy brought his trembling hands up, fists clenched, eyes blazing. "Leave me alone!"

But the girl just glared at her adversary, not afraid.

"I'll go with you," she said finally.

"No!" The twin let his breath out. "If your mother ever find out, she would lock you in forever, but not before she strangles me with her bare hands."

The girl stifled a giggle. "I would love to see that." Then she sobered. "You can't go there, either."

"Of course I can. I've been there twenty times and more."

"But not at night!"

"Who said?"

"I say." The girl tossed her head, triumphant. "Ocelotl sneaks from *calmecac* after darkness sometimes. No one else does that."

"I sneaked from *calmecac*, too!"

"But only once and not after darkness."

The twin scowled. "He is stupid. Stupid to do that and stupid to tell you about it."

"He tells me everything," said the girl smugly.

"That's what you think!"

But by that time, Tlalli had had enough. As another thundering pause ensued, she neared the fuming pair, her paces light, her hands on her hips.

"Where do you plan to go?" she asked firmly.

They looked at her, startled.

"Nowhere," said the girl readily, not deterred by the presence of a stranger, her chin up, the yellow gaze unwavering. She was not afraid of anyone. Mixtli was right about that.

"I want to help your family find your brother." Ignoring the silly girl, Tlalli concentrated on the twin, encouraged by his puzzled frown, liking him. "Where did you want to go looking for him?"

The boy hesitated. "On the marketplace," he said finally.

"At night?" She eyed the pleasantly round face, looking for signs of him being cagey.

"It's not even the middle of the night yet," he said, standing her gaze, still scowling. "Everyone is still out."

"Why do you think he would be on the marketplace?"

This time, the large eyes shifted, dropped, their innocence exaggerated. "I just think it's worth checking, all those places. Maybe he went to the marketplace for some reason."

"To steal things."

Amused, she watched both children gasping, backing away.

"He did not do that," called the yellow-eyed girl. "Whoever said that to you, lied."

Tlalli felt like laughing. "I saw him stealing arrowheads this morning. I saw it with my own eyes. He led a bunch of other rascals, and they almost got caught doing it." She narrowed her eyes. "I helped him get away, too. So he has a good cause to be grateful and so do both of you, if you care about him so much." Two pairs of widely opened eyes peered at her, taken aback. "So if I want to help you now, you better tell me what I want to know and keep your lies to yourself." Her piercing glare made the girl drop her gaze, at long last. She shifted her attention back to the twin. "He was not on the Plaza through the ceremony, was he?

Despite what you said to your mother."

The boy blinked, then shook his head.

"So I was the last person to see him," declared Tlalli, catching his gaze once again and holding it. "Now tell me why on the marketplace, and why now? I will go with you if I think I can trust you not to lie to me anymore."

He shifted his weight from one foot to another. "He goes there a lot. With his *telpochcalli* friends."

"To do what?"

"I don't know."

"Sure you don't." Stifling a chuckle, Tlalli decided not to push it any further. "So you plan to find some of his friends and make them tell you where he is."

He nodded, although she did not phrase it as a question.

"What if they won't?"

"Of course they'll tell him." Recovered from the former setback, Citlalli narrowed her eyes, looking fierce. "Coatl is stronger than any of them. He is the best student in *calmecac*. He is the best ball player, and he can do amazing things with his knife."

"So he'll beat the answers out of them." Not hiding her grin anymore, Tlalli nodded. "I see. Well, bring that knife. We'll take it along, just in case."

"I'm coming too." Citlalli's eyes were now mere slits in the gentle slenderness of her face, her legs planted onto the ground, wide apart, obviously set on fighting for her rights.

"No, you are not. You have more important things to do." Hurriedly, Tlalli raised her hand, preventing a flood of protests that seemed as though about to erupt. "Go and keep an eye on his mother. If she wakes up, keep her attention; make sure she doesn't look for Coatl. But if we are not back, say, after midnight, tell her everything. Can you do that?"

The girl's frown dissolved, her previous smugness returning. "Of course I can do that. You can take the whole night to return if you want to."

"What will you tell her if she asks?" asked the boy suspiciously, prepared to dive into a new quarrel, not trusting his stepsister, not even a little bit.

"It is none of your interest—" began the girl hotly, but Tlalli raised her hand, cutting off a new argument before it was born.

"Leave it to her and come. I want to be back before midnight. Market is not a place for any of us to spend the night."

And now, pressing against the cold stones of some filthy wall, she regretted her silly impulse to come in order to help. She was of no help, and the alleys they had passed so far were smelly, dirty, full of dangerous people, not a place to wander, neither for a respectable woman, the favorite concubine of the Mexica Head Adviser, nor for the underage son of the Texcoco Chief Warlord. They might be kidnapped, or worse, if detected, and she didn't trust the ten-summers-old *calmecac* pupil to protect her should they run into trouble. He might be tough enough to intimidate the little thugs his brother was mixing with, but he was no match for the hardy Texcocans, the frequenters of the nighttime marketplace, criminals most of them.

"Come," whispered the boy, pulling her into a narrow alley.

She followed hurriedly, concentrated on her step, unsettled by the thought that, like his ocelot-like brother, this twin could probably climb well, bolting for one of the stone walls if pursued, while she could do nothing of the sort.

"Ilhuitl does not live far away from the temple," her guide was muttering. "Maybe he knows."

"Who is Ilhuitl?" She didn't really care, but talking kept her attention off her fears.

"Ocelotl's friend. They wanted to throw him out of his local *telpochcalli*, so he had to behave well for some time."

A temple's wall towered ahead, unfriendly in the darkness, unlike the temples she had seen on the previous night, wandering pre-dawn Texcoco, excited and full of expectation. It seemed that a lifetime had passed between the previous night and this one.

"He has to be careful when he runs away from school, because his mother sells things in the food corner. She can see them if they are running around, or others could tell on them."

"So your brother sneaks out of school and comes here with them. Why?" She eyed the surrounding buildings, warehouses probably, wishing to be on their way back toward the more respectable neighborhoods.

In the darkness, she could sense the boy's shrug, could imagine his careful expression.

"I won't be telling on him. Or on you," she said absently, touching the temple's wall, wanting to feel the glyphs engraved upon its base. "I'll be leaving Texcoco tomorrow. Well, probably." Tlacaelel said they would be leaving for Tenochtitlan on the next day, but would he be taking her along? She suppressed a twinge of panic. Maybe he would let her explain this time.

"Where to?" asked the boy, curious.

"Tenochtitlan."

"Oh!" It came out as a gust of breath. She remembered the conversation at the evening meal.

"Have you been to Tenochtitlan?"

"Yes."

"When?"

But the small hand grabbed her arm, pressing it, signaling her to keep quiet. She froze. The wind howled loudly, trapped in the narrow passage, concealing the voices. Yet, they reached her ears nevertheless, muffled but clear.

"I say we wait. Do nothing. Let the things happen." The men were rounding the corner, coming out of the temple as it seemed, two dark silhouettes.

Rigid with fear, Tlalli pressed into a small alcove in the wall, wishing to squeeze herself between the cold stones, to disappear into the hard blocks behind her back as a ghost would.

"No. I do not agree with that." Another silhouette joined the pair, taller and broader than his peers. "Waiting would help no one but our precious ruler. He was always good at that. This is how he got his realm back. By waiting and by being patient." There was something familiar in the man's voice, in the way he spoke, drawing his words out longer than necessary. "He is doing it now, too. Playing the waiting game. A full partner of the Mexicas, but hardly fighting in their campaigns."

"The Mexicas are not at war with anyone now."

The men slowed their step, halting close enough to hear the rustling of their non-decrepit cloaks, their heads bent.

"Not now, but did he join them in Xochimilco? No. He found excuses, preferring to skulk around his former provinces, taking his time re-organizing Coatlinchan and Huexotla."

The small palm brushed against Tlalli's arm, signaling her. She felt the boy slipping into the darkness between the warehouses.

Holding her breath, she hesitated, then turned her attention back to the enraged nobleman, for now she knew where she had heard this sort of a speech. In the Palace, this afternoon, while watching the Emperor and his sister. The tall man was the one who had spoken agitatedly back then, expressing the hope that their ruler would listen to the pleas of the beautiful woman.

"I see your point, Honorable Brother," said the first man in hushed tones. "But the deed is done, and our emperor has no choice but to act now."

"To punish the Mexicas, yes," the third voice joined them, bursting with glee. "I heard the warlord was running all over the city, screaming murder."

"And so he should." The tall man's voice was dripping with satisfaction. "He would have sailed for Tenochtitlan this afternoon, but for the Mexica Head Adviser. The damn haughty frog-eater talked him out of it." Spitting, the man snorted with rage. "Too bad the rotten Mexica, that would-be-emperor, was here for the ceremony. It was a bad development. They should have timed the deed for a few days after that."

"If you were the one to plan it, it would have been done in a better way." The third man's voice had a growling tone to it. "I told you not to trust the woman. She may be determined and experienced, but she is still just a woman. Tenochtitlan's empress once upon a time she might have been, but she possesses none of the wisdom a nobleman has. We should not have let her do the planning."

"Well, it was her idea, wasn't it?" The second man shifted his weight from one foot to another. "It takes a female mind to come up with such a devious scheme."

"The idea was good. No one argues with that," said the tall man impatiently. "But the execution could have been done better. I'm not certain it will work. I have a feeling our young emperor is not convinced, even if his Chief Warlord is. And with the filthy Mexica Adviser whispering in his ear, he may not act the way we want him to act."

Tlalli felt her heart coming to a halt, freezing inside her chest.

"Then what should we do?" The other two men peered at their companion, unsettled. "What *can* be done?"

The silence prevailed.

"Maybe it's time to replace our ruler with a better-fitting one." This time, the voice of the tall man came as a whisper, a light breeze dissolving in the darkness.

They all froze, aghast.

"Don't stare at me like that," he said more loudly, obviously angry. "We talked about it before, didn't we? He is too young, too meek, too indebted to the Mexicas. He can't lead our people to true greatness. We need an older ruler, a stronger man."

"Like whom?" breathed someone.

"There are many able, greatly fitting persons among the old Acolhua nobility." The man shrugged. "More than ten summers of foreign domination changed our *altepetl* in too many ways. Maybe it's time we start a new dynasty of rulers."

"Oh!"

There was a meaning to the quiet exclamation, a meaning that even Tlalli understood. The tall man was considering himself a fit contester for the Acolhua throne, as good as any, Nezahualcoyotl's bloodline notwithstanding.

She felt the hair on her nape rising, the fear seeping through her limbs, making them tickle. Those men meant bad, violent things, things that did not bode well for the people she knew, from the Acolhua Emperor through his Warlord and his family, to even Tlacaelel himself. Was he safe in Texcoco? It didn't seem so now. He needed to leave this city and fast. There must be a way to let him know.

The men resumed their walk, almost brushing against Tlalli as they passed her niche.

"Let us meet in this temple again, tomorrow at dawn," the tall man was saying. "Invite those who were with us tonight, but not all of them. Only the most trusted, a handful. It won't be anything violent. I'd rather have it look like a natural thing."

"A poison?"

"We'll see."

It was a long time before she dared to breathe again, watching their backs being swallowed by the darkness. Her heart was pounding, making strange leaps inside her chest. These were the same men she had heard in the Palace, not happy about the Emperor back then either, but not plotting to kill him, not saying outright how the stolen sword of the Warlord was to fool the ruler into blaming his Mexica allies. Not to mention...

She brought her palm to her mouth, to suppress a desperate groan. The Emperor's sister, the Warlord's wife, the woman she had shared her evening meal with. How was it possible? No, no, it had to be a mistake.

"They are gone." The boy appeared next to her as silently as a ghost, making her heart leap.

"Yes, yes, they are." She tried to concentrate. What to do? She needed to get back to the Palace, and fast. She needed to let Tlacaelel know. "Do you know the shortest way to the Palace?"

His puzzled look was impossible to miss, even in the thickness of their dark corner. "Why?"

"I need you to take me there!"

"To the Palace?" He took a step back. "But we are looking for my brother!"

Oh, yes, the missing twin. She had forgotten all about it after hearing those men.

"Listen, we need help. We can't go on looking for your brother all by ourselves. We didn't find him so far, and we've been to all the places you wanted to see already."

"We didn't go to Ilhuitl's house yet." His eyebrows creating a solid line above his troubled eyes, the boy peered at her, lips pressed tight, set on argument.

"We can't go to some boy's house at night."

"Yes, we can. I know how to let him know so he will sneak out and meet us."

Oh, this one was as bad a rascal as his wild brother.

"There are more important things now." She leaned forward,

putting her arm on the thin shoulder, trying to reassure, to relay a calmness she didn't feel. Her heart raced as wildly as before, and the tickling in her feet just wouldn't go away. What if not only Nezahualcoyotl's but Tlacaelel's life was in danger? "You heard these men. They plan to do bad things, hurt your emperor. And maybe your father, too." Oh, that must get through to him, and it was a fair possibility, anyway. "I need to talk to them, to let them know."

He freed his shoulder in a sharp movement. "You promised to help find my brother. I'm not going anywhere else with you."

Oh, the stubborn little thing!

"Just show me the way back to the Palace. It can't be too far away!"

She grabbed his arm, this time forcefully, but the boy twisted like a snake, surprisingly strong and as slippery as a creature from the lake. Nimble and agile, he leapt backward, out of Tlalli's reach, glaring at her out of the glow the torches behind his back cast.

The torches! She caught her breath, seeing the men nearing, blocking their way of escape, dark, threatening shapes. *The plotting nobles came back to silence her!* She was sure she could see the tall figure of the worst schemer among them.

Her panic welled, snapping out of proportion. Casting a wild look around, she darted back toward the temple and its protective darkness, although this way she could be caught most easily in the open grounds behind the relatively low building. Just to get away from the narrow trap, from the murderous people bent on killing them all.

The air swished, bursting from her lungs as she ran, the blood thundering in her ears, the cries of the people behind giving her legs strength. Just to get away from them. She crossed the temple's plaza in one desperate effort, the light of torches still distant, but not going away, not disappearing. She could imagine their warmth burning her back.

"Here!"

The twin's slender form shot past her, diving into the darkness of a small passageway, invisible from the main road. Not hesitating, she leapt after him, squeezing between the cold stones, scratching her arms.

The darkness enveloped her, but she pressed on, sensing the boy's presence and the reassuring warmth of his body. He knew what he was doing, a little marketplace rat just like his wild brother. Both seemed to be natural survivors. His family's worry for the other twin seemed to be unwarranted, judging by this boy's behavior.

By the time they spilled out of their tunnel-like route of escape, the shadows of the torches danced far away, mere dots in the night. The boy pressed on, steering their way between the rough buildings that looked like warehouses, with the moonlight lighting their way now. *Where were they?*

Over her panic, Tlalli began to think again, the memory of the overheard conversation returning, along with the sense of helplessness, of nagging worry, the pressing necessity to do something.

"Where are we?" she whispered. "Coatl, wait!"

He didn't stop, didn't even slow his step.

"There is this place where Ocelotl hides their things," he muttered, as though talking to himself.

"What things?"

"All sorts of things. They were planning—" Suddenly, the boy fell silent, as though remembering his company. "Just things. Things they find sometimes."

"Things they steal." The little beast thought her to be completely stupid, didn't he?

The boy shrugged, then halted.

"Here, I think it's here." He fiddled with the screen that covered the entrance of a small, unimpressively rough wooden construction. "Yes, that's the warehouse." A nasty screech accompanied the investigator's attempts to deal with the obstacle. "He may be here."

The smell hit her nostrils the moment she neared, a strong rotten odor, familiar from her last days in Azcapotzalco and Coyoacan. She winced and her stomach heaved.

"Wait!"

But the boy needed no warning, frozen by the doorway beside her, afraid to breathe. She tried to curb her urge to run away, away from the stench of the rotten bodies, unmistakable now.

"What's in there?" The boy's voice shook badly, all traces of self-assurance in it gone.

"I don't know. I think…I think there might be bodies of people there. We better go away." She fought her fear, her nausea growing. "Come."

Once again, he freed his shoulder from her grip, and she could hear him swallowing loudly, desperately. "We have to…have…to see, see who it is. We need to know…"

Shuddering, she realized what he meant. Oh gods!

"We need to get a light, somehow." She looked around helplessly, thinking about the torches of the people they ran away from. They could have come in handy now. "Listen…"

But the boy was not beside her anymore, disappearing into the foul-smelling darkness, a desolate shadow. Holding her breath, she followed him carefully, bypassing dark shapes of chests and objects, trying not to bump into any. It was so dark inside, and the smell was terrible.

"It's there," whispered the boy, his voice trembling. "By that wall."

As her eyes grew accustomed to the darkness, catching the little of the moonlight that seeped in through the gaping doorway, she saw the shapes, a heap of limbs, too many to belong to one person.

Afraid to come closer, holding the contents of her stomach in, but barely, she watched the boy nearing, like a small animal, ready to flee. He must have been really frightened, yet he went on, one hesitant step after another, determined.

Oh, Coatlicue, the Mother of the Gods, she prayed, *let it be someone else's corpse. Let the other twin be safe somewhere, maybe in trouble but alive. This family had been through so much.*

A strangled shriek brought her out of her prayer, making her cover the short distance in one leap, throwing her beside the kneeling boy, gagging. He was pulling frantically, dragging one of the bodies out by its leg, pushing the other away, choking audibly, barely keeping his own balance.

"Wait, wait, let me!" She grabbed his upper arm, pulling him away, as he slipped and fell, turning into a part of the revolting pile for a heartbeat, as though he had already been dead, too. "I'll get it."

"It's him," he was muttering, pushing himself past her, choking with tears. "It's him!"

The body, indeed, belonged to a boy of about the same age, judging by its form and the angularity of its limbs. It was stinking worse than the other, slippery, its clothes stiff, caked with a revolting mixture of dried blood and worse. She felt her stomach contents coming up, impossible to stop.

When the retching passed, she forced herself up, rushing back toward the boy, wishing to at least be there for him, to catch him if he fainted. He had dragged the body out by this time and was curled beside it, as it seemed, running his hands along its limbs and up its face.

"It's not him," he sobbed, his voice still strangled, still choking. "It's not...not..."

He backed away abruptly and would have fallen if not for her catching him, pressing his shoulders tightly, pulling him into her embrace, desperate to contain his shaking.

"Are you sure?" she whispered. "Are you sure it's someone else?"

He just nodded, not attempting to pull away, his trembling worse.

"Good, good. So your brother is still alive, you see? There is no need to worry."

But, of course, there were many causes to be worried, a conclusion confirmed in the next heartbeat, as the boy straightened up, gathering the remnants of his courage with an admirable swiftness.

"It's Ehecatl," he whispered, swallowing a sob. "It's him. I know it for sure. He has a scar on his face. And his turquoise piercing."

"Who is Ehecatl?" Tlalli's desperation was returning as well.

"His friend."

"I thought we were looking for Ilhuitl."

He didn't look up, not moving from her embrace, snug in there like the child he really was.

"Ehecatl is another of his friends. They were always together. All three of them. And the other *telpochcalli* boys from time to time. He was their leader. They were hiding things here, useful things. They were planning to run away to the Highlands."

"Why?" She felt his trembling lessening, but still, he stayed close, as though trying to hide in her warmth. Poor little thing. Her desperation welled.

"I don't know. He didn't want to stay in Texcoco. He hates it here. The school mostly." A painful pause. "He can't run well. He can't be a great warrior."

"He seems to be quite a warrior, the way he was running his *telpochcalli* bunch of troublemakers. A leader even."

"Oh, yes, they were all afraid of him, and they always listened to him and did what he said. He took care of them."

She stifled a sigh. "Then he seems to be a good enough warrior to me."

"The *calmecac* teachers don't know that."

"No, they don't." Gently, she began steering him back toward the entrance, desperate to get out, if for no other reason than to enjoy a gulp of fresh air. "We have to go back now, Coatl. We have to talk to your mother. Your father will know what to do."

He slipped out of her arms, as lithe and as soundless as a forest beast. His head up but his shoulders sagging, he went back toward the sprawling body, pulling his short cloak off, placing it over the dead boy in one swift movement. Then, without a word, he headed out into the blissful darkness with no stench.

CHAPTER 14

Mictia felt like breaking something.

"What do you mean the whelp is gone?"

The boat swayed dangerously, as Nacatl backed off, anticipating a blow. He would have, indeed, struck the man, but for his astonishment. How could something so silly have happened to a killer as hardened as Nacatl, the best of his people? How could the stupid boy of barely ten summers get away from this man?

"How?" he hissed in the end, moving away to stabilize the boat. They were lined up at the far edge of the long wharf, having sailed during the deepest part of the night, navigating by their instincts mostly, avoiding collisions with other boats and planks by a miracle as it seemed, although Nacatl had always been good at maneuvering on the water.

"The dirty rat just slipped over the side and was gone!" cried out the man, chopping the air with his hands, upsetting the boat once again. "He just plopped over. I hope he sank all the way to the bottom, and I hope he suffered before he died."

"He is not dead." Against his will, Mictia scanned the dark water with his gaze, the open patch of the lake behind their back and the small, murky waves under the wooden planks of the wharf. As expected, it revealed nothing.

"He can't be alive! Even if he can swim like a stinking fish, he can't do it with his hands tied."

Yes, indeed. What was the dirty whelp's game? Since first falling upon them uninvited, intruding with his filthy bunch of other little thieves, the annoying cub had brought nothing but trouble. Even if not directly, even while being useful, showing them the well-hidden paths out of the city, he had always been a challenge, a danger, a risk he, Mictia, should not have taken. He should have killed the wild thing the moment they were shown the boat instead of dragging the hate-filled, defiant whelp along, tying him for good measure, but hoping to tame him maybe, or to get some sort of a payment out of his influential father after all. The boy was too good to be just killed, but when had the quality of his victims stopped him from disposing of people? Was he getting soft? He cursed viciously.

"He must have cut his ties somehow, before dropping over," he said, taking a deep breath to calm his fraying temper. "He must have found a way."

"How?" Nacatl was staring at him out of the pre-dawn mist, still breathless with rage.

"And how am I supposed to know that? If I had known he was working on his ties, I would have cut his filthy throat faster than it would have taken you to tie that boat." He clenched his teeth, trying to think. "Well, maybe it won't spoil our plans. If the cub didn't drown, then he must be running as fast as his stupid limp will allow him, trying to get back to Texcoco. It would take him half a day or more, and by that time, we will be away, well settled." He nodded. "After midday, we will be off."

"Where to?"

"I'll tell you when you need to know." He measured his companion with a side glance, taking in the dark eyes and the tight jaw. He would need this man and his cooperation for at least one more day. "When I see that my plan is going to work," he added, turning to watch the passing boat.

And it will work, he thought, remembering the fat official, the leading man of Coatlinchan. Oh, that one was scared out of his senses, never imagining that his carefully concealed scheme would lead back to him, not counting on his hired killer being smart enough to devise his strategy. Most certainly, this man did not return to sleep peacefully after his uninvited guest was gone, not with the dangerous sword lying next to him and his secret scheming revealed in a no-nonsense way. He would make an effort and bring the demanded payment, knowing better than to try playing games.

There was no hitch to his plan, but for the filthy cub running loose somewhere out there. Not dead, for certain. Not this one. Maybe fleeing home, or maybe trying to find his father's revered sword, come to think of it. The boy had been watching the covered bundle all the while they were sailing, not taking his eyes off it, so very concentrated. Was he working on his ties in the meanwhile? Maybe, yes. He might have picked up that pitiful knife he had brought in the beginning, before falling into their hands, keeping it tucked in his palm, maybe, well-concealed. The resourceful whelp might have been that good.

He choked down another curse. It was his fault. He should not have succumbed to the temptation of taking a hostage. His inability to let an opportunity go unheeded yet again proved disastrous, as had happened several times before, on the occasions he didn't care to remember.

"Tie the boat and get ready," he said. "I'll lead you to a warehouse, and you will stay to watch it until I come back."

Stifling another curse, he leaped out of their vessel, welcoming the firmness of the wide, artificially made patch of land under his feet. It extended into the lake, making it easier to access Coatlinchan's harbor facilities.

He took a deep breath, trying to banish the tiredness. The sleepless nights were taking their toll. Combined with the previous day of worrying and running around, coping with failures, they did nothing good to his temper and his ability to control himself. He needed time, time to rest and to regroup, to rethink his plans, maybe. Tired people were impatient and careless. Tired people made mistakes. And he was tired, tired and angry, just when he needed his senses honed, his instincts at their best, with the next half a day being crucial. No more mistakes, no more misjudgment, no more taking chances.

"Hurry up!"

Nacatl glanced at him fleetingly, but said nothing, working on the rope, tying the boat. The man was doing his best, as always. Aside from letting the damn boy slip away, Nacatl had made no mistakes, being nothing but a reassuring, helpful presence throughout this entire mission. Damn it. He needed to get rid of the anger and the impatience. He needed to return to his cold, lucid thinking.

The dawn was not yet about to break when the litter came back, creating much noise in the deep silence of the night. Listening to the hushed voices of the litter-bearers filling the patio, Tlalli shivered, then tensed at the sound of brisk footsteps clad in high-soled sandals.

Unsettled, she glanced at Dehe. Those were not the Master of the House's steps.

"It must be Iztac Ayotl," said her companion quietly, not attempting to get up.

They had been huddled here, in the quiet alcove of the central room since Tlalli had come back, not touching the refreshments, speaking in whispers, trying not to wake the children up. Both Coatl and Citlalli sprawled on a nearby cluster of mats, turning and muttering, their sleep troubled.

Poor child, thought Tlalli, watching the curled-up twin, his legs pulled up, arms folded around them, coiled into a ball, as though trying to protect himself. How horrified he must still be feeling. It's a wonder he had managed to fall asleep at all.

"Why would she come here?" she asked, her stomach going rigid with fear.

Dehe raised her eyebrows. "Why not? It's her home."

"Yes, of course. But why now? Why in the middle of the night?" She felt her anger returning. She had come back here instead of going straight to the Palace and Tlacaelel. Didn't the woman appreciate that?

Yes, she needed to bring the boy back, of course. After the horrors of that warehouse even such a fierce little thing was in no condition to wander the night alone. Still, she didn't have to stay, didn't have to wake the Mistress of the House up and share her

unsettling news with her. Not about the warehouse and their
findings there – on their way back both she and the boy agreed
that there was no need to scare his mother to death until finding
more clues as to Ocelotl's whereabouts – but about the
conversation she had overheard. She thought the woman might be
of help, might have possessed the fastest way to contact her
husband, to let the Warlord and the Emperor know. Tlalli's
running to find Tlacaelel might have taken more time.

Well, she hadn't been sorry about that. The woman had
listened avidly, perfectly composed, responding with typical
efficiency by sending several servants into various directions in
order to locate the Warlord, to relay to him the urgency of her
news. Asking no questions, she had complied with Tlalli's request
to dispatch a messenger to Tlacaelel too, requesting a litter. She
didn't ask why her guest insisted on her own litter being sent for,
instead of using the vacant one, and Tlalli was grateful for that,
not wishing to talk about his anger, which, by now, must be
soaring to the skies. If he had sent her a litter, he would be
signaling her that she was allowed to come back. A reassurance
she needed desperately.

Yet, it took time, too much time, and as the night wore off, they
sat together, thinking and talking, wondering, trying to
understand.

"It must have been someone else, some other woman they were
talking about," maintained Dehe again and again, every time they
would return to this particular subject. About the despicable
nobles bent on destroying Nezahualcoyotl they had no quarrels,
united in their determination to prevent that. Yet, when it came
back to the Emperor's sister, her converser would lose every grain
of reasonable thinking. "They used no names, so it might have
been someone else."

"They said it was the idea of the woman who used to be an
empress. How many Tenochtitlan's empresses do you know of?"

"Itzcoatl's Chief Wife could be called an empress. She is the
emperor's wife. She qualifies."

"Oh, please! And why would Itzcoatl's wife, chief or minor,
huddle with the prominent Acolhua?"

The dark eyes flashed at her. "I don't know that, but I will find out. It must be someone else. Iztac-Ayotl would never betray my husband or her brother. She is loyal, and she loves them both." Another hostile glare of the narrowing eyes. "You may have misunderstood them."

"I understood it all perfectly," cried out Tlalli, forgetting to keep quiet.

She held her breath, eyeing the sleeping children. The woman just didn't want to see reason, and she would have refused to believe her insistent guest at all if not for the twin who had confirmed her allegations, having also listened to the plotting nobles, apparently.

"Your son heard them too, and he told you so!"

"No names were mentioned, so neither of you two can be sure it was about the person you accuse of a very serious crime." Dehe took a deep breath. "Let us leave it at that for now."

And so they would leave the subject, to get back to it again, because what else was there to talk about? But Tlalli kept listening to the voices outside, hoping her litter would arrive soon. She needed to talk to a *reasonable* person, and she needed to know that he forgave her and was not about to toss her aside.

However, now that the noise of the arriving carriage reached her ears, not her litter but that of the Emperor's traitorous sister, she jumped to her feet, feeling trapped.

"Why did she come here now, at such a time of night?" she asked again, frightened.

Dehe looked up, her face blank. "I sent for her."

"Why?" Her panic welled, like back by the temple, when she stood listening to the plotting nobles.

"She will be able to answer all our questions, won't she?" The defiance in the woman's eyes made Tlalli's heart flutter in anger mixed with fear.

"She will deny everything. Of course, she will. It will prove nothing. I know what I heard and it all makes sense, too!"

"What *did* you hear?" The voice of the Emperor's sister echoed between the plastered walls. "What makes sense to you?"

Turning to face the woman, Tlalli gathered the last of her

anger, clinging to it desperately, afraid to succumb to the wave of fear. "I heard many secrets, many of the Palace's plots; too many for one evening." Her voice rang as loudly, almost as self-assured, and it pleased her, made her head straighten proudly. "Tonight, I learned truth regarding what happened."

"Oh!" The dark eyes narrowed, turned freezing cold. "And what is this truth, woman?"

Clenching her fists tight, Tlalli did not take a step back as the royal woman came into the room, her eyes narrow, the generous lips pressed tight.

"I'm glad you arrived, sister." Dehe was on her feet, taking a step forward, as though intending to place herself between the two women. "We need to discuss a matter of urgency and utter importance. The three of us." The last sentence came out firmly, carrying a message. While clearly not liking any of this, the Mistress of the House was not about the let her guest be insulted, or thrown out, for that matter.

The royal sister whirled at her fellow wife. "What is it, Dehe? Why did you summon me in the middle of the night, and why should this Mexica woman be involved?" A groomed palm came up, brushing against the smoothness of the perfect face, running down the delicate cheek, in a showy manner. "It's well past midnight, sister, if you didn't notice."

Dehe's eyebrows flew high. "You were not sleeping in the Palace, Iztac-Ayotl. This is your home, and there is no need to make a scene over me sending for you in this time of the night. If eager to rest, you would be sleeping in your quarters here." Impatiently, the small woman gestured toward the depths of the house, her eyes sparkling. "Now, would you please sit down and listen, instead of quarreling? What we need to tell you is important, unless you are not concerned with your brother and his *altepetl*'s well-being."

For a few heartbeats, the two women glared at each other, again reminding Tlalli of two siblings anxious to dominate and not to be dominated; like Coatl and Citlalli, ready to argue and dispute each word the other said, but needing one another at the same time. She glanced at the children, who by now, of course, were wide awake, fully conscious, listening avidly, two messy forms of sleepy eyes and disheveled hair.

"Mother!" Citlalli's voice broke the tension. "I want to sleep here in the main room. Second Mother said we can."

While the Emperor's sister smiled at her daughter absently, Dehe's frown deepened.

"You two, go inside. Sleep together in the twins' quarters, if you want to. Or better yet, sleep next to Mixtli. Calm her down if she wakes up."

"But I want to stay here!" cried out the yellow-eyed girl, as the twin got to his feet with such obvious lack of interest that Tlalli's heart twisted. She fought the urge to take him into her arms, like back in the gods-accursed warehouse.

"Do as you are told, Citlalli," said the Emperor's sister softly, fishing what looked like a reassuring smile from the depths of her frown.

The girl's eyes sparkled, and she planted her legs wide apart, in the pose Tlalli had come to know well after spending a day in this household, a pose that promised no good to those who wanted her to do something.

"I'm not going…" she began, but Dehe cut her speech short with a gaze full of meaning, uncompromising.

"Both of you, go and take care of Mixtli. I need you to do this now."

Her tone brooked no argument, but there was something conspiratorial in her eyes, something that clearly appealed to the rebellious child. Scowling, the girl hesitated for another heartbeat, then slipped out of the room, following the twin, who was already gone, paying no attention to the argument.

The Emperor's sister arched her eyebrows, but said nothing, while Dehe looked around briskly, as though pondering their possibilities.

"We can speak out there on the patio, or here, in that alcove. I'm not sure where we have less chances of being overheard."

"Let's just talk about what you wanted to talk about, Dehe. Let us get it over with," said the royal woman tersely. "I'm tired and could use some sleep."

The glance Dehe shot at her fellow wife hinted that even her patience might have its limits.

"I sent a messenger to you, Iztac Ayotl, while other servants went to alarm our husband and your brother, the Emperor," she began, as the three of them squatted on the mats the maid spread in a sort of a circle before being sent away, instructed to make sure no servants were around to listen.

The Emperor's sister tensed. "Why?"

"Apparently, there are people who are plotting against our lawful ruler, nobles who may try to get rid of him, according to their own words."

That had the desired effect. Iztac Ayotl straightened up so sharply the obsidian comb holding her elaborately arranged hair fell, clattering noisily, rolling over the stone floor.

"Who?" she breathed, aghast.

"That's what I wanted to ask you." Dehe leaned forward with no hint of accusation reflecting in her wide open eyes. "You see, these may be the people who are frequenting your vicinity, Iztac Ayotl. You know who I mean? They were always vocal in criticizing Nezahualcoyotl, but now they may have gone too far."

The color drained from the beautiful face. "What did they say? Whom did you talk to?"

"I talked to no one, sister. You know I'm not mixing in any of these circles. But she," the light nod toward Tlalli was friendly, encouraging, "she overheard a very troublesome conversation."

"What did you hear?" The narrowing gaze shot at Tlalli, cold and accusing, making her regret sharing the news with the stupid Mistress of this House once again. Couldn't the silly woman see the obvious?

Shrugging, she said nothing, desperate to gain time.

"Would you please tell her what you shared with me earlier?" Dehe's voice was full of warm reassurance.

"I heard people, the nobles of your *altepetl*, plotting to kill your emperor."

"What?" The widening eyes of the royal woman lost all trace of her previously disdainful hostility, staring at Tlalli as though she just sprouted another head. "It can't be!"

"Yes, it can. They were very clear about it." She was so tired. Two sleepless nights in a row did nothing to enhance her patience with the troublesome dwellers of this *altepetl*, nobles and commoners alike.

"Who were those people? Where did you hear them talking?" The woman leaned forward, her chest rising and falling, eyes so wide that they bulged, threatening to pop out of their sockets, not especially beautiful anymore.

"Near the marketplace, in one of the temples. They didn't bother to conceal their intentions at all." Pursing her lips, she shrugged, actually beginning to enjoy herself. It was a pleasure to see the haughty *cihua* losing her composure, thrown out of balance in such an unexpected fashion. "They were very clear about it. The Emperor has to go. A new dynasty is to be formed."

"A new dynasty?" It was quite a gasp.

"Yes, a new dynasty. Their leading man said that most clearly." Puzzled and even a little compassionate, Tlalli watched the woman, expecting her to faint any moment, as the exquisite face turned chalky, draining of color. "I suppose he thinks his own bloodline must be good enough for this position. He seemed to be hinting this way. And his companions accepted it, too. They just nodded and said nothing."

The Mistress of the House put a reassuring palm on her fellow wife's hand. "I sent a trusted messenger to our husband, and another one to Coyotl himself. They'll know what to do."

But the royal woman kept staring. "Who were these people?" she whispered, as though having not enough strength to talk loudly.

"I don't know. It was dark. I could only hear them."

Something crept into the incredulous gaze. *A spark of hope?*

"Then how do you know they were actual noblemen presuming to harm the Emperor and not just marketplace commoners, drunk on *pulque*?"

Tlalli clenched her teeth, holding on to her temper with an effort. "I saw the same people in the Palace earlier through the day. The tall man who wanted to replace the Emperor was there in the crowd, watching you talking to your brother. He and his friends were watching you two very closely, speaking in whispers."

"What did they say?"

"Back in the Palace? Nothing incriminating. But in the darkness of the temple, they were very open about their intentions. They said your brother is too young, too weak, too friendly with the Mexicas, following their lead when he ought not do so."

The woman bit her lips. "Yes, there are nobles who think that. It's not a treachery to disagree with your emperor's policies."

"No, it's not," said Dehe, taking her hand away. "Until they do something to get their way."

"What are you trying to say, Dehe?" The Emperor's sister whirled at the other woman, her face coming back to life with anger, aggressive like a cornered animal.

But the Mistress of the House didn't even blink, standing her companion's glare, her own stony and firm. "I'm saying that you should forget your friendship with these men and back your brother in everything he does."

"You understand nothing!"

"I understand more than you think I do!"

A brief silence prevailed, accompanied by burning gazes.

"Whatever I do, it is done in the best interests of our *altepetl* and our people. Coyotl is not always right. Sometimes he is too soft, too accommodating, too well-meaning when fierce independence is more appropriate and needed."

"He is the emperor, Iztac Ayotl, and as such, he deserves loyalty; from his subjects, and most of all, from his family and friends, people whom he has never forgotten or forsaken." The woman's eyes sparkled fiercely. "He is right most of the time, sister. He is one of the wisest men in our lands. He is the emperor for a reason, unless you agree with those who want to replace him."

"I do not agree with the despicable people who may want to throw Coyotl out of his throne!" cried out the other woman, clenching her fists. "Stop trying to imply that. I may disagree with some of his policies, but I am loyal to my brother. No one is more loyal to him than I am!"

More thundering silence. Tlalli felt like contributing to the conversation. "They said he should be removed. They said it most clearly." Their gazes leapt to her, making her heart race. "By poison, maybe, they said."

Iztac Ayotl's gasp tore the silence, while Dehe pressed her lips.

"What did they look like?" asked the Emperor's sister, her fighting spirit dying rapidly, leaving her eyes black and empty.

"One was tall and, well, imposing. He spoke in a strange manner, drawing out his words longer than necessary. This is how I recognized him as the man I saw in the Palace."

"Yolocatzin," muttered the woman, looking more downcast with every passing moment, her eyes boring into the surface of the low table, as though trying to burn holes in it. "I have to talk to my brother urgently."

"I sent him a messenger," said Dehe. "And one to our husband, too. I hope he will come here shortly. He will know what to do."

"But he is not in the Palace." The woman was on her feet, wringing her hands. "He is busy organizing warriors. With all this trouble," she swallowed hard, "with all this trouble, he won't be in the best of conditions, to think, to do something swift, efficient…" Her fingers were crushing the fringes of her blouse, making a mess out of the decorated material. "I'll go and see Coyotl at once."

"There is more, Iztac Ayotl." Dehe rose to her feet slowly. "If you see your brother before my messenger or our husband does, let him know that these people were planning to meet again, tomorrow with dawn." She glanced at Tlalli. "They said that, didn't they?"

Tlalli took a deep breath. "Yes, they said that." She stared at the Emperor's sister, unable to fight the temptation. Oh, the royal *cihua* was so obviously unsettled, so torn. Couldn't the Mistress of the House see how frightened she looked, how *guilty*. "They also said you messed up their plans. They said your idea was good, but that you implemented it badly."

She watched the last of the color draining from the beautiful face, making it look gray in the flickering light of the torch. If she fainted, the woman would wreck the exquisite table woven from reeds, reflected Tlalli randomly. It would be such a loud fall.

The pale lips moved, but no words came out. Eyes enormous, unblinking, dominating the stark face completely, the Emperor's sister just stared, as though having not seen something like Tlalli in her entire life.

"Stop talking nonsense!" Dehe's voice broke the momentary silence that prevailed. "I told you to get it out your head. This matter has nothing to do with Iztac Ayotl. They talked about someone else."

But the reassuring words had a strange effect. Their eyes still locked, Tlalli saw the generous mouth beginning to twitch, and then, all of sudden, it was not a stone statue but a real woman, miserable and lost, not very pretty anymore. The mask was slipping, falling apart, revealing something desperate, a flicker of pain, or maybe agony, or desolation. Another heartbeat of staring at her accuser, and the woman slid down, to sit back on her mat, arms wrapped around herself, as though from cold or for protection.

The short moment had a strange effect on the Mistress of the House too, who now froze in her turn, turning into stone. Shifting her eyes from one woman to another, Tlalli held her breath, understanding too well.

"No," breathed Dehe finally, not attempting to move a limb, her lips colorless, clutched between the small teeth.

The Emperor's sister came back to life with a miserable groan. "You have to listen to me, Dehe. You have to hear me out," she called, her trembling voice pitched high.

"No!" exclaimed Dehe. "No." Shaking her head, she took a step back, hands up, as though trying to push away anything that might be said.

"No, please! You have to listen to me." The other woman was on her feet again, rushing toward her friend, grabbing the lifeless palms, holding them tight despite the feeble attempts to take them away. "It was for the best, Dehe. I did it for his sake. Don't you see it? The sword was cracked all over; it was rotting. It was no weapon anymore, but a relic. He should not have been fighting with it, but he insisted on bringing it into every battle. He fought with it, although he knew it might break on him. You knew it, Dehe, you knew it as well as I did. You were worried, too. You said it many times." The words were gushing now, like a powerful current, with no pause for breath. "It was for his sake, Dehe. He was not reasonable about that sword, but it was dangerous for him to use it now. His safety was at stake. You have to believe me. You have to listen to me."

The last phrase rang frantically, crashing against the blank face, falling apart at its empty expression, as Dehe stood there wide-eyed, her mouth gaping, no flicker of life reflecting upon it; dead, turned to stone.

"Please!" pled the other woman. "Please."

Tlalli felt her own desperation rising. The Emperor's sister was so frightened, so full of remorse. Not the arrogant, self-assured royal *cihua* she had come to dislike, but a panicked woman about to break.

"You have to believe me. It was for his sake!"

"You stole his sword," muttered Dehe finally, her eyes glazed, dominating her face completely now. "*You* did this."

"It was for him." Iztac Ayotl's voice had a firmer ring to it, a hint of her former forcefulness creeping back in. "I had to ensure his safety."

The change of tone had the desired effect. Dehe came back to life all at once, wrenching her hands from the firm grip.

"And to achieve your political goals along the way," she said sharply, challenging.

The Emperor's sister tossed her head high, more herself with every passing heartbeat. "I know what I am doing!"

"Like throwing your brother off his throne!" It came out forcefully, like a thunderbolt, bringing the other woman back into her previous panicky state of mind.

"No, no, never this!" Swaying, Iztac Ayotl took a step back. "Never!"

Dehe's glare was as cold as marble. "And yet your friends seem to be determined to have a new emperor now that you created so much trouble for both your brother and our husband."

There was the noise of many feet clad in hard-soled sandals

bearing down the alley, in an obvious hurry. Numbed and helplessly undecided, they all turned to stare.

"What was that all about, Dehe?" The Warlord burst into the spacious room, blocking the entrance with his massive shoulders, while his warriors stayed outside, crowding the patio. "Why did you send for me?"

"A matter of importance," said Dehe firmly, pulling herself together with an admirable swiftness that Tlalli had observed in this woman through this entire day. "There is a plot against our emperor." A warning glance shot at Tlalli. "Tlacaelel's woman happened to overhear a group of nobles planning to murder him."

"Who?" rasped the Warlord, not taken aback upon hearing such news. He clearly did not expect to be summoned in the middle of the night, interrupting the most important of his duties, for anything less than this.

"Yolocatzin and his associates."

"What exactly did you hear and where?" The dark gaze leapt to Tlalli, boring into her, sending shivers down her spine with the intensity of it.

She swallowed. "It was before midnight, on the marketplace. Beside a small temple, near the colorful wall. Where the loose women are." Licking her lips, she wondered, receiving another warning glance from the Mistress of the House. "They said the Emperor should go. A new dynasty should be started. They seemed to think it was the best timing, while you are busy organizing a war against the Mexica."

The man's eyes were now blazing murder. "What else?"

"They said—"

"These people said they will meet again with dawn, at the same temple." The Mistress of the House burst into Tlalli's speech in the most inconsiderate manner, cutting her off with not a glance of apology. "This information is reliable. Your son can confirm it. This is exactly what they said."

The man's eyes lit. "Ocelotl is back?" he asked eagerly.

"No." The woman's face fell, but again, she composed herself, pressing her lips.

"Then how?" The light went out of her husband's face as

rapidly.

"Coatl... Coatl was there too." A heartbeat of hesitation. "They went there looking for Ocelotl."

"Where is he?"

"In there. Sleeping, I hope..."

The man was gone, disappearing into the depths of the house, leaving them gaping. Unsettled, Tlalli glanced at the women, but neither of them moved, staring ahead, each in her own miserable thoughts.

The Warlord reappeared, accompanied by the boy, who had, evidently, been doing anything but sleeping – this entire household must have been wide awake – his arm wrapped around his son's shoulders, pressing him warmly, protectively, *sheltering*. Giving him strength, realized Tlalli, watching the boy's troubled face relaxing, its youthful lightness returning, after having been banished so thoroughly by their night adventures and the awful discovery. The courageous little thing kept the frightful secret to himself, she remembered, not wishing to worry his mother, but now he was going to spill it all, let the mighty warrior take the terrible burden. It was written all over his innocently fresh, pleasantly round face.

Dehe's cold palm was upon her arm, pulling her away, guiding toward the inner rooms.

"Please, say nothing about what occurred here before. Nothing." The troubled eyes clung to Tlalli, relaying the urgency of the request. "We will solve it between us, the women. Please."

"You mean about the Emperor's sister?" She found it difficult to form the words, too stunned to think clearly.

"Yes." Dehe's gaze did not waver. "I will have my litter take you back to the Palace. Tell Tlacaelel everything about the plot, if you wish it so. But not the other thing. Please."

"Yes, of course." She stared at the woman, taking in the intensity behind the troubled eyes, the pallor of the haggard face, the firm, courageous determination. "I will do nothing to harm your family."

"It's not that." The woman wrung her hands. "She is not involved in the plot against the Emperor. It is not possible, and if you knew what kind of a woman she is, you would believe her on that too. But..." A small drop of blood appeared, glittering on the full lower lip, where the woman's teeth tore into it. "We can't have my husband know about the sword. He will never forgive her, never. No matter how innocent her intentions were. He cannot forgive that."

Oh, yes, thought Tlalli, shuddering, remembering the man's bubbling rage this morning and through the entire day. The Warlord was beyond being furious now, trying to deal with so many troubles at the same time. The stolen sword, the missing child, the filthy nobles plotting against his emperor, and now his exalted wife being involved, doing something terrible behind his back, conspiring with the enemies, even if her motives were not filthy, originated in the worry for his safety.

"I will not talk about it." She listened to the quiet voices seeping in from the patio, too quiet to understand their words, but the tone of the Warlord was calm, reassuring, encouraging, enveloping the child in his warmth. "Coatl might tell him. I don't know how much he heard or understood."

"Yes, maybe." The woman beside her sighed, leaning tiredly against the wall. "Life has been too tranquil, too good for the past few summers, in the Highlands, and here in Texcoco. I suppose it was too much to expect it go on like that forever."

Taken with compassion, Tlalli reached out to caress the thin shoulder. "It will all be well. You'll see. Your husband will protect the Emperor, and Ocelotl will come back, mischievous and guilty, but unharmed. I will offer in the Mother of the Gods' temple tomorrow with dawn. I will ask her to keep Ocelotl safe."

The large eyes peered at her, glittering with unshed tears. "I thank you." A hint of a genuine smile lifted the corners of the pressed mouth. "You've been a great help and very kind. I wish I could let you know how grateful I am."

CHAPTER 15

She was lying next to him, her head on his shoulder, snug in the curve of his arm, curled like a small animal, seeking protection. Her breath brushed against his chest, caressing, pleasantly light. From time to time, she jerked and murmured, but he would press her closer and she would calm, not coming out of the dream but diving into a more peaceful one.

The dawn was upon them and he needed to get up, to eat hastily, as was his custom, while reading the papers his scribes had prepared for him from the previous day. No written document went out without his approval; he had been very strict about it. Even on this sort of a holiday, enjoying the hospitality of the Acolhua Capital, he had plenty of work to do. Especially now that he was about to detour through Coatlinchan; although, after listening to her tales, he knew they wouldn't be sailing with the first light as planned. Toward the high morning, most likely, and that was also only because he knew how angry his friend was, how furious, how pushed beyond the limits of self-control.

This additional plot against the Acolhua Emperor would be squashed quickly and brutally, not in a subtle manner as it should have been done. There would be neither court procedures, nor the traditional noble way of using a poison or a dagger, hastening someone on his Underworld journey but in a quiet, unobtrusive manner. This was the way of the nobility, this was what the ruling circles did, but the Highlander was none of those things, a law unto himself, and deep down, Tlacaelel agreed with Coyotl's policy of not interfering with his Chief Warlord's activities. The Acolhua Emperor's most trusted, most loyal friend and supporter always got the results, his unordinary thinking turning him into the priceless asset the Texcoco Emperor needed on his rise back to power.

Much like the first Tenochtitlan's Emperor, Revered Acamapichtli, and his unruly Tepanec Chief Warlord, thought Tlacaelel, amused, Texcoco needed an unordinary thinking and that somewhat barbarian ferocity to get back to power. Then, just like Tenochtitlan, once these things had been accomplished, it would revert to the old, more refined, ways.

Unwilling to wake her up, he shifted carefully, letting her slide into the cotton blanket that was previously entangled under their bodies. It was challenging to wrestle it free using one hand, but he was not in a hurry. To linger in her warmth was a blessing, and just as he thought he had lost her forever.

He frowned, remembering the previous day and his bubbling anger. She was impossible, reversing to her commoner's ways in the worst of timings, when he had absolutely no leisure to deal with any of it. Angry with her and her wretched independence, he had confined her to her rooms until further notice, but of course, she paid it no heed. Why would she, the wild thing from Azcapotzalco's dubious alleys? Returning from the meeting with Nezahualcoyotl and sending for her, he had not been surprised when the troubled slave told him that she was not there, having been missing for the entire evening.

Holding his temper, but barely, he had sent the frightened servant away, then cursed for a very long time, kicking some furniture and thinking of what he would do to her. Throw her out, he swore, to go back to the slums she belonged to. He was through with all of it. She was taking too much of his time, anyway, the precious time that could have been spent on working or sleeping, instead of loitering in her quarters, reading poetry and making love.

So he had arranged his scrolls and tried to work, drawing a plan of yet another Huitzilopochtli temple, to be erected next to Tenochtitlan's wharves. This special Mexica god was gaining ascendance over the other sacred deities, and it was a good thing. It put his Mexica people slightly apart from the other Great Lake's nations who all worshiped the same gods. And if apart, then why not above as well? With his people growing to regard Huitzilopochtli as the deity they addressed first, it would be easier to install the sense of destiny, of superiority, of belonging and pride in their rapidly growing city.

She turned around, throwing her leg over the blanket, revealing the gentle outline of her slender shin, the smoothness of her thigh, the delightful curve of it suggestive, hinting at the secrets it hid.

His heart accelerated its beating. Reaching out, he caressed the creamy smoothness, stirring his thoughts in a very particular direction. The resolution not to wake her up wavered. He might have a little time. Busy in the marketplace temple, the Highlander most certainly would not be ready before mid-morning.

She murmured and stretched, reacting to his touch by moving closer, not fully awake yet but already willing, inviting him into her warmth. Yet he lingered, prolonging the moment, enjoying the pre-lovemaking dalliance as much as the act itself. With others, it might be done for the sake of reaching the climax; with her, it was the gratification of all senses, to enjoy before and after as much as the lovemaking itself.

Unhurried, his fingers traced the curve of her side, sliding toward her breasts, semi-hidden by the way she pressed against him, as though concealing her treasures. It enticed him as never before. He had been so close to losing her.

Frowning, he pushed these memories away, remembering how the night had deepened and so had his inability to concentrate, his frustrating attempts to finish the sketch, to have his scribes make a copy to send to Tenochtitlan first thing in the morning. Instead, he had found himself staring into space, thinking about her. What was she up to? Where was she wandering at such a time of the night? Had she gone for good?

After a while, the possibility did occur to him. He had treated her harshly, having never yelled at her or ordered her about before. She might have not taken it well, not used to such treatment. She was not a slave, as she was very keen to point out.

Gritting his teeth, he went to the room allocated to her,

scanning it carefully, looking for missing items. No fine clothes, no jewelry, no expensive things disappeared, but the stash of *amate*-paper he had given her upon their arrival in the Acolhua Capital and the box of charcoal were gone, and so was her best pair of sandals and some additional clothing. Did she leave? It would be so much like her to do so.

He had felt his stomach twisting in a violent way. The damn proud *cihua*! So she was telling him she would not be yelled at or ordered about. Just who did she think she was?

He had stormed back to his rooms, but now his concentration was gone for good and two good charcoal sticks got broken, to be thrown to the floor violently, until he gave up on the idea of making anything worthwhile out of this particular drawing. The new temple of Huitzilopochtli would have to wait until he solved his private dilemmas.

In the end, he had sent some servants, accompanied by warriors for protection, to look for her, to find her in the vastness of this gods-accursed *altepetl*. To do what? He didn't know, wasn't sure of his actions, he, who had always planned ahead, who had never acted out of impulses and mindless desires.

Pushing the memories away, unwilling to fight the temptation anymore, he pulled back the remnants of the blanket, to see her revealed in all her naked glory. Such a satisfying sight. She never put on weight, remaining too thin, still close to being that always hungry, underfed creature of Azcapotzalco, yet for some reason, he found it most attractive, her slender curves alluring, making him dizzy with desire, trying his highly praised self-control.

Still, he took his time exploring, watching her lips curving into a smug, purely female, smile of satisfaction, and her eyes still closed, still peaceful, as though determined to get the best out of her other senses. A luxurious animal; something feline. Not a jaguar – she was too small and too thin for that – but probably some sort of a smaller creature out of the unexplored west.

She was watching him now, her eyes large and dark, dominating her slender face, radiating this typical spark of hers, challenging and encouraging, yielding but never entirely, not like her body did.

Drowning in her warmth, he had taken her slowly, savoring the feeling, giving in to the wave of desire but not like earlier through the accursed night, when she had arrived with the Highlander wife's litter, disheveled and agitated, hesitating under the coldness of his gaze, not sure of herself.

"I need to tell you something," she had said, not meeting his gaze, her fingers making a mess out the fringes of her dusty blouse. "Then I will go, if you don't want me anymore."

"Tell me," he said, his anger getting the better of him, pushing away the depth of his relief in seeing her back and unharmed.

However her tale made him forget their battle of wills, while he had asked her questions, the exact recollection of what was said and by whom, the location of the temple and the planned meeting there.

"You told it all to the Warlord, word for word?" he had asked, his thoughts racing, mind bursting with possibilities.

"Yes, I did. He asked me the same questions as you, almost all of them. Then he went to talk to his boy." Her smile flashed suddenly, flickering with mischief, making his heart beat faster. "His boys know every dubious alley, every shady corner of this city. They are real rascals."

"Yes, I know that." He could not suppress his own grin, remembering the wild twins a few summers ago in Tenochtitlan, doing everything they should not, from running wild and making mischief to trying to save their father on that fateful day when Tenochtitlan's Third Emperor died. He forced his thoughts off the irrelevant memories. "Did you find the other twin?"

Her face fell. "No, we did not. But," she swallowed, "we found bodies. One of them belonging to the twin's close friend. It was in the warehouse the other boy was frequenting. Or maybe both of them. Coatl knew too much about this place to be just the innocent bystander." She swallowed again. "The Warlord talked to his son for a long time. He made him feel better." A helpless glance of the glittering eyes. "The other twin, do you think he got hurt? Do you think he can still be found?"

"Yes, I think he will be found. But let us hope his disappearance has nothing to do with this entire mess." He shrugged, then looked at her again, coldly. "So you decided to be involved, against my wishes and my direct orders."

She dropped her gaze. "I just want to help. They are a nice family."

"I know how nice they are." He let the silence hang. "And Coyotl is a very *nice* emperor, and the Highlander is a *nice* warlord, and his sword is a *nice* thing to use in battles, and so is this *altepetl*'s relationship with our *altepetl*, a very *nice* relationship. Useful, too, but now threatened." He squatted more comfortably, fighting the urge to invite her in. She was still standing by the doorway, like one of the petitioning commoners, or a reporting warrior, maybe. "Tell me more about this family. What did the other wife do all this time? Was she around there at all?"

His suspicion was still solid, now more than ever, as Yolocatzin was the most vocal noble protesting against Coyotl's policies, one of those who were reported to frequent the vicinity of the Emperor's sister. Also, the additional questioning gave him the opportunity to make her stay. She was clearly not about to beg for forgiveness, which left him with not much choice but to send her packing.

She tensed visibly, her gaze back upon him, more troubled than before. "Well, yes, she was there at some point." Her face brightened. "We shared an evening meal, and the two women were arguing about politics. Dehe said the theft of the sword could not have been done by our emperor. She said it made no sense."

"She is the smartest person of them all," muttered Tlacaelel, rolling his eyes. "And the other woman?"

"She said it did make sense. She said she knows Itzcoatl well, and he is capable of worse deeds."

"Of course he is!" He shook his head, irritated. What a stupid argument it was! "But he would do nothing without a good reason, and there is no reason for him to touch the damn sword, or to ruin our relationship with the Acolhuas. We need them as much as they need us."

She nodded readily, curiously relieved.

"What else?"

"Well, nothing, nothing much. I was out with the other twin, and I don't know what these women did in the meanwhile." Her eyes were everywhere but upon him, refusing to meet his gaze.

"You are not telling it all to me, Tlalli," he said curtly, the leading man of the Mexicas taking over. "What else did Iztac Ayotl do or say?"

She was so miserable, standing there, chewing her lip, watching him from under her eyebrows, her hands clenched tight.

"Tell me!" He got to his feet, mainly to gain another advantage, to tower over her, to intimidate her into telling the truth.

She dropped her gaze. "Nothing! She said nothing." Drawing a convulsive breath, she looked up, her eyes glittering with tears, but determined, full of defiance. "I told you everything already."

And what can one do with such obvious lies? he asked himself, frustrated and amused at the same time, the leader and the lover in him at odds. Torture her for information?

"What do I do with you, you wild thing?" he asked, coming closer, relieved now that the decision was made. "How do I make you learn to act civilized, like a woman of high status should? How do I make you forget your wild commoners' ways?"

She pressed her lips, but when he came close, she glanced up in such a hopeful way, the last of his qualms disappeared.

"I thought you were through with hanging under people's balconies or killing rulers that displease you." He drew her into his arms with force, still angry but comfortably so, now that she was his again. "I thought I turned you into a respectable lady."

Her lips trembled, so he pressed them forcefully with his, parting them, enjoying their warmth but also wishing to relay a message. She belonged to him.

"I thought you forgot your marketplace ways," he growled, picking her up, to carry her into the privacy of his inner rooms, pleased with the way her arms locked around him, pressing with desperation, her body tense, trembling, all her energies expended in the efforts to suppress the crying. So much like her. He stifled a smile.

"Don't you ever run away like that again!" he told her firmly, laying her upon the cushions, his desire intensifying, impossible to control. "Promise!"

"I promise," she whispered, gazing at him out of those bottomless, tearful eyes, making his heart twist. "I won't do anything without telling you first."

And this was as far as she would commit, he knew, giving in to his need of her, to the powerful wave of passion and lust, not struggling to control his senses anymore. His anger was still there, and his disappointment with her, but his relief in having her back and unharmed was stronger, forceful, sweeping him into the raging water with nothing to hold onto, into the mighty lake of divine pleasure and thrill, comfortable in losing control once again, as it always happened when having her.

And now, with the dawn so near, and her body again wrapped around his, enveloping him in her warmth, sheltering, caressing, he let his spirit float, his happiness soaring, threatening to get out of hand. She was his talisman, his lucky charm, the gift of the gods from across the Great Lake, the spoil of the dying Tepanec Empire. How could one expect such magic to be accountable to the simple human rules, to the ordinary behavior, to the ways of men and women and the relationship between them? She was not to be handled as a regular woman, because she wasn't such. That's why she had found herself in the middle of the Acolhua Capital's turmoil, because she was meant to be there, to help solve this problem, to prevent the war between the allies.

"Tell me what you didn't tell me last night," he said, hugging her lightly, running his fingers along the curves of her body, now pleasantly slick, covered with sheen of perspiration. An enticing sight.

She stretched luxuriously. "Is this your method of extracting the missing information, oh Honorable Leader?" she purred, eyes glittering, lips trembling with laughter.

He pinched her lightly, pretending to be irritated, both knowing he was not. "There are better, more efficient ways of extracting information, you wild woman. I'm sure the Acolhua War Leader is using some of them in these very moments."

She sobered instantly, sitting up, leaning on her hand, her forehead furrowed with lines of worry. "He will catch those traitors, won't he?"

"Yes, he will. In that temple of yours, before the dawn breaks. Or maybe a little later, if they are late for their own meeting." He shrugged, sitting up and clapping to invite the slaves in. "Before the dirty bastards realize what happened, they will be tied up or dead. He is good at those things, the pouncing jaguar that he is. But I hope he will opt for the first solution. Those people are noblemen and should be kept alive for spectacular trials and public executions. Also, to make their information forthcoming." He measured her through his narrowing eyes. "Maybe the same information that you are keeping from me, eh?"

Her gaze dropped instantly. "I keep nothing from you." She cleared her throat. "Nothing of importance."

"The Warlord's Chief Wife and her involvement in this plot are important," he said, watching her closely.

She gasped. "How did you know that?"

He grinned and said nothing, pleased with the effect. The slaves came in, then went away, ordered to bring the food and wet cloths to have them cleaned.

He made his expression suitably grave. "Tell me!"

"It is not as terrible as it looks," she mumbled, looking pitiful, staring at him like a child caught doing mischief. "She did it for the Warlord's sake. She said the sword was all rotten, falling apart. It was dangerous for him to keep fighting with it."

"So she was the one to organize the theft." He made it a statement, satisfied to have his suspicions confirmed. He was always right, wasn't he? "Where is it now?"

Her gaze flew at him, panicked. "I don't know. Dehe was enraged so badly, and they were yelling at each other, and then the Warlord came so they had to stop." She pressed both palms against her mouth. "Yes, yes, she should have asked her that. But maybe she did, maybe she knows where the sword is by now."

"By now, the Warlord knows too. I don't suppose he took it good-naturedly. I wonder how he handled this."

Her eyes were again firmly upon the mat, boring into the blanket covering it. "He doesn't know."

"What?"

"He doesn't know about the Emperor's sister and the sword." Her voice trailed off.

"Explain!"

She looked up, the determination creeping in, bringing back the girl from last night. "Dehe doesn't want him to find out. She made me swear not to tell anyone."

He remembered the woman, his friend's First Wife, so small and fragile to look at, but only on the outside. She was made of the toughest sort of marble, strong and loyal and fierce, and *decent*. Why was she determined to save her rival? Was she involved, too?

"Why do you think she did that?"

Her eyes peered at him, their sincerity touching. "They like each other a great deal. They argue a lot, but they are doing it like sisters, getting all angry but not in a hateful way. I think they would not want to harm one another."

"And I suppose you want me to keep it a secret," he said, his eyebrows raised high.

"Would you?" She pressed both palms to her chest, imploring. "Oh please, please!"

He suppressed his grin. As though he would be so unwise as to run to the fierce Highlander, friend or not, with this kind of accusation against his beloved wife of many summers. Oh, no! There are things a man should be finding out all by himself, without the easier solution of directing one's anger and frustration at the unfortunate bearer of the bad news.

"What about the rebellion against the Emperor? Is she involved in that, too?" he asked, giving her no indication as to his decision, not yet.

"No, I don't think so. She was appalled to hear what I said." A heartbeat of hesitation. "Back on the marketplace, I thought she was guilty of everything possible, but now I'm not sure. Dehe would have known. She would not have defended her if she was truly guilty."

And this was as good an argument as any, he thought, shrugging. He trusted the Highlander's First Wife's judgment as well.

"I will not be talking to him about his wives or their dubious activities, as it is none of my business, anyway," he said, getting up, watching the slaves coming back, carrying trays with food and chests with their clothes. "But I'm sure he knows most of it by now. With her accomplices being in his clutches, I think he knows more than both of us can ever hope to find out."A glance at his head scribe, hovering at the doorway, made him shrug. "We will have our answers soon, I predict."

However again, those answers came sooner than he expected. He was busy talking to the leader of his warriors, instructing the man as to how he wished his forces to be divided, who were to sail back to Tenochtitlan and who were to accompany their leader on his detour through Coatlinchan, when the word from the Highlander came, asking for a meeting in the Palace's gardens, near the gates.

So the temple business was over, he thought, hurrying along the perfectly swept paths. And it didn't take the man much time to do that. The sun had barely enough time to begin climbing its usual path. Which meant the rebellious nobles had been disposed of quickly, in no fitting manner. He frowned, then shrugged. His friend's ways were different, but they had evidently worked, time after time. Texcoco was no Tenochtitlan.

"Coyotl said you are willing to come along," said the Highlander, barely waiting to reach the hearing range, but careful to have none of his warriors, or just passersby, close.

"I may do that, yes." Taking in the heavily-ringed, sunken eyes set in the haggard paleness of his friend's face, Tlacaelel decided against the usual bating jokes. The man was in no mood for any of that. "What is your plan, Warlord?"

A fleeting smile twisted the man's lips. "If you don't mind joining this particular enterprise, I would like you to sail there, in an impressive state, not hiding your advance. How many warriors can you bring?"

"I came here with two groups of twenty. My elite jaguar fighters, most of them. Not just warriors." He shrugged. "To my reckoning, this amount would be enough, sailing regular boats. Twenty of those, spread evenly, in an organized formation, are bound to make a lasting impression on whomever you wish to intimidate."

The Highlander nodded and his face brightened lightly. "Yes, yes. This would be the best way. Although we will mix our forces, so it won't look like a Mexica invasion to Coatlinchan's fishermen."

Tlacaelel nodded. "It will take you longer to reach this town by land, even if you intend to make your warriors run all the way."

The man's grin widened. "You know me well, Old Friend."

"Yes, I do." With a matching grin, Tlacaelel kicked at a small stone. "So I'll be there earlier than you, doing little else than spreading panic among certain elements?"

"We'll be there soon after you. With the roads open and my men rested and eager, we will not make you wait. Sometime after midday we will be in Coatlinchan. Not much later than originally planned, come to think of it."

"Your men might be rested, but you are not."

The red-rimmed eyes clouded. "I'll be all right."

"I know you will. But you will need to be more than that. You will have to make quick, important decisions, decisions that will affect the good name of your emperor, whom you represent." Coming closer, Tlacaelel stood the narrowing gaze. "You cannot just kill them all and be done with it. Those are noble people, the old Texcocan aristocracy. Traitors or not, they should be treated as such."

"I just dealt with a certain representation of this precious Acolhua aristocracy. They die like anyone else when cut."

"Of course they do, but their corpses smell differently. Coyotl doesn't need this sort of odium clinging to him for the summers to come."

"Coyotl was pleased well enough this morning."

"It took you very little time to take care of the temple business."

The wide eyebrows climbed high, shadowing the narrowed eyes. "How do you know about the temple?"

Tlacaelel snorted in exasperation. "You are truly not at your best, Old Friend! I heard this particular tale from the same source you heard it from."

"Oh, yes. Your Tepanec woman." The Highlander rubbed his eyes tiredly. "She seems to be everywhere, always at the right moment. Which might make one wonder, you know?"

The still-raised eyebrows made Tlacaelel angry. "If you want to look for suspicious actions, look elsewhere. My woman has nothing to do with it."

The Highlander's eyes flashed, then died away. "I suppose not. You, of all people, would have known if she did." A shrug. "I took quite a few filthy lowlifes from that temple; sent them to Coyotl with my compliments. I predict we will have our questions answered soon."

This time Tlacaelel gasped, unprepared for such sloppiness. "Why didn't you interrogate them yourself? We need their information now. Not after we are done in Coatlinchan."

"I did, I did. Of course, I did!" The Highlander brought his hands up, in a sort of a defensive gesture. "But I had not much time and that bastard Yolocatzin used his dagger before I was able to lay my hands on him. He and the other lowlife, Acatzin, were the leaders of the local opposition, so the other filthy lumps of meat in that stinking temple knew hardly anything, soiling themselves in fear, wailing loudly, unable to say anything worth hearing." He frowned. "Well, not all of them. There was this old man of the royal family and his son, both demanding to be killed, afraid of nothing. I should have tortured them, I know, but both were so brave and I had no time to spare, so I ordered them killed in an honorable manner."

"And this is precisely what you should not have been doing." Watching the warriors congregating at a distance, waiting for their leader's orders, Tlacaelel shrugged. "It is not the matter of honor, or of extracting information even, but the matter of legalities. You can't execute the citizens of your capital without a trial. You are not at war with these people, traitors or not, so this is an entirely different kind of procedure." He gestured at the hovering slave, motioning to bring his warriors' leader. "Not to mention that such men, as the ones whom you decided to grant their wishes, could have yielded you plenty of useful information.

You can't predict how people turn up under torture. The bravest and the loudest may be the first to scream for mercy, telling you everything they know."

"Oh, keep your *calmecac* lessons on the state affairs, laws, and human nature to calmer times." The Highlander's grin was light, his old unconcerned self peeking out for a heartbeat. "Coyotl will make the temple incident look legal enough, and we'll get all the missing information in Coatlinchan, you can be sure of that." A curt gesture set a new outburst of activity among the waiting warriors. "In the meanwhile, I better start moving. By sunset, I want this incident over and forgotten, with Coyotl not threatened in his own capital and upon his own throne, anymore." The broad face darkened. "I have my own problems to solve, so this annoying town better be settled by nightfall."

So you know, thought Tlacaelel, startled, staring at the closed-up face, his senses alerted. *And you take it surprisingly well. Were you tired of the spoiled royal cihua, anyway?*

"We searched through the entire city, looking everywhere." Turning to go, the Highlander shrugged, his shoulders stiff, lips pressed tight. "There is no trace, nothing. But it could be a good thing. There were quite a few bodies on the marketplace and on some dubious alleys behind the Plaza. More than usual, because of the Great Ceremony. And, well..." Another shrug made the formidable shoulders shudder. "It's a good thing. Means that the wild rascal is still alive, wherever he is and whatever he is up to."

Oh, yes, the wild twin. Tlacaelel's stomach twisted.

"Well, let us solve Coatlinchan first," he said, turning to go in his turn. "The boy may be back by then."

A curt nod was his answer, but the Highlander's back was stiff, rigid like that of a stone statue as he went away, calling for his warriors, reserved and foreboding, not his usual amiably forceful, breezy self.

CHAPTER 16

"You will have to get rid of the sword."

For the first time through many moons, Mictia found himself staring, lost for words. "What?"

The frightened man, clearly no more than a petty official, shuddered. "I brought your payment, everything you asked for," he said, glancing at the group of commoner looking types that lingered at some distance, their cloaks made of plain maguey, bulging with what looked like clubs hidden beneath the cheap material. "It's there in the warehouse, as you have asked. Take it, along with the sword, and leave. "

"You want me to take the sword?" repeated Mictia, incredulous, paying no attention to the man's pitiful efforts to bring reinforcements. He could deal with the club owners, and Nacatl was there, leaning against the warehouse's wall, as casual as any bystander, more dangerous than the marketplace bullies.

"Yes. I was told to ask you to take it to Tenochtitlan, or," the man's voice dropped, eyes darting everywhere, "or to dump it into the lake, if you wish it so."

Mictia narrowed his eyes, angered with the way this man's behavior unsettled him too, made him glance around more often than necessary. "What happened? What are you not telling me?"

"Nothing happened." Again, the frightened eyes darted, scanning the peaceful alley and the occasional passersby hurrying along in the heat of the high-noon sun. "You were paid to bring the sword to a certain place, not to…to the recipient's house. You have to take it back now. That is all." The panicked gaze clung to him, almost pleading.

"Did you receive a word from Texcoco?"

The man took a step back, his face losing the last of its color. "They are coming here," he mumbled. "The Warlord is coming."

"To Coatlinchan?"

Hating the stab of anxiety that made his stomach twist, Mictia weighed the circumstances. Grab the payment and sail, urged his instincts, the tickling sensation in his feet growing, making him wish to run. The damn owner of the sword was smart, smarter than the Acolhua opposition thought he was.

"By water or by land?" he asked, forcing his heartbeat into calmness. A panic would do nothing but harm. He must still have enough time, and anyway, the Warlord was coming for these people, the local opposition. What would he want with a simple commoner in a small boat?

"I don't know," muttered the man, wringing his hands. "The rumors are everywhere. Some said he executed highborn Acolhua already, those who dared to voice their displeasure with the Emperor."

"These rumors are false. There were no executions throughout the day of the ceremony. I was there!"

Glancing around once again, he frowned, trying to decide. If he refused to take the sword, the man might make trouble, start to argue, try to detain him by ordering his ill-fated commoners with clubs to do something. But a fight in the wharves areas was something neither of them could afford, not with the Warlord bearing upon them, rushing to take care of Coatlinchan's rebels. And yet, he delivered the dangerous cargo and was not about to take it back.

"He executed them this morning." The man peered at him, eyes terrified, wide open, their pupils enormous. "With no trial and no imperial judgment. He just slaughtered them like the last of the commoners."

Now it was Mictia's turn to stare. "This is nonsense. Your source is trying to scare you." He glanced at the warehouse, arriving at the decision. "Find me a good boat, and I will take everything you put for me in this pitiful hut."

"This is not a problem at all," exclaimed the man coming back to life at once. "Come with me—"

"Send someone to bring the boat here, to the nearest wharf, at once. I will be sailing in a short while, with or without the additional cargo." Disregarding the man's helpless gesture, he turned toward the warehouse. "Get one of your servants to help me carry the bags."

The wooden construction greeted him with its coolness, dim with the doorway and the openings in the roof being the only source of light, now wide open, helping with the illumination. He scanned the semidarkness, looking for traps. But, of course, there were none. Neither the terrified official nor his frightened master prepared anything of the sort. Unconcerned, Mictia leaned against the doorway, letting the man pass. From the corner of his eye, he saw Nacatl coming closer, ready to pounce. Good!

"Bring it all out."

A rapid exchange sent two of the servants toward the dark pile of bags in the far corner. Mictia paid them no attention, watching the opening near the roof, its shutter screeching with a slight breeze.

His senses alerting him for no reason, he went toward it, examining the chests piled one upon another in the way that made it easy to access it, to leap through it into the brilliance of the outside if necessary. Why would the owner of all these goods leave such a wide open gap? Didn't this area abound with thieves?

Leaning closer, he saw the footprints in the dust, too small to belong to a grown-up man. A piece of cloth hung from the sharp edge of the shutter, still fluttering, still holding someone's warmth. For the sake of the Underworld Spirits, he thought. It can't be...

The cry of the official made him jump, his hand straying for his dagger, tearing it free, ready to use it. The man was staring at the bags, aghast.

"It can't be!" he groaned, his voice vibrating, threatening to turn into a scream. "It can't be!"

In one leap, Mictia was beside him, grabbing his shoulders, shaking him violently. "Don't scream."

"But the sword...it's gone," mumbled the man, not struggling at all, his body limp, covered with sweat. "It's gone. It's not here. It disappeared. Oh, mighty gods!"

Mictia pushed him away with disgust, wiping his hands against his own cloak, noticing the slaves standing there trembling, ready to flee, not anxious to help their master in the least.

"Is anything else missing?" he barked, dashing back toward the wall opening.

"The sword, the sword, only the sword!" The man was clutching the nearby beam for support, gasping for breath. "We are doomed!"

Paying the moaning official no attention, Mictia mounted the piling chests in one leap, grabbing the windowsill, pulling himself up. The light enveloped him once again, making him blink. Behind his back, he heard the other men pouring in, the clubs owners probably, alerted by the wails. He didn't bother to look back, sliding through the opening with a customary ease, leaving no pieces of *his* clothes.

The filthy cur, he thought, his rage overwhelming, making his stomach heave. *Oh, I will kill you so very slowly.*

The dusty earth greeted him, hurting his knees with the impact of the jump. Not too high, not enough to make the dirty whelp break his other leg. Oh, but for laying his hands on the stinking piece of excrement!

He examined the dust, seeking footprints. Oh, yes, here the annoying cub must have landed, toppling most probably, unbalanced by his precious cargo. He hoped it hurt.

"Go back inside," he hissed, seeing Nacatl rounding the corner of the warehouse, eyes as round as a pair of plates, mouth gaping. "Make sure the bags are transferred to our boat. Tell the dirty scum to get us a new one in a hurry, as he promised. Intimidate him all you like."

"But—" The tall man was staring, wide-eyed. "What happened?"

"Later!" barked Mictia, eyes still upon the ground, looking for signs. "Do as I said, then wait. I'll be there shortly." His sanity returning, he looked up, measuring his companion with a piercing gaze. "Make sure the route is opened, so we can sail the moment I come back. And for all gods' sake, if you don't wait, you are a dead man. I will find you, and I will kill you slowly, cutting you piece by piece. And then I will do the same to that filthy family of yours. Is that clear?"

"Yes, yes, of course," breathed the man, aghast. "Of course I will wait."

"Good! Now go."

Alone for a moment, he scanned the sunlit alley with his gaze, taking in the smaller pathways between the clusters of warehouses, spreading in disarray. Cursing the mess of one-story wooden shacks that blocked his view, he forced his body into stillness, trying to control the vastness of his rage. *Think*, he ordered himself. *Calm down and think. Angry people make mistakes, and you have made too many already.*

He scanned the abandoned alley once again. Where would the filthy cub go? Where would he himself have gone in a similar situation?

To the lake shores. Where else? With his damaged leg, the dirty thing would have taken half a day to limp back to Texcoco, while stealing a boat would solve all his problems.

"We are doomed, doomed! The magical sword will kill us all." The moaning from the inside interrupted his line of thoughts, reaching him through the opening in the wall, making him wish to go back and kill the annoying official.

He contemplated doing it for a heartbeat. But that would mean a fight with the pitiful bunch of thugs, making noise, attracting attention. With the Warlord and his warriors bearing on Coatlinchan, this was the last thing they needed. Better to take the payment and go away, before the whole wretched town sank into the bloodbath the enraged War Leader, the fierce barbarian from the Highlands that he was, would be sure to drown it in. It wasn't wise to chase the accursed sword now that he had received the full payment, and he was yet to check the other bags, to make sure Acomotzin didn't try to cheat him. If it was all there, he had everything he wanted already. And yet...

Oh but the wondrous sword would fetch a huge price in the distant east, or at the north. Why, there was no telling what the lethal wonder covered with magical carvings would mean to the rich traders of the Big-Headed Mayans, or the fierce Tarascans. Even the people of Lake Chalco might wish to acquire such a relic, most probably aware of its existence, after decades of fighting with Tenochtitlan and its allies. Oh, they would pay mightily to possess such a thing. And there was also the boy. How dared the dirty cub cross his path once again, intentionally this time, with a clear purpose? Such gall! It would serve the whelp right to pay with his life for this cheekiness. It would teach him a much-needed lesson.

He remembered the object of his unrestrained fury, the round scowling face, the dark eyes narrow, wary, alerted, full of hatred, radiating power. An untamed thing. A true beast. It would be a waste to kill this one before he blossomed into something fearsomely good, and yet this time, he would have to do it. The boy was a real nuisance.

Watching the ground for clues, signs, maybe footprints, he slid away, heading toward the shores, moving with his usual speed and lack of sound. Somewhere around the wharves. The boy would be skulking there now, hindered by his precious cargo, waylaying a chance to steal a boat. Somewhere where it was not truly crowded, on the more secluded of the shores. Where it would be easier to intercept him.

The ground was too dry to leave clear prints, but his prey's peculiar way of walking helped. It was easy to track the uneven path, to follow as it twisted between the ugly huts, the low buildings tucked everywhere, in a decided disarray.

The nearest shores greeted him with a light breeze, teeming with people, the rumors not reaching the commoners and the businessmen element of Coatlinchan, or not touching it. What would the fishermen and the traders have to do with the aristocracy and their struggle for power?

Cursing inwardly, Mictia scanned the crowds, frustrated. It was too easy to disappear here, in the gushing river of people, in the loud exchanges and the noise of the toppling objects, in the yells and cursing and laughter, the hubbub the filthy whelp had clearly counted on, knowing all about blending with the crowds, disappearing in it, the dirty marketplace thief that he was. And yet, he could not slip away, not now. With nothing to pay for his fare back home, he would have to stay here until nightfall, until the opportunity to steal a boat would present itself. Good!

No, not so good. He, Mictia, had no time to spare. He could not afford to stay here for another day, not with the trouble the officials of this town were about to face, with him being involved, if not directly. He needed to sail away, and with no delays. The Warlord was most probably coming by land, but there was no telling what he would do once here. He may close the water traffic for some time, until he had dealt with the rebellious elements as brutally and swiftly as back in the capital. Had he truly executed highborn Texcocans without a trial? It didn't seem possible, but if he had, to Mictia's private opinion, it was a brilliant move. Frowned upon or not, this act would serve as warning to the rebels, would deter even the most courageous among the Acolhua discontents of the future.

Turning to go back, he heard the cries and then the people all around him stopped their activities, gasping and pointing, squinting against the fierce glow of the midday sun. Reflecting off the flickering water, not helped by the carpet of small waves, the sun made it difficult to see the canoes as they neared, bearing down on Coatlinchan's harbor like a deadly wave, or maybe a storm cloud, ominously organized.

"What's happening?" people cried out, hopping up and down, trying to see better.

Mictia didn't spend his time on the futile attempts. Elbowing his way out, he rushed toward the nearest building, a two-story-high wooden hut. In a few leaps, he was on its roof, stabilizing himself as he turned, his new vantage point offering a good view, the breeze cooling his sweaty face, calming his taut nerves.

However, what he saw did nothing to alleviate his anxiety. The Great Lake spread ahead, dotted by fishermen's boats and traders' vessels, now anxiously rowing out of the way, fleeing the closely formed fleet of canoes.

Heart sinking, he saw the warriors' colorful gear, the sun sparkling off the distant obsidian, the rich headdresses of their leaders standing out against the peaceful blue of the lake and the sky. His eyes counted the vessels, appraising their formation, seeking out their banners, something to recognize them by. Was it a foreign force or was the Warlord coming by the way of the lake?

The amount of vessels, about two times twenty of them, told him that it must have been the Warlord. A foreign invasion would be larger, and it would carry the symbols of their *altepetl*.

So the Warlord acted that swiftly, he thought, narrowing his eyes, trying to find the wharf by which they had left their boat earlier, a shabby side pier, out of the main traffic. Which should work to their advantage. The approaching fleet had no chance of covering the entire area. They might be able to sneak away anyway, maybe not now, as the whole place would be busy getting into a fit of panic and the Warlord would be busy making sure everyone was intimidated properly, but later, when the glorious leader would take his warriors into the city, to hunt down the opposition. No later than this afternoon.

Turning to climb down from his perch, he hesitated, his eyes catching a movement, a small figure rushing down one of the distant alleys, maneuvering around the baskets with fish, its uneven gait unmistakable. From his vantage point, he could see it most clearly, despite the distance. The wild thing was heading toward the city, not running but obviously in a hurry. Why?

For another heartbeat, he followed the boy's progress, his mind racing. Should he or should he not? It might not take him long to catch the little thief, certainly before the Warlord reaches the city. And hadn't he decided to wait before making an attempt to sneak through the approaching canoes, anyway?

Yet, Nacatl should be apprised of those plans, should be notified, told to wait patiently. What if he panicked, seeing the warriors nearing, with him, Mictia, not coming back? What if he tried to sail away, endangering their precious cargo?

The boy disappeared behind another curve of the road, and Mictia hesitated no more. A few careful leaps and he was back on the ground, not pausing to look, his instincts alerted, senses honed, eyes on the road, calculating, seeking the best ways to cut through the maze of the pathways, ready to pounce. A wolf on a trail.

He didn't look back. Nacatl better have enough sense to arrive at the correct solution to their problem, waiting patiently and doing nothing to attract the approaching warriors' attention. He had to trust his associate's judgment for once.

CHAPTER 17

Tlacaelel shifted, watching the nearing harbor and the frantic activity that seemed to burst out with their approach.

"Remember," he said, summoning the leaders of his mixed forces, the Acolhua man of the Highlander's choice. "We are not mooring on those wharves. We just stay where we are now and do nothing." He narrowed his eyes. "No harassment of the fishermen, no provocations, no contact whatsoever. Is that understood?"

The man nodded, having been briefed before they had set off this morning, and then again while on the journey. Trusting his subordinates to carry out his meticulously explained orders, unerring at appointing only the best fitting men anyway, this time Tlacaelel was uneasy, aware of the precariously sensitive nature of this particular enterprise.

Not enough that the Highlander was nearly out of his depth, dealing with the troubles that were clearly not in the province of his natural talents and inclinations, but he, Tlacaelel, actually had no right to be here. He was a Mexica leader, and with this whole mess originating at the disputably close relationship of the Acolhua with the Mexicas, his participation in putting the insurrection down could do the opposite, could escalate the matters into an outright revolt. It all depended on the Highlander's ability to handle the situation, and Tlacaelel's hopes were not high. The warrior and the leader of the warriors, though a smart, quick-thinking man, with wonderful abilities and skills, a politician his friend was not.

The Acolhua warrior nodded gravely. "Yes, Honorable Leader.

Your orders were made clear to every man in this force."

"Keep in close contact with our forces that stayed out of sight. I want to know of every vessel trying to sneak out undetected. Every one of them. Those are to be intercepted and detained for questioning."

"Yes, Honorable Leader. I will send their leading man a messenger to make sure they remember your orders."

"Do that." He shielded his eyes against the glow of the midday sun, watching the shore and the protruding lines of the wharves, its activity dying away. "Send some of your men into the city, to see if the Chief Warlord has arrived yet, or if there is any word of him nearing. I may wish to join him, so have an appropriate escort ready."

Hurry up, he thought urgently, watching the quieted harbor and the gaping fishermen all around them, their tools abandoned. *Solve your damn problems once and for all, and learn the lesson for future use.*

Oh, how could Coyotl be so amateurish, letting his opponents go free and unrestricted for moons or more, doing nothing to silence them? Did he truly think he was universally loved, the darling of the liberated Acolhua? No ruler, no matter how benevolent, good, merciful, or wise, could make the mistake of assuming something like that. Every sovereign had enemies aplenty. It took just a few dissatisfied nobles who thought they could do better, could occupy the throne with more flair, to stir the trouble, to make it look as though the entire capital or a province were in revolt. Just a few loudmouthed, enterprising fellows to ignite the hatred, and then it would spread like a fire in a dry grove, consuming everything on its way.

Luckily, the Acolhua discontents made a wrong move, hurried the events long before they were truly prepared. Stupid amateurs! To underestimate their Emperor and his most loyal follower, the Chief Warlord, was the peak of stupidity, but then, according to Tlalli, they might have realized that already.

He suppressed his grin. Oh, yes. The Highlander dealt with the capital nucleus of rebellion decisively and swiftly, departing to take care of the problematic province on the same day. So maybe he was underestimating his friend. Maybe there were merits to his style of doing things, politically subtle or not.

The closer he got to the Central Plaza, the more crowded the alleys and the pathways became. Pushing yet another wandering man out of his way, Mictia circumvented one more obstacle, this time a pile of fallen beams where, evidently, a stall had collapsed earlier on. The damn crowds!

Here, in the maze of well-to-do neighborhoods that spread between both plazas, the enterprising commoners were already erecting stands, prepared to sell foods and drinks and various trinkets to the passing crowds, knowing that every vacant space upon the main Plaza and between the temples had probably already been taken by the quicker and more influential traders' guild.

Tight-lipped, Mictia pressed on, disregarding the cursing of those whom he pushed aside, paying no attention to the indignant loudness of their protests. There was again no sign of the filthy rat, but he knew where the slimy bastard was heading, or where he would not be heading, to be precise. Not to the places with no people around, where it would be easy to catch and dispose of the cheeky cub. The little beast was smart enough to appreciate the protection of the unsuspecting crowds, the annoying marketplace rat that he was, just a ruffled, disheveled boy in torn clothes, an ordinary sight, sneaking in and out between milling people, drawing no special attention.

Zigzagging between the alleys, darting in unexpected directions, desperate to get out of Mictia's sight, the stubborn thing pressed on, not parting with his cumbersome, fairly heavy cargo that was evidently slowing him down, wearing him out, making his limp worse, looking as though about to collapse but never actually succumbing to the temptation of trying to rest. A man of less experience would have lost the track already, but Mictia was like a wolf on a trail of footprints, determined, unerring, finding his prey every time anew. It was now only a matter of time before the boy would make a mistake of letting his pursuer close enough to be grabbed without creating too much fuss. The ruffled cub was bound to grow exhausted soon enough. And yet, how soon? The wait was the luxury Mictia could not afford. With its harbor already invaded, this town would fill with warriors in no time, and he needed to return to their boat. Nacatl might not be able to deal with the problem the approaching warriors created. He was bound to panic and do something silly, like trying to sneak away despite the blockade. A good subordinate, his associate was not to be trusted with making his own decisions, not under such precarious circumstances.

With the larger plaza in sight, Mictia doubled his efforts, knowing that it would be more difficult for the boy now, in such an open space. The little rascal could always try to dart into various pathways between the pyramids and the temples, but it would isolate him, put him out of the protective crowds, make it easier for Mictia to find and catch up with him at long last. So the cub would have to stay in the open, under Mictia's watchful eyes, to wait for him to make a mistake.

Pressing on, he saw the torn cloak swinging between the stalls and the animated people, the rich colors of the still-clean-looking bag easy to pick out, not fitting with the tousled appearance of its courier. The idea struck.

"Thief, thief!" he screamed at the top of his lungs, waving his hands and pointing. "Help me. That boy stole my bag!"

The people next to him, a group of commoners by the hastily organized stall with tortillas, stopped their conversation and cursed, startled.

"Please, help me." With pretended humility but still shouting as loudly as he could, Mictia faced them briefly, not willing to lose sight of his prey. "That little thief over there stole my goods."

The already worked-up people, excited by all the happenings, paid much attention.

"Where? Where? What thief?"

They crowded him, blocking his view, making him lose the boy for a brief moment.

"Over there, that dirty little thing with a colorful bag!" He pushed his way through them, worried. What if the boy darted in another direction, not heading toward the Plaza as he assumed?

"Follow me!"

Beginning to sprint again, he saw the limping figure breaking into a frantic run, not making the mistake of assuming that the fuss behind his back involved anyone else. That one had too much experience with crowds and theft.

Doubling his efforts, Mictia pressed on, not trying to avoid catching the boy in the open now that the crowds were on his side. No one would bother to prevent him from retrieving his allegedly stolen bag, or dragging the offender away, struggling and screaming his innocence as he might.

Evidently, the boy had realized it too, as he seemed to be putting it all into the effort of reaching the Plaza in order to disappear in its crowds. As though he could outrun anyone. Mictia grinned, closing on his prey, his heart pumping in his ears, spreading excitement throughout his limbs. Almost there.

A litter sprung ahead, coming from another alley, blocking their way. Surrounded by armed slaves and some warriors, the litter-bearers paused, bettering their grip on the wooden poles, waiting for instructions. A familiar face peeked from behind the curtain. Acomitzin? What was this fat fowl doing here? wondered Mictia briefly, recognizing the pudgy form of Coatlinchan's leading noble.

Then the irrelevant thoughts disappeared as the boy, instead of running around the obstacle, dived beneath it, rolling between the sturdy men's feet, avoiding being trampled on with the swift elegance of movement only his limp rendered impossible. Scratched and dust-covered, he was on the other side, on his feet again, dashing toward the hubbub of the Plaza, gaining a clear advantage.

Forced to detour, Mictia cursed, bypassing the panic-stricken followers of the litter, paying them no attention. The Plaza was so crowded! Waving their hands, talking in a breathless rush, well-to-do citizens and commoners, traders in their colorful attire and a topknot, peasants with their hair tied behind their backs and their loincloths just a simple piece of cloth, they congregated everywhere, highly agitated, more excited than afraid, looking around, exchanging gossip.

The boy disappeared in the commotion as though by magic, but Mictia pushed the wave of helpless rage away, scanning the crowded space meticulously, group by group, working his way toward the central pyramid.

"There!" Apparently, some of his volunteered helpers from the alley had followed, not giving up. The thieves were a nuisance, to chase them – always an entertainment.

"Where?"

A non-committal wave indicated a strange, three or four-story construction with a temple atop it, not pyramid-like but for a wide slab of stone composing its base. The man and his friends sprinted away, in a frenzy of pursuit. Cursing, Mictia raced after them, not wishing to let these commoners lay their filthy hands on his prey, neither the boy nor his cargo. They were supposed to render the protection of the crowds impossible for the little bastard to use, but here, on the Plaza, they were nothing but a hindrance.

Maneuvering between the obstacles, he cut to his left, catching a glimpse of the, by now, familiar sway of the colorful bag. Unable to see the boy, he was certain that the little rascal was trying to make his way to the other side of the construction, hoping to dive behind it, gaining enough time to disappear into the nearby alleys.

The light, dimmed by the strangely high wall's shadow, poured in strange patterns, making the temple upon it look more ominous. The boy was nowhere to be seen, but the commotion behind the corner pointed the way.

Racing to round it, he almost bumped into the wild thing as the boy leapt into his path, his face smeared with so much sweat and dirt it turned unrecognizable, his cloak missing, limbs scratched, but his hands clutching the precious bag with the same grim firmness the determined eyes radiated.

"You are done for, you dirty little rat!" cried out Mictia, pouncing on his prey, unerring now, certain of his catch.

Yet, somehow, the wild thing twisted out of his reach, leaping toward the wide stones, while on the other side, his chasers already appeared, shouting and waving their hands, victorious. Trapped, the boy gave them a fierce look, then, before they surged forward, he leaped up the lower ledge, grabbing protruding stones with both hands, pulling himself hurriedly, climbing up like a monkey, the bag hanging upon his shoulder, swaying awkwardly, hindering his progress but not enough to make him lose his balance or slow his desperate dash for freedom.

"Drop the damn bag!" roared Mictia, catching the culprit's foot briefly, but slipping, left with a worn-out sandal to clutch.

"What a beast!" called people, the chasers and the bystanders alike, many with admiration.

"He doesn't want to face the courts, this one."

"Get down, boy. The judges may be more merciful than the priests up there," called out someone, making everyone laugh.

All the while, the boy worked his way up, not sneaking a single glance behind, in panic most probably. He was quite a climber, apparently, better at that than at running.

"Maybe he wishes to appease the Mother of Gods with some special offering," said a man who had participated in the chase, breathing heavily, laughing hard. The temple atop the strange construction, indeed, belonged to the revered goddess Coatlicue.

Mictia had a hard time restraining himself from killing someone. He could climb this wall swiftly, catching the dirty rat as easily as on foot, but for the sacrilegious nature of such an effort. The boy was beyond the law anyway, and he was a child, not accountable for some deeds, not yet. What he did made people laugh. Yet, if a respectable man like himself were to climb a pyramid, or any other temple construction, the crowds would grow angry, eager to catch him and drag him, and not the boy, to the judges. Or worse yet, to the priests.

He saw the boy slipping, swaying dangerously, regaining his balance as though by a miracle, as though the goddess of the temple above was on his side. Shielding his eyes, he watched the small figure clinging to the damp stones with his entire body, afraid to breathe but still pressing the bag, determined not to let it go.

Putting himself on the path of the possible fall, Mictia willed his heartbeat into calmness. At least he could try to catch the sword should the boy fall. Or he could wait for the little beast to get down, or maybe climb after him the moment the crowds would lose their interest and go away. He just needed some time and some patience, but this was the thing he could not afford, he knew, the shouts from the other side of the Plaza drawing his attention.

With people pointing and gasping, he held his breath, even from their far side, seeing the warriors pouring onto the wide square before the main pyramid, looking victorious against the glow of the high-noon sun.

CHAPTER 18

"The stupid rats barricaded themselves in that house, those who were stupid enough to follow their would-be a leader."

The Highlander spat onto the ground, his face a study of excitement and irritation, eyes sparkling. Dust-smeared and sweat-covered, the man nevertheless seemed to be full of energy and purpose, his forceful self again, the worn-out, cornered expression gone.

Tlacaelel hid his grin. Some people needed a good sleep to restore their energies; this one needed a good march in the head of his warriors and the prospect of a battle.

"Whose house?" He frowned, remembering his purpose. He was here to make sure his friend did nothing stupid or rash. And to bring him the news.

"Acomitzin's, of course. The highest of the local nobility, that fat lump of meat, may his filthy flesh rot until this World of the Fifth Sun ends." The spark in the widely spaced eyes intensified. "Don't worry. I'm not going to storm it. They can rot there for all I care. Sooner or later, they'll have to come out." The wide shoulders lifted in an indifferent shrug. "I left enough guards to greet them upon their exit, while rounding up those who had more sense than to panic that stupidly. I predict some of my 'captives' may see a certain clemency from Coyotl, but not those bastards."

The lake of people swarmed all around, spilling into the nearby alleys and the more distant corners of the larger plaza, a round affair of low pyramids and temples, dotted with fountains, odd statues, and stalls with food and drinks. The citizens of

Coatlinchan seemed to be treating the armed visit from the Capital more like a holiday and a chance of making an additional profit rather than as the reprimand from the higher authorities. They found no fault with their favorite young ruler, the legitimate heir to the Acolhua throne. The reported restlessness and discontent were probably limited to some nobles, not touching even the influential traders of the first and the second ranks.

So much for you and your exaggerations, you haughty Acolhua princess, lousy politician that you are, thought Tlacaelel, careful to keep these thoughts well-hidden while facing the lady's husband. *What will he do when he finds out?*

Echoing his thoughts, the Highlander grinned. "The citizens of this town know better." Strolling toward the main square, pushing his way through the crowds with firm politeness, he answered people's greetings, striking up brief conversations, smiling broadly, a perfect politician. What a surprise!

Reaching his destination, the main pyramid of Coatlinchan, a mediocre affair of unpainted slabs of stone and a temple, the Highlander paused, turning around, gesturing for the following crowds to halt.

"People of Coatlinchan," he cried out, leaping up the lower stairs, standing above the crowds, his hands spread, legs wide apart, his cloak swaying with the light breeze, his jewelry shining in the afternoon sun, enhancing the broadness of his arms and chest, the turquoise piercing in his lip glittering dully, the image of a perfect warrior. "Nezahualcoyotl, your mighty Emperor, sent me here, to visit this richest, strongest, and largest town of his provinces, to tell you all, his most loyal citizens, how proud he is of you, how satisfied. Yesterday, when mighty Tonatiuh, our Father Sun, was at its highest, watching proudly, your sovereign, the lawful ruler of Texcoco, was anointed to rule the Acolhua lands for many moons, many summers, to come. He is the greatest, the wisest, the strongest man of these lands, and he will rule you wisely, just and heedful of your welfare and your well-being." His voice peaked, rolling down the stairs, spreading upon the Plaza in powerful waves, reaching those who stayed too far, unable to push their way closer. "Serve your Emperor loyally.

Trust him to take care of you. Always remember that he has your best interests in his heart, his warm beating heart that he would give to the gods gladly should they request that of him in order to spread their benevolence upon you." A piercing gaze seemed to be reaching everywhere, traveling the lake of faces, forceful and sincere. "Do not listen to lies of malicious people bent on nothing but their personal gain. Do not open your ears to false rumors. Nezahualcoyotl will give his life for you, but as long as he lives, he will dedicate all his vigor, his strength, his wisdom, and his immense power to the raising of the Acolhua people. He will make you as powerful as you used to be before the Tepanecs, and he will take you to the greater glory. He had sworn to do so while accepting the sacred regalia, with the gods watching and proud, receiving their due, feeding on the blood of the captured Tepanecs."

Not bad, thought Tlacaelel, fascinated. The man was an orator, and not a poor one at that. Even the technique of pitching one's voice higher than usual was employed, making one's words reach far and wide, although this particular trick the Highlander might have learned through the last few summers, leading large forces and needing to address his warriors all at once from time to time. Still, it was a relief to see his friend doing so well, spreading confidence and elation instead of terror and fear.

Standing a few steps lower, but still slightly above the crowds, he glanced at the faces surrounding them, seeing their expectation, their hope, their excitement. They hung on the Warlord's every word, admiring the magnificent warrior and leader, trusting him. Quite an achievement in the reportedly discontent city, where some of the leading aristocracy had just been rounded up, to be hauled to the Capital for a trial in the Imperial Court.

The Highlander went on, keeping his speech short and crisp, matter-of-fact, stating his claims and promises, telling them how great Coyotl was, how lucky they were to be blessed with a ruler like him, young, vigorous, concerned with nothing but their well-being. Which was true enough, come to think of it, but he wondered how his friend managed to look so sincere, so unconcerned when all the man wanted was to charge full speed toward the wharves and the lake shores, following the encouraging and unsettling news Tlacaelel had brought and managed to whisper in his ear just before they entered the plaza.

He frowned, remembering the canoe that tried to break his blockade, sneaking along the low wharves and under the higher constructions, obviously anxious to get away. His warriors, under the orders to detain anyone who attempted to sail, signaled the man, but the stupid lump of meat reacted by starting to row yet more vigorously.

So the warriors pounced, boarding the stubborn vessel, frustrating the man's attempts to resist with the easy familiarity of seasoned fighters. Tlacaelel's personal forces were hand-picked, highly trained and experienced, as lethal as the best of the weapons, unerring in judgment.

Following the orders, they did not kill the disarmed owner of the loaded canoe, but dragged him all the way to where Tlacaelel was, presenting their leader with the prisoner and his unusual cargo. So many riches in one place made every eyebrow rise. Was the man a trader who just finished a successful deal?

A question Tlacaelel asked, receiving a dark glare for an answer. Not deterred but pressed for time, he inspected the boat, then went straight for the more forceful of the interrogation methods. A quick beating didn't work, but when a few of the man's fingers were cut off, and his manhood threatened to follow the suit, the tale came out, a treasure of information that made Tlacaelel's head reel.

A few heartbeats later, he was out of his boat, distributing rapid instructions to the Acolhua part of his forces, sending them to comb the harbor and the city, as apparently, both the sword and the twin were here, in Coatlinchan, unharmed but in danger. The other black-clothed killer, the leader, according to the bleeding man, was out there, determined to get both escaped possessions back.

He had caught up with the Highlander only when the man was already nearing the Plaza, full of purpose and in great spirits, about to talk to the expectant crowds, having dealt with the worst of the crisis already.

Unwilling to upset his friend before the delicate mission was completed, Tlacaelel had related only the basic nature of his news, that the sword and the boy were around, running lose somewhere, probably unharmed. And now, standing near the base of the main pyramid, listening to the deep voice rolling down the Plaza, enveloping the crowds, working them up into an excited frenzy, he was glad he didn't make his friend worry more than necessary. The improvised address to Coatlinchan citizens was exactly the thing this largest of the Acolhua provinces needed. It looked good, appropriate, that the newly anointed Emperor sent his Chief Warlord to talk to his subjects, to encourage them and to promise them a great future. Not yet a day had passed since the ceremony in the Great Capital, and here was this most important leader of the warriors, thanking them for their continued support, assuring them that the Emperor cared not only for Texcoco, but for all his Acolhua subjects. A good move.

Watching the Highlander beginning to descend the wide stairs, nodding to people, answering them briefly, Tlacaelel pushed his way forward, letting his warriors clear his path in the pressing crowds.

"Not badly done, Warlord," he said quietly, when the Highlander was beside him, having as much difficulty progressing forward.

A non-committal wave of a hand was his answer. "I'm off for your boats."

"Why there?"

"Ocelotl will be somewhere around, trying to steal a boat. Or maybe he already got one. How long has it been since he got away?" The dark eyes were upon him, strained, worried, the broad face again closed and unreadable, full of shadows, its pallor back.

"When we get to the wharves, you'll have your chance to question my witness. He is still alive, I believe." Tlacaelel narrowed his eyes, puzzled. "Why would the boy try to do something as complicated as stealing a boat? I would be running back to Texcoco following the regular roads, if I were him."

"He can't run as well as you do."

"Oh." Following the wide back, as his friend charged forward, ignoring the swarm of people, Tlacaelel nodded. "Well, my warriors may have found him by now. I sent nearly all of your Acolhua forces to search around the wharves as much as around the city."

"Good!"

They had reached the outskirts of the Plaza when he recognized his Mexica minor leader, rushing toward them, gesturing ardently.

"Honorable Leader!" The man halted at a respectable distance, not daring to come closer than permitted in the vicinity of the Head Adviser, Tlacaelel's personal guards barring his way.

"What is it?"

"We may have found someone fitting the description."

"Where?" The Highlander, who was already some distance ahead, halted so abruptly that his sandals made a screeching sound, and two of his warriors bumped into him, muttering apologies.

"Here on the Plaza, Honorable Leaders. There is a commotion around the goddess's temple over there..." The man froze at the act of pointing, as the Acolhua Warlord was already away, charging back toward the square, shoving the people aside, his warriors running after him, desperate to keep up, having no chance.

"Take me there," said Tlacaelel, nodding at the stunned man. "And hurry up."

Thinking himself prepared for any sort of trouble involving the wild twin, he still found himself gaping, staring at the steep wall and the small figure perching upon a narrow ledge, half way up it, clinging to the damp stones, peering at the crowds down below. Bruised and half-naked, the boy looked bizarre, belonging anywhere but in the sacredness of such a place, clutching a large cumbersome bag close to his body, sheltering it, as though unwilling to let it neither fall nor to bump against the hard stones of the wall. Down the paved square, the priests were waving their hands, shouting indignantly, while the people around them pointed, amused and expectant, welcoming the show.

And into this scene, assumed Tlacaelel, broke the Acolhua Warlord like a lethal whirlwind, sweeping away everything in his path. By the time Tlacaelel neared, he was down the wide base, evidently done shouting instruction.

Grabbing the protruding ledge of the lower slab, the dignified leader pulled himself up, beginning to scale the wall with the familiar easiness, sacrilege or not, his warriors gaping, staring like the rest of the crowd, lost for words. Even the priests stopped their shouting.

The boy up the wall relaxed visibly, gathering enough courage to attempt climbing down, lowering himself carefully, fingers of one hand digging into a crevice between the stones, one of his feet sliding along the wall, seeking a new foothold.

"Don't. Stay where you are!" shouted the Highlander, himself already partway up, sure-footed and graceful, a spectacular vision of swaying cloak and well-muscled, glistening body, making the climb look like an easy work.

The boy froze, then tried to pull his leg back, wavering dangerously, the swaying bag weighing him down. For a moment, he looked as though about to fall, then he regained his balance, flattening his limbs against the cold stones.

Tlacaelel let out his breath, willing the boy to succeed, to hold on, not to let go, not until his father reached him. Just how the Highlander was to take himself and the child down safely he didn't know, but there was no doubt that the man would manage. He always did.

His eyes wandered toward the bag, guessing. How, in the name of the Underworld Spirits, did the wild thing manage to get involved?

The people stopped pointing, watching spellbound, exchanging excited whispers. Many moved, careful to stay away from the path of the climbers should one of them slip and fall down, many but a squat, broadly built man, who positioned himself just beneath the wall, his eyes on the boy, narrowed against the blazing sun, very concentrated. For a moment, Tlacaelel studied him, noticing the richness of the man's girdle as opposed to the simplicity of his loincloth, the knife tucked in it expertly, an expensive-looking thing, not fitting the picture of the regular commoner the rest of the man's attire suggested.

Back upon the wall, the boy resumed his climbing down, disregarding his father's previous orders. For a while it went well, then he wavered, struggling not to fall as his leg slipped and only the strength of his fingers seemed to be holding him glued to the dusted stones. The bag strap was slipping from his shoulder, and he flopped one of his hands frantically, trying to stabilize his cargo.

"Drop it," called the Highlander, doubling his efforts, climbing swiftly, but not swiftly enough. "Let it fall."

The boy's voice rang hysterically, trembling with tears. "I can't, Father. It'll break!"

The Highlander hesitated for only a heartbeat, his back as tense as the stones he clung to.

"It won't, Ocelotl. It's magical, remember?" he called out, his voice dripping with warmth. "Nothing will happen to it. Let it go."

Tlacaelel caught his breath, feeling his own body straining, as though fighting for his life up the pyramid's wall too. *No*, he thought. *No. Don't let it fall. Don't let it finish like that.*

"Drop it!"

It was an order, a firm order from the War Leader whose commands were followed by every dweller in these lands, thousands of warriors and many more Acolhua citizens.

Like in a dream, he watched the bag's strap sliding along the thin arm, yet the small palm closed around the torn material as it reached it, swinging the bag back up, the muddied fingers seeking a new fracture between the old stones, a new crevice to dig into.

For a heartbeat, it looked hopeless, with nothing but his desperation and the mesmerized gazes of the crowds below keeping the boy glued to the wide stones. Then, the courageous cub regained his balance, wincing as the bag banged loudly against the wall. Not daring to breathe as it seemed, he moved his arm slightly, trying to prevent another clash, but as he did this, the bag tilted and the sword began sliding out, as though reluctant to face its end stuffed inside the suffocating material.

Sparkling against the glow of the strong afternoon sun, the obsidian spikes caught the light, sending it back in the brilliant glitter that hurt the eyes, the ominous carvings too distant to see, but obviously there, filling the air with their presence.

Incredulous, Tlacaelel watched the boy twisting his body, struggling to prevent the fall of the carved magic with his leg, succeeding at slowing it down. Pressing into the wall, he reached for his precious cargo with one hand, releasing his grip of the peeling stone, wavering precariously.

Heart pounding, Tlacaelel stared at the small figure, willing it to hold on. Slowly, the boy managed to close his fingers around the carved hilt, and now froze, catching his breath. The Highlander doubled his efforts, not wasting any more words on trying to make his son listen, having a difficult time of his own on the steep wall, which was old, but sturdily built, the stones fitting closely, their plaster mostly intact.

Tlacaelel beckoned one of his warriors' leaders. "Take your men and bring here as many mats from the traders as you can carry." He waved toward the Plaza. "Hurry!" With the cold stones offering no hope of a softer landing the earthen ground might have, he could at least spread some of the straw rags to try and soften the impact should the Highlander, or the boy, fall.

Up on the wall, the boy cried out, his fingers claws, burrowing into the cracks between the stones, one of his bare feet slipping, brushing against the wall frantically, seeking a new foothold.

"Ocelotl, let it go!" The Highlander's voice shook, the fear in it obvious, mixing with desperation. He had never heard his fierce friend displaying so much uncertainty, so much tension or fear.

The boy was slipping, his fingers scratching the old stones, making the old plaster peel, showering the climbing Warlord and the crowds below with clouds of dust. Still, he didn't let the sword go. One hand gripping the broken edge of a bulging brick, the bleeding fingers clutching its sharp rims, slowing his slide downwards, he froze for another heartbeat, making the crowds gasp.

The Highlander was leaping up the wall like a cornered

animal, with no consideration for his own safety anymore. It might have been built of wide steps the way he pushed with his legs, finding a new foothold every time anew, as though by some miracle, as though planning his moves, his arms powerful, pulling up, no sword hindering his progress. He must have untied his own weapon before beginning his climb.

The boy's fingers were slipping, one by one, and still, he didn't let the sword go, the magical object now a part of him, ruling his mind. Or maybe it was the power of the sword, thought Tlacaelel in desperation. Was it determined to take the boy with it, not about to go down all by itself?

In desperation, he ground his teeth, seeing the boy beginning to slide again, unable to hold his weight on the strength of a few bleeding fingers.

"Let the damn sword go," he breathed, unable to hold his tongue anymore, his muscles cramped, fists clenched tight.

The fall stopped again. Clinging to yet another crack, this time supported with his legs, the boy flattened his body against the wall, not even breathing anymore as it seemed. The sword screeched, banging against the dusted stones. Then it froze, too.

By the time the Highlander neared, the silence was so profound, only the buzzing of insects were left to remind them that the world was still alive, still functioning.

Letting out his breath, Tlacaelel watched the man reaching up, propping the boy from below, his palm large and strong, radiating power. He wished he could hear the words his friend was most certainly saying, climbing closer, supporting, giving the boy his own strength.

From the corner of his eye, he saw his warriors coming back, carrying armloads of rough straw mats, the traders in their wake, indignant but not daring to protest. Before taking his gaze back toward the figures on the wall, with the sword now safely in its rightful owner's hand, not hindering his progress at all as it seemed but protecting and adding to his strength as always, he noticed that the strange-looking commoner with the knife was gone.

CHAPTER 19

The moon shone brightly, lighting his way. It was still very near to being full, like on the night of the theft, a mere two days ago, although back then the benevolent deity was barely there, obscured by the gathering clouds.

Mere two days? It seemed like a lifetime now. He spat upon the ground, then hurried on, diving into the darker pathway, careful to keep in the shadows. The moon made his progress easier, but it also exposed him more than necessary. Unlike many people, he could see well in the darkness, and the silvery light was more of a hindrance, especially since he still wore his regular outfit, a loincloth and little else, with his black clothes gone. Gone along with all his possessions, everything he had – his gear, his weapons, his riches, his associates, his honor and reputation, his self-respect, even.

The black wave was back, threatening to shatter the painfully gained semblance of self-control he had reached with such an effort, working to force himself into lucid thinking for the remnants of the afternoon, since he had returned to the harbor, to discover that everything was taken, robbed from him, going into the greedy hands of Tenochtitlan warriors and their filthy leader, the Head Adviser, who felt the need to shove his long aristocratic nose into the Texcoco affairs.

The harbor was buzzing with rumors, so he had heard it all, wandering around, blind with fury. Every possible version of the afternoon's events reached his ears. So many stories! From the Chief Warlord conquering the Plaza with little else than his words, to the same man flying up the temple's wall in order to retrieve the sword that had appeared up there magically, brought by the Mother of the Gods herself.

How stupid! As though he had not seen it with his own eyes, watching the precious weapon being taken from him; that and his hostage, the filthy boy determined to save the damn sword even against his own father's orders. He should have been dead, so many times over, fallen off the wall, drowned in the lake, cut by Mictia himself or his associate in that dirty warehouse back in Texcoco, on many, many other appropriate occasions, yet the cub seemed as though charmed, as magical as the sword itself, sent there to disrupt Mictia's mission, to make it fail.

Back on the wharves, he had cursed venomously, indifferent to the people's stares. It made them stop talking, sometimes. Which was a mercy. He did not want to hear any of these anymore. He had had enough! He needed time, and some peace and quiet. He needed to think, to decide what to do. But what was there to think about? What was there remained to decide, besides going away, defeated, with nothing but his skills to carry him into a new life, a filthy commoner with no means and no reputation.

He hit the pole of the nearest wharf again and again, until he could not feel his arm anymore. The pain refreshed him, made him concentrate, channeling his thoughts. The sword might still be here in Coatlinchan. If he were the Warlord, he would not be rushing back to Texcoco on the same day. He would have stayed to tidy this province's affairs, to drive the learned lesson home. It would be unseemly to just turn around and leave, not on the same day. And if so...

With his interest piquing and some of the clear thinking returning, he had wandered toward the marketplace, listening intently, careful to draw no attention from the warriors who now abounded all around. There was no telling if his description wasn't circulating among the Acolhua forces. The boy knew what he looked like, no one better.

The rage came back, subdued again, but with much difficulty. The filthy cub! But he would be made to pay. If he, Mictia, was lucky; if the gods were on his side. Maybe he should find revered Tezcatlipoca's temple and make a private offering to the mighty god before embarking on this last attempt to best his fate.

For the mission ahead of him was difficult, dangerous – impossible even. The Warlord would be guarding his sword and his child zealously now, alerted. And yet it was Mictia's last chance to gather back some of his dignity, the last of his self-respect. If successful in stealing the sword once again, he would go away satisfied, promisingly rich, avenged. And if the gods were to offer a chance of killing the Warlord, or his annoying son, he would thank the mighty deities and would never look back in regret.

The two-story house towered ahead, triggering the memory, igniting his anger anew. The night before, he had approached it clad in his black clothes, invisible, a part of the night, a confident man in control, with power, means, and purpose, regarded in fear, even by the local nobility. He ground his teeth. Now he was just a commoner sneaking along, bent on a desperate attempt to salvage the last of his pride.

For a while, he stayed still, huddled in the shadow of a wide-branched tree, watching the dark mass of the fence. Two armed silhouettes guarded it, leaning tiredly against the tall poles. At this time of the night the guards were usually sleepy, he knew, not alerted, uninterested, looking forward to the end of their mission. He watched them for another heartbeat, then slipped away, circumventing the familiar grounds. Taking his knife out, he crossed the patch of the open earth, hurrying toward the protective darkness of the wall.

It was eerily quiet, like always in this part of the night. Pressing against the high poles, he listened. There seemed to be no warriors in the courtyard, but he waited for some time, making sure.

His senses alerted, he scaled the fence hurriedly, not lingering on its top, although it might have given him a clearer view of the gardens. The moon shone brightly, too brightly. Even had he worn his special outfit, he would have been outlined clearly against the illuminated sky; but his clothes were gone, together with his riches and everything he had. Another wave of anger crashed against the firmness of his willpower. Later. After he had had his revenge.

Crouching in the thick shadow, he watched the warriors guarding the back entrance, leaning against the wall, obviously tired, their eyes on a small balcony of the second floor. Watching it. He counted them briefly, assessing their state of alertness and their gear. Satisfied, he waited, patient, in his element now.

Twenty more heartbeats. A hundred.

Two warriors got up and left. Another one was stretching tiredly. Bettering his grip on the club, he strolled away, scanning the darkness. The last remained where he was, alone now, pacing back and forth, guarding the balcony. It was time.

Mictia slid forward, the terrace above casting its shadow, helpful, his knife out and ready, its hilt comfortable, fitting his palm. No sound disturbed the silence as he launched, burying the chopped blade in the man's throat, just below his chin. Catching the twitching body, he eased it to the ground, then listened.

No alarm sounded, and no hurried footsteps could be heard. Satisfied, he straightened up, then, kicking the body into the thickest of the shadows, he eased the wooden partition away.

The next heartbeat saw him crouching in the dark corridor, breathing with relief. He always felt better in the darkness. Soundlessly, he slipped along the plastered walls, careful not to brush against the partly shot screens. Quick inspection confirmed his suspicion. Those rooms were full of warriors, now sleeping, enjoying their well-deserved rest.

Farther down the corridor, he could see armed silhouettes, standing next to the shut screen, guarding it. Was this where the Warlord was sleeping? There was no ready answer to that, but his instincts urged him on, whispering that his target would choose the higher floor, probably the one adjacent to the balcony that the warriors from the outside were watching.

The staircase was empty, easy to ascend, but the voices reached him as he neared the top, giving him barely enough time to dive into a small alcove, pressing behind a statue of a giant serpent, holding his breath. No torches lit the darkness, but without his special outfit, he felt naked, helplessly exposed.

The voices neared, two warriors, going down, talking in whispers. He let them pass, not trying to hurt them. They were very close, temptingly unheeded, but their fall down the stairs would create noise and, anyway, he was here for another purpose.

Waiting for a few more heartbeats, he retraced his steps back toward the balcony, reaching another set of main rooms. Oh yes, this doorway was guarded as well. He smiled grimly, pleased with his instincts.

Huddled in the shadow of yet another alcove, he waited, patient now, in his element again. The time of failure and indecision was over. He would sail away, the owner of the revered sword before the dawn broke. And he would have his revenge before he left.

One of the warriors shifted to better his position, leaning against the wall, obviously sleepy. His companion nudged him with an elbow, then got to his feet. A few paces down the corridor brought him into perfect range. Mictia pounced as the man began turning away, his knife slashing upward, in a perfect thrust, disappearing in the depths of yet another throat.

It was over in a heartbeat. The other man didn't even manage to gasp before Mictia was beside him, stabbing him in between his ribs, his free palm pressing against the gaping mouth, easing the twitching body to the floor, letting the blood soak into the polished bricks.

The partition moved reluctantly, yet it made no sound, the wood being of the best quality, well-oiled. As silent as a shadow, Mictia slipped in, assessing the room, searching for signs of danger.

There were none. A light breeze came through the open shutters of the balcony, relating strange peacefulness. The moon streamed in, silvery, generous. It lightened scattered chests, piling mats, some weapons, not reaching the sleeping figures curled in the farther corner, concentrating on a low table, instead.

He caught his breath, watching the carvings bathing in the shimmering light, glowing eerily, having a life of their own. Unable to take his eyes off the luminous images, the jaguar baring its teeth, the serpent-like form twisting between the obsidian spikes, Mictia came closer, not even noticing that he was walking. He just *had* to touch the magic, to take hold of it. Carrying it for two days, stuffed in a stupid bag, he'd had no idea what a wonder it was, did not realize the real extent of its power.

From up close, the patterns glowered at him, as though warning him, yet the wish to wrap his hands around the carved hilt, to feel its weight and its warmth, or maybe its coldness, grew. Would the dark power it held flow into him the moment he wielded it? He needed to know.

Like in a dream, he reached out, his senses honed, instincts alerted, limbs trembling, heart racing. The carvings glared at him, alive in the moonlight, now unmistakably. They called him. The jaguar on the base of the shaft stared with its hollow eyes, challenging. Its bared fangs were dark, having soaked in many summers of blood offerings; all the lives that the sword must have taken.

Engrossed in the staring contest, he didn't notice the change, yet something warned him of the looming danger. His hesitation forgotten, he grabbed the sword with both hands, jumping back, toward the safety of the opened shutters and the balcony behind it, both offering the route of escape.

The knife hissed close by, cutting the air. It crashed against the wall and fell, clattering on the stones of the floor. Mictia's palms wrapped around the wide shaft tighter, feeling the carvings, not trembling anymore.

"You came back!"

To his surprise, the Warlord did not leap forward but stayed where he was, as deadly and alerted as the carved jaguar, ready to pounce, or to evade the attack, yet keeping still. Why?

The answer presented itself readily as Mictia's eyes took in the small tussled form, propped on one arm, frozen in shock. An attack on the intruder would force the Warlord to leave his cub unprotected. He felt the surge of relief washing through his body.

"Yes, I came back to kill you and to take the sword," he said quietly, not coming closer, taunting, seeing the frustrated rage spilling out of the dark eyes. "After I kill you, the sword will become mine, the sword and the power it holds."

"You will not manage as much as to wield it," bellowed the man, frightening in his impotent fury, his eyes darting toward the other, regular, sword, thrown carelessly on the pile of clothes, not far away.

Ready to pounce, Mictia took a step forward, enjoying himself, his grin provoking, difficult to hide. He could attack the man the moment he tried to dart for the other sword, or he could pounce toward the momentarily unprotected boy, killing the cub or taking him hostage once again, both options delightful, both clear to his enemy as well. The smoldering fire in his rival's eyes told him so, boring into him like the hollow orbs of the sword's carving, with the same destructive, unrestrained hatred.

Yet, of course, he had no time for this play. What a mistake! He realized that the moment the voices outside grew, as the strong hands tore the wooden partition open.

His own rage overflowing, filling with the same sort of impotence as that of the Warlord before, he let his instincts guide him, the draft from the balcony beckoning. One powerful leap and he was beside it, squeezing through the half-closed shutters, one hand pushing, the other still firm, clutching his spoil, not about to let go.

The courtyard not far below was filling with warriors too, the Mexica and the Acolhua, with that other dung-eater, the Mexica Head Adviser, in their lead – so this is who was sleeping downstairs, in the guarded main rooms – his cloak askew, hair tussled. Still he jumped with no hesitation, having no better option, the footsteps of his pursuers thundering behind his back, tearing the shutters open.

The loudest thing he heard, landing upon the ground, was the roar of the Warlord, rushing toward the stone parapet, about to jump, too.

"Don't touch him. He is mine!"

Tlacaelel felt his heart racing, trying to leap out of his chest, not prepared to be torn out of his sleep in this way, by wild running, confused shouting, and commotion. Never sleeping too deeply, he was immediately on his feet, grabbing his weapons, rushing out.

"What happened?"

"There is fighting up there." His guarding warriors looked at each other, wide-eyed. "Our men discovered dead warriors. Someone, some killer. Or maybe—"

He rushed off before the man finished his sentence, his stomach as tight as a slab of stone. The black-clothed killer, the thief!

He remembered the tale of the twin he had listened to with mixed feelings, after settling the most pressing of Coatlinchan's problems and finding the Highlander here, appropriating this expensive, rich dwelling belonging to one of the revels, for himself and his warriors to rest; doing this mainly because of the boy, Tlacaelel knew, not needing the luxury of spending a day or two sorting this town's affairs. But for the twin his friend would have taken care of this all by himself, through this same afternoon, rushing back to Texcoco before the nightfall, maybe. Yet, as it was, the rounding up of the last rebels fell upon Tlacaelel, while the Highlander had been busy with his son, making sure the boy had been seen by the healer, then fed, washed, and made to rest, not leaving the twin's side for a heartbeat, reassuring, protecting. Something the boy evidently needed.

He shook his head, remembering the wild thing. So much courage and determination, and in such a young cub. He should have let the sword go, up there on the wall, or before, while trying to get away from his captors. The whole tale made Tlacaelel's head spin. Retold by the Highlander, in a crisp, matter-of-fact manner, as when Tlacaelel had arrived the boy had been fast asleep, it still stunned him, the wildness of it all. If not for the twin's antics on the wall of Coatlinchan temple, he knew, he would have been inclined to doubt some of this story, assuming that no boy of so little years and experience would be capable of surviving and then defying such a highly-trained killer.

However, after witnessing the struggle upon the temple's wall, he found it easier to accept. The boy was his father all over again, but in a slightly different, maybe even fiercer version; courageous, unpredictable, living by his own laws, abiding to none of society's.

"The killer is still alive and running loose somewhere here in the city," the Highlander had told him grimly, when the dusk fell and the three of them reclined on the patio, feasting on the best food Coatlinchan had to offer.

"He had left long since. He would have been a fool to stay." Raising his eyebrows, Tlacaelel watched the warriors milling around the gardens and outside the fence. "So this is why you filled this place with so many warriors until none of us can move a limb?"

The Highlander shrugged, deep in thought. "I wouldn't have left if I were him. You captured his goods. You left him with nothing, no sword and no payment."

"Is that what *you* would have done?"

The dark eyes didn't waver, one hand stroking the boy's hair, the other toying with the beautiful goblet, the *octli* in it untouched. "Oh yes, I would. If I thought I had nothing to lose and everything to gain."

The twin was watching his father, wide-eyed. Bruised and scratched, he looked better now, wolfing the food down, his eyes glittering, regaining some of their boyish glint.

"Will he come here?" he asked quietly, moving closer to the Warlord's side, his frown deep, sitting well with the air of grim resolve his whole being radiated.

The Highlander shrugged and pressed the boy tighter. "If he does, we will be ready."

But they weren't ready, thought Tlacaelel now, racing down the corridor, his teeth clenched tight, the body of the slain warrior by the back entrance disturbing like never on the battlefield. There was no point in heading up the stairs. The fighting there was surely taken care off.

The moonlit night jumped on him, illuminated too brightly, in a disturbing way. His eyes assessed the layout of the gardens, mainly out of habit, taking in the warriors and their disoriented state of mind, their eyes on the balcony and the man posing on its parapet, lingering for less than a heartbeat before jumping down with the grace of a person used to conquering heights.

Unscathed, the intruder straightened up, charging for the patio and the fence like a hunted animal, in a desperately concentrated effort.

"Get him!" cried out Tlacaelel, coming out of his trance, gesturing wildly.

The warriors sprang forward, blocking the man's way. This made the intruder halt. Pressing his back against the nearest column, he faced his pursuers, bringing the sword up, holding it in an expert manner, the carvings on full display, glowering in the silvery moonbeam.

"Don't come any nearer," he growled, his voice trembling, but not his hands. "Unless you wish to fight the magic of this sacred weapon."

The warriors stopped dead in their tracks. The rest held their breath.

The Highlander appeared on the balcony like a storm cloud, unstoppable in his deadly rage.

"Don't touch him. He is mine!" he bellowed, jumping down with the same inconsideration to the height the intruder displayed earlier, although not landing as well, grabbing the protruding stone of the wall to catch his balance, his face twisting. Yet, hurt or not, there was no stopping the man, his rage spilling like the flames of the Smoking Mountain, Tlacaelel knew. Worse than that!

"Move!"

It was quite a roar. Charging like a jaguar on a hunt, the Highlander was between the warriors, pushing them away, limping slightly, sparing his twisted ankle an effort.

"So you wish to fight with my sword!" he growled, stopping a hairsbreadth before the razor-sharp spikes. One more step and he would have bumped into the man, jamming him into the column, getting cut by his own sacred weapon.

Confronted with so much uncontrollable fury, the stranger did not waver, his hands tightening around the carved hilt, his gaze blazing with a fire of his own.

"Yes, I wish to fight with your sword, Warlord," he hissed. "When I kill you, I will be the rightful owner of the power it holds."

"You will die long before that!" breathed the Highlander,

snatching the nearest warrior's sword, sparing the man not a glance. One moment it was in its rightful owner's hands, the next it was in the air, glaring dully, absorbing the moonlight, another lethal beast thirsty for blood, not as powerful as the weapon it faced but demanding the warm flow to be released nonetheless.

It swished in the air and would have cut the thief in two, crushing his ribs and tearing his insides, if not for the man disappearing from the spot, not pressed against the column anymore but standing to the left of his attacker, bringing the sacred weapon down as swiftly, with the same sort of strength. It seemed to be a miracle that the Highlander managed to avoid being cut in his turn, throwing his body sideways, using the branches of a nearby tree to stabilize himself.

The warriors held their breath as the two rivals stared at each other, breathing heavily, suddenly wary, gauging one another's strength. Tlacaelel's mind raced in panicked circles. What to do? The honorable hand-to-hand was never, never to be interrupted. Once upon a time he had been appalled with his friend, this same wild Highlander, for contemplating something like that when he, Tlacaelel, had challenged the Tepanec Warlord at the walls of Azcapotzalco. Now he was considering a similar solution himself.

The knot in his stomach as tight as a rubber ball, he watched along with his and the Acolhua warriors, helpless, cursing his friend for challenging that stranger, an unknown quality, a warrior who was not afraid of stealing the sword no one dared to touch. The Highlander was an exceptional fighter, but he was far from being at his best now, the sleepless nights, the mounting exhaustion, the worry for his boy, and now a twisted ankle; perhaps worst of all, being forced to fight against his own beloved sword.

He watched his friend pouncing, directing his blow at his rival's ribs again, clearly trying to finish the man without harming the precious weapon. It didn't work. The foreigner twisted, escaping the razor-sharp spikes, answering with a blow of his own, a blow that the Highlander avoided by leaping aside, having every opportunity to block it with his weapon and maybe try to use his superior strength in pushing his less-impressive rival down.

The carvings upon the sword glowered. Mesmerized, Tlacaelel stared at them, feeling the salty taste in his mouth where his teeth sank into his lips. Would the sacred weapon turn against its owner now, thirsty for the blood of its creator? The carvings seemed to suggest that, and he muttered an ardent prayer, asking for Tezcatlipoca's help and protection. The god of the night and the warriors might take heed and help.

The warriors cheered as the Highlander tricked his rival into making a wrong move, faking an offensive from one side, while swinging his sword from another. A crimson line crossed the intruder's upper ribs, but the man twisted away from the worst of the blow, blocking it with his weapon, barely able to keep his balance.

The Highlander disengaged quickly, and Tlacaelel's heart sank. His friend should have been pressing his advantage, he knew, should have been pushing his wavering rival off his feet, hard wood against hard wood, pinning the man he fought down, giving him no respite, no chance of recovering. Instead, the veteran of so many battles stepped back and waited, regaining his breath, leaning on one foot, sparing the other an effort.

Tlacaelel swallowed a curse. *Stop trying to save the damn sword,* he wanted to scream, biting his lips in order to say nothing. *Save yourself, instead. Kill the filthy bastard by whatever means. Don't sacrifice your life in an attempt to save the damn relic.*

The other man recovered, and waited too, peering at the Warlord darkly, gauging his strength. His next blow was directed toward his opponent's weapon, as though testing a theory. Of course, he arrived at the same conclusion.

Tlacaelel's hands tickled, his fists clenched so tight he could not feel them anymore, watching the Highlander avoiding the engagement of weapons again, darting aside, not as cat-like and agile as usual, tired, his limp getting worse. A crimson line stretched across his upper arm, glaring angrily, dripping blood.

The fencing went on, hopelessly balanced. The silence was so heavy, one could hear the night insects buzzing somewhere in the darkness. Even the breeze ceased, and the sky clouded a little, making the moon dim, communicating its displeasure.

The Highlander gained another advantage, managing to crush the flat side of his sword against his rival's shoulder, sending the man reeling, crashing against the building's wall. Pouncing to deliver another blow, he managed to avoid hitting the outstretched sword with his own weapon, but in directing a part of his attention on this irrelevant maneuver, he missed the opportunity to hit his rival outright, trying to reach his exposed side instead, which gave the assaulted man a much-needed heartbeat of respite. Sliding along the wall, the foreigner slipped away, cut only lightly, with the edge of the Highlander's sword brushing against the hard stone, causing one of the obsidian spikes to break.

Not deterred by another failure, the Highlander attacked, relentless, as lethal as always, but again circling around the man, not pressing a frontal assault. Was he hoping to tire his opponent? It didn't seem like a good strategy, not with his own forehead glittering with sweat, his limp becoming more prominent, his exhaustion showing in the pressed lips, in the grayish coloring of his cheeks, in his frustrated attempts to finish it all. His opponent, although bleeding from several cuts by now, looked better, calmer, more in control. Who was trying to tire whom? Tlacaelel ground his teeth, feeling his stomach tightening, turning into stone. Was he going to witness the end of the legend this man and his sword had become?

The warriors by his side gasped as the Highlander disregarded another opportunity of a frontal attack, the carved sword waving temptingly before his eyes, inviting him to confront it, to strike hard. Clenching his teeth, he retreated, stumbling over a crack in the pavement, managing to avoid being cut by falling and rolling away. The magical sword hit the ground where its owner's torso was still imprinted in the dusted stones, two of its spikes breaking, and the hilt creaking ominously, in a strange manner. The Highlander leapt back to his feet, reeling but ready to fight, growling something inaudible as his rival smirked, a savage grin stretching his lips.

I will have him killed oh so very slowly, thought Tlacaelel, his heart pounding in his ears, as though he were the one doing the hopeless fighting. He wiped the sweat off his brow. *If he dies, I will make the despicable killer wish he had never been born!*

The incident made the killer gather enough confidence to initiate an attack of his own. Rushing forward, he didn't let the Warlord regain his composure, his sword up, the carvings sparkling, on full display. Eyes wide, the Highlander followed its progress with what seemed like a shocked fascination, before his instincts took over and his own sword came up, blocking the mighty blow at the last moment, holding on with desperation, his hands trembling, giving in bit by bit.

Tlacaelel felt his own heart coming to a halt. *Oh, mighty Tezcatlipoca, please give him of your strength.*

It was too late to disengage, but as the foreigner, his own limbs trembling, the carved sword creaking louder, tried to kick his rival in order to bring him down faster, the Highlander's instincts took over again. Clenching his teeth until his jaw seemed to crack, he pushed with the last of his strength, his own foot sliding against the man's shin, causing him to waver and lessen the pressure.

For a heartbeat, both rivals, still engaged, seemed to be fighting to keep their balance, the Highlander's damaged ankle not doing well taking the man's weight. Recovering a fraction of a moment too late, he pushed forward, but the foreigner's shove sent him crashing into the dusty stones, his own sword still thrust forward, still defending his position.

The carved magic rose, its images sparkling against the moon that peeked again from behind the clouds, as though reluctant to miss the climax. All eyes were upon it, spellbound, beyond words or thoughts – the Highlander's eyes too. A warrior to the very end, he brought his sword up to fend off the attack even when on the ground, not having much chance to stop the accumulated drive of the blow from above. His body twisted, struggling to get to the best of positions in the fraction of a heartbeat it took his attacker to bring the mighty weapon down, to crash against the hard wood of the other sword, heading for the softness of the flesh it protected.

A gasp escaped many throats, and Tlacaelel's heart stopped,

then threw itself wildly against his ribs. The snap of the breaking wood echoed as a mighty thunder, bouncing off the walls, spreading everywhere, filling the enclosure, or maybe the entire world, with the vision of the impossible, as the carved magic broke in two, falling around its rightful owner and upon him.

The silence prevailed, a deep, ethereal silence, a silence that follows the first moments of disaster. No breeze moved the air. Even the gods went numb. Incredulous, Tlacaelel stared at the larger of the pieces, the broken face of a jaguar, still baring its teeth, still ominous, but lacking its former vitality, a part of the wonderful image missing, taking its dignity away. The magic was gone!

He saw the Highlander leaping to his feet, blood dripping from a cut upon his cheek, his chest rising and falling, his eyes huge, dominating, the only feature enlivening the grayish pastiness of his face, spilling over with ferocious rage.

He didn't spare a glance for the remnants of his sword, but brought the one he held in a forceful sway, wielding it as though it had no weight, swishing viciously, cutting the air. A slight twist of the hands, and its flat side crashed against the temple of his stunned rival, making a dull, revoltingly wet sound, familiar from so many battles. The sound of crushing bones.

The man fell as a cut down tree, his limbs twitching, jerking uncontrollably, hands still clenching the carved hilt of the broken sword. Again and again the other weapon rose and fell, not a sword anymore but a club, crushing the head of its victim into a pulp, long after all movement ceased. No clean death for the lowlife who had done the unspeakable. Revolted, Tlacaelel could only watch. As did the warriors, and the onlookers, all holding their breaths, not daring to even gag.

Finally, when there was nothing but a headless body lying upon the ground, and most of the obsidian spikes of the assaulting weapon missing, scattered everywhere, the Highlander stopped. Wiping the blood off his face, he took a deep breath, then looked up, meeting the stares.

Lips pressed into a thin line, eyes as dark as the moonless night, and as clouded, he stared back for a heartbeat, then bent down and wrenched the remnants of the revered weapon out of the lifeless hands.

Straightening up, he went toward the other half of the dead sword and stared at it for another heartbeat, as though comprehending it only now, before picking it up.

Tlacaelel gestured to his warriors. "Get the slaves to clean this mess. Then shoo them away. They had seen enough entertainment."

His heart as heavy as a slab of a pyramid, he went toward his friend, not knowing what he was going to say or do.

CHAPTER 20

This time, she came here in a litter, with all the pomp of a high lady, preceded by warriors and attended by servants. The shadows of the afternoon stretched along the wide alley and across the clean, spacious patio, so familiar by now. She had spent more time here, in this house, than in the room allocated to her in the Texcoco Palace.

"We are here," she said, smiling at Tlacaelel, who didn't pay much attention to the litter's sways, or to the fact that it had stopped, being lowered to the ground. Crouching above yet another pile of papers, he had read all the way, marking the glyphs he didn't approve of, muttering to himself.

It was a report of funds needed for this projected southern campaign according to his aides' estimation, she knew, having peeked into his reading materials already, curious, as always. But that evaluation was too high. Tenochtitlan could not afford to spend so many resources on an unnecessary campaign. The revenue the former Tepanec provinces yielded was not satisfactory, not yet. He would have to find the way to cut on the costs, she knew, leaning back on her cushions, letting her thoughts drift. His campaigns were not as fascinating as his building programs, or his reforms. Or this last crisis with the Acolhua allies.

Shutting her eyes, she relaxed, enjoying the monotonous sway of the litter, at peace now that the troubles were behind them, prevented in a timely way, with him being involved, solving the problem, forceful, wise, not afraid of the challenge, knowing the right course of action, as always. Oh, he was the brightest star in the new world that he and his allies were busy creating. The brightest and the most desirable.

She tried to hide her grin. Well, maybe she was not impartial or detached enough to claim that, but he was one of the most important men in the rising new power, the founder of the Triple Alliance, the conqueror of the Tepanecs. It was a fact, nothing to do with her love for him.

The smile became impossible to conquer, and she let it out, knowing that he was too busy to notice and ask her about it. Oh well, maybe she was too in love with him to see clearly. Maybe Dehe, if asked, would say that the Acolhua Warlord was the brightest star of the Triple Alliance, the founder, the conqueror of Azcapotzalco. And then her fellow other wife, the royal woman, would add that her brother, the Acolhua Emperor, played a certain role in making that dream come true.

The Emperor's sister! Her smile gone, she remembered the woman, the extent of her misery, the depth of her regret. Spending an entire day and another agonizing night in this house, playing with Mixtli on the patio or curled in the alcove of the main room, she had watched them and listened, consumed with compassion. Oh but what a dreadful night it was, with the boy still missing, and the sword missing, and their men now missing too, out there in Coatlinchan, trying to solve all these problems. No more light, delightfully cozy, cheerfully argumentative atmosphere that made this house into what it was – an island of sparkling liveliness in the lake of well-mannered, aristocratic Texcoco. Now it was all gone, with both women downcast, moving like shadows, having no spark of life in them, talking sparingly, and the children huddled inside their quarters, quiet and cheerless, under the strictest orders not to go anywhere unless given specific permission.

It was all because of Dehe, she had realized, trying to be of help, mainly by keeping Mixtli occupied as much as she could, so the girl would give her mother respite from the endless inquiries if Ocelotl was dead like Nakaztli or not. By that stage, the poor woman was thinking about nothing else, caring not a bit for the stupid sword or the silly Acolhua-Mexica crisis, a shadow of her brisk, confident self, radiating none of her pleasant liveliness.

An observation that clearly worried everyone in the house, the Emperor's sister more than anyone. Regaining her businesslike, energetic ways after skulking for half a day, keeping appropriately low and quiet, the beautiful woman became herself toward the second part of the day, taking the lead when the Mistress of the House would not. Many delegations of slaves were sent to comb the city, many theories contemplated, plenty of possible explanations brought up as to the boy's whereabouts, every one more cheerful than the others. And more implausible.

"Please, Dehe, please stop worrying so. You will be sick!" implored the royal woman again and again. "Please, don't decide that the boy is gone. He is not. It's not his first time to get into trouble. Remember Tenochtitlan! He will be all right, you'll see. Our husband and Coyotl will find him. I know they will." Having been greeted with yet another gloomy silence in response, she would take the lifeless hand into hers, pressing it urgently, as though trying to bring it back to life with the sheer power of her will. "Please, eat something. You haven't eaten since yesterday. You will be sick. Let me order the foods you like the most. Remember this white fish with chili sauce you liked so much? I'll send the kitchen slaves to the markets right away, before the food sellers are gone. What do you say?"

But Dehe would just shrug, not taking her hand away, but not reacting with her usual warmth, either.

"I'm not hungry," she would mutter, staring ahead. "I will eat later."

And so it went on, with the dusk turning into the night, and no word coming from the Palace, or from Coatlinchan. It was nerve-wracking, this lack of information. What if things went badly? What if their hurried rush to Coatlinchan made them fall into some sort of a trap? And what about the Emperor's sister? Watching her covertly, Tlalli had found herself wondering. Was this woman truly innocent, not a part of the plot against the Emperor? Did she truly just act silly, without thinking things through, not understanding the implications, not behaving like the politician she claimed to be, bragging of her past as

Tenochtitlan's Empress on every occasion?

Trusting Dehe and her judgment, Tlalli regretted having told Tlacaelel about any of it, although he had tricked her into revealing her information. He said he wouldn't tell, but she knew he would if he thought it necessary. There was nothing Tlacaelel did without a good reason. So the other question was more difficult, more complicated. Was this woman's involvement in the affair of the sword still a secret? Would both these wives manage to keep it as such?

They needed to know what was going on, what was truly going on. To send groups of slaves was not enough. However, with the royal woman's reluctance to summon her litter and pay yet another visit to her brother, there was not much they could do. Tlalli's volunteering would be of no use, she knew. She had no spies in the Palace and no status to approach important people. She would discover nothing.

Shaking her head to get rid of the gloomy memories, she slipped out of the litter, then glanced back, her smile baiting.

"We have arrived, Honorable Master," she said, leaning backwards. "Will you stay here in the litter, poring over your papers? Shall I send here the best of your scribes?"

He looked up, his eyes twinkling, lips curving into a smile. "There is no need. I have a scribe here with me. Not badly skilled, I must to admit, this person is wild, not entirely reliable. Not badly looking, though." He beckoned one of the slaves, who hurried to take the paper, placing it carefully in a wooden box full of other scrolls. "Maybe I'll use this person, instead of leaving her free to gossip with the Warlord's wives, her newfound Acolhua friends."

She tried not to giggle. "Dehe is no Acolhua," she said, brushing against him lightly as he got out of the litter, unwilling to scandalize him or anyone else but showing her wish to be alone with him and do more. He was so handsome, even if tired-looking, with dark rings surrounding his eyes and his face still pale and haggard, but not as pasty gray as when he came back from Coatlinchan on the previous morning. "She comes from the wild highlands."

"Oh, yes, I know where this lady comes from," he said, his grin light, reflecting his desire. He too wished to be alone, in the privacy of her Tenochtitlan quarters. "She is an impeccable woman, nobler than many I know of." His eyes twinkled again, peering at her, full of mischief. "If you intend to let your newfound friends influence you, learn from her and not from the Acolhua nobility element of this household. Who knows? The Warlord's First Wife may yet turn you into a great lady."

Watching him crossing the patio, she followed, amused and indignant at the same time. "Maybe I should learn from your household," she muttered, making sure he did not hear. "Your Chief Wife gives a great example, such a filthy-tempered foul-mouthed *cihua*."

The central room of the house greeted them, unrecognizable, transformed into a merry affair of colorful covers, mats, and cushions, prettily carved low tables and wittily embroidered cotton rags hanging from the walls, adding to the cheerful atmosphere. Many of the guests were already there, squatting comfortably, served refreshments, enjoying themselves, the trilling flutes putting everyone in the right mood.

Quick to move out of sight, as she had most certainly not been invited to this warriors' gathering, she still found it hard to fight the temptation of peeking in, recognizing some of their Mexica minor leaders, mixed with quite a few Acolhua of the same rank.

The Warlord was on his feet, greeting his guest of honor, guiding him personally toward the seat in the center of the gathering. Tlacaelel, she noticed, was assessing the room, apparently pleased with what he saw.

Consumed with curiosity, Tlalli watched the Warlord, having not seen him since his return, since the terrible vigil two nights before until the word came from Coatlinchan, informing them of the twin's whereabouts, reassuring them that the boy was safe and that the other trouble had been taken care of. It was Tlacaelel who had sent the word, while informing the Emperor about the developments. The Warlord didn't bother.

Remembering the vastness of their relief, Tlalli frowned. It had been already near dawn again, and when both women finally had settled to sleep, after Dehe had cried her heart out for the first time since the troubles began, Tlalli had gone back to her quarters in the Palace, to rest and to wait for her man to return. It was he who had solved all these troubles, she believed. Without him it would have been bad.

"Oh, here you are!" The familiar voice broke into her reverie, making her smile widen. "Come. Let us leave the men to their devices. They can do without our company for some time."

The Mistress of the House's smile shone brighter than the midday sun, her eyes sparkling, lips stretched into the widest of smiles, revealing a row of small, perfect teeth. An image of well-being and inner peace, beautiful in a bright bluish-green gown, the woman stood there smiling, looking like a young girl ready to attend her first ceremony, the long turquoise earrings hanging down her shoulders, with matching bracelets and anklets encircling her delicate legs and arms.

Tlalli found herself staring. "You look beautiful," she said, gathering her wits. "I…I barely recognized you."

The woman chuckled, a melodious, thrilling sound. "Who did you think I was?" she laughed, eyes twinkling. "Did you think the Warlord brought a new woman from his raid on Coatlinchan?"

"Oh, no, I didn't think that." Unable to keep from doing so, Tlalli grinned. "But yes, it might have explained the change."

"Let me see that everything is well and then, we'll retire to my rooms, to sit and talk and eat all the delicacies my servants were able to hunt through the markets this morning." Another conspiratorial grin. "The glorious Acolhua and Mexica warriors did not get the best of the spoils this time. I can assure you of that."

Eyes busy assessing the room, like a leader watching the battle of his planning developing, the Mistress of the House beckoned the main maid, hurrying to meet the heavyset woman halfway, distributing her instructions in hushed tones, setting frenzied activity among the servants. More refreshments came in, and additional cushions and mats were spread, while the hostess smiled, answering greetings politely, her expression warm, genuine, well-meaning. The Warlord, noticed Tlalli, glanced at his wife, stopping his conversation briefly, his eyes clearing of shadows, sparkling proudly, filling with warmth.

"Come."

It was a pleasure to dive into the depths of the house, exchanging the masculine haven for the refinement and the tranquility of the inner rooms, which bore such an obvious sight of the Mistress of the House's delicate touch.

"We will be safe here for some time." Smiling, the woman guided Tlalli toward the cozy arrangement of mats. "Until Mixtli discovers that you are here, that is."

"Where is she?" With a sigh of relief, Tlalli sank into the pile of cushions.

"Out there, on the Plaza." Squatting gracefully, busy arranging her skirts, Dehe waved in a non-committal way. "There are special dances to be held, to honor Revered Tlaloc, the guarding spirit of the Acolhua."

"Oh, yes, I heard about that." Eyes upon an old maid that came in carrying a tray of prettily arranged plates and bowls, Tlalli shrugged. "I wanted to go and watch too, but when I heard that the Adviser was invited to the Warlord's gathering, I thought it better to come here."

A warm smile was her answer. "I'm glad you did."

"So all the children are out there? I hoped to see them before we leave."

"They will be back soon. Neither Iztac Ayotl nor the servants would be able to handle the wild bunch for too long. Especially Mixtli. With the troubles of the last days, she turned into my shadow again, like she used to be when smaller. A very demanding shadow." A fleeting, somewhat apologetic smile stretched the generous lips. "She will grow out of it."

Tlalli nodded absently, not caring for child-rearing dilemmas. "So the Emperor's sister took the children to watch the festivities?"

"Yes, she did."

It was too tempting not to ask. "How is she?"

"She is well." Not pretending to misunderstand the essence of the question, Dehe dropped her voice. "She has seen better times, but she will be all right. Eventually. When her fears and remorse will let her be."

"You did a very noble thing." Tlalli smiled again, liking the woman in front of her a great deal. Yes, Tlacaelel was right. Out of all people, this woman was worthy to be called a friend.

"I did nothing a sensible person wouldn't have done," said the Mistress of the House, her face closing, the cup of steamy chocolate drink getting cold, forgotten in her palms.

"But people don't always act sensibly. Especially women."

That provoked laughter, and the atmosphere cleared. "Well, yes, that is true too. Women are prone to do silly things, aren't they?"

"Yes, they are." Reaching for the other cup of chocolate sweetened with a generous amount of honey, Tlalli brought the foamy drink to her lips. "I always preferred to make friends with boys when I was little. Girls were silly and empty-headed." She thought about Tlacaelel's wives and concubines. "And they don't get any better as they grow up."

Her companion nodded, deep in thought. "I didn't get along with my fellow women either, certainly not after," the woman swallowed, "after I moved to Huexotzinco. It was the worst there." She shook her head, as though banishing unwelcome memories. "I agree with you, women do tend to be silly, spiteful, unreliable. But not all of them. You are not like that, and I am not. And some other women, too. Iztac-Ayotl among them. She may be reckless, impulsive, sometimes not very reasonable, but she is a good person, loyal and kind." A defying smile dawned. "And this is why one doesn't throw a friendship away lightly. There are relationships one should cherish and protect as much as one can."

Yes, thought Tlalli, *but there is more to it. You are not telling it all to me, because you think me a stranger, but Tlacaelel knows you too well.*

This woman had done it to protect her man and her family before anything else, he had told her this morning, when she had asked him about it, puzzled. The Highlander's First Wife was a beautiful *quetzal* feather beyond price, kind and generous, and very, very smart. She loved the Warlord, and she loved her life, being too wise of a woman to succumb to the temptation of getting rid of her rival.

The Highlander was passionate about both of his women, maintained Tlacaelel. He had loved them for many summers, since being a mere youth. To inform him of the treachery committed by one of them was to break his heart, something his sensible First Wife would not do, preferring to share his love if his well-being was at stake. She was one of these rare people, people who put their beloved's private happiness before their own. She was that priceless.

Watching the dreamy expression that softened his sharp features, making him look younger and more of the boy he must have been once upon a time, Tlalli had sworn to herself to be just this sort of a woman for him, loyal and full of love, putting his happiness before her own.

"I see what you mean," she said now, coming out of her reverie, watching the woman with somewhat different eyes. "Still, what you did was very generous and kind. Tlacaelel thinks highly of you."

Her hostess's smile held a measure of embarrassed delight. "He does?"

"Oh, yes! He praised you higher than I heard him praising anyone else, ever." She grinned. "He says I should learn from you."

"Oh, please!" The laughter of the Mistress of the House was untypically loud, her embarrassment obvious. "He doesn't know everything about me. Ask Iztac Ayotl. Our mutual history goes back to the days when I was as young as you are, but not as confident, full of stupid ideas." Her face darkened. "She keeps my secrets as well as I keep hers."

For a while they kept silent, each in her own thoughts. Tlalli eyed her plate thoughtfully.

"How does the Warlord take the loss of the sword?"

"He takes is relatively well, all things considered." The woman put her cup back, unsettled. "The accursed thing almost cost him his life! I'm glad it's gone."

"Tlacaelel says it, on the contrary, saved his life."

"Maybe." Dehe's shrug held a measure of clear resentment. "It was a magical sword. There could be no doubt about it. But all the same, I'm glad it's gone. It brought us all too much trouble this time."

"Yes, it did." Uncomfortable to attack her plate when her hostess paid no attention to hers, although it was full of all sort of delicacies, Tlalli watched her companion, wishing she had not brought up the troublesome subject. This woman had been so pleasantly lively, so animated before.

As though reading her guest's thoughts, Dehe smiled. "But now all is well, so I have no cause to grow angry, do I? They are all back and alive."

"How is the twin?"

The lovely face lit. "Oh, he is better, in greater spirits than he used to be for moons, since before we came to Texcoco. The poor boy was so angry, so frustrated, his inability to live up to everyone's expectations, when his brother did so well, drove him positively mad. But now that his father is so proud of him, praising him to the skies, telling him that it was he who had saved the sword, and his family's honor into the bargain, that boy is glowing brighter than Father Sun on the summer days."

A proud mother, she was shining as brightly now, reflected Tlalli, having received a somewhat different account of the events from Tlacaelel. The boy, indeed, was brave and enterprising, impressively fierce, but if not for his involvement in this whole affair his father might not have come into so much danger at all.

"I'm glad to hear that. He needs to go back to *calmecac* and start behaving reasonably, like his brother does."

The glow dimmed slightly. "I'm not sure he will do as well." At last, Dehe paid attention to the food, picking her plate up, eyeing its contents somewhat dubiously, deep in thought. "But I sincerely hope he will do better than before. No more marketplace escapades, and no more stealing."

We'll see about that, thought Tlalli, remembering what Coatl had told her. The boy did not steal for the sake of stealing. He was preparing to run away, taking his little band of marketplace thugs with him, leading them to a brighter future that, according to these boys, lay somewhere there in the Highlands. Would he forget his questionable plans now?

The answer came in not much later, when the children spilled in, entering the house through the back door, not allowed to disturb the noble gathering in the central rooms and the patio. The feast was still on, filling the entire house with merry clamor, the guests talking and laughing, drinking to their hearts' content.

The peacefulness of the inner rooms broke.

"The boys wanted to go to the lake, but Second Mother told them not to," cried out Mixtli, bursting in with her typical inconsideration to the privacy of her mother's quarters.

Her eyes took in the sight of their guest and lit like a pair of torches. "I knew you would come back!" she yelled at the top of her voice, running to Tlalli, jumping into her lap, almost pushing her off her cushions. "You should have come with us to the Plaza. The priests danced so well, and there were clouds around them. I coughed all the time."

"Good for you, little one." Not minding being assaulted in this way, Tlalli pressed the plump little thing closer. "And I guess there were sweetmeats all around, weren't there?"

The sticky lips stretched into a widest of smiles. "Second Mother bought us tortillas with honey. There was so much of it that it was spilling on my clothes. It was so tasty!"

"And I can forget about trying to feed you today," commented the First Mother, getting to her feet, her own smile as wide, not matching the pretended frown. "Well, first of all, let us change your clothes, before you make our guest as sticky as you are, little honeycomb." Still smiling, but uncompromising, the woman made the girl follow. "Where is the Second Mother?"

"In her rooms."

Dehe's frown deepened. "I wish she gathered enough courage to visit the Palace already," she muttered. "It doesn't look good, the way she hides here. Please, treat yourself to the food," she added, glancing at Tlalli. "I'll be back shortly. Come, Mixtli."

Alone at long last, Tlalli attacked her plate, famished, sorry to lose her pleasant company but glad to have some privacy to eat and think. So the Emperor's sister was safe, and the troublesome twin was safe and maybe not about to get into troubles anymore.

And the sword was gone but in a spectacular way. If it was doomed to break anyway, then why not while saving its owner instead of harming him?

Shivering, she thought about the duel. Tlacaelel had described it to her in his regular crisp, matter-of-fact manner; still, the way he had talked about it made her stomach twist in fear. He had been unsettled by this whole incident, the entire crisis culminating in the most bizarre hand-to-hand. She could see it most clearly, but knew better than to ask. The ominous weapon was no more, and it was enough to make her, and probably Tlacaelel himself, and maybe even the dwellers of this household, breathe with relief.

The children's voices reached her, coming from the outside, ringing loudly, unconcerned. Unable to fight the temptation, she slipped toward the opening in the wall, gaining a clear view of the small garden at the back of the house, with blossoming rows of tomatoes and various greenish plants she did not recognize, lined by flowerbeds aplenty, everything weighted against each other in a perfect accord. The garden bore evidence to the Mistress of the House's unmistakable touch, now invaded by the young inhabitants of this dwelling, banished from the patio and the main rooms.

Amused, Tlalli watched the boy from the marketplace putting finishing touches to the drawing upon the clear patch of earth, making a sketch of a bean game board. Citlalli and Coatl hopped around, impatient, the wooden figurines clutched tight in their palms, the dotted beans piling up on the ground.

"Come, Ocelotl. Stop messing with this thing. It's ready and good as it is," cried out the yellow-eyed girl, kicking at a small stone, careful to make it roll nowhere near the precious drawing. "We want to play before tomorrow comes!"

"It's not," said Ocelotl curtly, busy shadowing the middle squares of the drawing, which he made to look like a pair of crossed spears.

Pressing closer to the windowsill, Tlalli tried to see better, impressed with the boy's drawing skill. The little rascal was a true artist, as good as a scribe designing a wall image instead of a regular book.

"If you don't let us play now, I'm going to make a simple board over there and we'll play it without you!" The girl stomped her foot, then glared at Coatl who paid her no attention, watching the drawing, fascinated, evidently not about to cooperate. "Oh, you two are impossible."

But as she made an attempt to storm away, Coatl, standing next to her, caught her arm. "Calm down, Citlalli," he said, laughing, not impressed with her halfhearted attempts to break free. "Let him finish. It's going to be a pretty thing."

"It's going to be stepped upon before we start playing. Why would he make it look so perfect, drawing in the dust?" Her eyes narrow, she stopped struggling, but glared at the crouching painter, instead. "We won't have enough time to finish one game."

"The way you play, I'll have enough time to beat you twenty times and more before it's dark." Coatl's laughter was unbearably smug. It made even Tlalli, the invisible watcher, wish to challenge the annoying little bragger to a game with high stakes.

"No, you won't. Not this time," cried out Citlalli, clearly sharing the same sentiment. She tore her hand from the boy's grip. "I will beat you this time, like I did on that day before we left Huexotzinco."

"She still remembers that," muttered Ocelotl, chuckling. "Here, Citlalli. Have your drawing and go on, beat my brother like you did many moons ago. I'll be cheering you on." Nimble but not as graceful as the other twin, he jumped to his feet, putting more weight on one leg, sparing another the effort.

Welcoming the chance to study the object of so much worry and thoughts, Tlalli peered at the boy, curious. The twins did, indeed, look astonishingly alike, two tall, impressively broad-shouldered forms and long angular limbs, with their yet-uncut hair surrounding the roundness of their pleasant, look-alike faces. Just two mischievous boys, an exact image of each other. And yet, the differences were there too, impossible to miss. While Coatl's eyes gleamed with calm, good-natured mischief, Ocelotl's face was closed, dark, the bruises upon it still fresh, his lips twisted in what looked like a permanent defiance. As good-looking as his brother, he radiated a different glow, watching the world with wariness and suspicion, not about to trust anyone, not as readily as the other twin did. In this, he had something of Citlalli in him.

"You are not going to play?" asked the other twin, puzzled.

"I'm going to watch you two playing, so go ahead."

Pressing her lips, Citlalli gave the boy a look that bode him no good, but he paid it no attention, squatting next to the nearest flowerbed, his limp almost invisible but still there, marring the grace of his movements.

Poor thing, thought Tlalli. He might have been glad to be home, with his family that he clearly liked and enjoyed, and his father being proud of him, yet he was anything but glowing with happiness as his mother claimed. He would be back in the marketplace, up to no good, before long, she knew. Nothing had changed.

"You just don't want to lose any more games," said Coatl, picking up the beans, studying them carefully, in a showy manner. "Citlalli is boasting that old game that she won ages ago, but you can't boast anything at all. You never win."

Something flickered in the other boy's eyes, something fiercely dangerous, a fire that blazed for a heartbeat, then died away. "I don't care for your stupid games," he said, shrugging. "I'm busy with more serious things."

The provocative smugness cleared off Coatl's face all at once. "You are not going back to your *telpochcalli* friends," he said, half asking, half demanding.

Another indifferent shrug was his answer.

"You can't, Ocelotl! You have to be good now. You promised Mother."

Citlalli narrowed her yellow eyes. "You both are lucky to be in *calmecac*. I wish I could go there, too."

The squatting boy snorted. "You can take my place any time."

"You don't know how it is to be stuck here at home." The yellow-eyed girl stomped her foot. "Mother wants me to weave and decorate cloths, and draw glyphs and learn to read them. She made your mother promise that she is going to supervise my studies when we move to the great house by the Plaza." She crossed her arms, her frown deep, lips twisted in an unpleasant manner. "They'll make me learn everything boring, and they won't let me out at all, until the time of the temple training comes. And I heard that the temple training is even more boring." Enraged, she glared at both boys, challenging. "And here you are complaining. See how you would like it to be stuck here all day long!"

"Maybe I would like it very much." Ocelotl shrugged again, not impressed. "I want to see you being kicked out of sleep way before the sun is even thinking of coming up, to be yelled at and slapped and ordered about all day long. That is when you are not beaten and locked up with no food forever. I bet you would run back to your weaving and drawing as fast as you could."

"It is not like that!" Coatl straightened abruptly, angry now too. "You are yelled at and slapped and locked up because you don't do what they tell you to do. You argue and you pick fights, and you don't do your duties. That is why they punish you all the time. Not to mention that you are barely there, sneaking out the moment you can, to do all the stupid things you do."

That made the other twin bounce onto his feet like a rubber ball. "What I do is none of your dirty interest, you stupid piece of dung. I don't play at being the best boy in *calmecac* because it's stupid. Who cares for their orders? No one but you. You are so perfect one could vomit, or maybe just wish to beat you up from time to time." He spat upon the ground, fists clenched, legs wide apart, obviously ready to withstand the attack, if not to mount one. "You think it's all about being the best *calmecac* student, but it is not so. Father was never in *calmecac*, and he is the greatest warrior of them all!"

"Oh, yes! You keep running around the marketplace and the warehouses, stealing and doing all the other stupid things you do with your dirty commoner friends, and you will grow up to be just like Father." Facing his brother in the same ridiculously similar pose, Coatl positively glowered, now spoiling for a fight, his good-natured, easygoing attitude gone. "At least I do what Father wants me to do. I make him proud. You make him ashamed!"

"Stop yelling, you two. Stop it!" Eyes wide-open and as enraged as these of her stepbrothers, Citlalli shot forward, positioning herself between the boys, ready to stop the fight. "Stop it. They will hear you out there, so shut up, just shut up!"

Shifting her gaze from one trembling-with-rage adversary to another, the slender girl positively glowered, not about to step back or to let them go for each other's throat. Smaller than them, she looked ready to beat both her impressively broad-shouldered stepbrothers into listening, if need be.

It had the desired effect. They still stared at each other, but the worst of their anger was gone, with their shoulders relaxing, and the general air of the pouncing predators dissolving into the warmth of the afternoon, with only the hum of the festivities on the patio invading the quietness of their corner, and the sweet aroma of vanilla wafting in.

"Forget it," said Ocelotl, letting the small stone he held in his palm, the stone he had drawn the game board with, slip onto the ground. "Just forget it."

Listlessly, he turned around and was gone, disappearing behind the corner of the house, careful not to step on the flowers and the plants.

"Cuauhnahuac would have to wait until we dealt with more pressing problems." Stretching, Tlacaelel sighed, resting his back against the pleasant coolness of the plastered wall.

Many of the guests had drifted onto the patio, to enjoy the warmth of the afternoon sun, with others reclining all around, replete with food, sipping their drinks, talking loudly, enjoying the music. For the first time through this pleasant afternoon they had been left alone, to converse privately, which pleased both of them, Tlacaelel knew.

"I would never believe that Cuitlahuac, this filthy town, would dare to make trouble. They must have been thinking with the back exit of their bodies and not with their heads." The Highlander fiddled with his pipe, stuffing it in a leisurely manner. "Stupid people. Will they never learn?"

"They will, eventually. But not before we teach them a lesson." Shrugging, Tlacaelel glanced at his own pipe, abandoned for the sake of the colorful arrangement of fruits that had just been distributed among the guests, loaded on various plates, a renovation to the regular course of dessert. "Itzcoatl will be furious."

"Will he argue?" The Highlander's glance was swift but unmistakable, its wariness obvious.

"Maybe." Picking an accurately cut half of a red fleshy fruit, Tlacaelel studied it, curious. "But he rarely interferes with my policies, so the fertile valley of Cuauhnahuac will have to wait."

"Good. It'll give us time to take care of Acolman. I want all Coyotl's provinces back and settled before we embark upon any further expansion." The familiar spark was back, flicking out of the dark eyes, making the man look young and as mischievous as either of his wild sons. "Since we are bent on creating an empire, we can do it in an orderly manner and a grand style. Not like Tezozomoc, the lousy conqueror that he was."

"Tezozomoc was not that lousy. He ruled for twice twenty summers, carving himself quite an empire. Didn't the old Tepanec, that favorite uncle of yours, teach you any history?"

"Oh, yes, he did." The grin upon the man's face was wide and full of warmth. "What a man he had been. I went to see him not long before he embarked upon his Underworld journey, when we came back from Azcapotzalco. He wanted to hear all about that *altepetl* and the battles around it. He asked many questions. I think it made him sad, just a little. He grew up in Azcapotzalco, after all. He *was* a Tepanec." The smile upon the handsomely broad face deepened. "So near the beginning of his journey, but he was still himself, very lucid, wise and witty, sparkling with mischief, a pleasure to listen to. I stayed for nearly an entire market interval, when I planned to spend only a day or two on your island. It felt grand to relax in this exceptional man's company." A sigh. "He was a great man. I wish he could have stayed in our World of the

Fifth Sun for a little longer." The twinkle was back, banishing the sadness. "He was no admirer of Tezozomoc. He had a personal history with that power-hungry bastard. He told me all about it."

"The old Tepanec was a law unto himself," said Tlacaelel, not hiding his own smile. "I learned a great deal from him. He is missed in Tenochtitlan. To be forgotten is not the fate that awaits him." He glanced at his friend, pleased with what he saw. "You remind me of him not a little, you know that? Our First Emperor Acamapichtli needed a wild, fiercely independent Chief Warlord to put Tenochtitlan on its feet. And I think our friend Coyotl got himself just that sort of a man to return Texcoco to its former glory." Laughing openly now, he watched the frown and the smile fighting each other across the prominent features. "Oh yes, your family seems to develop a sort of tradition, of serving emperors in need. I wonder whom your sons will be busy rescuing. Especially this wild thing that did everything to worry you all to death while trying to save your sword."

The Highlander's face darkened, but only for a heartbeat, the cut upon his cheek, the reminder of the terrible duel, still glaring, dry but angrily red, refusing to calm.

"Ocelotl will do many great things, but it won't happen here in Texcoco." The smile won, lighting the dark eyes, igniting the warmth in them. "Yes, maybe he will carry the family tradition, supporting this or that rising power. The Highlands might have their own scores to settle, you know? Against your Mexica, most probably, as I'm sure Itzcoatl will not stop with your immediate neighbors. One day, it will come to your confrontation with my people, so I might be doing right by sending them reinforcements."

Puzzled, Tlacaelel looked up. "What do you mean?"

"The wild twin. I'm taking him to the Highlands. My father is still alive and relatively well. He will be glad to take care of the boy, to teach him all he needs to know while not breaking his spirit the way the *calmecac* teachers do. He was a great Warriors' Leader in his time, and he is still a great man, right up there with the old Tepanec, his full brother."

"You must be joking!" Unable to take it all in, Tlacaelel found himself staring. "You are sending the twin to the Highlands?"

The widely spaced eyes hardened. "Yes, I am."

"You are setting the wild thing free, when all he needs is to be disciplined. The boy has great potential. And while the best school of Texcoco is ready to do all the work for you, you are turning away and sending the wild thing into the wilderness." He shook his head. "I don't understand you."

The Highlander pursed his lips. "Huexotzinco is no wilderness. Along with Tlaxcala Valley towns, those places are fairly large, influential, full of civilized people that can teach you, arrogant Mexicas, quite a few things." The generous lips stretched into a mirthless grin. "And I'll tell you another thing, Old Friend. They played an important role, helping you take the Tepanecs down, but it will not be the last that you hear of them. They will not turn into a part of your future great empire, tamely or otherwise. They will defend their independence more fiercely than any people you will try to subdue. They will never lay down under the Mexica domination. Remember my words, Tlacaelel, and take them to heed. Whether you become an emperor of Tenochtitlan one day, or whether you remain ruling from the shadows, do not underestimate, neither Huexotzinco nor Tlaxcala Valley. They are too strong even for Tenochtitlan to swallow." The smile turned warmer as the hostility left the dark eyes. "It is a friendly advice given to you as a friend, not as the Acolhua Warlord or the representative of the Highlands. Coyotl knows it, and so should you."

"I see." Tlacaelel shook his head, surprised with his friend's perception.

The Eastern Highlands, indeed, might be turning into a problem one day, he knew, having heard young Moctezuma talking about an expedition into the east and the rich areas beyond those mountains. The traders' reports had been most interesting, telling of fertile lowlands rich with rubber, cotton, *quetzal* feathers aplenty, and much more. Huexotzinco and Tlaxcala would be on the way of such military undertaking, and yes, they might not wish to cooperate, not without risking a conflict.

"I will cherish your advice, Old Friend," he said, trying to camouflage his thoughts, seeing the generous lips quivering, fighting a grin, the large eyes reflecting too much understanding.

Shaking his head, he watched the Mistress of the House as she entered the spacious hall, assessing the guests and their well-being with an experienced gaze, managing her little army of servants, distributing orders, a stern commander, but at the same time such a pleasant sight in her greenish-blue dress and the matching jewelry.

One problem at the time, he thought, seeing the Highlander's gaze following his wife's progress, his eyes clearing of shadows, glowing with warmth. When the time came, they would deal with the Highlands one way or another, although, for the sake of his friend, he hoped there would be an easy solution. An agreement, maybe. A share in spoils, perhaps, like in Azcapotzalco. The eastern lands would yield much if the traders were to be believed. But to maintain the growing trade, he would need to ensure the Mexica travelers' safety, would need to make the eastern people fear and respect the Mexicas, commoners and warriors alike.

"We will deal with the problems as they come," he said quietly, not willing to lie, not to this man. "Haven't we always?"

The Highlander's grin held nothing but affection. "Yes, we have, Old Friend." His eyes strayed back to his wife, as she made her way toward them, graceful and lithe, glowing with happiness, irresistibly pretty because of it, drawing the attention of many. "It won't be easy for her."

Tlacaelel did not make the mistake of assuming that his friend meant military matters. For a mother to part with her son, and just as the boy came back after she might have despaired for his life.

"Another reason not to do that," he said, raising one eyebrow.

But the Highlander shook his head firmly. "The boy will go from bad to worse, if he stays. She will understand that. Out of all people, she will appreciate my reasons, better than anyone."

Jaw firm, gaze unwavering, he sprang to his feet, standing there, tall and impressive, watching his guests, nodding at their greetings, in perfect control, a man in his thirties, a leader in his prime. The Acolhua Chief Warlord.

Remembering the pair of wild youths he had met more than half twenty summers ago, Tlacaelel shook his head, pleased. They had gone a long way, all three of them, and it was still just a beginning. They hadn't yet traveled even a half of their designated paths, and the future spread ahead, beckoning, sparkling with challenge, but in a friendly manner.

Oh yes, he thought. They would go far, and in the end, the world as they knew it would be so changed, no one would recognize it anymore. And no one would remember. New books would be written, telling history in the way it should be told. And then his Mexica Aztec Empire would spread its wings.

He watched the proud profile of his friend, measuring the man, gauging his newly discovered strengths. Yes, the Acolhua Emperor and his loyal Chief Warlord would remain great allies, and when the trouble with the Highlands arose, well, they would deal with it, somehow.

One problem at the time, he told himself, remembering the old Tepanec and his advice. One problem at the time.

AUTHOR'S AFTERWORD

Re-conquest of Texcoco did not happen immediately after the fall of Azcapotzalco. It took nearly two years for Nezahualcoyotl, the Acolhua Emperor, to install himself back upon the Texcoco throne.

Reported as being a man of great learning and taste, he must have accomplished it in grand style, beginning even back then to develop Texcoco into what it was reported to have become later the cultural center of the Mexican Valley and beyond it. 'The Athens of Mesoamerica' some post-conquest and modern-day historians had called it. Maybe with a good reason, maybe not. We'll never know, as the spectacular Texcoco library, along with the rest of the Mesoamerican book repositories, were burned at the time of the Spanish conquest, a century or so later after the mentioned events.

The troubles Nezahualcoyotl might have faced with his own old aristocracy and some more independent-thinking provinces are mentioned in, at least, one source, by the 16th century Acolhua historian, Fernando Ixtlilxochitl, who claims an access to the original sources he never produced. According to him, some Acolhua citizens of Nezahualcoyotl's times seemed to dislike his continuous cooperation with the Mexica-Aztecs of Tenochtitlan. Whether the dissatisfaction was strong, or rather vocal enough to bring up the crisis described in this novel, we'll never know. Historical fiction genre leaves the writer with a measure of literary license to think up mission connections, details or developments.

What we do know is the fact that the Acolhua and the Mexicas, along with their third junior partner of Tlacopan, who represented the defeated Tepanecs but in a small, humble manner, continued to cooperate very closely, developing their city-states into spectacular capitals, fighting in plenty of mutual campaigns, expanding their rapidly growing reach and influence.

However, not all wars were fought together. For one, Tlacaelel did, indeed, conquer the *altepetl* of Xochimilco while his Acolhua allies seemed to be busy elsewhere, probably recapturing the old Acolhua provinces, such as Coatlinchan and Huexotla, and Acolman later on. Or maybe those towns and cities were never the Acolhua provinces before, but after the destruction of the Tepanecs and the rise of the Triple Alliance, they might have been left with no choice.

Finally, with the troubles in the provinces and on the borders settled, the allies turned their eye to the greater distances. The fertile lands of Cuauhnahuac and its surroundings in the south were reported to be a mutual enterprise, with the Mexica and the Acolhua acting in tandem, conquering side by side, sharing the spoils and the tribute, leaving little for their junior partners of Tlacopan to pick up.

Still relatively young men in their prime, Nezahualcoyotl and Tlacaelel worked hard to adjust their *altepetl*s to their rapidly growing importance and riches, each in his own way.

Nezahualcoyotl was *tlatoani*, the ruler, the 'emperor,' the engineer, the poet, the lawmaker, a highly refined man, second to no one in the Acolhua lands. Tlacaelel, on the other hand, although reportedly holding the main power, working on shaping Tenochtitlan into what it became only half a century later – the greatest power of Mesoamerica – was *cihuacoatl*, the main adviser, the 'prime minister,' the man second only to the Mexica supreme ruler, but still a second.

Why Tlacaelel didn't claim the throne for himself no one knows. He had the birthright, the power, the charisma, the vast intelligence and a wonderful capacity to work hard, making his undertakings succeed, the more farfetched and the broader the better. His reforms, political and religious, were the ones to allow Tenochtitlan to grow into what it became without toppling over from too much conquest like it happened to their predecessors, the Tepanecs. The power was always at his fingertips, but never officially. Why?

Perhaps he had been loyal to his half-uncle, Itzcoatl, the emperor, the conqueror of the Tepanecs. Perhaps he liked wielding the power without the need to face the representative side of the emperor's job.

However, by the time Cuauhnahuac had been subdued, Itzcoatl was well into his late sixties, no longer a young man. A new emperor for Tenochtitlan was to be sought soon, the possible implication of which I addressed in the next book, the seventh and the last book in the Rise of the Aztecs Series, "**The Triple Alliance**".

ABOUT THE AUTHOR

Zoe Saadia is the author of several novels on pre-Columbian Americas. From the architects of the Aztec Empire to the founders of the Iroquois Great League, from the towering pyramids of Tenochtitlan to the longhouses of the Great Lakes, her novels bring long-forgotten history, cultures and people to life, tracing pivotal events that brought about the greatness of North and Mesoamerica.

To learn more about Zoe Saadia and her work, please visit www.zoesaadia.com

Made in the USA
San Bernardino, CA
09 May 2017